Ain't that America

Ain't that America

A novel

Sean Hoade

Writers Club Press

San Jose New York Lincoln Shanghai

Ain't that America
A novel

All Rights Reserved © 2000 by Sean Hoade

No part of this book may be reproduced or transmitted in any form or by any
means, graphic, electronic, or mechanical, including photocopying, recording,
taping, or by any information storage or retrieval system, without the
permission in writing from the publisher.

Published by Writers Club Press
an imprint of iUniverse.com, Inc.

For information address:
iUniverse.com, Inc.
620 North 48th Street
Suite 201
Lincoln, NE 68504-3467
www.iuniverse.com

ISBN: 0-595-09529-1

Printed in the United States of America

For—but not about—Ann

Acknowledgements

I am deeply indebted to the Indiana University South Bend Undergraduate Research Fund (SMART) for its funding of the research used in writing this novel. Specifically, I'd like to thank Brenda Knowles, Erika Zynda, Frances Sherwood, Tom Vander Ven, Lyle Zynda, and everyone involved with the URF program. Also thanks to Eva Day, Sean Conner, Dr. Michael Bartberger, Greg Pius, and most of all my patient and loving wife, Ann Charles Hoade.

One

The day before Gordon Mitchell was going to kill his wife, dreams of the life awaiting him tickled his mind like silent, playful caresses. He held the silence close, then, slowly, allowed in the sound of waves slipping onto the sand. He closed his eyes and could see the sun fat and orange and low in the sky, just dipping its oval in the water of the horizon. No Wanda. No worries. Never have to think twice about bills, about buying a round of drinks for your pals, about making a big—

"Down payment?" The chunky guy's eyes were almost bulging out of his glasses. "The ad in the paper said 'No down payment.' What kind of a scam you runnin' here?"

Gordon came back down from the clouds, remembering now where he was and who he was talking to: He was at Major Dale's RV World in Elkhart, Indiana—recreational vehicle capital of the world! And he was talking to a major burr in his saddle.

Of course, Gordon had been in this situation hundreds, quite possibly thousands of times in his fifteen years at Dale's. But just in case, he switched off his autopilot and assumed the controls of his well-oiled pitch machine.

"Okay to call you Dan?" he asked his beefy quarry.

Chunky Dan gave a half-shrug. "Whatever. The ad said 'No down payment.'"

"Why is that important to you, Dan?" He casually leaned up against the side of the mini-home's cab, forcing Dan to look at the beautiful machine he was nickel-and-diming himself away from. "A thousand dollars to drive home in *this* doesn't sound like much to me."

"Principle means something here."

Gordon leaned forward. "Principal, like money?"

"No, *principle,* like the bigger picture."

He leaned back. "Look, Dan, I want to sell you this mini-home. You want to buy it. All I need is a thousand bucks cash and you got it. What's it gonna take to do this? It's Friday afternoon, quarter to six—fifteen minutes and I'm gone for the weekend."

Dan chewed his lip.

Runway up ahead, Gordon thought with a smile. *Bring 'er in easy.* "You mean to tell me your wife's gonna be happy about not having this baby out tomorrow, all for a lousy grand?"

"How do I know it's worth it?"

A bigger smile spread across Gordon's face. Ask a salesman *How do I know it's worth it* and get ready for the show. "Rambling RVs are the best-built, most reliable coaches in the world, Dan. We take pride on doing things the best, things that the average customer—hell, even the sharpest customer, like you, Dan—wouldn't think about. Watch this."

Wagging a finger at his chunky customer, Gordon stepped over to the next row of vehicles, the giant bus-like Vacationeers, and tugged on the metal tubing holding the huge side mirror in place. Then he grabbed on and lifted his bulk off the ground, hanging a little over two hundred pounds on the tubing and bouncing on it a little for good measure. "Tell me that's not fine workmanship," Gordon said as he let himself back onto the asphalt and came back next to Dan. "Huh? Tell me."

"Yeah, it's fine. Lemme talk to your sales manager."

"You got him," Gordon said, still smiling but feeling a little turbulence in this landing.

"Then I want to see Major Dale. You guys said there was no goddamn down payment."

Mayday! "Look—Dan. How much we talking about for this baby?"

"You said seventeen." Mr. Principle was looking interested. "Seventeen nine."

"Make it twelve. Just give me a thousand dollars. Today."

Dan looked like a kid walking into a surprise birthday party, only with five thousand bucks sitting amidst all the streamers and balloons instead of a cake. "Really? You serious?"

"We aim to please," Gordon said. And knocking five *g*'s off the price is guaranteed to hit the mark, knock it dead. *Dead.* His thoughts turned to Wanda again, and a peaceful smile spread over his face.

Dan swung out a bank envelope, something Gordon had seen more times than a farmer's seen shit. "Got it right here. Don't we have some paperwork or something?"

Gordon looked at his watch, although he knew exactly what time it was, down to the second. "Do you really want to fill out forms right now or drive off in your new RV?" He took the cash, felt its silky beauty in his hands for a moment, checked to see none of the other employees of Major Dale's was looking, and slipped the wad into his shirt pocket. "Come back Monday and take care of that stuff, okay?" He wouldn't be there Monday, of course, or Tuesday, or ever again.

"You bet I will," Dan said with a wide grin, and shook Gordon's hand. "Thank you so much. No hard feelings about the down payment thing?"

"Forget about it."

The grin got wider, which hardly seemed possible, and that was that. Dan took the keys, got the fifth-wheel hitched to his pickup, and was gone.

Gordon beamed as he slipped the cash into his wallet. Perfect three-point landing. Maybe the last one of his high-flying career on the RV lot, for tomorrow, he had to get out of Dodge if he hoped to avoid a hanging.

Hanging. Death again. It made him think of Wanda, his wife, and that warmed his heart. He whistled softly as he strolled back to the deluxe manufactured housing office to formally list Chunky Dan's Mayan Berry-colored mini-home as being out on a test drive for the weekend—

His cell phone chirped. "Janey, I thought you were gonna call earli—"

"*Janey?* Expecting someone else?" Wanda barked through the ether. "Don't tell me—the little chippie's a customer."

"What is it, Wanda? Finishing up here."

"Well, I just talked to my sister. She's letting us stay over at her place during the trip."

Gordon reminded himself he was on a cell phone. "It's not a *trip*. We have *business* to take care of, remember? There's a very wealthy person waiting for this RV in New Mexico, and we wouldn't want to be late, right?"

"Wealthy person? What are you talking about? I thought this was the weekend we were taking the cash and—"

"Jesus, we're on a cell phone here."

"Well, we've got to stop sometime, Gordon. It's a twenty-six-hour drive."

"We'll find a motel."

"We're staying at my sister's. It's halfway there."

"Ron Mitchell," the loudspeaker outside the dealership boomed. "One-one."

"Gotta go," Gordon said. "That whole job thing."

"My sister's," she said again. "It's not up for discussion—"

He pressed a button and shut her up. Before he could even take a step toward the office, the phone chirped at him again.

He swept it up and shouted into it, "Goddamnit, Wanda—"

"*Wanda?* Were you expecting someone else?" the small voice on the line, younger and smoother than his wife's, strained to yell.

A hand went over his eyes. "Janey. Sorry. That bitch has me crazy."

"Well, you won't have to worry about her much longer." Gordon could feel her smiling all the way from Las Cruces.

"Cell phone, honey," he said. "I'm a bit rushed, sweetie—what's up?"

"Just wanted to hear your voice, Ronny. Oh, and I got my ticket with the money you sent."

"Fantastic. That makes life easier. I'll call you on the road, okay?"

"I'll be waiting, sugar."

"Love you, babe."

"Oooh, love you," she purred. "Oh, and Ronny? If you ever call me Wanda again, you know I'll rip your fucking throat out, right?"

"Perfectly understandable, baby," he said, and disconnected.

The loudspeaker sounded again. "Ron Mitchell, one-one. One-one. *Now.*"

He winced. Five minutes left before he could escape and he gets a one-one. Which meant Dale wanted to see him. And that couldn't be good.

As he himself liked to say, Gordon "Ron" Mitchell had been a lot of things to a lot of people, many of whom shaped him in their own images, which suited him just fine. He was the football star, the backseat Valentino, whatever—people looked at him and fit him into categories, categories which usually translated into meaning he was what they wanted to be. As a child, he was friends to almost everyone except the skinny, nerdy kids he felt could do nothing for him, the kids that as eight-year-olds went crazy for Sputnik and flying-saucer movies while he was more interested in girls (even then—Christ) and work, at that tender age odd jobs that didn't pay much but still facilitated relations with the girls.

Of course, he didn't even know what to *do* with girls back then. But he found out soon enough.

What he found out was that girls responded to *talk*. Action, sure, they liked strong, silent types as well. But what they *really* liked was being swept off their feet by a silver-tongued devil that made them feel like they were on top of the world.

The nerds taught him that. How, he never told anybody, but he remembered the day he learned talk could get him into or out of *anything*. Gordon and his buddy Leon were getting ready to traumatize this geek— you know, stuff him in his locker or stick him in the trunk of a car or something—when the kid said to Gordon, "Hey, I bet you could beat the *shit* out of Leon, huh?"

Gordon stopped, a grin half-cocked on his face, and sized up his pal. "Hell, yes," he said.

"The fuck you could," Leon said, smiling himself but dead serious, and he gave Gordon a playful little shove.

Gordon shoved back, and before he or Leon knew what was happening, they were slugging each other, knocked down on the floor of the hallway. The nerd was gone and forgotten—until later, when Gordon sat him down and listened to every word he said. Because if words worked that well on two toughs getting ready to pound someone, imagine how well it would work on some pretty little thing.

He never acknowledged the geeks in front of anybody, naturally, but he knew from then on that their ability to talk circles around anyone, their verbal slickness, their mental smoothness—transplanted into his body, these made up the skeleton key to any door he might care to open, and certainly to those of girls and money.

In high school, he discovered "Ron" worked better than "Gordon," even though he couldn't stand the sound of "Ron" (and he would never tell his sainted mother, who gave him his name, that he would so carelessly replace it). Ron Mitchell had no interest in football until he noticed talk alone wasn't doing it anymore—he needed some stature, and playing tail- back at Elkhart Memorial gave it to him in spades.

Then came Wanda.

Gorgeous, not too smart, entranced by Gordon's considerable charms. They met in his sophomore year at Indiana University in Bloomington and married four months later.

He had no junior year at Bloomington. He moved his new bride back up to Elkhart and, after ten years driving semis and getting laid in some of the prettiest spots in North America, started selling RVs at her uncle's lot. Her uncle, a decorated veteran of the Korean War, was Major Dale.

"Paged me, Dale?" Gordon asked as he half-knocked on the door.

Major Dale, stroking his white mustache as he gazed out onto the shimmering concrete of the sales lot, motioned for Gordon to sit. This didn't bode well for getting out of there in a hurry. "The lot's looking a little light," Dale said.

The tongue-twister hung Gordon up for a moment; then he got what Dale was saying. "End of the week. You know, plenty of deliveries."

"We're missing vehicles, Gordy. I want to know where they are."

Smooth, Gordon told himself. *Think silk, good Scotch, white skin—*

"Jeez, Dale, you know how I am with paperwork when the weekend's here. Have that for you Monday, no problem."

"Today. I want to know where every vehicle is *today.*"

Gordon could feel sweat beads pulsing on his forehead. He looked at the clock: ten after six. He had to meet Morihita at seven-thirty and not a minute later. The Japanese were bitches for punctuality. "Test drives. Couple of those."

"Fine. Write them down with the deliveries. Whenever you're done, I'll be here. I'm always here, you know that. Sixty-eight years old and you don't see me running off around the country, taking it easy," Dale said with a pronounced sniff.

It was amusing how a businessman as successful as Major Dale could have so much contempt for one of his core customer bases, retirees. They plunked down cash for new RVs—Class A's, none of this fifth-wheel stuff for them—like there was no tomorrow. Of course, for the Methuselahs they got in there, there probably weren't too many tomorrows left.

Silk, skin, Scotch. *Smooth.* "Look, Dale, I want to give you those numbers, and I will. But you know I've got that delivery to make, the

Vacationeer down to New Mexico *tonight*—leaving in a couple of hours," he said, looking at his watch for effect. "Back Tuesday, though. Wanda's coming with me—we're making a little vaca ... *trip* of it." Gordon knew Dale hated his people, especially his nephew-in-law, taking *vacations*. "See what I mean?"

"We've got a floor-plan checker from Rambling coming in here tomorrow—we're gonna be closed a *Saturday*, our biggest day of the week—to make sure everything's kosher. He'll freeze us if it isn't. I'm sorry, Gordy, I need those figures, all of 'em, tonight, before you leave."

Dizziness swept over Gordon. If he missed meeting Morihita, he wouldn't get his traveling money. If he didn't get his traveling money, there was no point even going down to New Mexico. And if he didn't get down to New Mexico—then over the border—he would be in jail by the end of the week, as soon as the floor-plan checker noticed a dozen VINs didn't match up with the vehicles on the lot. Then Wanda, who had thrown in with him to cash in and get away from it all, would have no choice but to turn witness on her husband to save herself from going down. It was the risk he took enlisting Wanda as protection against her uncle's suspicions—Dale's little Wanda would never do anything like this—until he could get her alone and get her dead.

He had to beat the Rambling floor-plan checker. He had to buy time.

"Tell you what, Dale. I want to get everything in order and you want everything in order, so we're on the same page here. The Rambling guy isn't gonna freeze a dealership of this size—"

"The hell he isn't. I need it *tonight*, Gordy. Or is there some reason you don't want the numbers known?"

His hair stood on end. This was impossible. Gordon had covered his tracks. Unless Wanda had said something to her uncle—that *bitch!* When he finally got her where he wanted her—

"The checker, name's Johnson, has already stopped by, Gordy. He found some discrepancies. Big ones." Dale cleared his throat. "Now, I know how you are with paperwork and letting folks have long test drives, and so does he, so he agreed not to freeze us until he does another check tomorrow. We're getting a break. See why I need this tonight?"

Gordon ignored the attempt to reason; Dale wasn't half the salesman he was. "What about the delivery? A touring Class A, two hundred eighty thousand and change. You wanna just let the sale go?"

"Gordon! What's got into you? Of course not. I've got another salesman to deliver the vehicle—Timothy."

"*Timothy?*" Gordon said, eyes bugging. "Not Tim, right? It's *Timothy.*"

"He's a good kid. He can get the coach down to New Mexico and get all the papers signed. It's not that hard, Gordon."

"Greenhorn. Guy's a greenhorn." Gordon scoffed as well as he could with all of the blood draining from his vital systems. "He can't shut this sale."

Major Dale leaned forward in his huge chair, the oiled leather squeaking incongruously. "You are going to stay here until every vehicle that is supposed to be on this lot is accounted for. Call in every one of your extended test drives. Get every scrap of paperwork from every sale you've made in the past month. Account for all of the cash from the Japanese sales. I am going home. You will do…it…*tonight.*"

Gordon looked at the clock. Six-thirty. He had an hour until Morihita, cash, freedom—if he made it. One hour. "Mind if I grab dinner?"

Dale nodded. *Bye, Dale!* Gordon's heart soared.

Then his wife's uncle said, "Take Timothy with you. I want you back here."

And with that, any opportunity for further smooth talking was lost.

Anger and frustration fried his brain. Months planning this out, nearly a year, the triple crown of lots of cash, Wanda deader than eight-tracks, and a new life away from hawking RVs to Mr. and Mrs. Methuselah every day dancing before him, and *pow!* The one month he picks, Rambling calls the dealership to the carpet hours before he's gone.

All that, and he's stuck with Jonny Quest the tenderfoot salesman, part of the new breed mostly seen at the manufacturer lots: Clean-cut, service-oriented, looking towards management in the company. *Christ.*

As they drove in silence to dinner in Gordon's customized converted van—made in Elkhart, van conversion capital of the world!—he noticed that Timothy was lustily admiring the conversion work, especially the audio system. This could be an opening, he saw. Everybody's got an opening. He jumped in.

"Like it? Four thousand bucks for the whole job."

"Gee! I love stuff like this," Timothy said as he took it in.

Gee? Did the kid actually say *gee,* as in *gee whiz golly willickers?* "Um…look, Timothy, you sure you know how to handle a Class A? Like a bus, you know?"

"Oh, sure. My pop was a trucker. I've handled the big rigs before. You don't think I can do it, Mr. Mitchell?"

"Call me Ron," Gordon said automatically, although he actually would have preferred the little dork call him Mr. Mitchell, get the pecking order well-established. "Far as handling it goes, I'm sure you'd do just fine, Timothy. But maybe I *want* to take it down to New Mexico. Talking motivation here."

"I don't follow you, Mr. Mitch—Ron."

Gordon fired up the bullshit props on his finely crafted mental P-38. He loved the hum of his mind's engines as he zeroed in on a target, be it a sale, a lay, whatever. "I want to drive the RV down, son. It's my twenty-fifth with the wife. Wanna take her on a little trip."

"The Major must have his reasons for keeping you here, right?"

Got that right. "Old men like Dale don't need to keep young wives happy, Timothy. Young ones do."

"I don't follow you, Mr. Mitchell."

Gordon shook his head and realized that hell, to the tenderfoot, he probably looked older than Moses. "Talking about *me.* I need to take the coach, get me?"

Timothy pondered this for a moment, seeming to weigh the implications of everything Gordon had said and what effect it might have on his brand-new career if anything went awry. Then he looked around the cabin of the van, checking out the teakwood trim, the color TV, the Rockford Fosgate unit, the sunken speakers, the power amps, the cherry rose carpeting on the floor and walls, even the Chevrolet key ring hanging from the ignition.

"You gonna help me out, Timothy?"

"Gosh, Ron," he said in his Dennis-the-Menace lilt, "what's it worth to ya?"

Gordon's lips curled into a toothy smile. Wasn't gonna take the van with him anyway.

3

Major Dale did not go home after talking to Gordon, instead calling his wife and telling her to hold dinner until he called again. Then he swiveled in his finely upholstered leather chair to face the sales lot and the Mediterranean Aqua Vacationeer, over a quarter of a million dollars' worth of cruising luxury that was scheduled to go down to New Mexico tomorrow with Timothy now instead of Gordon.

When he saw Timothy pull up—*hey, wasn't that Gordon's van?*—and climb into the Vacationeer, he almost turned his back to the window and told his wife to go ahead and heat up whatever the hell she planned on making.

But then he saw Gordon climb out of the van and skulk into a Coyote Tan Class A Luxliner Junior, driving it right off the lot after Timothy in the Vacationeer.

He picked up the phone but not to call his wife. He followed the series of voice-mail instructions made by the police department's phone system.

Finally a human answered and Dale said, "Yes, Detective Gann, Dale here. It turns out you were right all along."

4

Gordon always thought it was hilarious that the Japs would come ten thousand miles, fly for fourteen hours, to see America and the first place they had to go was Elkhart, Indiana, to pick up their RV. Of course, every other place in the country would look better after seeing Indiana first.

He swung the Luxliner into the Ramada Inn lot, taking up thirty feet of the fire lane as he let off the brake to that satisfying *hiss*. He brought up his watch: Seven-thirty on the dot.

But no Morihita.

He wriggled down to make himself comfortable in the captain's chair and counted his traveling money in his head. Two thousand from earlier in the day, plus the grand from Chunky Dan—and now the Japs would come through as they had for the past month, getting ready for the big summer traveling season by slapping down big bucks to "rent" giant coaches. Really, they were buying the RVs and selling them back as used after a summer of sightseeing, 'cause what the hell did the Japs need a coach for back in Tokyo or whatever? And really renting one would get you a second-rate vehicle for the same amount as buying a brand-new one and selling it back. This was Gordon's grand plan, and it was working fine. Six coaches at just about three hundred grand apiece, and now this little beauty to Morihita for eighty—

A rap at the window lifted Gordon out of his seat.

"Mr. Mitchell?"

Mistuh Mitchurr? Gordon almost laughed. Fucking Japs.

He popped the door open and swung down, hand extended for immediate shaking. "Mr. Morihita, please call me Ron. Ready for the summer of a lifetime?" he said, slapping the side of the coach.

Morihita looked starched even in his red polo shirt and khaki slacks, but a smile broke across his stern features as he scanned the Luxliner. "This is the vehicle we spoke about?"

"That's right—the Rambling Luxliner Junior. All the luxury and convenience of the Luxliner, but—as you requested—even easier to handle than our six-axle original Luxliner." Gordon could recite all of the pluses of the Junior over the original in his sleep, then turn around and list the pluses of the original over the Junior. All he had to do was keep talking. "Eighty thousand dollars is quite the bargain for this, but I do like to cater to my Japanese friends."

"Very good," Morihita said, and pulled out his checkbook. "My family and I are looking forward to seeing the United—"

"Wait!" Gordon stepped forward, speaking before Morihita's pen could touch the paper. "Cash only on these transactions, Mr. Morihita, please. Remember, that was part of the deal for the sales-return policy we discussed. My apologies."

Morihita stiffened, then slid the checkbook into his back slacks pocket. "It is very difficult to bring that much currency into the United States, Mr. Mitchell."

"Ron. Yes, I know, but—"

"Ron Mitchell, what if I told you I did not have that much currency, because it would require declaration through United States Customs Department?"

He was pulling the Customs routine? Everything swayed for a second, stopping just in time for Gordon to keep himself from falling over. He could feel pinpricks of sweat on his face, his arms, his back. It would be so easy for Dale to check Customs records for cash brought into the States, and it would be so easy to track that right down to the missing coaches...

"Mr. Mitchell?"

Nonchalantly, Gordon made a slight bow to his customer. Slight, but unmistakable. Then he said, "Mr. Morihita, I would ask why you did not bring thousand-dollar bills, which your company can transfer to accounts in the U.S. through internal documentation. This would save you from having to declare the money, sir."

Morihita's lips pursed, and he nodded sternly at Gordon. And then he laughed, sweeping out an envelope fat with bills. "You are a very smart salesman, Mr. Mitchell. Count this—you will find eighty of those thousand-dollar bills."

Gordon counted. He found them. "You're good to go, Mr. Morihita. I got the faxed contracts back at the office, so there's nothing more to do except hop on that horse and ride," he said, and with a hearty cowboy smile gripped Morihita's hand and shook.

The Jap smiled too, and gave him a little bow of his own. Gordon chuckled, and hoped Morihita could at least see the rest of Indiana before the police took back the coach. Timothy pulled up in the Vacationeer, and Gordon hopped in and rode west, into the sunset.

Gordon dropped Timothy back at the lot, then popped across town and just sat in the Vacationeer, listening to the ten-CD system, grinning through narrowed eyes.

There had been some obstacles shoved in his way at the last minute, but, like the former football player he was, he finessed his way through what he could, then dropped his shoulder and rammed through the rest. Even though Morihita had given him the huge bills, useless for traveling money, he still had three grand in smaller denominations for trip expenses.

Time to celebrate.

He pulled the thirty-five-foot Vacationeer across six parking spaces of the Kitty Klub, Elkhart's premier strip club and one Gordon knew…well, intimately. This was his last night in the United States, his last chance to down a few and get laid, show what he was made of. After all, the giant bills weren't totally useless.

"Ever seen anything like this?" he asked the brunette, who called her-self "Angie"—the chick had a name from a Stones song, that had to be a good omen. She came and sat on his lap, taking a look at the green piece of paper with a one and three zeros in each corner and Grover Cleveland right in the middle.

"Is that for real?" Her eyes went to the money but her arms stayed wrapped around him. She was firm. God, was she firm. "A million-dollar bill?"

"Thousand." His prick was rising up against her firm, firm thighs as she sat on his lap. "Just a thousand dollars."

"That's still a lot," Angie said, and whipped off her top just like that, bouncing her tan (and firm) breasts in Gordon's face. They were so close he could smell his boozy breath bouncing off of them. "You ever seen anything like these?"

He had seen breasts *like* them in that they were bulbous and nippled, but never any so…magnificent. "Can I touch?"

"I don't think my boyfriend would like that."

"He likes you sitting on men's laps with your tits in their faces?"

"I'm mostly a dancer," she said, not answering the question. But that word hung in the air like a promise: *Mostly*. "I got bills to pay."

Gordon wiggled the Cleveland. "And I'm here to help you pay 'em."

She put her tan, firm breast in his fingers. Better than a handshake.

The rest of Angie was just as firm and tan, the impossibly skinny strips of white where her bathing suit once lay against her just serving to enhance the effect. She was duly impressed with the Vacationeer, as it was one hell of an impressive machine, if Gordon did say so himself. Starting from the front, it had a dashboard like the cockpit of a 747, a nineteen-inch remote-control color television between two full-swivel captain's chairs, a full-size sofa (available in over two hundred stain-resistant fabrics) and recliner, central roof-ducted air conditioning, full overlay cabinetry (available in three distinctive hardwoods), full-size bathroom with marble countertop and full shower, kitchen area with microwave, gas stove and oven, a dining room with seating for four, tons of "basement" storage space, and the *pièce de résistance*—a huge bedroom with thirteen-inch TV, beveled mirrors, security safe, and more storage located underneath a full queen-size bed, the final thing Angie was impressed with as Gordon laid her down and started peeling her already slight clothing off of her.

Firm. Young and firm. To Wanda as day is to the dead of night.

Dead! He chuckled to himself.

She kissed him; it was a good kiss, full of interest and creativity. Gordon appreciated that and returned it with gusto. Her legs were spread up against his slacks and he liked that, too.

"Ron," Angie said as she started unbuttoning his shirt, "I've really never seen one of those dollars before. It's really real, right? Not that I'm doing this for the money."

Right. "Don't worry, sweetheart, it's real. You can't just spend it, though—"

"What?" Her legs slammed together like the covers of a book.

"Wait! Gotta take it to a bank and let 'em exchange it for hundreds, that's all. Took it out of circulation, honey, that's all. Take it easy. It's good money." He eased her legs back apart and nestled himself between them.

"Well, why do you have one?"

"Got more than one, sweetheart."

She unbuttoned him faster. "Okay, but why?"

"See, I sell these beauties," he said, motioning at the gorgeous surroundings. This one would take three hundred of those bills you got there."

"Thirty thousand dollars? Wow!"

"Whatever," he said, but dumb, beautiful women got his blood going. He was aching for this little sweetie. "Point is, I deal in big, big amounts of cash. In fact, goin' down to New Mexico tomorrow to get my hands on a huge stash." *Jesus—why was he telling her all this? Why did he have to blab to these chicks?*

His pants were yanked off by Angie, who was now visibly excited. *Oh yeah, that's why.* "I'll come with you," she said as she slid his jockeys down

and off, leaving his member standing proudly, like the flagpole in front of
Fort Knox.

"Ooh, can't, honey, sorry." And he was. "Gotta take the wife—"

He slapped his hand over his mouth. Fort Knox's flagpole began to fly
more at half-mast. Time stood still. Angie stared at him with an expression of growing bemusement. "Wife, huh?"

"Got a boyfriend yourself, don't ya?" He said in a "we're all in this
together" tone, not accusatory. Never make a sale that way.

"I sure do, Ron," she said, and took him into her hands. "Got another
one of those million-dollar bills, don't ya?"

He sure did.

Ecstasy. His last night on earth, his last night as a married man enjoying
the fruits of another woman, his last night as a working stiff, couldn't have
been better spent than in the arms of Angie, although her questions about
the money…and then his wife…and then New Mexico lasted throughout
the evening.

One day he would have to learn to keep his mouth shut around
women, keep his damn trap shut and save himself a lot of trouble, but as
long as the rewards of having a woman listen rapt to you and the costs so
relatively small, he didn't know when that lesson would really be worth
bothering with.

6

Wanda Polska Mitchell started wearing makeup when she was seven years old. She got into her mother's makeup case and became enthralled with the many colors, the different textures, the exotic names (Desert Bloom, Irish Rose) for different shades of pink and lavender, the way her mom would delicately apply just a bit of each to create a unique look for her father's return home. *Less is more*, her mother would say when it came to makeup.

Her dad would come home, drop his case on the chair by the front door, and hold Wanda's mom's shoulders in his hands, drinking her in. "Aren't you beautiful?" he would say, every day the same words, and give her a big kiss, smearing even the little bit of "wonderful war paint," as he called it, but it didn't matter at that point. The effect had been created. Her mother had succeeded again.

Of course, when dad didn't come home one day, or the next, or the next, Wanda knew it wasn't just a business trip because her mother didn't constantly cry during those, didn't stop putting on her wonderful makeup even though dad wouldn't be walking through the door for a few days.

After a few weeks, Wanda and her little sister, Peg, learned the truth from her mother: "Your father's left us for his receptionist, for that made-up hussy."

Wanda didn't know what a "receptionist" was, nor a "hussy," but she knew what "made-up" was. It meant his receptionist was more beautiful than Wanda or her mom—wore more makeup than did her mother, and was consequently that much more desirable.

It was a lesson well learned.

Wanda Polska started dipping into her mother's makeup case and coming out looking like a million bucks, right from the start. She had an intuitive knack for matching colors, textures, styles. She could just look at a fashion magazine and know how to apply every bit. Even if she did have a tendency to apply the makeup a little thick, more like an artist does to a canvas than a woman usually does to her face, the overall effects were still nothing short of stunning.

She did her mother from the time they moved from Elkhart to Bloomington (when she was seven, when her dad left) to the time she left to go back to Elkhart with her new husband, the dashing and promising Gordon "Ron" Mitchell. Her mother cried at the wedding, but her makeup stayed perfect. Wanda was a genius with mascara and eye shadow, everyone said in the '60s and early '70s, when more was better. She worked as a cosmetologist and beauty consultant, had lots of clients who were all very pleased and took her advice to heart, only applying the war paint (now Gordon called it that) a good deal less generously at home than Wanda did at the salon.

That was more than ten years ago, after Gordon started selling RVs at her uncle's lot but before he became a big shot there. Before the other women, before the drinking with the other salesmen, before Wanda gave up and became a childless housewife. The good times.

Now, maybe the good times were back. Gordon's little scam (not so little, really—he could end up put away for a long time; hell, they *both* could) had socked away over a million dollars in the past month. So what if it was from her uncle? She never cared much for him anyway, and the feeling was mutual, she knew.

Over a million dollars. Splitting it with him fifty-fifty (her price for flying the cash down to New Mexico and stuffing it in that safety deposit box for Gord's contact to launder), she could finally get free of him and start her own life, her own salon even. Bring whatever family she wanted near down to South America.

Of course, Gordon would take his half and spend it on cheap bimbos (or not-so-cheap ones) and booze, like he had always spent their money. Which reminded her that she had one more job to do before she sent him packing in Mexico.

With that, she finished up her nap and got to work.

Two hours later, Wanda pulled the zipper closed on her fourth and final suitcase. Gordon walked in, looking surprisingly alert and sharp considering the drinking and probable screwing she knew he was doing until ten at night.

"I have more belongings than bags," she said, and crossed her arms.

"Leave some belongings, then," Gordon said, and proceeded to grab his own packed suitcases. "Don't care what you bring anyway."

"No, Gordon."

"Be happy, Wanda. This time tomorrow, we're millionaires. Buy new stuff."

"No."

He let out a sigh and put his own suitcases down. He was counting the minutes until she drew her last breath. "We've had ten months to plan this, *dear*. You saying you couldn't have gotten more bags before now?"

"I need more room. I don't have any of my cosmetology materials, none of my teaching stuff. I've got to bring it, Gordon—I want to start up my own business again."

"That junk's fifteen years out-of-date, maybe more! We'll buy more. Besides, Venezuelan women wear their war paint a little different than Americans. Lighter, for one."

"I get more bags or I'm not going."

Jesus! If anything, she had gotten *more* obstinate over the past year, as freedom approached. Like she wanted to get her last digs in before she died or something. In any case, he wasn't going to have her getting goofy on him.

He dumped his suitcases open on the floor. Clothes, after shave, shoes in a heap. And on top of it, a bag, now spilled open, of thousand-dollar bills.

"That ain't the *Racing Form*," Wanda said with her trademark sneer, one reserved just for him. "Is there something you want to share with me?"

"*Something you wanna share with me?*" Gordon spat back. "Got one last sale in last night. Tell you about it later."

She trudged over to him, arms still crossed. "Now."

Just twenty or so more hours, he reminded himself. He could put up with it for twenty-five years, he could put up with it for one more day. "What do you want? Made one last sale tonight, to another Jap. Eighty grand, cash money. I was gonna tell you."

"My half. Now." The woman could bark orders. She stuck her hand out.

He slapped the bag in her hand. "You hold onto it. Gesture of goodwill."

As he kicked as much of his stuff as he could into just one suitcase to leave the rest of them for Wanda, she began counting the bills one by one, finishing at seventy-eight. "There's two missing."

Gordon didn't know what to say. His silver tongue had tarnished to the point of uselessness with Wanda years ago.

"Was she cute?"

"Firm," Gordon said, giving up.

"Two thousand dollars worth of firm? You spend *two thousand* on a goddamn *hooker?*"

He waved his hands at her. "Listen, this money's to grease the wheels for the trip. We get pulled over, some hick cop with a bug up his ass—two thousand bucks is nothing compared to what we got coming, get me? But it *is* enough to startle somebody into leaving us alone."

"You didn't spend two thousand to get some slut to leave you alone, Gordon."

He stopped then and dropped his chin to his chest, turning all solemn on her. "Leaving all that behind now, sweetheart. Last time, I swear to God."

Not terribly original, but the best he could do on the spot. When he sneaked a glance at her, however, he could tell right away she wasn't buying it.

"You know, one time I'd like to—" Wanda started, then stopped short as the doorbell rang. Someone was there. Someone who was not supposed to be there was there.

Quickly, Wanda hid the money as Gordon zipped downstairs, noticing they could still work as a team when they had to.

7

Lieutenant Detective Douglas Gann had been with the Elkhart, Indiana, Police Department for two years, since his graduation from the academy after graduate school. He had been assigned to the Mitchell case when he got a call three weeks earlier from Major Dale himself, owner of Major Dale's RV World. ("Major Dale's makes Major Deals," the ad went.)

Dale knew who was stealing RVs from his lot and even knew how he was doing it. What he couldn't understand, he told Gann, was *why* his sales manager, Gordon Mitchell, was doing it. The man made eighty thousand dollars a year at least, sometimes more! The boy's wife—Dale's niece—was, at forty-three, still a slim and beautiful woman. And Mitchell could look forward to being part-owner of the lot someday!

Major Dale told the detective all of this out of confusion and feelings of betrayal and despair. Gann understood that well enough. He had seen men with perfectly good jobs, even great ones; nice wives, even perfect ones; and promising futures, even sparkling ones, give it all up for what they saw as one big score, or what they saw as a better woman, or what they saw as a more worry-free future.

Gann didn't know if Gordon Mitchell had another woman on the side or if he needed the money for gambling debts or what, but he did know that after Dale's call the night before telling him Mitchell was heading to New Mexico with his wife in tow, he knew Wanda Mitchell's life was in serious danger.

He'd seen it before. A wife is a dangerous witness to leave behind, so the husband would plan a trip somewhere, turn on the romance, then kill the poor woman before skipping the country. He had definitely seen it before, especially in cases where, as Major Dale had told him on the phone, the magic had been gone for some time.

Poor Wanda probably didn't even know what her husband was mixed up in.

Lieutenant Detective Douglas Gann noted the beautiful bus-sized motor home parked on the street as he walked up to the house and rang the doorbell. He'd seen all this before.

"Help you?" Gordon asked with a smile, his head barely poking out of the cracked door.

Gann flashed his badge. "Detective Doug Gann, Elkhart Police. Taking a trip?"

"Sell RVs. That's a delivery."

"Almost midnight—seems kinda late to be heading out on a trip. *Are* you going on a trip, Mr. Mitchell?" Gann asked, smiling to himself that he was using Mitchell's name without the poor bastard knowing how he knew it.

"Delivering the coach. Can I help you with something, Detective?"

"You haven't answered me. Are you taking a trip or not?"

"Why? Listen, you know my name, you obviously know what delivering a coach is. What do you want?"

"Is your wife home, Mr. Mitchell? Or is she out delivering a coach?"

Gordon cocked his head at Gann and took a slow drag on his cigarette. "Home."

"I need to speak to her."

Gordon Mitchell then gave Gann the most insincere smile he had ever seen. If this was the expression he used with his customers at Major Dale's, it was a wonder the guy had ever had a job to steal from. "This about those parking tickets?" he asked with unconvincing jocularity. "I've told her a hundred times—"

"Please bring Mrs. Mitchell to the door, Mr. Mitchell." Gann made no attempt at returning the smile Gordon was pitching at him, had no interest in buying whatever it was he was trying to sell. "Or may I come in?"

"I'll bring her," Gordon said, and shut the door in Gann's face.

Wanda finished zipping up the last of the suitcases Gordon had dumped out for her. In one she had their dirty bed sheets; in another was all of their towels they didn't use anymore, except for company; and the last was filled with nothing at all, just an empty zipped-up suitcase. She smiled at the pile of personal effects Gordon had been forced to leave behind in giving her his share of the luggage.

She started as the door swung open. "It's the police," Gordon said, out of breath from taking the stairs almost three at a time. "Wants to talk to *you*."

She had to admit she was surprised by this, and then maybe a bit worried. Had her role in this somehow come uncovered? She was the one who took the money down to the safety deposit box in New Mexico every time, after all—maybe she had been caught on surveillance cameras!

Or maybe her son-of-a-bitch husband had turned on her to get out of having to pay her share of the money. But that wouldn't make any sense— he'd be out his money, too, and money was his prime motivating factor. She'd just be happy as long as Gordon was miserable. What with the trip approaching, it hadn't been easy being happy lately.

But the detective was waiting, and no matter what nasty surprise might be in store, she had to go down and face him. "Let me just put a face on," she said.

She watched Gordon roll his eyes at her. He was such an asshole.

Even though he was just in his late twenties, dark brown hair sometimes falling into his eyes and making him look like little more than a skinny kid of average height, Douglas Gann had seen all of this before. So he did exactly what he had done dozens, maybe hundreds of times in the past two years; he waited in a family's sitting room for someone to come down and talk with him. He fiddled with picture frames. He noted layers of dust behind things. He resisted the urge to plunk a few random notes on the piano. But mostly, he planned what he was going to say. He had waited downstairs to arrest people before, had waited downstairs to tell families their son or daughter, sister or brother, husband or wife had died in accidents, murders, suicides.

But never had he come to urge someone not to go on a vacation.

This was a first. It was also the first time he felt he could use his position as a police detective to directly save someone's life. It was a nice feeling, one he got all too seldom on this job.

"Officer?"

He turned at the voice, a pleasant if flat female tone, and saw Mrs. Wanda Mitchell descending the stairs. For a forty-something woman, she was in good shape; she obviously spent time at the gym or doing stepercize or whatever. But her face... Something seemed wrong with her face. She looked like a Kabuki performer, or the Joker from Batman. She was wearing the heaviest makeup of any woman he had ever seen, and that included burn victims.

But the shock—that long-forgotten shock of connection—hit Gann, and hit him hard.

"Good—ah, good evening, Mrs. Mitchell, sorry to be calling so late. I'm Detective Doug Gann from the Elkhart Police. Is there somewhere private we can talk?"

"What about my husband?" Her mouth looked so odd to him as she talked. The funny thing to Gann was that she actually looked very inviting still, like she was using the cosmetics to somehow accentuate...*Oh heck*, Gann thought. *I have no idea what I'm talking about.*

"It has to be private, ma'am."

"Is it about Gordon?"

"I'm afraid it is, ma'am."

At that she smiled. And Gann could tell right away it wasn't fake. He followed her into the sun room and closed the door behind them.

Gordon busied himself with shoving everything he could into the basement storage of the Vacationeer. He took no time to admire the workmanship of the gliding compartment doors, the coordinated color scheme of the riveted fiberglass sidewalls with the stylish acrylic patio awning. He didn't think once of the interlocking, double-welded aluminum studs around the frame-mounted windows and doors or about the construction of the walls: one-piece high-gloss gel-coat fiberglass backed by an inch and a half of fiberglass insulation, a vapor barrier, three-quarters of an inch of bead foam insulation, and a final layer of fine wood veneer paneling. All of this escaped his notice, although at any other time he might have stopped to savor their beauty.

Because his mind, in order not to freak out about Detective Gann's surprise visit, was focused squarely on *the plan*. He had worked the plan out in such perfect detail, not leaving a single element to chance, that once he got on the road, it ran virtually no risk of failure. He had the exact route picked out to his destination, which was Truth or Consequences, New Mexico, the town named after that game show. He would deliver three hundred thousand dollars worth of recreational vehicle in exchange for the wonderful banking services provided by his contact in that cozy little tourist town. He had every stop along the way picked for maximum visibility for Wanda and himself—for just this contingency of a cop wondering what's going on! He congratulated himself on that one.

He also had the exact spot where he would kill his darling wife of twenty-five long, wasted years picked out, and had had it picked out for ten months. The steepest drop off the most remote lookout on the road to T or C, as the locals called it. No one would find her body until he was ensconced snugly in Venezuela, collecting twenty percent on his full million and a half.

Again, the thought warmed him as he worked. He slid the hatches closed on the storage compartments (some of those bags had seemed pretty light) and gazed back at the house where Wanda was talking to Detective Needlenose, a house he would never see again.

A tiny yelp escaped his throat, but of joy or panic, he couldn't say.

"No one's gonna kill me, Mr. Gann. I can fend for myself."

Gann shook his head. "Wanda, I'm afraid that's not the case. I have seen this all before. Did you know anything about the thefts at your uncle's RV lot?"

"Thefts? No, of course not," she lied.

"Did you know your husband has purchased a single ticket to Caracas, Venezuela, from Mexico City? I have a friend who did me the favor of checking for any travel-related activity on Mr. Mitchell's credit card. Gordon bought an airline ticket, a *single* ticket."

This was news. "Just one?"

"He's not taking you with him for the rest of his trip, Wanda. He's visiting Venezuela alone."

"I—I didn't even know there *was* a rest of the trip," she lied, at least remembering to do that as she reeled from what Gann was telling her. "Why would he buy one ticket? What's in, um, Venezuela?"

"They have no extradition treaty with the United States, Mrs. Mitchell. And—please excuse me for saying this—he is trying to escape prosecution, maybe for crimes he hasn't even committed yet. That's why I'm here to try to persuade you not to accompany him on this road trip—you're not going as far as Gordon is, he's going to make sure of that."

A tiny, tiny smirk crossed Wanda's lips, so small Gann might have mistaken it for a simple twitch if he had seen it. *Son of a bitch wants a divorce,* she thought with amazement. The insinuation the detective was making didn't make a whole lot of sense—not one bit of Gordon's plan would have been possible without her. The lot was her uncle's. She shuttled the money down to that weird little town in New Mexico. She covered for him constantly. The idea that her husband would want to kill her—not just want her dead, which she guessed all spouses wished for their partners occasionally, but to actually want to *kill* her—skipped past her like a friend's recipe suggestion for a dish to which she was deathly allergic. She gave it barely a first thought, let alone a second.

No, Wanda just let out a weary sigh and thought, *The son of a bitch wants a divorce. He wants to leave me, after all I've done for him.* It was the only reasonable thought—he was going to flee the country without her, let her face the music for what they together had done. What a guy.

"Your life is in danger. Let me take you into protective custody. You shouldn't be traveling alone with Gordon Mitchell. He's not the man you think he is."

You mean he doesn't *screw around?* she almost said, but thought the better of it. Best to have this young officer feeling like she herself thinks she's in the model marriage. She was far from any suspicion that way. "It's hard to believe, Doug. I love my husband. And he loves me. He must just think I want him to drop me off at my sister's in Oklahoma City."

"I know you love him, Wanda. If he's on the up-and-up, great; the worst is that we will have inconvenienced you for nothing. I know you're looking forward to this trip, but honestly, you could be in grave danger."

Young or not, he talked like what she guessed a regular police detective would, she had to give him that. "I'm going on the trip," she said at last.

Gann sighed. "I had hopFed I wouldn't have to use this," he said, reaching into his coat pocket.

Her heart jumped. She was under arrest! *Her!* Goddamn Gordon robs, cheats, screws—she's the faithful wife, and this is how things end up!

Gann took a folded piece of paper from his pocket and handed it to her. "It's a subpoena for deposition in this case, Wanda. I'm afraid we're going to have to have you come in and tell us anything you might know about the thefts at your uncle's lot."

"When?"

"Next week," he said, and added, "and I hate to say this, but—that's only if you're still alive, of course. I have good reason to believe your husband will try to hurt or kill you on this trip and make it look like an accident, try to eliminate you as a witness."

"*Kill* me?" Wanda said with a laugh. "Why would you believe something like that? He's never so much as raised a hand to me."

Gann patted her on the shoulder. "Wanda, I know it's hard to accept, but I've seen all of this before. This is how these things work," he said, and added emphasis with a nod. "Now, are you sure there's nothing you might know that Gordon wouldn't want you telling us?"

If you only knew. She nodded, looking appropriately regretful.

He nodded as well. "Here's my card. Please call me if you change your mind, even on the road. I'll come. You have a cellular phone on that monster, right?"

"And fax, and satellite TV."

"Great. I hope you enjoy them," Gann said, but she could tell he wished she wouldn't get near the coach at all. "Call me."

"Thanks." She hesitated. "Um, Detective—I have to ask: If you're so sure he's going to do something bad, or that he did something bad, why don't you just arrest him?"

Gann cleared his throat. "Your uncle…"

"Dale?"

"He won't move forward unless you've got immunity to testify. Would you like immunity?" Gann said this very slowly, not looking her in the eye.

Wanda stared at the floor. For months she had dreamed of her and Gordon, on the beach, without the worries that had fucked up their marriage for so long. She wanted to make him pay for all the shit he had done to her, but there was still a chance to work things out, wasn't there?

Finally she said, "I told you, Detective—I don't know about any thefts."

Gann looked at her again and nodded. They rose and she showed him to the door, closing it behind him. She leaned up against it and let all of her air out.

Detective Gann seemed like an earnest and nice young guy. She had been attracted to him; it was obvious he had been attracted to her. But he was way off-base about everything—almost everything. He wouldn't be much of a worry.

She had heard Gordon come back into the house and wondered if he had eavesdropped on any of the conversation. "Gord! A word with you!" she yelled up the stairs.

He wasn't going to like this, and that was just fine. Lieutenant Detective Douglas Gann had just put a very powerful weapon in her hand, one she intended to use to its full squirm factor on her husband— soon to be *ex*-husband? She'd *rather* be dead than go through the embarrassment of a divorce, be left like her mother was.

"Not so fast," she said with a smile, and held up the subpoena. "It's time to take another look at our arrangement."

8

Detective Gann was thankful Class A touring motor homes were so darn big. If they weren't, he wouldn't have been able to climb up on the side of the RV opposite the house and slap a transmitter at the base of the Mitchells' cellular antenna without anyone seeing a thing, under cover of the near-midnight darkness.

He stepped back, satisfied with his work. Whenever the Mitchells used their phone or fax—actually, as long as the cellular antenna was powered up, which was probably whenever the vehicle's battery was charged, their global positioning system would send a signal that gave the coach's location, a signal Gann could access and decipher with his new department-owned laptop. It was a system used mainly for tracking stolen cars—Gann was sure there was an on-demand system inside for the rich retirees who bought these things, maybe with a backup too that could be tracked with an access number known only to the owner and the Rambling company—but tracking the Mitchells seemed to Gann like the perfect use of a system meant to stop crime.

Gordon Mitchell would not get away with whatever it was he planned on doing. And Gann certainly was not about to let him kill his beautiful and charming wife.

9

"That's right, jerk-off," Wanda said, "Sixty-forty or I'm talking to the cops."

"Don't do this. We're almost home-free."

"*Free?* That's a word you're not going to know for a while if you don't stop being so cheap."

"Giving you nearly a million dollars already is *cheap?* Get a subpoena and you think you own me, Wanda? There's nothing you can say that won't point a finger back at you, babe."

"You are the cheapest son of a bitch I have ever known. You should be *thanking* me, Gord." She gazed out at the RV, probably just for effect. "They've known about your scam from the beginning. I told you Dale was no fool."

Gordon steamed. *No fool? I've got a lot of money in New Mexico for no reason if Major Dale wasn't fooled.* "My scam, huh?" he started, and then caught himself. *Wait a minute...* "Sixty-forty, Wanda? That what you want? That gonna get you on the bus?"

"No, I mean it. You better not try to rip me off later, either."

"Not a problem. In fact, keep the seventy-eight grand as a down payment."

She hesitated, and that almost made Gordon laugh. He knew damn well it wasn't like him to give in right in the middle of an argument (or at the end of one, for that matter), so she was caught off-guard. Maybe even disappointed. All the better. For he had just realized: *Why am I arguing?* By the end of the day tomorrow, Wanda would be dead. She could ask for all of it and get her wish right now!

"Why?" she asked warily.

He fought to keep down a smirk. "Isn't that what you wanted?"

"Yeah…"

"Owe it to you, right? Isn't that what you said?"

She had no position to argue from here, and she couldn't *stand* it. "Right."

"Then take it," he said, and actually put out his hand for her to shake. "Sixty-forty."

She ignored his hand, but said, "Fine. But Detective Gann is right— something's not right about this." She didn't look happy.

"Not right? How about, we're stealing a million and a half dollars and fleeing the country? How's that for 'not right'?"

Now she had the smirk. "*Fleeing the country*…I forgot that part. Got the tickets out of Mexico City?"

"Got 'em."

"Both of them, right? Two tickets? To Venezuela?"

He hesitated. She *couldn't* know. "Sure."

"Great! Can't wait to see them!" she said, and beamed, grabbing his extended hand and shaking it until it hurt.

"Something cheered *you* up in a hurry," Gordon said, his smirk gone.

"You ain't seen nothin' yet."

Somehow, he believed that. But he got her in the coach, fired it up, and they were on their way. Gordon didn't bother looking back as they rounded the corner and left behind the house where he had spent the past fifteen years. He was busy thinking about a few things he still had up his sleeve for Wanda.

And at that, he could feel *his* little smirk return.

10

Gordon Mitchell pulled Major Dale's Rambling Vacationeer onto I-80 heading towards Chicago and settled in for a long night of cruise-controlled comfort. This was life as he had always seen the rich folks he sold to lived it; this was luxury.

Jeez. He was buying his own sales pitch. *Smooth, smooth, smooth.*

Twenty-six hours of driving the nation's ribbons of shimmering concrete, all night and into the next day—hell if he was stopping in Oklahoma City to see Wanda's sister—and he would be reunited with his money, a million and a half dollars of it. Just before then, he would drop Wanda off (literally, *hee-hee*) and, as they said to prospective customers at Major Dale's, freedom would be his.

Meet Janey in Truth or Consequences, make a quick jaunt into Mexico City (buying a used car for cash if need be to remain inconspicuous), catch a plane to Venezuela…why hadn't he done this years ago? Well, he wasn't getting any younger, of course, though he could still charm the ladies. Take Angie…

Wanda must've seen him smiling to himself, because she broke his rev-
elry with: "Gann says you only bought one ticket to Venezuela."

The motor home swerved on the highway, then straightened out. "Just
one, huh?" *Oh, shit,* he thought. *Think fast. On your feet, soldier!*
"That…that what he said?" *Great—who was that smooth talker again?*

Wanda rotated her seat so she was facing Gordon while he drove. She
had a relaxed, confident grin under her geisha-girl visage. It was discon-
certing. "Is there something you want to tell me, Gordon?"

Confusion enveloped him. That damned Gann! *Ten months* of planning! But she didn't look upset…she looked *happy.* "That's weird.
Should've gotten two. Meant to get two."

"Not if you wanted a divorce, Gord," she said, and smiled when he shot
a shocked glance her way. "I can't believe it. I put up with twenty-five years
of your shit—some of them were good, okay—but now, just when you
make something of yourself, bang. You're casting me aside like an old tube
of lipstick."

"Just forgot to get two tickets, Wanda, that's all. Or, I mean, *I* didn't
forget. Charged 'em—to pick up at the airport. You know. Must be a
computer fuck-up."

Her smile widened as she listened to him squirm. Now she leaned in
close to him. "Detective Gann had something else to say, too, you know."

He could hardly wait. "Gonna share it?"

"He says you're going to try to kill me tomorrow."

The Vacationeer swerved across three lanes of traffic and up onto the
median before straightening out this time.

Gordon Mitchell met Wanda Polska in Bloomington, Indiana, one early-'seventies evening in May, at a mixer designed specifically to bring together promising young college students and girls from town who had an eye on marriage. He was an engineering major, a sophomore, with a crew cut like everyone else he knew then. There were hippies, sure, but the guys he knew had haircuts like his, wore clothes like his, and dated girls like he did.

Wanda Polska was one of those girls. Blonder than the driven snow, with what he thought were tasteful rings on just about every finger and clothes so tight they looked like beds made by the Marines during basic training. She didn't have the annoying country accent of so many townies, instead speaking with the flat tones of the northern Indiana girl that she was.

She also had the best, the most creative, makeup of any of the girls his friends hung out with. Her lips looked like ripe fruit, ready to bite; her eyes were like a cat's when it's in the throes of heat; and with the foundation she wore, her skin looked as smooth as it probably was underneath all of that foundation.

Twenty-year-old Gordon was taken with her, and as they danced and drank from the flask he sneaked in, their eyes met more and more, their hands roamed more freely, and by the end of the night were making love in his dorm room with a ferocity that rivaled anything either had known before.

They married four months later, Gordon in a borrowed blue tux, Wanda in a short white wedding dress and eye shadow and lipstick that brought out the flowers in her bouquet. Her pregnancy, which hurried the nuptials, turned out to be a false alarm, as did every one during the first ten years of their marriage, until they stopped trying.

They were bad for each other, Gordon and Wanda, and they expressed that badness in the strongest way possible. Other women were a constant for him; for her, well, she did what only a truly disappointed wife can do: She worked diligently to separate her man from his dreams. Mostly it worked. When it didn't, it simply made him keep his dreams a secret from his bride.

As material possessions piled up around them, as the trappings of twentieth-century life became theirs, they became only less satisfied with each other. Too much now seemed like not enough; there seemed nowhere to go but down. Each had kept their real selves tucked so far away from the other for so long that when Wanda asked Gordon eleven months before their trip to New Mexico, "What would happen if the money the Japs paid for a coach just disappeared?" they both saw an opportunity to cash in the chips of their lives and start over with a new hand.

12

"I'm stopping him," Lieutenant Detective Douglas Gann said, and stood with his arms crossed at the door of the duty chief's office. "I need your authorization."

Duty Chief Marcus Brown rubbed his eyes and looked at the clock ticking off the seconds until he could get away from the station. There was almost six hours to go in his shift, which ended at seven a.m. And now he got Doug Gann. A perfect evening.

"Listen, Gann—you know damn well I don't have the clout to okay you going over state lines to arrest somebody who hasn't done anything yet—"

"Hasn't done anything? He's ripped off Major Dale's for over a million dollars!" Gann uncrossed his arms to gesture and then crossed them again.

"And you're waiting for what before you arrest him? Why didn't you bring him in before he left the state?" Brown said, but he knew why, perfectly well. He just liked to see Medal Boy squirm a little bit.

"The floor plan checker won't be done until tomorrow afternoon—that's why Gordon left the state."

"You mean *this* afternoon. It's Saturday now, Doug. Us uniformed flatfoots are sensitive to that kind of thing, you know."

"Fine—*this* afternoon. He's trying to make it out of the country before the checker finishes his count. Come on."

Brown raised his eyebrows. "So he fled? Or...did he have business outside the state? Business you can't interfere with, Lieutenant?"

"I'm stopping him, Mark. Don't make me go over your head."

Brown laughed. "Feel free," he said, and swung his phone around. "Want me to dial? I'm sure the chief would love to hear this at one in the morning. *Please* call him."

Gann bit his lip. "You can give me the okay, damn it. I just need to follow him, make sure he knows I'm watching, so he doesn't kill his wife."

"So he doesn't *what?*"

Clearing his throat, Gann said, "I have reason to believe Gordon Mitchell's wife is a witness to his criminal activity and he's using this RV delivery as an opportunity to get rid of her."

"You are out of your fucking mind, you know that, Doug?" He rubbed his eyes again and wished he was home in bed, out at a bar, anywhere but there with Medal of Valor-winner Douglas Gann staring at him with that holier-than-thou attitude of his. "If you really think he's going to off his wife, call the FBI. This would be their jurisdiction, not ours. You know that."

"My case."

"What was that?" Brown said, although he was afraid he heard it right the first time.

"It's my case, Mark. I'm the only one who can handle—"

Brown waved his arms. "Nope—I'm not gonna listen to this. Call the chief if you want authorization to go over state lines and harass some moron because of your *hunch*. Call the chief—then he can tell you to shove it himself."

"He's going to *kill her*, Mark—don't you care?"

"Not without a fucking shred of evidence, not a thousand miles away from here, not at one in the morning, Doug. No, I really don't."

Gann shuffled out of the doorway, arms still crossed, and went to his desk to steam. Brown shook his head and looked at the clock again. When he looked back out his door he could see Gann dialing the phone, and wondered if there was anything the guy wouldn't do to get another medal and handshake from those whose asses he was always bending to kiss.

The phone next to Elkhart Police Chief Harold Roberts bed shrieked, practically lifting the captain out of his bed. He looked at the clock, and it quickly hit him that there was only one reason anyone would be calling at this hour: Something was up, something big.

"Roberts," he croaked into the phone.

"Chief, this is Lieutenant Detective Doug Gann."

"A train better've derailed."

"No, Chief…I need permission to pursue a suspect over state lines. Right away."

Roberts blinked sleep out of his eyes. "*Who* is this?"

"I hardly have time to explain, Chief. They've already left."

"Who?"

"I have reason to believe a suspect in a string of thefts is transporting his wife over state lines to kill her."

"There's plenty of good places to kill somebody right here, Dann."

"Gann, sir."

"Whatever. Look, if you're so concerned, call the FBI. This sounds like a job for them."

"No, no—*I* need to do it. I know this couple, how they work, their dynamics…"

"My advice, Dann? Go back to bed."

"I haven't been to bed, sir. I've been tracking them all night."

Tracking them? Oh, boy. "Has the wife requested assistance?"

"Not as yet."

Damn if he wasn't waking up. *Who the hell gives out my number, any-way?* he thought with a scowl. *I'll fire the sumbitch.*

"Chief, I need permission to take a car and go after them. I need it right away—this woman's life is in danger."

"How do you know all this?"

"The guy—it's Gordon Mitchell. The one who's been ripping off his RV lot."

Roberts sat up. "Don't we have the checker coming in on that one?"

"Yes, sir—he's finishing later today."

"And you want to blow this whole thing by picking up Mitchell *now?* I don't think that's a good idea, Dann."

"But there's no time to—"

Enough already. "Forget it, son. You're not going anywhere until the checker's finished and we can actually *arrest* Mitchell on something. And we don't have the manpower to send one of our detectives out of state."

"Then chief," Gann said, "I'm on vacation. You won't be losing a man."

Roberts let out a rough breath. "No, but you'll be losing a job if you take off before that checker is done making a count of the lot. Understood, detective?"

"Understood, sir," Gann said, sounding completely deflated. "But I'm going to keep a close eye on their location—I won't lose them, Chief."

"Whatever," Roberts said and clunked the phone down, slipping back under the covers with the vague hope that this had all been just a bad dream.

Lieutenant Detective Douglas Gann had never in his two years in the plainclothes division ever been so frustrated and angry. He took the phone receiver and slammed it against his desk so hard it cracked down the middle.

He had been working on this case ever since Major Dale had alerted the Department that something was amiss on the lot, and now that his investigation had turned up something truly ugly, no one was interested. Now, he knew, not only was Mitchell going to get away with grand larceny, but he was going to do something bad to his lovely wife, Wanda, as well. Kill her, probably. And no one wanted to do anything about it! Why was he on the case anyway, if not to protect Mitchell's victims from further harm?

Well, he was going to do something about it, that was for darn sure. He left the office, the last one to go at five in the morning, and stepped out into the Indiana night. He would go home, grab a few things, and hit the trail in his unmarked Crown Victoria the second the RV floor-plan checker said that Major Dale's was one coach short.

He gazed into the darkness. That Vacationeer motor home was barreling down the highway somewhere with Gordon Mitchell behind the wheel, probably laughing and thinking he was going to get away with murder.

13

In the middle of Missouri, as the sky behind the Rambling Vacationeer slowly turned from black to purple to pink, Gordon's knuckles had turned bone white, wrapped in a death grip around the steering wheel, all the blood drained from his hands as he thought about what Wanda had said. His face was pale as bathroom Formica and beads of sweat dotted his forehead like bubbles on a peeling RV sidewall. Dark circles hung beneath his reddened eyes.

She knew. Goddamnit, she *knew*. That little punk Gann told her he fit the profile of a man on the run about to kill his wife before she found out—that was the funny part: Gann had everything else wrong! He had no idea Wanda was in on it, no idea at all! But he had stumbled on the fact that Gordon planned to kill her on the trip.

His one saving grace was that Wanda wasn't actually aware that she knew anything real—Gordon knew that she would never believe her husband, her wayward but in the end whipped husband, would ever actually do anything to get rid of her. No doubt she thought Gann and his theories were crazy, but she was using it for every ounce of annoyance she could get out of it, watching Gordon squirm like he was on a hook.

Which he was, in a way. Wanda always saw to that, didn't she?

Well, he would see to something, too. He would see that Wanda took a long, nice gaze at the New Mexico scenery on the precise lookout spot Gordon had chosen for its remoteness and steepness, one that, according to his calculations, they would arrive at in the late afternoon but well before sunset, just at the spot's least popular time.

He would continue on as planned. By the time Gann found out about it, he would be sipping rum in South America as his twenty-two-year-old lover rubbed his shoulders, and he just unwound for the rest of his life, completely non-extraditable.

His fingers loosened on the wheel a bit. The dark circles under his eyes remained, and he was quite confident they would as long as Wanda drew breath, whether it was in the front seat giving him grief or in the queen-size bed in the back, snoring like a congested rhinoceros.

The cellular phone tweeted. *What the...?* Gordon thought as he debated over picking it up, then figured it would look more suspicious if he didn't. "Yeah?" he said with more than a hint of caution in his tone.

"Gordon Mitchell?" the male voice on the other end asked.

"Help you?" Gordon said, then there was a beep and a click and silence.

He replaced the phone warily. Full daylight couldn't come fast enough. There was the next part of his plan to take care of, and the interstate tourist traps didn't usually open until folks hit the road for breakfast.

Gann waited until Gordon picked up the phone, then punched a couple of keys on his laptop computer, his eyes watery and red from skipping sleep to make out *his* plan.

"Gordon Mitchell?" Gann said.

"Help you?" Gordon muttered, and Gann set his little cell phone into the socket attached to the laptop. He then clicked on "Position" and the computer did the rest of the work, keeping the line with Mitchell open while it dialed the Geo-Find computer in Indianapolis, which sent instructions to the four geostationary satellites ten thousand miles up to tell it where the RV with Gann's transmitter was at that very second.

Seconds later, Gann had his answer. A U.S. map opened up in a window on his screen, and crosshairs intersected somewhere south of Illinois. He selected the little magnifying glass with a plus sign in it and clicked where the crosshairs met.

The Mitchells were just outside Springfield, Missouri.

Gann sat back and rubbed his eyes. They hadn't even stopped long enough to gas up that monster or eat breakfast yet. He'd know if they had, too: He'd been checking their position every ten minutes since he got off the phone with the chief, and he'd check it every ten minutes until he found a place where they stopped. The software could tell him the RV's position within a hundred yards anywhere in the United States.

If Gordon Mitchell stopped to fuel, eat, shit, or kill his wife, Gann would know exactly where he did it. There was no hiding from him—if the bastard killed his wife, Gann would know just where the body was. This was far from the best situation—he wanted to lock Gordon up before the S.O.B. could lay so much as a finger on his wife's head, but as long as he was stuck by protocol in Indiana, he would do what he could.

The thing that kept Gann amused was that nobody had to answer the phone at all—as long as it was operational, he could get a lock on their position. He just liked to fuck with Gordon's head by calling him and hanging up, letting him know somebody was keeping tabs on him.

He rubbed his eyes again and looked out the window at the brightening morning, which reminded him that Gordon would have at least a day and a half on him, plenty of time to kill his wife and skip the country. The son of a bitch had a ticket to *Venezuela*, for Christ's sake, and no one would move to stop him because they didn't have the *evidence*.

Wanda's body would be the evidence. That was just great. That was just typical.

Gann looked at his watch. Seven minutes until he could check again.

14

Stuckey's, Shoney's, Cracker Barrel, Waffle House—these and a hundred others like them are the lighthouses of American navigators, pegs in the great board of the plains to steer by. Buses always welcome. Tourist information always available. Gift shops always open. This much could be counted on like the mariners of yore counted on the frequency of the lighthouses' beacons to orient them to land.

And they made a great place to be seen as happy *touristas* on a happy vacation, as a couple getting along great, as a couple in which the happy husband would never have any reason to shove his loving, happy wife off a sheer New Mexico cliff. That's why the billboards counting down the miles to the next restaurant couldn't click by fast enough for Gordon.

"Okay, it's eight o'clock—we're in plenty of time to stop at my sister's place and have breakfast," Wanda yelled to him as she checked herself thirty feet away in the bathroom mirror.

"Oklahoma City's five hours away. You really wanna have breakfast at one in the afternoon? Come on, we'll stop at Cracker Barrel."

Wanda poked her head out and yelled at the back of her husband's head. "*Cracker Barrel?* What the hell do you want to fight the crowds there for? We should stop at Burger King or something, get a Croissan'wich to tide us over till Oklahoma."

Gordon shifted in his seat. "On a schedule, Wanda. Not a vacation. Your sister'll have to wait for next time," he said, and allowed himself a half-smile at the knowledge that there wasn't going to *be* any next time.

Now she stepped out of her cosmetics shrine to yell in his face, but he cut her off before she made a sound. "Stop right there, *dearest.* Told you when we started planning this little caper—"

"Goddamn you, we are spending the night with Peg and her family! The goddamn bank doesn't even open until Monday morning! What are we gonna do, go sightseeing?"

A grin rose unbidden on Gordon's face. *You bet your ass we are.* He pretended to be fascinated with the drab Missouri scenery until he could regain his poker face.

"I swear to God, I'll talk to that detective if—"

Fuck! "Fine, okay, stop at your sister's, okay, Christ. But do me a favor and eat with me at Cracker Barrel, all right?"

"I'll wait for lunch." This time she glanced away at the scenery for a few seconds before turning back.

"Feel better with a good breakfast in you."

"Since when do you care how I feel?"

He sighed. *Getting along, we're the happy couple getting along for all the goddamned world to see.* "Actually, honey, as I think about it, I'm looking forward to seeing your sister. You're right—we got plenty of time."

Wanda eyed him. "What are you buttering me up for?"

"Just want to have a nice breakfast, get along a little bit," he said, and tried his hardest not to bat his eyelashes at her. "Slips my mind sometimes we're starting a new life. Just fall into those old ways of relating, you know?"

She smiled and said, "Okay, we'll have breakfast at Cracker Barrel, for goodness' sake. But Gord?"

"Wand?"

"I know you're full of shit."

He sighed again. "And how might you know that?"

She gave him a deadpan look and repeated his word: "*Relating?*"

He grinned, and this time let her see it, because he couldn't deny it: Sometimes, she just had him pegged. It almost felt like getting along.

Gordon's ass was a sweaty, numb mass of deadened flesh after an entire night of nervous driving. He tried to stretch his limbs as he disembarked the Vacationeer, but his muscles really wanted to cramp. "Come on, Wanda, see what they got."

"I've eaten at Cracker Barrel so many times I can read the menu in my sleep, Gordon, we've got one not two miles from Dale's lot."

Nothing was easy. It wasn't enough just to go in and eat—he had to get her inside the gift shop, let them be seen by a few people, getting along, vacationing. "Order what you see, then," he called to her, feeling a bit foolish standing out here talking to the wall of an RV, even if it was a luxury liner in itself.

"Okay, you win. Let me put a face on."

"Christ, you look like a goddamn witch doctor with that stuff on your face."

"You want me to come out or not?"

He zipped his lip. Just a few more hours. They were at the bottom of Missouri now, lumpy as one of Wanda's pancakes and just as appealing. Soon they'd be in New Mexico. It wasn't far off. *Patience.*

He strolled around the parking lot, sat in one of the rocking chairs out front of the restaurant like some kind of goddamn hillbilly grandpa, read the paper while he waited for her to finish getting ready. When she stepped off the Vacationeer fifteen minutes later, looking to all the world like she had just walked into the path of a paint roller, she gave Gordon an actual, honest-to-goodness, good-morning-to-you smile and allowed him to open the doors for her.

Perfect. He couldn't wait to kill her.

"Ever seen such a selection of Jack Daniel's collectibles, honey?" he asked when they were close enough to a pudgy family for them to hear him. They had been milling around for ten minutes and hadn't made much of an impression on anyone, in his opinion. "Don't have anything like this where we're from."

"How about at the Cracker Barrel in Elkhart?" She wasn't even looking at the stuff. "Are we going to eat or not?"

"Said there was a twenty-minute wait."

"But there's just one family ahead of us! *I'll* ask them this time."

"No!" Gordon snapped, blocking Wanda with his body, then collected himself. "I asked the guy and he said twenty minutes. Come on, it's our *vacation*. Shop a little."

Usually you didn't have to ask the woman twice, but this time he guessed she was feeling a little pumped up from her victories on the road the night before, and she wasn't giving any ground. "I'm sitting in the camper until they call our name."

No! he thought. That would be the worst thing—even if they were just eating, at least they were being seen together. "Let me ask the guy again," he said, and skulked through the aisles of Coca-Cola merchandise, of woven checkerboards, of stuffed country goose collections, of electronic parrots that spat back whatever you said, of root beer suckers, of marshmallow candies, of commemorative plate sets, of angels made of crystal and porcelain, of cinnamon brooms, of canning jars, of framed cute sayings like "Grandmas are God's way of saying 'I love you'," of X-ray glasses for kids, of locally published collections of area humor that no one actually from the area was even vaguely familiar with, of large boxes of mints, and of apple butter and seventeen kinds of marmalade—everything stacked artfully, haphazardly on every inch of shelf in the place—to reach the host's podium.

"Need to get seated after all," Gordon said.

"But the twenty bucks?"

"Keep it. Just use the P.A."

The host swept up the handset. "Mitchell, party of two. *Mitchell*, party of two."

Gordon gave him a thumbs-up as Wanda appeared from behind the racks of watercolor greeting cards. "Good timing," he said to her, and stood beside her as to frame to the two of them in the host's memory. "Love you, honey."

"Let's eat," she said.

Three times that Douglas Gann called the Mitchells' cell phone, there was no answer and the satellite pinned them in the same location, not moving a foot. He brought up his CD-ROM road atlas and used his skinny bubble-jet printer to make a hard copy of a list of all the businesses within half a mile. It was nine a.m., breakfast time, and right as rain they had stopped to eat. There was a Shoney's there, and a Cracker Barrel. He could hop down there and find out how the Mitchells were getting along, collect evidence that Gordon and Wanda were not getting along on the day of her death.

The day of her death. He was thinking that way already—giving up. But the day of her death was exactly what it would be if he didn't get on the road pretty freaking soon.

I'm sorry I couldn't stop him was the thought he sent to Wanda. Sometimes he would try to form a psychic bond with those he was trying to protect, warn them the only way he could, since the paper-pusher bureaucrats sometimes wouldn't let him do what was right. *Be careful, Wanda Mitchell. I will be there soon.*

He looked at his watch again, even though he had just checked the time five minutes earlier. He'd call Major Dale's in a few minutes, see if the floor-plan checker had started work early. As soon as the first damn VIN didn't match up, he was out of there and on the road after Gordon Mitchell.

Well—as soon as the first number didn't match up, and he got the okay from his "superiors." Protocol. The rules. Mitchell had no rules on him, and Gann had to wait for the bean counter to *tell* him what he knew all along and he was allowed to get the heck on the road after them.

He squeezed his eyes shut tight and thought: *Careful, Wanda. Hold on until I get there.* He knew she would get the message, even if she didn't understand right away. A good cop formed a psychic bond with those he was sworn to protect.

He admired the medals and awards he shared with the squad room by placing them in the trophy case for all to see. His psychic effort had worked before. It would work again.

16

Wanda Mitchell shuddered at the table. "Do you hear that?"

"What?"

"That song—'*She Got the Gold Mine—I Got the Shaft.*' I haven't heard that in years. That's the song my cousin was arrested for playing, remember?"

Gordon chuckled. *This was good—happy things!* "Wasn't just for playing it—it was for blasting it outside his ex-wife's window at three in the morning," he said.

Wanda laughed and actually reached over and held his hand. She said, "I've missed this. You don't really want a divorce, do you?"

"Who said anything about divorce?"

"Come on, Gord—one ticket to Venezuela?" She gave him a knowing smirk.

What an idiot. "Just…" *Just what?* "Just felt at the end of my rope. Didn't know what else to do. Just…thought we'd split the money and start life over."

"So the airline didn't make a mistake and charge you for just one ticket."

"No," Gordon said, then tried to think of something endearing, something he'd never really say, something romantic. *Yes!* "I—I'm sorry I lied to you. I was scared of my own feelings." *Oh, Lord*—it was almost all he could do not to laugh.

She patted his hand and said, "We're gonna start life over, all right, but we don't need to get a divorce to do it. All our problems are—"

"We—we should tell the waitress."

"What?" She wasn't patting anymore.

"I'm...just so happy at how we're relat—how we're getting along! I just want to tell somebody. I—" He could feel it slipping away. "I—"

Wanda's pancaked face was turning from a smile to a scowl. *Fuck fuck fuck*—he had to *show* her the depths of his love blah blah, a dramatic gesture like the geeks in high school did to the pretty girls in lunch—

Gordon's eyes went wide and he gave Wanda a conspiratorial smirk.

"What? What are you thinking, Gordon?" She sounded suspicious, but almost excited. Which was very good indeed.

He stood up suddenly, and he could feel every head in the room turn as his chair squeaked against the floor. "Everyone!" he bellowed over the music and conversation, and now all eyes in the room were on him in a mixture of curiosity and alarm, all the better to make this little scene stick in their memories.

"Everyone, tomorrow is my wife and I's twenty-fifth wedding anniversary. And..." He paused as he looked at Wanda's face. He wanted so badly to ring her neck most of the time, but now, with her looking at him with those blue-ringed eyes...

He still wanted to wring her neck, but at least make it quick.

"And I want everyone to know that I want this woman to marry me all over again! Wanda, will you renew your vows with me?"

The room broke into slightly embarrassed but definitely enthusiastic applause. And why not? It was probably the performance of his life.

One courageous tear braved its way down his wife's painted cheek as she stood and threw her arms around him. "Oh, Gordon, Gordon, I knew we could work out any problems! I knew it!" She cried into his shoulder.

He held her, even patted her back, all the while thinking: *Consider this problem worked out.*

Eggs, thick bacon, grits, home-fry casserole, biscuits in sawmill gravy, hot spiced apples in sauce, coffee, and juice make up the "Loosen Yer Belt Breakfast," a favorite of traveling folks everywhere Cracker Barrel serves it. With just the right amount of calories and carbohydrates a body needs for a day of sedentary, motionless activity such as driving a recreational vehicle cross country. Most people have to lie down for a while after eating the whole thing, which is one reason why the Vacationeer, with its queen-size bed, was such a popular choice.

Gordon ordered the Loosen Yer Belt. Wanda chose the "Happy Sunny Good Mornin'," which was on the "light" menu since it left off the hot spiced apples.

Just as the plates made it to the table, the cell phone Gordon had brought in gave out its electronic chirp.

"Not now," Wanda said, looking genuinely disappointed.

"Been ringing all morning. Think your detective friend is having his fun harassing me. I haven't been answering it for hours."

Wanda nodded at that and dug in, but the phone continued to ring. Heads turned again to look at them: Why weren't they answering their phone? It was probably creating a memory Gordon would just as soon prefer people didn't have.

He looked at Wanda and shrugged. "Gordon Mitchell," he said into the phone.

"Ronny!" Janey cried from the other end.

He watched Wanda's eyes bug as his bugged, and he scrunched his face to erase any tell-tale signs of guilt. Too late.

"Who is it, Gord?"

"Ronny?"

His eyes were bugging again. He stood up suddenly again, and their fellow diners looked at him, no doubt wondering if he was going to break into more spontaneous protestations of love and devotion. "Got to take this call, Wanda," he said, the syllables putting out like air bubbles from a drowning man.

"Who is it?"

"Dale—knows something's up. The checker…" *The checker what?*

"Ronny? Are you there, sweetie?"

"Just a second, hon—" He froze. Wanda cocked her head at him. "—*honey* is here with me."

"Uncle Dale wants *me*?" Wanda whispered, looking suddenly stricken, and slid back in her chair, waving her hands in a *no way* gesture. Then she pointed toward the bathroom and skittered off, head down as if Dale could look through the phone and peg her as her husband's accomplice against him.

"Thank God," he breathed into the phone. "Bad timing, sweetheart." He glanced at the diners sitting within earshot and quickly added, "Um, *sweetheart* had to run off to the ladies' room." That gag was going to get old quick.

"Uh-huh." She gave him a couple of seconds of silence, then giggled. "Aren't you gonna be glad when all this is over? No more sneaking around, that bitch dead—"

"Cell phone, *cell phone.*"

"Whoops. Sorry. Anyway, tomorrow I see you? In the morning, right? You kill—kill—*time* in the morning in T or C and then we spend Sunday together, packing and stuff, then Monday we zip by the bank and head south, right?"

Gordon kept his eyes laser-focused, past racks of cozies and inspirational needlepoints, on the ladies' room door across the gift area, and chewed his lip.

"Ronny? I remembered the plan, see? And you thought I was too—"

"Hold up. Been a little change."

"Oh, *fuck* me. What is it? You're not gonna go through with the—"

He half-barked into the phone to shut her up. "Just got to stop by her sister's place in Oklahoma City, spend the night."

"*What?*" He could almost feel her spit flying at him. "You said no more nights sleeping with her! No more!"

"One more, that's all. I mean, she still *is* my wi—"

"Don't you fucking say that to me, Gordon Mitchell. You said you *hate* her, that you *can't wait* to get rid of her."

"Cell phone, Janey."

"Fuck that! I'm twenty-two years old, and never been married, waiting for you, and now you're having a *sleep-over* with that cunt! I fucking shouldn't even meet you in T or C! I should fucking just…just…*god-damn it!*"

Gordon kept the phone plastered close to his ear, even though her yelling was giving him a headache, so his neighbors wouldn't notice he had a young woman screaming at him while his wife was in the bathroom; that simply wouldn't do. "Calm yourself—it'll just be late afternoon instead of early morning. No big deal."

"No big deal? If you ain't at the Pine Knot Saloon in T or C by ten in the morning, I'm history. You can go to Venezuela by yourself—I'll get a refund on my ticket and keep the cash."

"You don't mean that."

"Wanna bet? Just keep trying me, Ronny."

"Don't have to do this. Just talking a couple of hours."

"I'm sick of her coming first. She always comes first! You love *me*. Not her—*me*. Why can't you put me first?"

Jesus fucking Christ. Gordon almost wished it *had* been Dale; at least that would've been quick. "You *are* first, babe—um, *Dale*. Don't go nuts on me now, okay?"

"You shouldn't spend the night with her ever again. You were gonna help me pack, Ronny." She sounded more disappointed now than angry, which was a vast improvement. "We were gonna make a day of it."

"Lots of days ahead. Whoa—Wanda's coming. Call you back."

"*I won't be here!*" He cut her off.

Wanda slipped into her seat and put her hand over her food to see if it was still hot. "Does he know?" she asked, digging in.

"No," Gordon said, then searched for more to say…and found it. "Atchison wants the coach down to him in Truth or Consequences in the morning Sunday—Dale just wanted to make sure I had it there first thing in the morning tomorrow, that's all."

Wanda stopped mid-bite. "But that's impossible. I mean, God, he's getting the coach for nothing—"

"Not for nothing—he's waiving his fee for taking care of the big bills for us, remember," Gordon said as quietly as he could. No one could hear him in the general clamor of the place, but Wanda probably couldn't, either. "We're letting Major Dale spring for Mr. Atchison's service charge."

"We can't drive there by Sunday morning. It can't be done."

"It *can*—got fourteen hours to go, if we drive straight through, and if we pull off for a couple of hours' sleep, we still get there by—"

"First thing tomorrow morning, we'll just be leaving my sister's, Gordon."

"Afraid this is a little more important, dear. Got a coach to deliver."

She smacked her lips into a scowl. "What's Dale gonna do, fire you?"

Gordon whispered, "Got to look on the up-and-up, you know that. Don't attract any suspicion till we're over the border."

"We've got five hours until Oklahoma City, and then we're stopping and visiting until the morning." She scooped up a big spoonful of potatoes to slap a period on the end of her declaration.

"Gonna fuck this up, Wanda, all to see your sister."

He was minding his volume, but Wanda wasn't, and as she spoke, he glanced around, pinpricks of sweat breaking out all over his body. "You want to see me fuck it up? Just try to skip going to my sister's."

"Honey, keep it down. We're just in a hurry, that's all. We'll buy Peg and her whole brood tickets to Venezuela when we get settled in, okay?"

She pointed a fork at him. "We're stopping."

"Fine, we're stopping. Hell with everything. Your sister can visit you in jail."

"You're a prick."

"You're a bitch."

"Coffee?" the waitress chirped.

Gordon nodded through a hand spread over his face, hoping to God she hadn't heard them. Sometimes he wished he could give axes to his wife and his girlfriend, let them do this dirty work, let them do the killing, let them go at it against each other until only one was left standing. Maybe not even that many.

17

Ten a.m.

Gann's fingers drummed on the laptop as the satellite took its sweet time collating the position data. Finally, the crosshairs pinpointed the RV a mile down the road from where it had sat for an hour while the Mitchells ate at Shoney's or Cracker Barrel. They were moving again.

He swept up the phone and hit one button to speed-dial Major Dale's. "Page Mr. Johnson for me, please," he said to the receptionist.

The eternity of a few seconds ticked by before Johnson picked up the line. "Johnson."

"Detective Gann here. How goes the count?"

Johnson cleared his throat and said, "We've only just started, Detective."

"Sure, of course. But are any VINs not matching up yet? Anything missing?"

"There are a couple of discrepancies I'm looking into. But—"

"That's all I needed to know," Gann said quickly, and hung up. He looked again at his watch: four past ten. He hit another speed-dial button.

"Chief, this is Gann."

"I thought you were on vacation."

"I am, sir, but I thought I'd let you know my destination."

He could hear a small groan from the other end. It was still early for some folks—he must have been waking him up. "Do tell," the chief said.

"I'm heading to New Mexico to pick up Gordon Mitchell. The floor-plan checker at Major Dale's has let me know there are vehicles missing. We've got the evidence we need."

"Well, that's terrific, lieutenant. I think Judge Stone should have some time Monday morning to issue the warrant."

"Monday? But sir, I've got to go immediately. He could—"

"You're on vacation, Dann, said so yourself. I'll contact our man in the New Mexico State Police down there to bring him in. You just sit pat and enjoy your latest collar, okay, detective?"

"I'd like to go down there, Chief."

"Hey, it's your vacation. Just don't go interfering with the cops down there. They're perfectly capable of apprehending a forty-five-year-old RV salesman and his wife."

No, not the wife, Gann thought. *She's got nothing to do with this. Besides, she'll be dead by then.* He didn't know what to say. Finally he squeaked, "It's vital that I—"

"It's vital that you keep your butt planted until you really do have the evidence you need. I've been with the Elkhart force eighteen years, and I know an RV dealership the size of Major Dale's takes more than an hour to floor-check, okay? Maybe come five o'clock, they'll have enough to say something one way or the other, but five o'clock is seven hours away, all right?"

"But—"

"All *right?*"

"Yes, sir," Gann said, and hung up before the jerk could ask him again. Seven hours was a long time, an eternity when the fact was that Gordon Mitchell would take about twenty seconds to kill Wanda.

Wanda. His thoughts turned to this woman he didn't even know, had spoken to only once, and who he knew now he would do anything it took to protect.

It was ten-fifteen. He checked their position again and saw they were fourteen miles farther down the road; at that rate, they'd be in Truth or Consequences by evening.

His hand shook as he disconnected the cell phone from the laptop. Wanda was as good as dead. As good as dead.

Ten-sixteen. *As good as dead.* Gann sat and chewed his fingernail, watching the seconds sweep by. With every minute that passed, he knew Wanda Mitchell was as good as dead. The thought pulsated in his mind like a growing tumor.

But why? he asked himself. Why did he give a care one way or the other about Wanda Polska Mitchell? He was a police officer, sure, a lieutenant detective, but why did he care about *this* particular potential victim so much? She was beautiful, but there were a lot of beautiful women he came across in his line of work. She was no doubt oppressed by the life she'd had to lead with that lying, murderous bastard of a husband, but he'd seen that dozens, if not hundreds, of times in his couple of years on the force.

No, it was something else, something Gann had felt only a few times before in his nearly thirty years on the planet: He and Wanda shared a psychic bond.

Gann knew his psychic abilities, the way he could feel out the truth and guide him in an investigation, were what had brought him such success in the department and were what allowed him to pursue his career with such passion and satisfaction. But to feel that he *knew* another person instantly, just by seeing her, just by talking to her—this was something he had done maybe twice before.

And both times, it had been life-or-death situations.

The first time was when he was just ten years old and playing with friends near the St. Joseph River right there in Elkhart, not a mile from where he currently sat chewing his nails and watching the minutes go by on the clock. He had just met the new girl in the neighborhood—Jennifer something, but that name shimmered in his mind: *Jennifer*—and instantly felt a link to her that told him she would be in great danger very shortly, and that he would be the only one who could save her.

He didn't know what to think or do. He just watched her, and when she was about to dive into the river, he stopped her. He made an excuse that he wanted to talk about something—they ended up kissing a little, Gann following her lead as she got ideas about what he wanted to "talk" about—and led her away from the water.

Fifteen minutes later, two of their friends swimming in the river were hit by a speeding motorboat.

They died.

Jennifer lived.

And Gann knew he had been given a gift.

The second time was when he was at the academy and he met another cadet named Liz, a beautiful brunette who sent an electric charge through his body when she shook his hand.

He felt that bond again, had that feeling that she needed him to protect her and that he was the only one who could do it. He watched her for a while, trying to deduce how she might be in danger, and then figured it was just a false alarm.

The next day, Liz was killed in an accident at the firing range not ten feet from fellow cadet Douglas Gann. He had not been watching, so he never knew if her death was something he could have prevented.

He never *knew*, but he had a pretty good feeling. He had a psychic gift, and if it went unrespected, it was a curse. From then on, he respected it. From then on, he kept close tabs on any psychic rumblings he might detect, vibrations which occurred often on important cases and put him in the right place at the right time enough that he couldn't see how those without access to their "third eye" could even *think* about doing productive police work. He had lots of psychic experiences, but never that electrifying surge of absolute *connection* that he had gone through with Jennifer and Liz.

Until now.

He was having that feeling, that beautiful sense of psychic oneness, about Wanda Mitchell now. She was in serious danger, and luckily for her and for Gann, he thought, it was pretty easy to identify the source of the threat this time.

It was ten-twenty-five. There was a long time to wait. He checked their position again, and set the computer to check it every ten minutes, figure everywhere they stopped to do so much as take a look at the scenery, and he would check every single place out as soon as he left Elkhart at five o'clock sharp.

He took off his shoes and lay on the bed, and before long he slept and dreamed of Jennifer, and Liz, and Wanda.

18

The food and the driving were taking their toll on Gordon as he guided the Vacationeer down the highway out of Oklahoma and into the Texas panhandle, home of the western hemisphere's largest free-standing cross, the whole area sun-baked and dusty and to Gordon right at that minute the most beautiful thing he'd ever seen. There was no time for him for sightseeing, though—everything was right on schedule and every minute counted. Stop at her sister's! *Ha!*

Despite the heaviness of his eyelids as the road glare increased with the steadily rising sun, he had plenty of room to laugh, because he remembered something Wanda didn't: Heavy food and the soothing rhythms of highway travel knocked her out surer than a double shot of Halcion. She was gone not two hours out of Springfield, and once again, Gordon could hear the sound loggers everywhere had come to know and love: that of a finely tuned chain saw, and it was coming from the bedroom.

He flipped on the radar detector, popped the cruise control up to ninety, and cut through Oklahoma City like a hot hatchet through ice cream. He watched the skyline come up around the interstate and then fade into the distance behind them as the highway straightened out for the long pull to the Texas panhandle. Fuck if he was gonna blow everything with tight little Janey so they could hang out all afternoon and night with Wanda's retard family. Just thinking of all the opportunities for fuck-ups and slips of the tongue that would allow made him shiver with dread and relief.

And then, just as they were getting away from that Godforsaken city—and his wife's family—just as they were leaving behind the place he most wanted Wanda to sleep through, the cell phone gave off its shrill ring.

Shit! He told himself he wouldn't answer it again—the damn thing had been ringing every ten minutes until he shut it off. But then he worried Janey would get pissed off if she tried to call and he didn't answer…

He picked it up and whispered, "Yeah?"

Beep. Then a click.

What *was* that? He looked around for a place to throw the damn thing, but had to finally settle for the noiseless option of banging it against his leg in frustration.

But to no avail. Wanda was stirring. "Gordon? Are we there yet?"

"Let you know," he called back sweetly. "You can nap."

Too late—she pushed her way up into the shotgun seat and peered out at a highway sign through puffy eyes. "'Shamrock'? Where's Oklahoma City?"

"Back a few miles."

She turned to face him then, and for the first time in their twenty-five years of marriage, Gordon wished she had taken the time to put on some makeup. "Turn around."

"Too late now. Didn't know what exit for your sister's, and you were sleeping—"

"Gordon, turn this goddamn thing around, or you'll regret it."

"You want to go to jail? That's where we'll both be unless we get the hell out of the States, get me?"

"I want to see my sister. You said we could stop."

"Fly her down to Venezuela, for Chrissakes," Gordon snarled. "We're running out of time."

"For what? The bank doesn't even open until Monday!"

Oops. Time to change tacks. "Wasn't sure which exit to take, so—"

"Turn around and I'll show you."

"It's been half an hour—I'm not taking twelve hours out of our trip to go see your sister, sorry."

Wanda trudged back to the sectional and plopped down. Was she crying? She was. This was a new wrinkle.

"Listen, if we…" He stopped. "Come on, it's…we…we'll have her down as soon as we get settled. Be a vacation for her. Whaddya think?"

"I think you don't give one shit about anybody—I think you don't love one person other than yourself. That's what I think."

"Hey, come on—I love *you*, Wanda. I care about *you*."

"One day you're going to have to prove it. Right now, I don't think you care if I live or die—if *anyone* lives or dies." She paused and sighed, then looked at him looking at her in the rear-view mirror. "Now turn this thing around or I'm calling Uncle Dale and telling him everything—including a certain account number at a certain New Mexico bank."

Gordon stared at her for-once-unpainted face for a few seconds, then cussed under his breath and started looking for the next exit back to Oklahoma City.

"Just keep it quiet about the plans, okay?" Gordon said as they were pulling around the last corner to Peg's. "No need to give anybody anything to say to the cops."

"I'll say whatever I want, Gordon. She's my closest kin."

Kin? "Fine, Daisy Mae. See your *kin* during visiting hours the next twenty years you don't keep your mouth shut."

That put a dent in her hat. She sulked for all of five seconds before her sister's house appeared through the wraparound windshield.

Peg and Bob Hake actually lived on the east side of Oklahoma City, so Gordon had to truck all the hell the way back through town to get to their place, a low-slung ranch house littered with sachets and a lawn goose and who knew what else, things Gordon couldn't even identify. Peg shared her sister's "gift" for useless ornamentation, and Gordon thought Bob might even have dabbled in it a bit himself from the looks of him—skinny desk jockey, a *chemist*, for Christ's sake.

Peg ran out and whipped her arms around her sister the second Wanda stepped out of the coach, and Bob was there on Gordon's side, all smiles with a weekend drinker's light beer in his hand. He extended his other mitt for the "manly" shake with his brother-in-law. "Gordy! Welcome to *chez* Hake! God, I always love to see one of these machines coming up the drive. Usually means fishing!" he said, and let out what Gordon was sure he thought was one hell of a laugh.

He took an inventory of Bob and himself: He outweighed Bob by a good seventy-five pounds, he was pretty sure Bob didn't have a million and a half dollars in the bank, and Gordon was one day away from being a merry widower. Yeah, he had it pretty good over Bob. But you wouldn't know it to look at Bob—son of a bitch was too busy chortling and chatting to notice he wasn't half the man Gordon was. Oh, well—Gordon would find a way to remind him.

"So where you headed in this beast?"

"Delivery," Gordon said, and tried to give a nonchalant smile. "Sometimes the customer wants to see the coach before buying. Nice to get out of Indiana."

"I bet, I bet." Bob walked slowly around the Vacationeer, all thirty-five feet of it, no doubt noting the superior detailing and construction of a Rambling Class A. "So, where you headed? Peg and I couldn't *believe* you guys were passing through."

"Decided, 'Ah hell, make a vacation out of it.' Both been out time to time, but never together. She really wanted to see her sister this time."

"I bet," Bob said, finishing his inspection and facing Gordon again. "Where you going?"

You're going down *if you ask me that again*, Gordon thought, but tucked that away. When the time came, the police would definitely be talking to the Hakes, and it wouldn't do to give Bob a punch in the mouth just for asking where they were going. No, all he had to do was fire up the props on his mental P-38—

"Bob! They're going to New Mexico!" Peg cried as she ducked around the front of the coach. "Isn't that romantic?" Then, to Gordon: "That's where Bob and I honeymooned, you know. Taos and Santa Fe—the north part. We never made it down to Truth or Consequences, though. God, I remember it like it was—"

"*Wanda!*" Gordon yelled, and when she poked her head around, he flashed them all a *delighted* smile and cocked a finger at her to come. "A word with you. *Sweetheart.*"

Of course, Bob and Peg had three children—two boys, one girl, the girl the youngest at thirteen—and they all joined Uncle Gordy and Aunt Wanda at dinner, all of them sitting around a Value City-issue dining room table with its leaf added to make room for the guests.

"Uncle Gordy, how do you get back after you drop off the RV?" Greg, the seventeen-year-old, decided to ask before dinner had even made it to the table.

Questions. Great. Gordon glanced at Wanda, and hoped his look was all he needed to remind her to keep her trap shut and let them get through dinner without giving their forwarding address directly to the Elkhart Police Department.

"Yeah, do you fly back?" Pete, their bucktoothed fourteen-year-old, chimed in.

"Usually," Gordon said, and tried like hell to think of what to say next. He stared at the doorway to the kitchen, hoping for the Hakes—Bob, naturally, was just a *whip* in the kitchen—to come back with the food and rescue him from the prying minds and fantastic memories of their kids. "Maybe take in a few sights this time."

"Where?" Pete asked.

"The general...area in general, you know. The desert. Rocks and the whole general desert."

"Mom says you're going downtown to see the Murrah bombing site tomorrow morning."

Wha—? Gordon bit his lip as he looked to Wanda for confirmation. If this was her idea, he'd...Okay, so he was going to kill her anyway. But maybe he'd make her suffer a bit now first. "That right?" he said to his wife.

Now she looked at the kitchen door, but the Hakes must still have been fussing over their noodle casserole and Jell-O. "We *are* in Oklahoma City, Gord. People come from all around to see it. I thought since we aren't ever—"

"Good idea!" he yelped, cutting her off. "Fine. We'll go downtown tomorrow. Maybe make a picnic of it. Not like we have a *job* to do here, right? Delivering the coach, right?"

Wanda nodded, and looked at the kitchen door again for her reinforcements.

"Aunt Wanda," asked Tip, the girl with a name like out of a Dickens novel, "how come you went with Uncle Gordy this time? What about your job in Indiana?"

"I didn't—" she flicked a glance at Gordon—"*don't* have a job, honey."

Tip did a double-take. "You don't have a job?" She looked at her brothers for explanation, and getting none, said, "Then how do you maintain your feminine self-esteem in a working person's economy? What's your role in the home?"

Wanda looked stricken, but Gordon couldn't stifle a laugh. At least they were off the subject of travel arrangements. "That what they're teaching you in middle school, kid? 'Feminine self-esteem'?"

"Women have important roles to fill in society, Uncle Gordy," Pete said. "These aren't the *eighties* anymore."

Even Wanda laughed at that. Everyone had a good chuckle, and then Greg looked back at Gordon and said, "So you're flying back? What airline?"

Peg Hake never liked her big sister's husband. Peg was only fifteen when Wanda married Gordon—or Ron, or whatever he was calling himself these days—but she knew a snake when she saw one. He grabbed her rear one time, right before the rehearsal dinner, then played it off like he was teasing.

Like heck he was teasing. If she hadn't been fifteen and would have spoiled the wedding, she would have told somebody. Or maybe not—Wanda was a cosmetology student with prospects, but no one ever thought she'd nab an athlete like Gordy Mitchell. Her family wouldn't take too kindly to the kid sister trying to stir things up just because the groom was trying to be friendly.

Besides…part of her kind of liked Gordy's touch. Maybe she couldn't say she never liked Gordon, because she did have quite the crush on him up until she married Bob. A little after, even. But now, seeing Gordon sit across her fancy dining room table watching every word her sister said, she was glad she had never been the one to walk down the aisle with him. He kept interrupting Wanda, cutting her off, finishing her sentences, not letting her speak for herself. Even Tip thought he was being—what was her word?—patriarchal, which meant being a typical bossy man.

And Wanda—something wasn't right with her big sister. Had Tip's little comment Greg had mentioned, the one about not having value in the home, hurt her? Peg herself had gone and found work after Tippy, her youngest, had started junior high—and thank God. The way Tip talked now, she'd be giving her mother holy heck if she wasn't working part-time for Mary Kay.

No, that wasn't it. Wanda had proudly declared herself an Elkhart domestic goddess and always kept the ambition of setting up her own beauty salon. She sure had the talent—even now, when something was clearly wrong, her makeup, although maybe a bit heavy around the eyes and the cheeks, maybe a bit much, was still perfectly and carefully applied. No, Wanda still had her ambition, and that would shield her against any idealistic liberal talk from her niece.

Idle "how you been" conversation trickled around the table as they ate their supper of ham, potato casserole, and green beans (French style, for the company), but Peg played only a small role in it—she was busy watching Gordon and Wanda. Bob and Gordon were doing the usual man-talk, who fixed what and who saw what on the television, but Wanda generally kept her eyes down and ate, which just wasn't her. Whenever one of the kids would pipe up and ask her a question—she raised them right, her kids, they were friendly and curious—she would look at Gordon before she said anything, and Gordon would watch her even closer, ready to jump in the second she said anything about...about...Peg couldn't quite pin it down.

Peg watched Greg, her oldest, ask Wanda, "How long you staying in New Mexico?"

Of course, Wanda looked at Gordon while answering. "Maybe just a day. We—"

"—got a schedule to follow," Gordon said. "Don't know yet—depends on your Great-Uncle Dale and what he needs. Right, Wanda?"

She nodded, and looked down again before anyone might ask her another question. She had been so like herself when they first stopped, couldn't wait to spill where they were going, what they were doing, until Gordon called her over and shut her up.

He shut her up then, and shut her up every time she started to talk about...

Peg's eyes popped open wide. Going far away from where anyone knew them, didn't want anyone knowing where they were going, didn't know how long it would take, both of them so tense you could break them into pieces...

They were getting divorced.

Peg plopped her fork down on her plate and rushed to the bathroom to wash her face and cry in private.

"Honey? You—" Bob called after his wife, but she was already in the bathroom and shut the door. He looked at his sister-in-law and said, "I'm sure she's just overjoyed you're here."

Gordon watched Wanda say, "It's been almost two years. And it might—"

"—might be a couple more before—"

"*Would you let me finish a goddamn sentence!*" Wanda yelled in his face, and turned back to Bob, whose eyes were now as wide as the collectible plates on the dining room walls. "And it might be a couple more before we get back this way. I'm gonna check up on her."

Gordon reached at her as she stood. "Don't you think you should—"

"Gordon Mitchell, you are on my last good nerve and I'd get the hell off it if I were you."

He drew back his hand and looked at Bob and the kids with a little smile. "Just didn't want Peg upset is all," he said, but he could tell they didn't believe it for a second.

He looked back down at his plate and pretended to be incredibly interested in the casserole, but he watched Wanda stomp off. As she tapped on the door and entered, he could feel his blood turning cold and his fingers go numb. He could hardly breathe.

There was anything, absolutely *anything*, that woman could blab to her sister in there. Two fucking broads in the bathroom—that's practically a confessional booth for Midwestern housewives. He swept the oversalted food into his mouth and realized there wasn't a damn thing he could do to stop her, but there was something he could do to keep the rest of the family from picking at the corpse of his perfect plan like a bunch of buzzards. He'd get the kids to clean up and he'd drag Bob into the perfect American distraction.

He prompted his brother-in-law to ask the three teens to clear the table and said, "So, Bob—see what kind of set-up you got in the TV room."

Bob's face turned from worry about his wife to pleasure in showing off his entertainment center. Gordon smiled to himself: One more for the silver-tongued devil.

Wanda pushed the door open and slipped inside the bathroom, and saw it looked like her sister had already thrown up. Peg let out another great sob as she noticed Wanda, then put a hand over her eyes to wipe away some of the redness.

"Wanda, you got to tell me what's going on with you and Gordon. That's all there is to it."

Wanda stopped cold from getting any nearer her sister. Peg, who still went to church and who still had the love of her husband and who had three children, while Wanda had none. Peg, who wouldn't understand wanting to start over and get another chance at life, because she had done it right the first time. She couldn't tell Peg the truth. She had to tell her the truth. She would tell her the truth. God and Peg maybe wouldn't understand, but would love her anyway.

"Peggy, we—"

"It's divorce, isn't it?" Peg said it like you'd say *cancer*.

"Divorce?" Wanda echoed, and wondered at the sound of it. It sounded like a break just then. "We don't...we don't know."

Peg's tears were still wet on her face, but Wanda could recognize the setting of her jaw. "You're right to take some time out," she said, and put her hands on her big sister's shoulders. "You and Gordon can make things right again. Twenty-five years tomorrow, big trip—don't think I haven't noticed. It's 'take-stock' time, time to figure out what your priorities are, right?"

"I don't want a divorce, but I think Gordon does." She was almost believing this was what was wrong herself.

"He's a lot of man, honey. He likes to do things big, impress people, right?" Peg nodded on Wanda's behalf. "I seen him pull up in that rig, and

I could tell right away his mind was somewhere else. He wants to take you and go somewhere, like the people he sells those things to. Oklahoma City isn't where he dreams of being, right?"

Amazing. "No—Venezuela."

"Venezuela?"

Wanda clapped a hand over her mouth. Gordon was not going to be happy about this. It's not like the police could send them back to the U.S.—Gordon had told her that a thousand times when she complained about his choice of destination—but still, he wanted as little known about the plan as possible. But her sister was her sister, and it was an accidental slip.

"Wanda, you two are going to Venezuela? In South America? That's romantic!"

"It's just a thought."

"Just—? What do you mean?"

Wanda paused for a second, then thought: *Oh, hell with it. She's my sister.* "He only bought one ticket."

Peg's mouth dropped. "He *does* want a divorce!"

"I thought he did. But we've been together twenty-five years, since we were kids practically. We had some shitty—some bad times, and he never left me. He never did what Daddy did to Mom." She could feel her own tears coming now, and she let them come. "He still loves me, Peggy."

"One ticket, though?"

"He needs me to show him how much I love him. I can be pretty bitc—pretty mean sometimes. He needs assurance and stroking. He's a man."

"My Bob's a man, but he never threatens to leave me."

Wanda nodded. "That's the thing—he never said a word about leaving me. He played around—don't looked shocked, you know how he is—but he always included me in his plan. We maybe were even getting better as we got closer to getting away."

"Getting away? On this vacation?"

"It's not a vacation. We were gonna start a new life, Peggy. Him and me, in Venezuela. That's where we're going."

"You're *moving* to Venezuela?" Peg was smiling now, her tears just a memory and streaks down her face. "You weren't going to tell me?"

"It's kind of a secret," Wanda said, knowing she was saying too much. "Gordon and I have…come into some money. We were gonna be rich. We are rich, I guess."

Peg wasn't just smiling anymore—she was almost laughing, clutching Wanda's hands with excitement. "I *knew* that RV wasn't a darn delivery! That's your RV, isn't it? You two were dream-building, and now you've bought into the dream!" She hugged her sister, then looked her close in the eye and said conspiratorially, "It's Amway, isn't it?"

Wanda sat down on the closed toilet and sighed. "Gordon doesn't want anyone to know about it until we get out of the country."

Peg gasped and knelt down to examine her sister's face for clues. "It's something illegal?"

Wanda nodded, despairing. She had to tell everything now, because her sister wouldn't stop asking until she had it all. And if Gordon heard the kinds of things Peg was asking, he might just leave her behind after all. No, better to get it all out there in the bathroom. "Gordon's been embezzling from Uncle Dale," she said, trying desperately to avoid her sister's eyes.

"How much?"

"A million and a half."

"How?"

Wanda shrugged. Now that she thought of it, she really didn't know much about how Gordon actually got the cash in his hands. "He said RV dealerships let some customers—*rich* customers—take the coaches on what he called 'extended test drives.' But he's really selling them and taking the cash. A million and a half dollars over the past year or so."

"And now he has to get out of the country, before…" she said, letting it trail off into a question.

Wanda nodded again.

Peg sloughed down onto the laminate floor next to her sister. "I thought a lot of things about your bottom-grabbing husband over the years, Wan, but a thief? A *big-time* thief? They're gonna put him away for thirty years."

"That's why we're leaving the country."

"*We?* You can*not* go with him, Wanda Jean."

"He's my husband."

"They'll think you're involved!"

It was a long minute before Wanda finally said, "I am, Peg. I *am* involved."

Keeping it quiet, keeping everybody nice and distracted, that's what was important. Bob's entertainment nerve center was quite a showpiece, and it kept the skinny buffoon talking—and about himself, not Gordon and Wanda's business or their future travel plans. He checked his watch: Six-fifteen. A couple more hours among the Hakes, and then he could corral Wanda into a debriefing on the fold-out couch. All he had to do now was keep any of them—Bob, Peg, or their three teenage Inquisitors—from learning too much. He did the arithmetic in his head—if they left and saw the goddamn precious bomb site at maybe seven the next morning (plenty of time, since he was begging off as sleepy probably in two hours or so), they could be at the lookout outside T or C at four in the afternoon. Plenty of time to beat the dinner picnic crowd, which usually didn't heat up till five or so, according to Janey.

Until then, Bob.

"I'm not talking about quadraphonic, Gordy—I'm talking octophonic stereo," Bob said, leading him around the room to point out felt boxes sunk into the walls in some complex geometric arrangement that made Gordon's head hurt just to think about. "You see the subwoofers close to the carpet there? That gives you the rumble you'd feel—not just hear, *feel*—in real life. It's actually better than what you'd hear in real life. More authentic sounding."

"Must've set you back a bundle."

"You're not whistling Dixie there, boy. And it's all infrared, no wires to tangle or give you that hiss some systems have. I'm all DVD—I mean, what's the point of going digital if you've got analog wiring between the system and your speakers, right?"

"Just thinking that." Blah blah, keep this going for a few more hours, he was in the clear. "Install all this yourself, did ya?"

"You bet," Bob said, his hands on his hips as he admired his work and turned to face Gordon. "So, New Mexico, huh? I've never been, myself. How long are you staying?"

"Sorry, that's classified." *Ha, ha. Fuck.*

Bob leaned close. "Come on—you guys haven't taken a vacation the whole time I've known you. You're not going to share?"

"It's a surprise. Wanda doesn't even know all the details—I wouldn't want it to slip out. Twenty-fifth anniversary, you know. Want some surprise to it."

"Come on, how long you staying? Where all are you going? I won't tell, cross my heart."

And hope to die, pencil-neck? Gordon could feel his jaw clench in tension and anger. But he held himself, because he knew damn well that anything and everything he said and did would be examined and re-examined after Wanda's body was found. He had to say *something*, and obviously stalling Bob the chemist wasn't going to work for two more hours. Any lie he told would look mighty bad if Bob—who looked like he could be *Jeopardy!* champion five days straight, no problem—could trip him up on it. And of course, the truth was an unattractive option when the inevitable questioning reached Bob. Gordon chewed his lip and looked at his brother-in-law, and decided what the hell.

"Mexico City, actually." It was the truth, it was a lie. A smile crept across Gordon's face: Fifteen years in sales hadn't gone to waste.

"Ah, I think Mexico City's in Mexico, Gordy, not *New* Mexico."

"That's just to keep Wanda off the trail. Gonna see some ruins, do some touristy shit."

"Oh my," Bob said, and nearly doubled over with his suburbanite's silent chuckle. "And she doesn't know?"

"Nope—has no idea what's coming."

"That's terrific! That's really good. Heck, Peg and I always thought you were going to break her in half one of these days."

"How—what?" Gordon sputtered, and winced immediately at his desperate tone, hoping Bob didn't pick up on it.

But he did. "Yeah…" he said slowly, looking Gordon in the eyes with a concerned furrowing of his brow. "Wanda always used to say things to Peg…thought something bad was going to happen—like she thought you'd do an O.J. on her one day. But that was when things weren't going so well. Back when you were…"

Gordon crossed his arms, trying to look buddy-buddy and threatening as hell at the same time. "Were what? Back when I was enjoying life a little too much?"

Bob bopped him on the arm. "You always were one with the women."

Gordon bopped back. But harder. "Shucks." Now back to business—he had a bud in which something nasty had to be nipped. "Wanda thought I wanted to *kill* her? Like *kill* kill? She *said* that?"

"Sorry, Gor—"

"Can't believe it," he said, and brought a fist down on top of Bob's sound mixing bench, which would no doubt leave an impression of how very *upset* he was at this suggestion. "Just when we were getting it all back together."

"Hey, it's okay, man. You don't have to—"

"I mean, she just told this to Peg, okay, but if Wanda went saying I'm abusive and she feared for her life, then I got to cancel the whole damn trip." He moved for the door. "Better tell Wanda what you told me. She won't be happy, but…"

Bob skittered in front of him. "Hey now, Gordy! She never said you were *abusive*—she just worried that you wanted some little piece of, um, action more than her. She thought it would *kill* her if you left her—you know how she and Peg are at any sign of abandonment, with their father taking off on them and all. That's what she meant. I'm sure that's what she meant."

"Love that woman, you know that? Never laid a hand on her in twenty-five years. And she's been a real bitch sometimes, maybe even deserved it sometimes—"

Bob's eyebrows twitched.

"—from a lesser man. Lesser man would've taken her to the woodshed and shut her up. Not me. Bided my time, gave the benefit of the doubt, and now we're sitting pretty, going to Mexico City for a two—hell, *three*-week stay."

"Boy, that's terrific, Gordy," Bob said, and patted him on the back as he led him away from the door and toward his DVD movie selection. Gordon could see the flop sweat on Bob's forehead, and wondered how much of his own was pouring down his face right then. "Now let's watch something."

He looked over Bob's movies, the blood pounding in his head. That was a close one. He peeked a glance at his watch: six-thirty. Maybe an hour and a half until an early bedtime—shit, he hadn't slept more than an hour letting Wanda drive since they left Indiana.

He knew he was probably hoping for too much, but he looked for a war movie. Something with lots of guns and explosions. Something, with Bob's octophonic home theater set-up, that would make it much too loud to talk. With that, all he had to do was relax and pray that Wanda just kept her mouth shut.

Fear unlike anything she had ever felt before nearly froze Peg Hake as she wept on her sister's shoulder for the second time. How could Wanda let herself get talked into this by that husband of hers? Was there no end to what he would do to her? Cheat on her, keep her from useful work, deny her children—and now this, which was making her leave the country forever or go to jail for twenty years? Peg couldn't—*wouldn't*—stand by and let this happen. There was only one thing she could do.

"Wanda, I am calling the police. That man is not dragging you into this. They can come and arrest him, and you—you can testify against him. You'll be all right."

"All right? He can't go to jail—what would happen to me?"

"This isn't 1964—women do make it by themselves nowadays. We'll have Gordon hauled off and you—"

"I told you, they can't arrest him until the floor-plan checker is done and they have gone over all the results and show that Gordon could've stolen the RVs or the money. And besides, I've been taking the money down to New Mexico, flying once a week and sticking it in the safety deposit box so Gordon's friend can do whatever he does with it and put it in the box. That's where the tickets are—or his ticket. In the box."

"Which is in Gordon's name."

"Well, not *Gordon's* name—he's got a faked New Mexico ID under a different name. But Peg, listen—I *am* part of it. I got a fake ID like his. If Gordon goes to jail, I go too. I'd rather be in Venezuela."

Peg steamed. How could she see it so plainly and Wanda not see it at all? Gordon had everything set up so he could get out of town, leave her behind and take off with the money, let her face the police. *One ticket* to Venezuela? That wasn't the kind of thing somebody did accidentally. She would have to make Wanda see the truth, no matter how she had to hurt her sister right now to do it.

"I bet Gordon has a little honey all set to go south with him."

"No! He has been so romantic on this trip—he loves me. He can't keep his thing in his pocket most of the time, but—"

"Wanda!"

"He can't, but he loves me and he wants to make up for everything. I know he does. Maybe he was planning on leaving me at the border with seventy-eight thousand dollars as a divorce settlement," she said, ignoring

Peg's puzzled look. "But getting away from Dale, getting away from all the awful part of our life—he loves me again, Peggy. We're going to make this work. Why else would he take me on this trip?"

"He obviously wanted to keep you from talking."

Wanda shook her head. "No—he knows that he couldn't get out of Mexico City—where he could be extradited—before I could get to a phone and get him arrested, even over the border. Besides, there are a lot of ways to keep somebody from talking."

"You sound like an old con, Wanda."

She shrugged and said, "Just a lot of thinking and planning and talking. It's like this has finally brought us closer together after all this time."

"The heist of the century, huh," Peg said with a sad smile, and hugged her big sister. "I guess you know what you're doing. You're standing by your man."

"That's right."

"Too bad that man had to be Gordy Mitchell," she said, and they laughed. And as she washed her face and patted it with a lavender towel, she looked at her smiling sister and remembered what she had said: *There are a lot of ways to keep someone from talking.*

She almost said something, but looked again at Wanda's smile, so rare when she was talking about her husband, and decided to keep her peace.

The lights were barely out in the living room, the streetlights coming in through the bay window, when Gordon shifted around on the pull-out bed and said to Wanda, "Tell me our secret's still a secret."

"Gordon, what do you take me for?"

"The sister of a curious woman."

"I didn't tell her a thing. I told her we were going to Venezuela."

His eyes popped wide, then clamped shut like he was trying to keep from seeing bodies fly from a car crash. This could *not* be happening. "You're shittin' me."

"I told her we were going to Venezuela because we were starting everything over, getting romantic again after so many years, you know?"

"Why couldn't you say Argentina? Or the Philippines? Fucking Antarctica? Had to say the place I'm going?"

"*You're* going? You son of a bitch."

"Jesus, you know what I—don't change the subject. You had to say the actual place we're going?"

"What does it matter? They can't extradite us—that's what you said."

He sucked in his lip. They couldn't—well, *wouldn't*—probably want to extradite anyone putting millions in their banks, but he wondered if they would send out someone wanted for murder. Even though Venezuela lacked an extradition treaty with the U.S.—which is why he chose Caracas as his final destination—if the U.S. authorities knew where to look, and they could show it was murder, and Venezuela knew his real identity...

Well, they'd know where to look now, thanks to Wanda. But it was too late to change the plan—Janey had it set up according to his instructions, and he would have to act fast once he got over the border and into Mexico City.

That is, if the police weren't already waiting for him when he got off the plane in Caracas. He hadn't an hour to spare; the Rambling checker was definitely done with his count by now, and that meant Gann and the rest of them would be asking around—

Fucking shoot me, Gordon thought.

"I didn't tell her anything else about where we were going, honestly," Wanda said, giving him a start. He had almost forgotten she was there. "Nothing else about that at all."

"Trying to tell me you told her something about something else?"

"She didn't understand why we were leaving the country, Gordon."

His hands balled up into fists, and he would have bashed her to a pulp right fucking there if he didn't have to know more. "And you told her what?"

"Why we're leaving."

"Which is why?"

She looked at his fists made so tight his knuckles were obviously white even in the dim light of the darkened living room and said, "I told her we're leaving because you just can't stand the RV business anymore. And I'm not being left like my mother was. I'm standing by my man."

"Is that right."

"I don't lie to you, Gordon Mitchell."

He took another few seconds to look into the outlines of her eyes, scrubbed now of their sealing paint, and then relaxed a bit, letting the blood flow back into his hands. She seemed like she was lying, all right, but he supposed he was enough liar for the both of them in that marriage, and let it go. If he knew any more she said, he'd probably kill her right there in her stupid sister's house, and that wouldn't be good for anybody, least of all him.

Wanna stand by your man? he thought as he lay back down on the pillow and tried to ease himself into sleep. *Stand by me—right next to me—when I show you the view off the cliff tomorrow afternoon.*

It was just after nine p.m. That meant she had about nineteen hours to live, and that was fine by Gordon. This whole adventure had already gone on plenty long enough.

19

Four hours earlier, at five o'clock, Douglas Gann chucked his laptop and a bag of clothes into his Crown Victoria and floored it onto the I-80-90 Toll Road towards Chicago. He checked the Mitchells' position again and again and again and, by eleven p.m., figured they had stopped for the night near Oklahoma City.

He stopped for gas twice. Other than that, he drove. He didn't listen to the radio or admire the bright lights of any passing town. He drove.

By first light Sunday Gann had made it into the ass-end of Missouri and pulled into the lot between Shoney's and Cracker Barrel. He stepped out into the still-cool June air, stretching his legs and deciding it would be a fine day indeed—clear skies, warm temperatures, and some eyewitnesses to interview. Maybe even saving a life if he played his cards right and got himself in a position where he could haul Gordon Mitchell in before he killed that lovely wife of his.

As he made his way toward the Shoney's door, which was probably still locked at five-thirty in the morning—but would no doubt swing open with one flash of his badge—he allowed himself to wonder what it was about that woman that drew him so, what it was about a woman—it had always been women—that made him *connect* with her. Wanda wasn't the most beautiful he'd ever encountered, that was for darn sure; she wasn't bad to look at, for a forty-something lady, but no serious beauty queen. She had the most artful makeup he'd seen, but he was never much of a makeup man—his women, the few there had been after college and the academy, were way too made-up as it was, but that was desperate, the kind of makeup a woman sticks on to catch herself a man with a good future and a pension after that. Wanda was more…real? No, that wasn't it. He was only twenty-nine, but he was still bemused that he hadn't yet experienced enough in his life to put his finger on what it was about Wanda Mitchell that made him want to protect her, made him want to curl up with her and let her tell him what life was like in the early 'seventies. There was just this aura she gave off—maybe hers just matched his. He didn't know.

He came to the Shoney's door and shook it off, got himself "in character." Just as he thought, the door was locked, and a display of his shiny badge in its leather case got the floor-mopper opening the door right away.

"Hi—Detective Gann of the Elkhart Police Department. May I speak to your manager, please?"

"Elk*what*?"

"Elkhart. Indiana. This is police business—your manager, please, son," he said, and the teen skittered off in search of his boss.

Gann took the minute to look around the place. There were a lot of nooks and crannies with booths and tables crammed in them, plenty of places where the diners couldn't see each other. Customers, then, probably wouldn't remember the travelers, and the only ones who might would be especially eagle-eyed employees who happened by them. And that was only if the Mitchells left an impression, which they probably weren't too eager to do. Still, he had driven instead of flown so he could catch some clues on the way and figure Gordon's mindset, so he would ask around.

The manager, a ruddy-faced heavy-set man with a cretinous mous-tache—the maximum facial hair he was allowed, Gann was sure—minced out of the kitchen area and shook Gann's hand. "Officer, tell me this isn't about our dishwasher again. Not having him for three months last time almost killed me."

"No, nothing like that, sir," Gann said, and peered into the man-ager's eyes. "Just looking for a couple of…fugitives. Our investigation has led us to think they may have stopped here for a late breakfast, early lunch yesterday."

The manager's eyes rolled into his head as he thought. "Nothing unusual yesterday," he said finally. "What did they look like?"

"A man and a woman. Early forties. He has a beefy build, widow's peaks in his brown hair, which is turning gray. The woman has beautiful brown eyes, good features, wears artful makeup."

"Artful makeup."

"Yes—well-done makeup. She's a cosmetologist."

"Sure. What were they driving?"

"Driving an RV."

"An RV? These are fugitives, you said? A cosmetologist in an RV?"

Gann let out a chuckle, then stopped and gave the manager a stern look. Sometimes giving people mixed signals let them know you had seri-ous work to do. "I know, it sounds funny, but it isn't. Does any of this jog your memory?"

"Maybe I was helping out in back."

"Hmm. Is your same wait staff working this morning? Weekend staff?"

"Most of them, sure—come on back."

Gann followed him into the kitchen area, which bustled as the cooks and servers prepared for the Sunday morning rush. Slowly, as each employee noticed him—and his badge, which he had hooked onto his belt to ease cooperation and understanding of his purpose there—the activity stopped.

"Um, everyone? This is a detective from Indiana, and he's looking for a couple of escaped fugitives who stole an RV and may have come through here. The RV is for hostages, right, detective?"

What the heck? Gann stared at the manager for a few seconds, wondering what it would be like to work under someone like that, and said, "There's no cause for alarm. I just want to know if anyone noticed a fortyish couple, a man and a woman, acting strange yesterday around ten-thirty, eleven in the morning. The man may have seemed nervous. They were in an RV."

"We get a lotta people in RVs around here, mister," said one of the waitresses, a dark-haired wrinkle-fest who looked like she started waiting tables for chump change when she was fifteen and pregnant and she'd be doing it until she died, and turned back to wrapping silverware with napkins.

"I had a couple, looked like the woman was gonna kill the guy before they even finished their coffee. They were in an RV," another waitress said, this one a tiny blond teen-ager whose mission in life probably was to do anything not to end up like the first waitress.

Gann lit up. "Can you describe them?"

The teen thought for a minute and said, "All I really remember is that they were really acting mad at each other, and they were Black."

"Black?"

She nodded.

"Anybody else?" The sun was rising rapidly outside, and Gann still had another restaurant to check.

20

A couple of hundred miles down the road, Gordon's eyes snapped open as soon as his sleeping mind realized it was now the sun, not those damn streetlights, shining in his eyes. Immediately he made a half-roll and said, "Up, Wanda."

She was gone. The sheets weren't even warm.

"Holy fuck," Gordon mumbled as he swung his pale legs off the thin mattress and tried to get his bearings. He slapped himself in the face to get himself awake and was just turning to throw his pants on when he saw Wanda, fully dressed in a nasty purple pantsuit he'd never seen before, coming down the stairs with Peg and Bob, who were similarly dressed in clothes Gordon thought you might wear to a funeral if you didn't particularly like the person but couldn't come right out and say it.

"Oh, you're up. Want to come to church with us?" Wanda said with a smile.

"No church for us—schedule to keep, remember? Gotta get moving."

"Gordon, Peg and Bob are taking us to see the bomb site, remember?"

He wished there was still a crater there, so he could push them all in while they gaped at a vacant lot surrounded by a fence. "What about church?"

Peg said, "Church first, then a group goes downtown to lay flowers and give a little prayer."

"No time for that. Sorry, Peg, Bob, but got a job I have to do. That's three hundred thousand worth of machine out there, and the buyer's in New Mexico, real anxious to get it." He watched Wanda's face fall like one of her cakes when he said this; she must have been looking forward to entering the land of the Godly pretty bad. "Sorry about that, Wanda."

"That's a darn shame," Bob said. "Well, it's been—"

"You son of a bitch!" Peg yelled out of nowhere. "Why don't you let Wanda do something she wants for once in her life?"

Gordon blinked.

Peg looked back at Wanda and Bob, whose mouths were hanging open. "I'm serious—Gordon, when have you ever just done something for your wife. Hell, when have you ever done anything for another person? Have you ever just done something out of the good of your heart?"

He searched for words—*him*, the smoothest pilot that ever flew the good ship *Silver Tongue*—and couldn't find any. At least not until he looked at the smug grin filling Wanda's face. That's when he said, "Came here for you, Wanda, didn't I?"

That wiped her face clean. And he enjoyed immensely making Peg and Bob watch helplessly as he said to his wife, "Glad you're dressed already. Bob, want to help with our suitcases? Won't be a minute myself."

Far from the blabbery he had to endure when they arrived, their departure from the glorious *chez* Hake was silent as a death chamber telephone on election night. Gordon pulled the Vacationeer out of their driveway and watched Wanda watch her sister's family disappear in the passenger side mirror.

"Won't feel bad for long," he said, and almost laughed.

It was just after seven in the morning. They had five hundred miles to go, and he had to get Wanda to the scenic lookout by four p.m. if he wanted to be safe, five at the very latest. Plenty of time.

At lunch he'd slip away and call Janey, calm her cute little butt down. Once she knew he was in New Mexico, she'd be cool. She just never thought he'd get there, that was all. Once he was close she'd forget all about being pissed.

He looked at Wanda, who sulked as she looked out the window at the landscape, which was already empty of everything except grass and far, far-off buttes, and smiled. It was all going so perfectly; she had lost her will to bitch. Eight hours to go.

Wanda could see Gordon's head turned toward her in the reflection off her window. He was so happy he could put her in her place, get her stuck where she couldn't say anything because it was her ass on the line with his. He was so freaking happy, and his sister-in-law was right—he didn't give a good goddamn about anybody else.

What he didn't know is that she was that close to just staying with Peg and Bob and their nice kids, just letting him ride off with the money and everything else. She'd sell the house, move to Oklahoma City, start life over again with people who *cared* about other people, for the love of God. She was *that* close.

She'd give him one more chance, one more, when they got to Truth or Consequences. One more chance, and if he fucked that up, she'd get enough for a bus back to Peg's, and that would be that. She would let him show her that he cared about her—cared about *anybody*—and if he didn't damn well measure up, she would do what she swore to herself she'd never do: She'd leave.

Wanda turned back from the window, wiped the tear from her eye, and went back to the bathroom to fix her face. On the way she smiled at Gordon, and she could tell he wondered what about. He thought he had the upper hand, but twelve hours or so from then, when they had gotten the coach delivered and had settled down in the motel in T or C, she'd show him he didn't, not at all.

A couple of hundred miles north, just outside of Cheyenne, Wyoming, a young man, looking thirsty and hot, sat next to his motorcycle and watched for anyone coming down the lonely stretch of road. It was hard to find any part of the immense interstate that would qualify as a lonely stretch, even in Wyoming, but the biker had ridden a couple of hours and finally gotten himself a good spot. There was a clear sight line for miles, a nice straight stretch so he could see who was coming and so the drivers could see him by the side of the road, allow them plenty of time to slow down and pull off, help the poor stranded motorcyclist. He was young, dashing, safe-looking, you name it—hard to resist for elderly couples with a soft spot in their hearts and a blind spot in their safety precautions.

The biker's name was Spike. He had been waiting on this hot-as-Hades mountain road for an hour now, waiting for a suitable mark to stop. That was the problem, oftentimes: Hyundais would stop and offer help, but most Hummers and Winnebagos and the odd Lincoln Town

Car—anybody with anything worth taking, in other words—would just sniff and zoom past him.

At the first glint of metallic reflection at the horizon, Spike would leap to his feet and try to make himself look doubly desperate, his backpack slung over his shoulder, everything the way he imagined a genuinely broken-down rider would be. He kept his gun tucked into his pants behind him, his leather vest—suede, really, nothing too butch, nothing to scare anybody off—covering the handle.

Well, maybe not *nothing* to scare anybody—he probably had bugs in his teeth, sunburn, you name it, after six weeks of plying his new trade of highway robbery. Oh well, all the scarier, once the mark had stopped and gotten close enough that there was no turning back. Skinny twenty-two-year-olds, experience or no, needed all the help they could get in the instilling-fear department.

His gun helped a *lot*, once the mark got close enough.

The twinkle of reflection was a pickup truck pulling an Airstream trailer, Spike was sure. Airstreams were like oases in the vast desert of moving vans, four-door sedans, and RVs with the air-conditioning running full-blast: Inside their silvery shells, they held the promise of folks with nowhere particular to go, and who had to be there at no particular time. Airstream owners, usually retirees, did that kind of traveling.

And that kind of traveling took quite the reserve of spending money. Trinkets for the grandkids, magnets in the shapes of each state traversed for the refrigerator, three square Cracker Barrel or Big Boy meals a day—these weren't free. Travelers could use credit cards, true, but almost everyone kept a reserve of cash somewhere in case the computers went down or they wanted some glittery bauble at some roadside stand that didn't take American Express, VISA or MasterCard.

He squinted into the distance. It *was* an Airstream. That was good, because it was very hot out there, and he had a long way to go if he was going to make it to Mexico by sunset. He didn't know exactly what there was over the border, but this was the outlaw's life as he had always envisioned it—steal from some rich traveler, then hightail it down to Mexico, where he would find the closest brothel and liberate a poor village girl from her life of prostitution, give her back her dignity and the chance to go to a good school. Or something like that. After the robbery part, things got a little hazy.

That was okay, though—he would get enough money, a thousand or so, and go down to Mexico, which was after all the closest Third-World country, and the border the only place on Earth where one can walk from a Third-World to a First-World country. The main point was that he would get the money and do some good with it, that was all.

Spike set his backpack down and waved his arms at the pickup and trailer, which were getting close now. Were they stopping, pulling over? It was hard to tell through the shimmering glare.

In order to do some good with the money he stole, however, he would have to hang on to it long enough to give it to someone other than himself. Lodging was more expensive than he had accounted for back in his dorm room, planning all of this out on loose-leaf paper that he kept hidden lest his roommate find his scribblings and decide to turn stoolie—the "lingo" was becoming a real part of him, he noticed. He had spent most everything he had stolen in a month and a half of separating Fat Cats from their ill-gotten gains, spent it on hotels—motels, really—and meals and sport drinks that kept his electrolytes and sodium content in balance after a full day of riding his motorcycle in the summer heat. Now, though, he really would have to get some money and actually give it to those who he had promised to benefit through his life of crime. Who the beneficiaries might be was still unclear, but hopefully he could score a quick grand off of the approaching Airstream—which—*yes!*—was pulling to the shoulder to help him—and get himself down to Mexico and identify someone to bestow it on, like he was the millionaire on that old TV show.

He would never take the money and run, as he imagined most bandits would, since after all they *were* in it for the financial benefits; that wasn't the point for Spike. That didn't jibe with his philosophy, and his philosophy was all-important. His philosophy said—

"Some help, son?" the beefy grandfather type bellowed as he swung the red pickup's door open and launched himself out. The chunky grandmother remained in the shotgun seat and smiled at Spike and her thick-fingered husband.

This was someone who would know how to fix motorcycles, no doubt. And who would see in an instant that there was nothing wrong with this one. Spike reached back and felt the handle of his thirty-eight.

"Bike's busted," Spike said, doing his best to sound like an authentic desperate motorcyclist. The man was getting on the bike and trying to start it. "Anything you can do…"

"No problem, son—it's probably just—" Grandpa said, then stopped as he kicked the ignition and twisted the throttle and started the thing right up without so much as a hiccup. He fixed Spike with a quizzical smile. "Hey, it's working!"

Spike clamped his fingers around the gun and pulled it out, giving the Fat Cat a smile of his own. "How about that," he said, and pointed the gun at Grandpa's head. "Now stick 'em up."

"Roger!" Grandma screamed from the truck.

"You're shittin' me," Grandpa said, then, when it was obvious Spike wasn't shitting him at all, added, "You looked like such a nice kid, too."

"That's the idea," Spike said.

Six hundred dollars later, he was back on the road, taking I-25 south towards the border. One more "stop" and he would probably have his thousand. Heck, he could probably find a good spot in New Mexico before the day was done, and then that would be that.

Gann was sitting across from the Cracker Barrel manager at the table nearest the crackling fireplace, as homey there as it was in each of their two hundred and eighty locations. "All I need is to find out if these people ate here or not," Gann said. "It's of vital importance to the investigation."

"I see. And you think they ate here because of their above-average taste?"

"Of course." Gann gave a quick smile. "Seriously, though, we pinpointed the fugitives' location to the parking lot you and Shoney's share."

"Are they still here?"

"No, they've moved on."

"Then why—"

Gann took out his badge again. "Listen—I need to speak to any employees here who worked yesterday morning. Please."

"What jurisdiction do you have here, detective?"

Oh, boy. "What *jurisdiction?*"

"This doesn't look like Indiana to me. Maybe we can give a call to your supervisor and find out what—"

"Whoa! This is a criminal we're talking about. Don't you want to help us track him down?"

The manager eyed him. "I thought you knew where the fugitives are, with that satellite deal."

"We do," Gann said slowly, trying to think, "we do. We just need some…corroboration of their…state of mind. Witnesses. You know."

"We have forty employees here at a shift, detective. And we may look slow right now, but in an hour or so, when the churches let out and tourists are hitting the road…"

Gann let him talk for a minute, scanning the huge dining area. It had a thatched wall—heavy with knick-knacks, of course—separating the smoking and non-smoking sections. Other than that, any diner could see any other diner in the restaurant. He shut his eyes and pictured Gordon's smug face, then remembered what he looked like with a cigarette in his mouth. Right—he was a smoker.

He cut the manager off. "Forget it. I'll just get some breakfast, okay?" he said, then stood and moved toward the hostess. "One, please. Smoking."

It wasn't ten minutes later he had a positive ID from his highly coop-erative young waitress—there was no way she'd forget them, she said, because the man stood up in the middle of the dining room and pledged his undying love to his wife. They were celebrating twenty-five years of marriage, and wasn't that a sweet thing of him to do?

Gann agreed that it was, and had a solid stab at the Loosen Yer Belt Breakfast as his mind turned on the new information. There were two possibilities: One, Gordon was trying to make things look good—rather clumsily, if you asked him—and leave a trail of clues that would show he loved his wife and would never kill her; and two, Wanda really was in on the embezzlement scheme and they really were celebrating.

Either way, Wanda Mitchell was dead, because there was no way her husband was going to let her stick around as a witness. Unless Gann got to her first, of course, and took the choice away from him.

He waved a hand to get some more coffee, and said to the waitress, "Was there anything else, anything out of the ordinary? You may be saving a life."

She cocked her lips to the side and concentrated. Finally, she said, "Well, he did call her…" She seemed uncomfortable or unsure; he couldn't tell which.

"Called her…?"

She leaned in close so the other diners wouldn't hear. "He called her a bitch."

Gann coughed his coffee onto the place mat.

"And she called him a prick. It was so weird after they had just—"

"I've got to run," he said, and did. He left a huge tip.

In the car zipping down I-40 with the bubble going, Gann punched the speed-dial for headquarters. Being Sunday morning, he got Duty Chief Brown. "Mark—I've got evidence the wife knows about the Major Dale scheme!" he shouted into the phone. It was stretching things a bit, but hunches were what gave him the edge over those who weren't in touch with their third eye.

"I imagine she does, since she's going off with him."

"No! I mean, she had no choice—she thinks this is just a delivery. She's not part of the scheme. I have reason to believe she just knows about it and is allowing it to go forward out of love for—"

"What do you *want*, Doug?"

Gann snapped back like he'd been slapped. "I'm bringing her in as a material witness."

"You already served her with the subpoena, right? Let the poor woman be, for Christ's sake. The Rambling checker's reporting big discrepancies—we've got enough to charge the husband. Tomorrow morning we're going to the judge, Doug, okay? We're getting the warrant. We'll have the New Mexico guys pick him up for us. He's in the net, okay?"

"Tomorrow morning's too late. The wife'll be dead by then."

"So you've said. She's gone under her own power, by her own free will. There's nothing we can do about that. Or is this another one of your psychic flashes?"

Gann ignored that. "I'm intercepting them."

There was a long, long pause on the other end of the line before Brown finally said, "Where are you?"

"Maybe four hours behind them. I'm just passing into Oklahoma."

"You're not."

"I need an order to compel the wife to come in as a material witness." Gann swerved to get around a Camaro clogging the road at eighty.

"You want to arrest her?"

"Protective custody. I need the order, Mark."

"What, is the husband waiting for you to get there before he kills her? How do you know she's not dead already? She's not a material witness, Doug—she's a suspect. In the morning, she'll be on the warrant with her husband, okay? Then the New Mexico guys can bring them both in, safe and sound and heading for jail."

Gann darn nearly smashed his cell phone like he had his desk phone, but looked at his laptop and remembered this was his only key to where the Mitchells were. "She's not *involved*—she's been suckered by her husband, I'm telling you."

"She knows too much, enough that her husband wants to kill her."

"Right."

"But she has nothing to do with the thefts."

"Right, that's right."

"Goodbye, Doug," Brown said, but before he hung up he said, "You should get your ass back here before you do some real damage."

"What could I do that would be worse than—"

"Not to them. To yourself. The chief finds out you're out there, chasing them around without any authority, you're fucked. Not too many Medals of Valor get handed out on the traffic patrol," Brown said, and hung up.

Gann could feel his grip tighten around the steering wheel, and he blew right through the speed where he had the cruise control set. They wouldn't give him the okay to bring Wanda in as a material witness, fine; he'd take care of getting her away from her husband on his own. He knew they stayed the night in Oklahoma City, and a little research using his Phone Numbers USA CD-ROM along with a long-distance dip into the Elkhart PD databases, and he knew that they had stayed at the home of her sister, one Margaret Polska Hake.

If Gordon stopped there, then Wanda was still alive, that much was for sure. And their stopping for the night had allowed Gann to make up valuable miles. He would pop in for a visit to the Hakes, and then would pop back out, maybe with a clue to where Gordon might stop to do his killing.

It was just a couple of hours to Oklahoma City at the speed he was driving. Gordon could keep the noose from closing around his neck for only so long, no matter how much he charmed his wife.

23

As Gordon noticed that western Oklahoma turned into Texas long before any signs welcomed you to the Friendship State, he also noticed he was doing a piss-poor job of charming Wanda. She would sneak a look at him every few miles—not much to see out the window, true, but this look was something else. He could almost see the little gears in her head turning as she peered at him through the corner of her eye. He let her do whatever she wanted; this far along, his plan was likely to work perfectly just from inertia.

The plan really was simplicity itself, he had to admit: The only weak point was that it hinged on perfect timing. Having let people see that he and Wanda were traveling together, the police would have no idea there was any trouble until Gordon had already flown the coop—except for that Detective Gann, anyway, and he was more than a thousand miles back, in Elkhart.

They would stop at precisely four o'clock at the Coyote Jump Lookout, twenty-five miles north of Truth or Consequences, New Mexico, the lookout with the steepest drop of any in the area. At that time, in the heat of the middle of the day and long before any spectacular desert sunset, he would invite his lovely bride to peer over the edge…and push. All the guidebooks said the traffic didn't pick up along these scenic sites until around five p.m., so he figured as long as he did what he had to do by four, he'd be in the clear and no one would even notice her body for a week, if that soon. Then he would make it into town, sleep, and on Monday morning at nine sharp would retrieve the money placed in a dummy account by his contact in T or C—for which one Mr. David Atchison of Sierra Savings and Loan got a *very* generous twenty percent—then launder the last seventy-eight thousand and be on his merry widower way.

The afternoon stretched out lazily as they passed through New Mexico, mile after sunny mile, through Santa Rosa, through Albuquerque, through Socorro, south on I-25 like they were slipping down the throat of the land. Twenty miles or so from the lookout, about fifty from T or C, they passed a steaming car with a dejected-looking family staring at the father, who looked even more dejected than they did.

"Now that would suck," Gordon said with a mournful chuckle.

"That's *it!*" Wanda yelled, making Gordon jump and nearly yank the coach off the road. "You don't give a *shit* about anybody but yourself! Stop this damn thing—I've had enough!"

Gordon leaned over the wheel and, as nonchalantly as possible, covered the keys with his hand. It would not do at all to have her yanking them out of the ignition and wandering off, especially not in sight of the interstate.

"We've passed at *least* five cars in the past half-hour that you could've stopped and helped."

He couldn't believe this. "Ever hear of something called a *schedule?* What am I, a tow truck?"

"Stop the coach, Gordon. I was giving you one more chance and you blew it."

"Look, get into Venezuela and I'll give a thousand bucks to the…Venezuelan Orphan Fund, okay? Sound good?"

"Sounds like the only person you care about is yourself."

Somebody's gotta do it, he thought, but kept it to himself. "That's not fair. I care about you."

"You don't care about anybody. All I want is to feel appreciated and admired for who I am. But that's not gonna happen, because you never do anything out of the kindness of your heart. I could love you again if you'd do that."

Whoa! Where'd this come from? And what made her think he could love *her* again? And who gave a rat's ass if she loved him or not? In half an hour, she'd be dead at the bottom of a dry river bed.

But not if she decided she was getting off the bus early.

"I swear, I'd give up my share of the money and make sweet love to you if I just could see you do one thing for another person. I'd go to the ends of the Earth for you if you'd do just *one* thing for somebody, not even me. Just *somebody*," she said with a sob, and threw her head back into her hands.

He could do without the sweet love, but keeping her on board definitely interested him. If she meant it, it would be worth the trouble. He checked the dashboard clock—three-fifteen and they were fifteen miles from the lookout. Plenty of time to do a good deed. But what? The dry ribbon of highway stretched ahead like a line straight to T or C. Not a soul in sight, much less a soul in need of a selfless helping hand.

And then, like a winning lottery ticket just peeking out from a Christmas stocking, the chance to show Wanda what she wanted to see appeared, far off down the highway but close enough that Gordon could see exactly what it was: A stranded motorcyclist standing by his bike, waving for help.

Cue the cherubs, he thought, and smiled at Wanda, who was still crying. *It's hallelujah time.*

"Think I don't care about people?" he said as he pulled over to the interstate shoulder. "Watch this."

He flipped the hazards on the huge bus and locked her down so she wouldn't roll back down the rocky mountainous road, then cracked his fingers, stretched his legs, and, making sure Wanda was watching, swung the door open to selflessly help his fellow man.

For Spike, it had been one heck of a long day. Heat, bugs, jerk drivers who didn't respect the commandment *Thou shalt share the road, especially with vehicles much more fuel-efficient than your own*, everything had added up to a miserable search for the right spot. Finally, he had settled—it was a bit more populated than he would have liked, but rich folk didn't travel the blue highways and he wasn't about to spend another baking hour looking for a more secluded bit of interstate.

But now, this big luxury liner of a motor home was putting on the brakes and the hazard lights—to help him! He felt against his back for the comforting bulge of the thirty-eight.

The guy getting off the RV looked like hell, like he hadn't slept in a year. That was okay—Spike himself probably had looked like sunshine half a dozen hours ago when he thought he looked so scary for the benefit of the Airstream travelers.

"Need some assistance?" the guy called to him. "I'm in kind of a hurry, but I always want to help folks."

"Great! My bike's broken down! Can you take a look at it?"

The guy walked strangely, like he was being watched. Big strides, with his arms out like a cowboy taking his ten paces before a duel. Once he got there, he said, "I don't know a damn thing about motorcycles, okay?"

Spike was reaching for his gun but stopped. *What was up with this?* "Um…okay."

"But look, you need something and I need something, right?"

"Are you some kind of salesman?" Spike found himself asking. His mother, when she was bored one time, had dabbled in "network marketing," and she used to talk like that.

"RV sales. Gordon Mitchell," the guy said, and stuck out his hand.

Spike shook it. Something wasn't right here. The guy, Gordon, hadn't even glanced at the motorcycle, which, of course, didn't have a thing wrong with it.

"Call me Ron."

"Ron."

"Exactly. Got a name there, son?"

"They call me Spike."

"Cool. That your real name?"

"No, my real name's Trent. Trent Jones." *Oh, shit*—he nearly slapped himself in the forehead. *What an idiot.* But there was something about this guy that made him want to talk all of a sudden.

"So you're Spike Jones?" Gordon said with a chuckle.

"Yeah…" *What was he laughing about?*

He stopped chuckling. "Never mind. Look, getting this bike going again isn't what you really need, is it?"

Spike took a step back. This guy was spooky as hell. "Well…"

"Tell me what you really need, Spike. Just not too loud." He stole a glance back at the RV.

Spike eased his hand back to touch the handle of his gun.

"Need money, dontcha?"

His hand swung back around to the front. It was empty.

"Could replace this lousy bike if you had enough cash, couldn't you?" Gordon asked him, smiling as Spike nodded. "Well, there's something I need, too."

Oh my God, Spike thought. *The guy's a queer-baiter.* He'd read about these burly guys who would travel around beating up gays, and people like Spike—young men who were traveling alone—were often mistaken for homosexuals. "I—I'm not into that."

"Wha—?" the guy said, then a light went on in his eyes and he barked a laugh that echoed for miles. "No, no—see, my wife's in the coach. She wants me to be a good Samaritan and help people, so we chose you. Truth is, I don't give a good goddamn about stranded motorists—no offense. But I do wanna help you."

Spike was definitely listening.

"So, I'll tell you what." Gordon peeled two bills out of his wallet, showing them but not handing them over. "These are thousand-dollar bills—take 'em to a bank to exchange for regular money. Go in there and tell my wife what a wonderful guy I am and they're yours. Get yourself a new motorcycle."

Spike almost pinched himself. Two thousand bucks. And he didn't even have to show his gun. "Wait—you're *giving* me two *thousand* dollars, just to say you're a good guy?"

"Deal?"

"Deal," Spike said. He had his thousand—way more than his thousand—but now he was watching the salesman motion for Spike to follow him into the giant, expensive RV, and before he even realized it he was thinking: *I'll bet there's more where that came from.*

Spike grabbed a handrail and hauled himself up into the Vacationeer, stepping on the plastic protectors of the first two steps and immersing himself in the plush, air-conditioned comfort of Class A motor home living, Gordon right behind him.

He was prepared to do exactly what the rich guy, Ron, asked him to do, just say thanks to the lady and tell her what a wonderful man her husband was—

But then he saw Wanda.

Spike was a young guy, just out of college, and so had seen a lot of girls, a lot of women, and sampled a good number of them as well. But never had he seen a woman with every feature so perfectly highlighted, her attributes so utterly on display, as the rich guy's wife. Her makeup, her jewelry, her shimmering platinum hair...she smelled like money to Spike, but more than that, she looked like an angel.

"Honey, this is the motorcyclist I helped, Spike."

She took his hand in her smooth, cool fingers and shook it. "Did Gordon do a good job for you?"

"Gor...? Ron?"

"Oh, right. I forgot he likes to hide his real identity. *Ron.*"

She had spice! "He did a great job," Spike said, his eyes never leaving her face, "Your husband's a very lucky—uh, a very helpful and kind man."

She cocked her head like a puppy hearing a squeak toy. "He is?"

"I might've died out there if it wasn't for him." *A bit thick, but hey.*

"Really? On a major road like this?"

Gordon stepped in and said, "Okay, *honey,* we'd better let Spike get on his way. We don't want to keep you, son," and ushered him out the door, slipping him the two Clevelands as he shook his hand again. "Take care now drive safely bye." The door slammed shut and the RV was off in seconds, heading south.

Spike stood on the side of the road, clutching two thousand dollars, and he wondering what the hell just happened and why the woman of his dreams was married to such an obvious fake and creep. He wondered if Mr. and Mrs. Ron would care that the bucks, even thousand-dollar bills, weren't what motivated a guy like him—and that he hadn't yet gotten what did. He thought they'd probably care about that, once they found out.

And so he wondered where they were heading with their big bucks and their Richie-Rich lifestyle. He hopped on his bike and cranked it in the direction the RV was heading. It was this kind of experience that made Spike value his decision to enter a life of crime.

As he took a leak, Gordon checked the color-matched clock over real-porcelain fixtures of the bathroom: Three-thirty-five. They'd have to hustle a little bit to make it right at four, but no problem. He'd finish going to the can and then would head on up the mountain to Coyote Jump and the rest of his life.

As he flicked off the light and stepped out of the full-size bathroom, he heard that familiar flat voice say, "Gordon."

He turned. Standing between him and the driver's seat was Wanda, who had slipped out of her day clothes and into a slinky little lavender nightie that showed off the toning she had done at the gym over the years. Not bad, but...

"You showed me, I have to admit it. That kid would've been in big trouble if not for you," she said, slinking right up to him and running a hand around his neck.

"Told you I wasn't such a bad guy," he said, sneaking a glance at the clock again. It was three-forty. They'd have to hurry now. "Got to get going, sweetheart."

"What's the rush? Remember, I owe you a little something."

"Owe me—" he started, and then remembered she'd promised to jump his bones if he helped somebody. Shit, he was just trying to keep her on the bus. "That's nice, but no time right now. Why don't we—"

"Gordon Reeve Mitchell, I want to make love to you. This *is* our vacation, isn't it?"

"Rest of our lives is a vacation. This is still work."

She shrugged off the nightie. *She has really been working out,* Gordon thought in spite of himself. The last time he had really looked at her naked was…it had been a long time, and she hadn't looked like this! Now she looked thin, tan and…firm. "Let's go," she said, and showed him what she had hidden behind her back: the keys to the Vacationeer. "You're not getting these back until you show me how much you want me."

He glanced at the clock again, and thought, *what the hell.* There was no way they were making Coyote Jump by four o'clock, but goddamn if they wouldn't be there by five.

He took her hand and let her lead him onto the bed. If Atchison in Truth or Consequences knew how well Gordon was breaking in his bed, first with Angie and now with Wanda, he'd either cancel the sale or want to shake Gordon's hand.

Ferocious. That was how Gordon had described the way Wanda had sex from the very beginning, talking with his college pals about the hot blonde with the sexy cat eyes before they got married, and that was how he would describe it now. Maybe a hunger, maybe a drive to impress, but always with one hundred percent.

The problem was, as much when they were together two weeks as when they were married twenty years, that Wanda simply could not keep her mouth shut during lovemaking, apparently feeling the overwhelming and undeniable urge to insult her lover, be *playful*. It was like sexual Tourette's. She insisted on making the most dick-shriveling comments at the most inopportune times, and their romp in the Vacationeer was no exception. The problem now was that he needed to finish up in something of a hurry—the deadline to make Coyote Jump loomed like a mother-in-law peeking through a bedroom window—and Wanda's mouth had a tendency to prevent that from happening. It was mood killer along the lines of a sack of dead kittens being slung through the bedroom window.

Despite the central A/C chugging away at full capacity, Wanda's face was pink and sweaty, her makeup trapping some of the moisture to give her a pudding-like appearance at close range. She writhed and grabbed and groped, throwing her torso at Gordon, giving herself to him and making him take it. "Oh, yes! Let me have that little cock! Make it so I can feel it for a change! Come on!"

And this was her *enjoying* it.

Gordon plugged on, loving the feel of her newly, amazingly slim, firm body but unable to block totally the stream of abuse that came from her painted lips. Every time he would near orgasm, she would let loose another flurry of emasculating comments and the moment would pass.

The funny thing was, it felt *terrific*. If he could just find something to focus on, something to take his mind off of her mouth…

"What, are you running out of steam? Come on, pencil dick! Be a man for a change!" she howled, clearly in the throes of intense pleasure.

Scanning the small room, his ken falling on the bag of thousands that Wanda had left out. The money spilled out of the sack, scores of Clevelands frowning at him presidentially. Thousands and thousands of dollars, seventy-six thousand dollars, just a drop in the bucket of what was waiting for him…

"Oh God…" Gordon yelped, and clutched Wanda tightly as orgasm rushed through him.

She held him affectionately, clearly enjoying every spasm of his body and shuddering in ecstasy as he filled her. Lovingly, she said, "Happy anniversary. I knew you couldn't keep it up very long."

He hopped up and was dressed and guiding the Vacationeer toward Coyote Jump in less than thirty seconds. It was just after four—he still had time to beat the dinner picnic crowd if he allowed for no more interruptions. And then he'd never have to bear her mouth again.

He stuck a CD—the Stones, yeah—into the deck and tapped his toes to the music as he drove up the mountain road. Less than an hour till he could begin the rest of his life. And he was doing it freshly laid, to boot.

Fully loaded, the Rambling Vacationeer weighed about thirty thousand pounds. Taking that up the steep grade to the lookout was slow going indeed—in fact, in all the years Gordon had sold and sung the praises of Rambling RVs, he had never taken one up a steep mountain grade.

Now he knew why. Climbing uphill just the fifteen miles to Coyote Jump chewed time off the clock like a real coyote chewed up…whatever the hell it was coyotes chewed. Sheep. Roadrunners. He had no idea, but slow was not the word for how the Vacationeer moved as soon as they were off the interstate and onto the scenic route uphill; it was more like stopped, with active scenery.

Almost before he knew it, it was a quarter to five in the afternoon and they still had four miles to go. Five was the absolute latest, the absolute, because then picnickers would be hitting the site and waiting for the sun to go down, anxious to get a good spot to see the colors and hear the coyotes wail.

Five, no later than five, or it would have to be Plan B.

Which he didn't have.

"Get your face on," he growled to Wanda, who was still basking in the afterglow without important matters like Gordon's running through her mind.

"For what?"

"Want to look pretty for the picture, right?" She always wanted to look pretty for everything and everyone, holding him up as she dabbed on her features, but today she needed to hop out as soon as they got there so he could push her off the cliff and be done with it. "Using the panoramic camera."

"Oh, I don't like heights, Gord, you know that. You go look at it if you want."

His knuckles tightened around the wheel. He managed between clenched teeth to say, "I did for you—do something for *me*, okay?"

"What was that in the bedroom just now?"

Just wondering that myself. "Very nice," he said, "but I wanna…take a picture of you at the lookout. Capture the moment."

"There's film in the camera? Did we even bring the camera?"

One mile to the lookout. "Go put a face on. I'll get it. I want to remember this moment for the rest of my life," he said, and thought, *Film!* There was no film in the damn camera—Jesus, what was he thinking?

Five minutes and it wouldn't matter anyway—it would just be too damn risky. *Five minutes, five minutes, five minutes.* He repeated it over and over to calm his nerves and block her pasty face out of his mind.

She sat there looking at him for what seemed like an eternity. Finally she touched his arm and said, "You have gotten so sweet all of a sudden. Maybe we *can* get another ticket to Venezuela, you think? Give things another try?"

Hmmm…fuck, no! "Maybe," he said with a strained smile and patted her hand, whisking it off casually as he did so. "Now hurry."

She sauntered back toward the bathroom. He gunned the gas, making her lurch toward the back a few steps.

"Hurry!"

Coyote Jump Lookout was a popular stop for Sierra County tourists and even townies to bring a blanket, have a picnic, the warm breezes actually serving to cool visitors if the sun wasn't too high in the sky.

Most popular times, according to the Mobil guidebook Gordon had been treating as his Bible the past ten months: Dawn to ten a.m., five p.m. to sunset.

It was five minutes to five when Gordon Mitchell pulled the bus-sized Vacationeer halfway off the road at Coyote Jump. There was not another vehicle in sight as he set the parking brakes and opened the door. "Ready?" he called to Wanda in the bathroom.

"Just a minute," she called back.

Okay, okay, everything seemed to be okay even though they had missed his target time by nearly an hour. He wrung his hands—*oops, grab the camera*—and stepped out onto the dusty, narrow shoulder.

The view really was magnificent. A textbook southwestern vista of browns and reds, rolling hills and mountains, New Mexico at its finest. The air was dry and sweet. Paradise. Just what he had—

He froze, his heart gripped in his chest by the iciest terror.

Two people were setting up a picnic.

A blanket, wine, cheese, sausage—two slim twenty-somethings, a man and a woman, had their bicycles leaned up against a tree and were just sitting down to enjoy a meal and the view.

All the blood drained from Gordon's face. Wanda would be getting off that coach any second and would want to see the view so she could go back inside. And once she was back inside, she wasn't coming out again.

Gordon's book of thought automatically flipped open to the page headed *Everybody has a price.* Just bribe them, give them a couple of thousand to take their beach blanket somewhere else. Hell, it's what the traveling money was for in the first place, and it had already come in mighty handy. He reached for his wallet and—

The money was still in the bedroom. No dice.

He swallowed hard. They had not yet noticed him, but when they did, they were going to wonder what the hell he was doing standing there staring at them. They looked like nice enough kids, maybe he could go over and sweet-talk them.

Maybe? Ha! He could sweet-talk anyone. He almost believed that right then.

Steeling himself—he had to act quickly—he trotted over to where the couple was hunkered down. "View's great, isn't it?" he said as casually as possible.

The young man, his long hair framing his glasses and goatee, swiveled his head to look up at Gordon. "That's why we're here."

Gordon nodded and crouched down to the hippie's level, always a good sales tool. "Look, I've got a favor to ask of you—"

"Is that thing a diesel?" the girl asked, motioning towards the Vacationeer.

"Yes, yes it is," Gordon said, unable to help himself, "It's optional, but the three-hundred-horsepower engine really gives it the extra *oomph* to get up these hills."

"I hate diesels," she sniffed, and turned back to face the view. "They pollute worse than any other kind of engine."

Tree-huggers, Gordon realized. *Great.* "Uh, I wanted to ask you…tell you, really…it's the wife and my twenty-fifth wedding anniversary today, and we had our first picnic together right at the spot where you're sitting."

"Uh-huh," the hippie kid said, unimpressed.

O-kay… "And, well, we were wondering if…if we might sort of ask you if we could picnic here ourselves, now."

"Sure, set yourselves up anywhere, man. The outdoors belongs to everybody."

"No, I mean, right where you are. And we picnicked by ourselves back then."

"A lot's changed, pops. *Share the land*—ever hear of that, Diesel Man?"

Little punk. "Thanks for your time."

"Why don't you just have a microwave dinner and watch TV in your biosphere, *Diesel Man!*" the girlfriend yelled as he walked away. She and her hippie cracked up.

It was straight-up five o'clock now. The time for games was over. Gordon got to the door to get back inside just in the nick of time, as Wanda was getting ready to step out. She looked like someone who forgot to take her Halloween scare makeup off. "No sightseeing?"

"Gotta move the coach," he said as he swung himself into the driver's seat. "Blocking traffic."

Without even closing the door or letting Wanda get herself sat down, Gordon fired up the Vacationeer and moved it about fifty feet so it sat not five feet away from hippie and bitchy.

"Just a sec, hon," he told Wanda as he locked down the parking brake, slammed his foot on the gas and went through every gear he could over and over again. *Don't try this at home,* he thought, *if you want to keep your transmission intact.*

The optional three-hundred-horsepower diesel engine groaned and farted huge toxic bursts of exhaust out its backside, blanketing the Coyote Jump Lookout in noxious gray clouds of poison. *Diesel Man strikes again!*

Hippie and bitchy screamed at him to stop, calling him names Wanda usually reserved for during sex, but he could barely hear them over the engine's roar. After a minute or so of this, and feeling a couple of rocks whack against the coach's riveted fiberglass sidewalls, he cut the ignition and looked outside.

No picnic, no bikes. They had the place to themselves. It was five past five.

"Come on," Gordon said to Wanda, stretching out his icy hand.

"It's going to stink out there."

"Come *on*," he snarled, and yanked her out into the New Mexico sunshine.

Wanda had to admit that despite the stink of the diesel, this was one nice place to stop. She felt a little guilty about resisting his efforts to visit a romantic lookout. What was she thinking? One nice roll in the hay didn't erase years and years of neglect and disappointment—this was something they'd have to work at. It had been so many years, so many years of putting each other last...

Of course, that was before the money came into the picture. She had always delighted in tweaking her husband, but she had to hand it to him: This he had done right. They were going to be millionaires. Fugitive millionaires, true, but still... The finer things in life—any jewelry on QVC she even looked at (she hoped they had cable in Venezuela), a house in a classy-type subdivision, as many dogs and cats as they could buy—were within their grasp.

Money changes everything, she had heard. Now even Gordon was acting romantic. There was still a chance.

She gave him a huge, long hug and kiss and followed him, a little nervous about the height, to the edge of the lookout to see what her husband promised would be a once-in-a-lifetime view.

Tears formed in Gordon's eyes as he held the hand of his bride of twenty-five years and led her to the edge of the cliff.

He had never been so happy in all of his life.

"Waited a long time for this," he said, and put his arm around her shoulders, then stepped behind her and wrapped his arms around her waist. "I need to tell you something."

"Oh, Gordon." Her hand came up to stroke his face as she choked with happy tears on the next few words. "I love you, too. It's all come together. We're working it out. We're gonna make it!"

He cleared his throat. "Yeah. What I need to tell you is, well…there's no way in hell I'm sharing a dime of that money with you."

Utter silence. Even the breeze stopped.

"I have wasted the most productive years of my life looking after a stunted weed of a wife, and I'm not gonna do it anymore."

She was rock-still. He might as well have been holding a statue.

God, this felt good to finally get off of his chest. "Gonna push you right off of here, grab all of that money for myself, and fly away from the train wreck of my life, fly away from *you*," he said. "Goodbye, Wanda."

"Okay."

If she said anything other than what she said, he wouldn't have hesitated, wouldn't have waited that split second to shove her worthless ass off Coyote Jump and drive away a new man, free and with the world at his feet. If she had said *anything* else.

But she went kind of limp and just said, "Okay."

That's what got him—Okay? *Okay?*—what made him wait that one split second, that instant—

And then a voice interrupted them.

"Ron?" Spike the stranded biker said, walking around the RV. "Wanda? You guys okay?"

"We're *fine*," Gordon said, slapping a hand over Wanda's mouth so the kid couldn't see, craning his head to give him a smile.

"Great," Spike said, and reached back into his belt to pull out his thirty-eight and point it right at Gordon's head. "Then stick 'em up, I guess."

Two

Trent Jones was born December 25, 1976, in Pittsburgh, Pennsylvania, the only son of an architect and a law student. He grew up with a silver spoon in his mouth, he'd admit it, and that's one reason why he rejected all of that after graduating from Carnegie-Mellon, the best technological university in the area, with a degree in sociology.

His degree was fine, but kept life at arm's length—he never experienced the excitement, the raw naked thrill, of life on the edge. He didn't even know where the edge *was* most of his life. He attended prep schools, spent two weeks in Europe with his auntie and uncle each summer, and led a generally boring, if comfortable, life.

That all changed when he bought the gun. A thirty-eight caliber pistol, tucked in his belt behind him, became the symbol of the new him. He put a motorcycle on the platinum AMEX card his dad gave him as a graduation present, learned to ride it, and kissed their bourgeois traditions goodbye.

He had studied how native people suffered, how indigenous populations were driven out of existence and assimilated, how rich fat cats (like his family, yes, but not him—he had an *awareness*) subjugated the land and the poor...

He had studied all of that. And what he came up with, the single defining thought he came away with, was that the people—and when he said "the people," of course he meant the poor and the *aware*—would be empowered. His thirty-eight and his motorcycle were his empowerment. Ironic, he knew it was: He rejected money but now depended on his robbery income—always off the fat and the rich, never the downtrodden—to finance his "living experiment," as he called it.

The first time he held someone up, an old couple in Kansas tugging an Airstream trailer, he flashed the gun and then could put it away. They handed him fifteen hundred dollars and a sandwich, then took back the money when they talked with him for a few minutes too many and realized they were in little danger of violence from this young man. He thanked them for the sandwich, then threw up.

After that, he tried to be a little more intimidating.

Ron hadn't been intimidated. He hadn't seen what this was all about.

And never, *never,* in his five months of living as a traveling bandit, had Spike seen a wad like Ron's. *Thousand*-dollar bills? And the guy just *gave* two of them to him! This, clearly, was a situation to be exploited. He hadn't intimidated the guy, hadn't made him understand what he was trying to say. He wanted more than a sandwich from this particular highway traveler. He had the money to liberate the young prostitute or whatever in Mexico, sure, but how much more would he end up with if he followed this to its logical conclusion, which was this: If Ron gave him two thousand dollars just to make himself look good, wasn't there so much more that could be wrenched from him once he was made to understand the philosophy behind Spike's life of crime?

Trent "Spike" Jones was going to make him understand. And he was going to get another look at the beautiful vision that was the Fat Cat's wife.

He had sped ahead, waited at a nice secluded lookout for the giant RV to pass, then followed it at a conservative distance. When it stopped at Coyote Jump and blew diesel fumes all over that progressive-looking couple, he knew his time had come.

He parked his motorcycle—which had a scratch in its paint, he noticed; he'd have to get that touched up—slapped the clip in his pistol, and made tracks to visit Ron and Wanda once again.

2

"A stickup?" Gordon said with a shrill laugh, keeping his hand clamped over Wanda's mouth. "Saved your life, remember? Now you're holding us up?"

The kid seemed unsure of himself, with the gun held out in front of him like a charm to make his victims keep their distance. It only enhanced the effect when he peered around his own gun to look at them more closely. "Why are you holding her like that, Ron?"

Out of reflex, Gordon's hand popped off her face. She immediately ducked down and crawled on the ground all the way to Spike behind him to safety. "Thank God!" she cried, and hid behind the man who had been holding a gun on her. That figured.

Gordon's mind shrieked curses to the sky. That close, *that* damn close, and now she had found her savior in a skinny kid, one awfully clean-cut looking to be a wandering robber. "Look, son, don't know what you th—"

"He was going to kill me!" Wanda yelled, and scrambled a few more feet away from him. "He was about to throw me off the cliff, Spork!"

"Spike," the robber said gently, and looked into her eyes in a way Gordon wasn't sure he was entirely comfortable with. Then he gazed over at Gordon with a look Gordon *knew* he didn't like. "That true, mister? You planning to kill this nice lady?"

Gordon didn't feel good about this, but he couldn't have a guy with a gun taking Wanda's side. "It's a ruse, kid. She tried it last time we got robbed and it almost got us killed. I'd rather give you the money than have anyone get hurt."

Wanda zipped her head around to stare hatefully at Gordon, and in that instant, they both knew that nothing could be farther from the truth.

"How about you just tell me what you need, son," Gordon said. The sooner he took control of this situation, the better. "We just want to be left alone."

Wanda shook her head violently. "Don't leave us alone! Don't leave *me* alone!"

Pumped up by Wanda's act, the kid seemed to be warming to his job. "I don't know what I *need*, Ron. How about *you* just tell *me* what you've *got*? How's that sound?"

"Money?" Gordon said.

"Okay, you've got money. That's a start."

"Let's not play games, Spike."

He wiggled the gun. "This look like a toy to you?"

Gordon sighed. He noticed that the kid's gaze kept falling on Wanda and her smeared war paint. When he'd look at her, his pistol hand got less rigid, like he was turning all warm and buttery inside. Clearly, the kid was insane.

But it left him an opening. "Honey—"

"Don't call me that, you scumbag," she spat at him. Even with that, Spike looked like he savored every word.

Gordon cleared his throat and said, "Maybe Spike would like it if *you* asked him what he wanted."

Still sitting on the dusty gravel, Wanda turned to look right into Spike's eyes. "Spock—"

"*Spike*, honey," Gordon offered.

"Shut up," Spike said, keeping the gun trained on a spot that moved farther and farther away from Gordon as Wanda held his eyes.

"Spike, what is it you want to do with me?"

The gun fell completely to his side as he melted into her mime-like face. Seeing his chance, Gordon stepped up slowly and moved for the gun, just about there—

Beep! A little rice-burner's horn—Gordon reflexively wondered how it made it up that mountain on a Honda's two cylinders—stopped him dead. Picnickers were pulling into the lookout area.

He looked at his watch: Five-fifteen.

Spike whipped the gun up and under his shirt. Now it was pointed dead at Gordon's head again. "Okay, Mr. Fat Cat, Wanda—a little too much company for our little transaction. In the RV," he said, and opened the door for them. "Quietly."

Gordon's fists clenched and he steeled himself to make a lunge at the biker kid, but the gun, the people in the Honda who Wanda would run to and tell everything to, all of that kept him trembling in place, unable to contain his rage and unable to do one damn thing about it.

"Come on," Spike said again, and motioned with the gun. "In you go."

Finally, Gordon made his leaden feet move, and he shuffled forward and aboard the coach, shifting his eyes back and forth between the gun and the newly arrived picnickers. As he sat down in the driver's seat, he realized that whatever Spike did didn't matter really now anyway. Picnic time had begun. Gordon's moment had passed.

3

A few hundred miles east, Gann rocketed across the New Mexico border at nearly a hundred, fueled by the knockout punch Peg Hake had provided for her brother-in-law when Gann had stopped and asked her a few questions. Now he knew the Mitchells were headed for Truth or Consequences, exactly where they were supposed to go to deliver the RV. Gann had to hand it to Gordon—he knew exactly what he was doing. Every step of the way Gordon had slipped in enough ambiguity—a paper trail that looked fine from one angle, totally crooked from another—that he was very close to getting away with it all. Getting rich through double-dealing: a salesman if there ever was one.

But, he thought with a big grin as he nodded to a speeding police car that he flew past, bubble flashing overtime, Gordon no doubt hadn't counted on a little hitch in his plan, a little hitch by the name of Lieutenant Detective Douglas Gann. He would be bringing Gordon in just as the smug bastard thought he had won.

He had entered the Sierra County New Mexico State Police post in his phone, and now he punched the speed-dial with his thumb. After a few rings, there came an answer: "State police, Perez here."

"Officer, this is Detective Gann of the Elkhart, Indiana Police Department. Remember we had spoken about a stolen-RV ring someone was ready to cash in on?"

"Oh, yeah," Perez said, "they told me you were gonna call. We've got it under control, detective."

Gann could feel the rings under his eyes blacken. He was so damn tired, and this wasn't helping. "I've been tracking the RV they're using."

"Glad to hear that. We, uh, don't have the warrant yet, though. Your chief said it would be going through tomorrow morning—"

"We've got a potential murder on our hands here, they told you that, right?"

"Nobody said nothing about a murder. Is the FBI involved?"

Gann slapped himself in the face.

"We can't do nothing until we get a warrant or the FBI says go." Perez hesitated, then said, "You know this already, don't you, detective?"

Gann could feel that this Perez was a good person, a good officer. He probably stood for the forces of good, and justice; and he probably thought having every single *i* dotted and *t* crossed was part of making sure justice was served. Gann could feel it through the phone.

"Detective?"

Gann squeezed his eyes shut and concentrated every ounce of his aural energy through the phone, to let Perez know that he would be doing good by arresting Gordon even without a warrant, let them get a warrant the next morning. He telepathically sent his strategy: Say Gordon had been driving erratically, or was driving with a taillight out, or whatever. Just *bring him in.*

He willed the New Mexico officer just to listen, and feel…open his heart…open his mind…open his soul…

The line went dead. Perez had hung up.

"Cell phones," Gann said, and hit the button again. They were no good for transferring energy—something with dispersal of radio waves. He supposed he could just *explain* the strategy to Perez and see if he could get some assistance.

As the phone rang, Gann tried to blink the glare out of his eyes. The road was swimming in front of him; it was all he could do just to stay in his lane. He was exhausted—eighteen straight hours of driving, and that on a night of very light sleep, was kicking his butt. He wished he could go to sleep, even just for an hour, but with every second he took, he knew Wanda Mitchell was one second closer to death.

He rubbed his eyes and kept driving.

4

It didn't surprise Gordon one bit that the kid with the gun, Spike, ordered him to drive north on the interstate, towards Albuquerque, away from Truth or Consequences. It didn't surprise him that the robber was in the spacious living room, chatting amicably with Wanda even as he was tying her up. What was it with these guys and their fixation on his wife? They could have her, for Christ's sake; but, of course, she always played the loyal spouse and never gave him the peace of mind that would have come with her leaving him.

As Gordon drove, his mind raced for a solution. His gut was clenched tight as a fist. His eyes felt like they were going to pop right out. He could feel the veins in his forehead twist and tighten. He hadn't come this far so some lowlife robber could derail the whole damn plan. There was something he could do. He wasn't sure what, but there had to be *something*.

He chewed his lip and thought. Spike never put the gun down, so Gordon couldn't exactly stop and ask the police for help, and even if he somehow could get a hold of the cell phone and call the cops, Wanda would probably have some interesting information to share with them after they were done talking about Spike.

No, he'd have to go this one alone. Maybe he could sweet-talk the kid—hell, give him a big chunk of the money in the coach—to get him to go on his happy way. There was no way Spike would be able to *do* anything with the cash, anyway—one or two Clevelands might raise an eyebrow, but seventy-eight would bring in the Treasury Department. At least, without the right banking industry connections, it would.

"Hey, Spike, don't want any trouble here," he called back to him. "Got plenty of money in this thing—"

"Gordon!" Wanda yelled.

"—and you can have it. Just let us get on our way, huh?"

He could see Spike look at him in the wide-angle mirror above the windshield. He stared at him for what seemed like an hour, and then sighed. "You think I'm in this for the money, don't you?"

Nobody said a word. Gordon looked at Wanda in the mirror now, and she looked just as confused as he felt.

Spike came up through the living room and plopped himself down into the shotgun seat, then swiveled with his back to the windshield so he could keep an eye on Gordon and Wanda at the same time. "This isn't about *money*," he said finally. "This is about teaching Fat Cats a lesson."

"Fat Cats?" The image of an obese man wearing a white three-piece suit and smoking a cigar popped unbidden into Gordon's mind. "What is this, *Guys and Dolls?*"

Spike seemed to make it a point to casually point the gun at Gordon as he said, "More like *Rich Man, Poor Man*. I'm the poor man, and you're the Fat Cat driving the half a million dollars worth of touring bus."

Gordon couldn't help but chuckle. "Got the wrong cat, Spike—this coach is a delivery. Just taking it down for a customer. We're working folks."

"Working folks don't usually flash thousand-dollar bills to stranded bikers."

Fuck, Gordon said to himself, but then his fifteen years of looking for openings in what people said told him this was just the opportunity he'd been after. "More where that came from, you know."

"Oh, I know."

"Then why don't you just take it and leave us alone?"

"I told you, Ron—this isn't about the money."

Gordon's lip twitched. "Bullshit."

Spike brought the gun up and said, "Excuse me?"

"It's always about the money. You may want to beat us up or kill us or whatever, but it's still about the money. Saw your eyes light up when I showed you those two thousand-dollar bills. Come on—don't bullshit a bullshitter."

This time, Spike didn't seem to know what to say.

So Gordon kept talking. "Don't want any trouble. Take the money. We just want you to leave us alone."

Spike looked back at Wanda. "Is that right, Wanda? Do *you* just want me to leave you two alone?"

Gordon's eyes shot up to the mirror, where he could see Wanda shaking her head violently. She found her voice and said, "Please don't leave—he was going to…"

Spike nodded, giving her a warm, comforting smile of understanding. "Well, Ron, it looks like two votes for staying, just one for leaving," he said, and reclined a bit in the passenger seat, the gun never wavering from aiming at Gordon. "But don't worry—I'll be glad to take the rest of your money."

An hour passed. Two hours. Spike moved from the shotgun seat to the couch in the living room, keeping up the patter with Wanda as they talked about everything, just everything—about her and Gordon's early years in a trailer park, how she bought jewelry and exercise equipment off the television, what kind of makeup and costume jewelry was right for what kinds of occasions. The kid seemed totally enthralled.

"Quite a woman you got there, Ron," Spike said with a wave of the gun. "Can't believe you were going to try to kill her."

"Then don't believe it," Gordon said. "Told you it was a ruse."

"You know that every time a representative of a culture dies, a little bit of that culture dies with him?"

What? The robber talked like he had just graduated from college, and still believed everything they told him. "Don't really care, son."

Spike ignored his comment, instead seeming to concentrate on the fine wood veneer paneling that was standard with the Vacationeer. "This machine is another beautiful piece of work," he said, winking—*winking!*—at Wanda as he said it. "Hope you appreciate *it,* at least. I wouldn't mind having one of these someday. Of course, I wouldn't drive it."

"Of course."

"No, sir—too much damage to our environment. How about you, Wanda? Are you an environmentalist?"

She turned her cat-eye gaze toward the ceiling. "Yes. You could call me that, Spike."

"Christ," Gordon spat out, "you buy Styrofoam cups, throw trash out the window while you're driving, and use makeup they test on rabbits. Woman calls herself an environmentalist."

Spike said nothing, just cocked a look at her.

"Well…I am at heart. I just haven't always been able to do it in practice."

"Good enough for me," Spike said. "How about for you, Ron?"

"Don't care, dickhead."

Spike whipped the gun around and stuck the barrel right in Gordon's face. "You care now? How about you *tell* me how much you care."

Gordon's eyes were puffy with fatigue and red from the glare, but they opened wide when the business end of the thirty-eight came within inches of his face. He could reach out and grab it right now, right that second. The barrel shook a little, like the kid was pumped up, which could be good or bad, depending.

If he got the gun away, the kid would be nothing, neutralized. *Neutered.* He used the gun like a pecker anyway; take it away and he was the man no longer.

The gun swung back around as Spike eased himself back into the leather of the passenger seat. "I thought you might care after all," he said. "Amazing how a weapon levels the playing field, isn't it, Wanda?"

Oh yeah, Gordon thought. *The gun was his dick, no doubt about it. Time to cut it off. Time to grab that gun away and—*

He paused. Grab the gun and...

A tic sprang up under his right eye. An idea was forming. After a few seconds, it sprang full-grown into his mind, and a tranquil smile washed over his features.

Grab the gun and shoot Wanda dead.

Gordon threw a quick glance at Spike, who was still jawboning with Wanda. If he could wrest that gun away and blow Wanda's brains out, he could pin it on the kid—he was an *armed robber*, after all—and be rid of two problems at once.

The police could test to see who had fired a gun, but Gordon could get around that simply enough—make Spike fire off a round afterwards, tell the cops he himself got Spike's gun and accidentally shot Wanda while aiming at Spike, whatever.

The road ahead was looking brighter indeed, and it didn't have a thing to do with the rapidly setting sun.

He looked again at Spike—who was letting the gun rest for a change, and at Wanda in the mirror, and then concentrated on the road, his mind racing. There were cliffs aplenty in this area, buttes and sudden drop-offs and dry lake beds, all manner of things to fall into, so he made sure the coach was on a straight stretch of road before he cleared his throat and said, "Drop that gun and I'll show you a level playing field, pal."

Whoosh—the gun was back in his face. Perfect.

Spike sneered. "You'd like that, wouldn't you, Mr. Fat Cat—"

Quickly, Gordon slapped the barrel of the gun away with his left palm and in a flash was out of his seat, trying to twist the thirty-eight out of the little punk's hand.

"Gordon!" Wanda screamed. "Don't hurt him!"

The kid, apparently distracted by her voice, loosened his grip on the gun just enough for Gordon to yank it and bring it up against the base of his jaw. Spike stumbled backwards against the steering wheel, spinning it as he fell to the floor.

The Vacationeer lurched off the road, barreling through a drainage ditch and a speed limit sign before the wheel straightened out. Diesels don't slow down too quickly, so it continued on through the rocky scrub, racing away from the interstate, almost at full speed.

As the coach swung around suddenly, Gordon flew into the fine wood veneer paneling and Oaklike cabinetry, taking a sharp corner in the top of his head. Spike regained his footing as the path straightened out, leaping past the octagonal end table to yank the gun away from Gordon, who was still trying to shake the stars out of his head.

Gordon jumped at the gun leaving his hand, but the room was swimming from him hitting his head, and now he lurched forward, smashing his forehead against the cabinet frame. Bloodied, he staggered over to Spike, who now had the gun pointed right in his face once again.

"Better kill me now if you're gonna do it," he said, blood dripping into his eyes.

Spike hesitated, and that was all Gordon needed. He whipped the gun out of the kid's hand and tried to point it at him. But Spike grabbed the barrel in time and they quickly found themselves in a stalemate, no one moving, neither releasing his grip on the pistol, no one at the wheel, the Vacationeer slowing down, but still trampling over dirt, rocks, and brush.

"I don't want to kill you, mister," Spike said. "I just want to teach you how to treat a lady."

"Listen, kid," Gordon panted in his face, "you don't know this woman. You don't want to know this woman. If you did know her, you'd be pointing this gun at her, not me. And you'd pull the goddamn trigger."

Spike tightened his grip on the barrel. "You're not killing anybody, Ron—*if* that's even your real name. Tell you what you're going to do: You're going to sit back down behind that wheel and take us wherever I—"

"*Jesus Christ! It's the edge!*" Wanda screamed, unable to look away from the windshield even as she struggled against her handcuffs to move toward the back.

Gordon and Spike whirled to see what she was looking at. Spike let out a little squeak as he saw it; Gordon didn't make even that much sound.

What they saw was their deaths screaming at them. The wide area that girded the interstate ended less than a hundred feet ahead—ended with a drop-off as steep as Niagara Falls—and the coach was barreling towards the abyss. In ten seconds they would be crumpled in a fireball four hundred feet down.

The two men reacted at exactly the same time, Gordon diving for the steering wheel and Spike rushing back to Wanda and fumbling with the key to the handcuffs.

Gordon wrenched the wheel around, but fifteen tons of motor home doesn't change its direction of momentum that quickly and skidded sideways, threatening to turn over, threatening to keep spinning and plunge right off the cliff anyway.

Fifty feet. Gordon slammed on the Rambling standard hydraulic ABS braking system, all eight 11R 22.5 Goodyear tires groaning in protest, tearing out weeds and clearing a path of ruin behind them as they locked-released-locked-released their way toward the edge.

Thirty feet. The thirty-five-foot, thirty-one-thousand-pound, two hundred eighty thousand dollar Rambling Class A Vacationeer, the biggest and best, the pride of Major Dale's RV World, was now careening at a forty-five degree angle with its ass end sliding towards the edge. Gordon threw all of his weight, all of his driving experience—ten years with the big rigs, fifteen with motor homes of every shape and size—all of his hope for a future without that bitch, into keeping the wheel turned and the brakes on. The coach tipped, but didn't fall; and it slowed, but didn't stop.

Ten feet. It was turned around, sliding completely backwards now. The bedroom with its queen-size bed, thirteen-inch TV, beveled mirrors, and safe box for valuables now was pointed toward the abyss, moving closer each second to pitching over it. The wheels, locking and releasing again and again, weren't slowing the tremendous mass of the bus fast enough.

They were going over the edge.

Suddenly, Gordon's panic, his blind scrabbling need for survival, gave way to a moment of understanding at least as clear, if not as satisfying, as the thought he could shoot his wife and pin it on the kid. Without lifting his foot off the brake, Gordon cranked the stick into second gear and slammed on the gas as hard as the shaking muscles of his other leg could manage.

He lifted the foot off the brake and punched the accelerator with it, lifting his butt off the seat as he threw all his weight into jamming the pedal *down.*

For a horrible second, the wheels spun, throwing up rocks from the very last inches of level ground, rocks which *tinked* against the extended rear of the coach and fell away the hundreds of feet to the valley floor below.

But then they caught, hurling the bus and everything in it forward, hard against the inertial direction of motion, four drive wheels grinding against the last few feet of solid ground and pushing the Vacationeer away from the end of the world.

Gordon couldn't stop his hands' shaking; the sweat running into his wide eyes stung; and he had, yes, he had wet himself. But he made it. Of course, they did too, but at least *he* was still alive.

He stopped the coach and let out a ragged sigh. He turned to look into the back and realized he had forgotten all about the gun in the excitement.

But Spike hadn't. The gun in Gordon's face told him that right away.

"Ever heard of gratitude?" Gordon said.

Spike grinned. "I haven't shot you yet, have I?"

Somewhere in the night, between Albuquerque and Truth or Consequences, the Vacationeer and Gann's Chevy Caprice crossed paths, the RV going north, the Caprice going south. In the glare of headlights and the fatigue of driving, neither driver could see enough to recognize the other vehicle, and they both kept going on their separate bits of ribbon running through the desert darkness.

6

The shift had started out so well for New Mexico State Police Sergeant Luis Perez—the day was beautiful, the boaters on Elephant Butte Lake were staying relatively sober, and he had to man the phones with another officer for just an hour or two while the chief checked out some trouble down by Las Cruces. A good shift, three to midnight.

Then Detective Gann called.

A murder was *going* to be committed? Perez checked with the Indiana police, and they said the wife had never filed so much as an assault charge, let alone any kind of restraining order—and she was taking a cross-country trip with the husband, wasn't she?

Gann also said he was going to bring the husband in for embezzlement, theft, all this stuff—but Indiana said no warrant was going to be issued before morning, and Gann was supposedly on vacation! On vacation, hell; the guy was breathing down Perez's neck to *do* something to stop this heinous person—well, what exactly the hell was he supposed to do?

He wished he had never picked up the damn phone in the first place; when he called the chief, the chief told Perez this was his to deal with for the rest of his shift.

He looked at the clock over the front entrance, and felt a wave of relief wash over him. It was quarter to ten. He had only a couple of hours left on duty, and Gann would have to stop to sleep somewhere along the line, so—

Bug-covered headlights swept into the parking lot, and Perez's stomach sank. Of course Gann didn't have to sleep; that might interfere with busting up the Crime of the Century.

"Sergeant Perez?" the intruder asked, looking weary but still dressed up in a blue suit and black tie. He was blinking a lot, no doubt trying to clear his bleary eyes from an entire nonstop day on the road. "I'm Douglas Gann, from the...um, Elkhart, Inniana, police department."

"You okay, detective?"

Gann swept the question away with a wave of his hand, and cleared his throat. "Ready to go."

"Go?"

"You, uh...witnesses?" Gann said, and cleared his throat and rubbed his eyes. "You have witnesses? I'm looking for that RV with the husband and wife in it. If he's already done it, we have to stop the RV and apprehend his ass."

"Detective, like I said to you on the phone, we have whole *towns* in southern New Mexico where you got nothing but RVs. People retire and live in 'em down here, you know?"

"That's how Gordon Mitchell could get away with this scheme for so long, running money down here."

What was this guy talking about? It was time to nip this shit in the bud, as far as Perez was concerned. Embezzlement, theft, murder—*possible future murder* even—soon Gann was going to have him arresting people because they might jaywalk or could be thinking about speeding at some time in their lives. He didn't become a cop to start thinking like a Nazi. "I talked to your duty chief back in Indiana," he started, slowly, letting the words penetrate the sleepy man's brain, "and he says that not only there's no warrant been issued in this case, but you ain't even supposed to *be* here. You're supposed to be on *vacation*."

Gann stood there, tottering, for a good ten seconds before he straightened himself and said forcefully, "Maybe this is one I had to solve on my own."

"No offense, detective, but you seen too many movies."

"They don't give the Medal of Valor—*twice*—for watching movies. This is going to sound crazy, I know, but I get in tune with the ether, with the frequency of minds and hearts, and that helps give me the hunches I go on."

Perez decided to ignore most of that. "And your hunch, it's that this Gordon Mitchell is going to kill his wife."

"Or maybe already has. We have to find that RV. That's all I'm asking for, sergeant—just help me find the RV and make sure the wife is all right. I know there's no warrant yet, and even if there were it would be for theft and fraud, not murder—but I haven't been wrong yet. That's all I want— just help me find the RV."

"I thought you had that satellite thing tells you where they are."

"The, uh, satellite thing. Right, the global positioning system."

Perez cocked his head at him. Is this what all the cops in Indiana were like? "Right. You know where they're at, don't you, detective?"

"I'm really tired. It would really help me if you—"

"You don't need us to help *find* your suspect, do you? You want us to help you *arrest* him, without a warrant, and hold him here till the warrant, it comes through in the morning. That's right, isn't it?"

Gann stared him down with his bleary eyes for a minute, then sighed and said, "I'd like nothing better than to be wrong, believe me."

"Why do I doubt that?"

"Look—if he hasn't killed his wife yet, you'd be saving her life. If she's not on the RV, you'll be the one who brings this guy to justice. Isn't this what you joined the force to do, catch the really bad guys?"

Perez chewed on that one. He had grown up poor in the gutter sections of Las Cruces, picked up again and again as an illegal until his mother could come by and curse out the police to let her son—a second-generation American—out of jail. The young Perez wasn't a "bad guy," and he wanted to make sure the distinction was always clear. That was probably why he wore a badge now. Gann was right: Whose side was he on, now that he was the law?

He guessed there really wasn't any harm in helping the guy locate the couple and just *make sure* there was nothing going on…"But you know we can't arrest him unless we got some kind of witness, somebody who's gonna say something like *He is gonna kill her*—you know this, right?"

Gann bit his lip as he stared hard into Perez's face. Just stared at him.

"Um, what are you doing, detective?"

"Nothing," he said, and relaxed. More like deflated, actually. Then he said, "No one's reported anything strange—no sightings of a guy acting weird with his wife, trying to get her to say she loves him or something in front of a group of people?"

God help me, Perez thought, and looked at the clock. Barely ten minutes had crawled by since Gann showed up. "We can check the log book. No arrests or nothing, but maybe somebody called something in. Saying *I love you*, that's pretty suspicious behavior, 'specially in front of lots of people."

Gann nodded with a small smile and said, "You think this is pretty crazy."

"That's how you get that Medal of Valor, right?" He was trying so hard to be patient and nice, but he couldn't go on absolutely *nothing*, even if that's how they did things in Elkhart, Indiana. He picked up the thick log book, a clipboard stuffed full of handwritten reports filed by every officer assigned to the post, reports of loud stereos, wild animals, reckless drivers, flashers, public pissers—in other words, anything they couldn't really do a damn thing to stop but which made the public feel better to complain about.

Gann took the heavy clipboard and immediately started ruffling through the pages, scanning them for what, Perez had no way of guessing.

He figured that would take the detective up to at least midnight, when he could go home, or until Gann would fall asleep, as surely he had to before too long. But for some reason Perez was barely even surprised when, not fifteen minutes after he started, Gann barked "*Ha!*" and yanked out one of the reports to give to him.

"Two picnickers reported a nuisance up on Coyote Jump, which is what, a scenic lookout, right?" Gann said with amazing energy, considering how tired Perez was from just being around him.

"Yeah, near T or C. Truth or Consequences, you know? But I don't see—"

"Look, the couple said the man—in his forties, with an RV—was desperately trying to get them to leave the site *so he could be alone with his wife!* He pestered them until they had to abandon the site! He could have done it there!"

"Done what?"

"*Killed Wanda!*" Gann yelled, then got a hold of himself. "He could have killed the wife there, tossed her off the cliff or something."

"But this report says it was at five o'clock. That's just when the lookouts start getting busy. I don't know, detective..."

"Sergeant Perez, please—just bring them in and let me talk to them."

"Now? At almost ten-thirty at night?"

"I swear to God, if they have nothing to say, I won't go any farther. I'll just wait for the warrant in the morning. But jeez, maybe we can save a life here."

Perez stared at him for a good minute and a half. They were about the same age, late twenties, early thirties, and had chosen the same profession, law enforcement. So how was it that this had turned into just a job for him and it was obviously the very blood in the veins of this Detective

Gann from Indiana? He didn't know, but finally he decided that even if he had lost the spark, there was no way in hell he was going to stand in the way of someone who was living, eating, breathing his job and duty to do whatever he could.

He called the couple's contact number from the report and was actually happy when the man said they'd be overjoyed to help stop this polluting jerk and would be over in an hour or so. Actually *happy* to be doing something outside of the rules that might bring him a Medal of Valor someday. Maybe he could find a way to help.

He was about to say something along those lines to Gann, but when he looked up from the telephone, the detective had already fallen asleep in one of the waiting room chairs. Perez got him a blanket.

7

"If we make the rich afraid to show off their wealth, then we have effectively ended the age of 'conspicuous consumption,' just by definition, right?" Spike said to Wanda as they sat on the sectional sofa.

"Oh, yes, I see that," Wanda said.

Gordon scoffed at them in the rear-view mirror. "She has no goddamn idea what you're talking about."

"Shut up, okay? Nobody's talking to you," the kid said, not even turning to look at him.

"Wh-*what?*" Gordon sputtered, his vision nearly blocked as his head pounded in sudden rage. He'd been driving them north, toward Albuquerque, when everything he needed, everything important to him, was south, in Las Cruces and T or C.

"Yeah, Gord, he still has the gun. Let's be careful," Wanda threw in, and that made it too much. Gordon slammed on the brakes, sending the coach sliding onto the shoulder, and shut the whole thing down.

"Hey, Fat Cat, just what do you think you're doing? I'll let you know when you can stop this thing—"

"Fuck you, sonny. Wanna play rough? Wanna use that thing? Well, go the fuck ahead, 'cause I'm not driving you and that cunt anywhere else. Wanna prove you're a man, you got a dick, go ahead—shoot me. I god-damn fucking dare you."

Spike sat turned around on the couch, his body facing Wanda, his face towards Gordon, and didn't say anything for a few seconds. Then he said, "You call this woman a cunt? I should shoot you."

"*That's* all you have to say? Shouldn't call her a cunt?"

"You wouldn't be in this mess if you knew how to treat your lady here."

"*You gonna shoot me or what?*" Hearing the wonderfulness of Wanda the Queen Bitch extolled, he probably would have shot *himself* if he were holding the gun.

Spike sat and thought about this one, too, and as he did, Gordon took stock.

Wanda, sitting all pretty and painted on the sofa, no longer hand-cuffed, a frozen strawberry daiquiri made in the coach blender in her hand, knew all anyone needed to know to send Gordon away for a long, long time, the rest of his life. She knew where he was going and how he planned to get there. She knew who he worked with to launder the money. And she could trade all of that knowledge for maybe six months of time, which would probably let her get out, oh, say forty or fifty years before Gordon did—and that was only if he was "lucky" enough to live to his nineties. He wished he had "accidentally" knocked her off the cliff when Spike showed up, but his fear of witnesses stole his thunder, and now here he was, maybe forty miles south of Albuquerque, far, far north of where he needed to be. *Fuck.*

Finally Spike said, "I don't think shooting you would teach you a darn thing."

"What are you, Professor Outlaw?"

"Get off the RV."

Gordon blinked. "Come again?"

Motioning with the thirty-eight, Spike said, "Open the door, go down the steps, and get off the vehicle."

"Goddamn desert out there, Spike."

"You're going to learn a lesson—so get going. And leave the keys."

Trying not to give in to panic, Gordon looked wide-eyed at Wanda, but she seemed to find the fabric of the sofa suddenly fascinating.

"Get you for this," Gordon said, and stepped down off the coach, into the chill of the New Mexico night. "I can track this thing, you know."

"That's fine, Ron, because I'm going to leave it in a real easy-to-find place anyway, with your wife's dead body in it." He paused, then smiled. "After I get done raping her."

Wanda looked up from the sofa. Gordon stood there with his mouth hanging open, finally getting out, "The hell, you say."

"That's right, Fat Cat. I told you I wasn't in this for the money. And I told you I was going to teach you a lesson."

"You're so full of shit, boy. Don't believe you for a second." But he did.

"Your lips say *no*, but your eyes say *yes*, don't they?" Spike said, and smiled even wider, waving the gun at him. "Now go on, get out of here."

Gordon stepped onto the rocky shoulder of the highway and turned around just in time to watch Spike sidle up to the front of the bus, close the door and lock it, and ease himself into the driver's seat. "Say goodbye to your lovely wife! You should've appreciated her when you had the chance, Fat Cat!" Spike yelled, and fired up the coach.

A few seconds later, they were gone up the highway, melting in with a hundred other sets of taillights.

It was quiet. Distantly Gordon could hear the drone of the highway, that constant beat of vehicular surf, but that was far away.

It was dark. There was no moon, and as far as he was from a town of any size, an ocean of stars blazed from one horizon to the other.

And it was all over. Wanda was gone, kidnapped by a "gentleman bandit" who now swore to rape and kill her. And when the police saw what the kidnapper had done to her, they'd never stop looking, looking for...for...

Wait a minute...

For the kidnapper. They'd never stop looking for *Spike Jones.*

The kid had stolen Gordon's albatross, and it felt so strange to be free of it that he had almost missed the freedom he'd been waiting twenty-five years for! Unable to believe his luck, he played the thought over and over again in his mind: Spike was going to kill Wanda! *Spike* was going to kill Wanda! Spike was going to *kill* Wanda! Spike was going to kill *Wanda!* And all Gordon had to do was just be seen tonight, get an alibi, and when they found her body, her wonderful and totally *dead* body, he would be the one person in the world they'd know *didn't* do it!

In the middle of the desert night, forty miles from anywhere, Gordon jumped up and down and whooped so loud he wondered if the stupid kid could hear him five miles away. He hoped so.

8

The robber—now Wanda guessed she should call him the kidnapper—was still driving north, but Wanda had no idea where they were headed. He had handcuffed her again, this time to the handle next to the passenger-seat armrest, and he had a rigid determination in his eyes as he drove down the pitch-black interstate. It scared her a little.

"Um, Spike?" she said quietly, the words squeaking out. "Should I be worried?"

"About what?"

Her mouth was so dry. "Rape, murder, you know."

He cast a sideways glance at her and said, "Maybe I should make you sweat it out a bit." And smiled.

She smiled back nervously. "That was a *no*, right?"

Spike threw his head back and laughed, then reached over and patted her knee. "Right, that was a 'no'—hey, do you think I'd save your life just to kill you myself?"

"I—I don't know *what* you're doing, Spike." *Careful...* "Do *you?*"

He laughed again. "That's a good question—they didn't teach Robbery 101 at Carnegie-Mellon. I'm kind of rolling my own here."

"Carnegie-Mellon? What's that, a prison you were in?"

Again, Spike laughed, harder this time, and said, "God, Wanda, you are so *refreshing*. Not like the society wives I've run into before."

"You think I'm a 'society wife'?"

"I've been on the road, trying to make a statement, trying to teach Fat Cats a lesson, for over six weeks now. I've noticed some patterns; really, it's all sociology."

"What are you, a college graduate?"

"Gosh, you are *sharp*. I graduated in May, just hopped on my bike with nothing but my L.L. Bean bag and equipment and headed out."

"Robbing people."

He gave her a disappointed look. "Evening out the haves and have-nots, Wanda. Taking from the rich and giving to the poor."

"I'm not rich."

"I'm not poor. It all hasn't fallen together at once, that's true. It's a work in progress. *I'm* a work in progress—and so are you. You've got something special, I could tell the first time I saw you."

"My husband and I were heading to Venezuela, to start a new life."

He didn't say anything, just drove.

"We're not rich, Spike—this really was a delivery. We were dropping it off before we went down to Mexico to catch a plane." Boy, they were really telling each other a lot. His college, her escape plans. "We did some bad things."

"It looked like your husband was about to do one more when I showed up."

She dipped her head. "He only bought one plane ticket."

"See, it's people like that that need to be taught a lesson."

"You keep saying that," she said, not wanting to get him upset. "What does that mean? What are you, an evangelical highway robber?"

"This is the only gospel I need to share." He held up the gun. "The Great Equalizer. Actually, what I teach is that although the Fat Cats of the world—I love to say that, *Fat Cats*, it's so Thomas Nast, so Boss Tweed— although they may have the money and the power in macro, the little people, the guys with guns, have it in micro. I put a gun in your asshole husband's face, suddenly *I* have the power, and when I have the power, I soon have the money as well. They may have it all in the big picture, but at any moment a guy like me can come into their lives and mess up the works. That's the lesson I make the Fat Cats learn."

"Are you a genius or something?"

A schoolboy grin erupted on his face. "I have principles and I work to imprint them on the world around me, if that's what you mean."

"You know you'll probably end up in jail."

"All geniuses do at some point. But I don't hurt anybody, so I doubt I'd get much time. Besides, it's noble to suffer for what you believe in."

Wanda could feel her face getting flushed. A couple of hours ago, her husband had tried to kill her. Then she had been kidnapped and threatened with rape and murder. And now…

And now she reached over as far as her handcuff would allow her and clasped her kidnapper's hand gently. "Spike," she said softly.

He gave a start as she touched him, then looked at her with surprised, eager eyes. "Wanda?"

"I sure could use a glass of water."

It took him a moment to process what she just said. Then he said, "Of course," and stopped the coach by the side of the road, flipping on the hazards as he went back to the kitchen to take care of what she needed. Not for a second did she take her eyes off her young kidnapper; not for a second did she want to, as he poured her a glass of water, and walked back to her to put it in her hand, and let his fingers trace over hers for just an instant as she took what she needed from him.

Spike watched her sip her water. Everything she did had a dramatic quality to it: She didn't just ask for a drink, she caressed his hand and gently requested a glass of water; she didn't just bat her eyelashes at him, she flirted with everything she had.

He liked that, but…"I still have to rob you, Wanda, you know that."

"I don't have much on me," she said. "Gordon made sure of that."

"Ron—Gordon—made some comment about a lot of money here he'd be willing to part with if I'd take off, presumably so he could then kill you. Do you know anything about that, where that money might be?"

"What if I said *no?*"

"I'd be disappointed."

"What if I said *yes?*"

"I think that would do wonders for you on the karmic wheel."

The RV was stopped, so he could really watch her as she watched him. Maybe she really thought he had meant to hurt her and so was trying to get on his good side, maybe she was just passing time, but as she tapped her teeth with a fingernail and looked to all the world like she was puzzling over what to do, Spike knew she was trying to entice him.

But into what? *He* was the one representing the criminal element here. Still…when he looked at her, red strokes of blush running up her porcelain white face, he saw a woman completely different from those around which he had grown up—she had a rough side, maybe the very side her jerk husband didn't like about her, but at the same time was all woman, all feminine, and much in need of his help, judging by the way her husband was treating her.

He smiled at the thought that she could probably entice him into anything she wanted him to do. Carnegie-Mellon and all those pony-tailed, backpack-wearing, perfect-tan girls were behind him now. He was living on the other side now, and Wanda was an other-side kind of woman.

"What are you smiling about?" she asked, breaking his train of thought.

"Just—just thinking about how you said you weren't rich."

"I'm not. The seventy-six thousand dollars in this coach doesn't belong to me, or Gordon—it's stolen."

"Seventy-six—stolen?" he mumbled, the words fighting over each other to get out of his mouth first. "You stole seventy-six thousand dollars? Stole it?"

"We have more in common than you thought, huh?"

He let this sink in, then said, "Is that why your husband was trying to kill you? To take your share of the money?"

"I don't know why he was gonna kill me, Spike. I've always tried to be the good wife, you know? Kept house, waited on him—"

"Hand and foot?"

She nodded. "Hand and foot. And all he did was cheat on me, day in—"

"And day out. God, I love the way you people talk."

"You people?"

Whoops. "Yeah, the, uh, more gray-collarish social stratum. Very interesting group from a sociological standpoint. I mean, I've seen it—read about it—so many times: The male, simply because he acts as the sole financial provider, feels that his opposite number lacks any value—economic or otherwise—and so can be treated at his whim," he said, and looked at her. She wasn't following; that was just fine. "But he was cheating on you?"

"Constantly. Actually, I think he wanted me dead so he could run around with his little chickie I know he's got somewhere in this part of the country."

He nodded, kind of glad he had managed to wrangle her out of flirt mode; it wasn't easy to just rob someone you were attracted to. Since most of the couples he ran into were septuagenarians or older, it wasn't something that he had ever thought about. "So anyway, Wanda, I'm going to have to take that money, and at least get the RV back to Truth or Consequences so I can get my bike. Then I'll let you go, okay? You can just carry on your trip from there, like before I showed up."

"And then what—go off the cliff like I was supposed to?"

He smacked his forehead. "Right, right," he said, trying to guess what it was exactly she expected—or wanted—him to do after he robbed her blind. "*Duh.* Um, do you want a ride somewhere?"

She finished her water and handed him the glass, caressing his fingers as he took it. Then she said, "Don't leave me behind."

"Wanda, I'm a *robber*. Yeah, I'm a gentleman bandit and everything, but my mission is to change people's lives through violent demands. I'm robbing you, changing your life—that's all I can do. Please don't ask me for more."

"You're right—you've changed my life! But I wasn't rich, I'm not a Fat Cat! Now you've changed it into...*I don't know what!*" she said, and let out a sob that sank right into Spike's heart. She crumpled in the shotgun seat and stayed motionless until he started the RV up again, then said, "At least take these damn handcuffs off me."

It was the least he could do, considering. He left the engine running and got up and bent over her, unlocking the cuffs in one swift move.

But even more swiftly, Wanda's arms came up around his neck, and she pulled him into a kiss, a wet kiss in which he could feel the older woman's mouth, her lips, tongue, everything. They all felt rough, and he loved it; they were like nothing he had ever touched before. He kissed her back, hard, and right in the middle, feeling this taut and experienced woman wriggle and moan at his touch, realized that it wasn't just Wanda's life that had been changed now.

Douglas Gann's good pals at the force, men and women who had dedicated their lives to protecting citizens and fighting back against the dark forces of our age, popped open the champagne and doused him in it, their hollers rising over the mad fizzing of the bubbly as it coated Gann's hair, his face, all sopping wet in the celebration of his arresting Gordon Mitchell and saving the unsuspecting Mrs. Mitchell's life.

No Medals of Valor this time—just his best friends lifting him up on their shoulders, spontaneous displays of affection that almost embarrassed him, rising up and up so everyone could hear what a good friend Douglas Gann was to them personally and to citizens everywhere, what a valued friend, what a friend…

A hand reached up from the crowd and nudged him. Nudged him again.

"Detective," Perez said, shaking him lightly to consciousness, "your witnesses, they're here."

Gann's eyes fluttered open, and he sighed. Of course, a dream.

The twenty-somethings didn't look any worse for the wear of being dragged away from their bong this late at night. The guy, goateed and wearing faded overalls right on his white skin, and the girl, tube-dressed and with tiny sunglasses, it was obvious to Gann that these were two of that type that came to the Southwest for freedom from responsibility, parents, and careers.

Oh, from crime, too.

Gann introduced himself and got the general story of what happened at Coyote Jump, then asked them, "Do you have any idea why he wanted you to leave the area?"

"There are problems with this investigation," the guy said by way of an answer.

"That's—what?"

"I said, There are some problems with this investigation. The issue isn't *why* he wanted us to leave the area. It's *how* he went about forcing us to leave the area."

Gann shook his head, trying to knock loose whatever was causing this hallucination. "Um…"

"Do you know what kind of haze diesel emissions cause in this area?"

"Stop it," the girl said, her mouth as tight as her sandals. "He gets like this when…"

"When…"

"When he's around, you know, *authority* figures. Anyone with a badge or a gavel, he's got to try to convince them to take up the cause." She didn't seem too annoyed, though—probably she thought it was noble.

Gann could relate—he *was* an authority figure, it was true. He made an impression, he had to agree, with his short professional haircut and perfect tie knot, which stayed done even while he napped and waited for these people to come. "I understand, and the way he got you to leave was reprehensible" he said, "but, um, could you tell me why you think the RV driver wanted you to leave the area?"

The girl took it this time. "I think he wanted to dump his garbage at the most beautiful lookout in the area. He's a *polluter*."

"Couldn't he just toss his garbage there without running you both off?"

"We inspire assholes," the guy said.

Gann nodded, chewing this over, then had his *eureka* moment. "So let me get this straight: The man—the *polluter*—was behaving threateningly and talking about his wife in the RV, yes?"

"Yeah—it was their twenty-fifth anniversary, he said."

Gann smiled and wrote: *Witnesses reported Mitchell was being threatening, talking about his wife.* Ambiguity was the crusading detective's friend.

"So, you think there's a chance of citing him for the environmental assault?" the guy said as he and the girl stood and got ready to leave.

"Have to see about that," Gann said. "But I sure do appreciate the information."

The couple didn't seem too terribly pleased about that, but at least they had made their stand and could tell their fellow progressives about it.

"Hippies, right here in River City," Perez said as he knocked on the door and entered the room. "They help you? I hope so, 'cause I'm getting ready to—"

"Mitchell was threatening his wife, right in front of those witnesses." It wasn't exactly true, but exactness wasn't going to get Gordon in jail *tonight*. "He ran them off—I bet the body's down at the bottom of Coyote Jump. That must be where he killed her."

"We don't know she's dead, detective."

"If she's dead, we'll find her down there, I know it. I can feel it."

"You going to check it out?" Perez said, inching back out the door.

Gann closed his eyes and concentrated, put every ounce of his being into telepathically convincing Sergeant Perez to take him down there in an NMSP squad car, make it official...

A minute later, he opened his eyes and ran down the hall to just *ask* him. The man was an absolute psychic brick wall.

Perez was less than shocked at the lack of a body at the bottom of Coyote Jump, but the motorcycle up at the top took him by surprise. What was this, an actual clue? Who left a brand-new Honda motorcycle, gassed up and working fine, at a scenic picnic area—with the keys still in the ignition, no less?

"The hippie kids didn't mention a motorcycle," Gann said, kicking a rock.

It was so dark Perez wasn't sure Gann wouldn't just walk right off the edge and put an end to all of their misery. His warm and fuzzy feelings about this "case" had been chilled out and shaved, and now he was feeling more and more anxious to just get this over with.

The bike was shiny—it did look right-off-the-showroom-floor new—and had been carefully set up on its kickstand. But the keys...was this someone in a hurry or not?

"Obviously, the husband had an accomplice. The accomplice rode the bike here."

"Accomplice to what?"

Even in the darkness, Perez could see Gann's *Are you stupid?* look. "To kill the wife," he said. "The motorcycle rider must have been here to help him."

Perez would have given him a look of his own if he had thought it would make any difference. "Detective, the wife, she wasn't killed."

"We don't know that."

"There's no body."

"We don't know that, either."

"What?"

"Look," Gann said, and stepped close enough that Perez could see his eyes reflecting the starlight, "you're right, there's no body *here*. And I said that if she were dead, her body'd be here, I know that. But I didn't realize there was an accomplice."

"There ain't no accomplice, detective, there's a motorcycle. Come on."

"Mitchell has a cellular phone."

Perez didn't even know what to say to that.

"He could've called this accomplice when he realized…"

"Realized what?"

The starlight glinted in Gann's eyes, but no light appeared in his expression. "Realized…that he needed help. That he couldn't do it alone."

"Shit." Perez turned for the car.

"Wait!" Gann said, and ducked in front of him. "I need to check Mitchell's cell phone records. Hey—please."

"Then you can use my phone to call your department in Indiana."

"I can't—you know I'm not officially on this. *Please*."

Perez got in the car, leaving Gann to scramble around to the other side and get in. He turned on the lights, the white lights exploding in their eyes after the meager beams of the flashlights. Finally he said, "It's almost midnight. You get some more sleep, when you wake up, the judge in Indiana, he'll have the warrant for you. Then we can go get Mitchell, okay?"

"But he's going to kill her."

"We're back to he's *gonna* kill her? We come here, I thought she was already supposed to be dead."

"It was a hunch…I don't know what happened."

Perez sighed. He wanted Gann to just disappear, fuck off, anything, but the guy was such a goddamn Boy Scout, checking every corner for old ladies to help across. Which was a good thing—he wished he could be more like that. Of course, Gann probably ended up getting them run over half the time—

"You're smiling. Is that good?" Gann asked.

Perez grumbled noncommittally. "We check the phone records, and then what?"

"See who he's been calling—the accomplice, right? Put an APB out on all vehicles owned by the accomplice, and on the RV. Mitchell probably dumped the vehicle with Wanda's body still in it—that's why we can't find a body—and is out cruising God-knows-where, *with the accomplice*."

Gann's face radiated excitement at his own quick sleuthing. "The phone records are the first step."

The first step. Perez did *not* like the sound of that, suggesting as it did a whole shitload of steps afterward. He looked at his watch—ten till midnight. By the time they got back to the station, his shift would be over, and he wouldn't have to be back until eight a.m. Getting the phone records would be his *only* step. "All right," he said at last. "We get the phone records, you make your call—*if* there's anyone *to* call."

"Yes!" Gann shouted, and pumped his fist in the air.

"And the home team *scores*," Perez said as he pulled the car away from Coyote Jump, unable to keep the Boy Scout mood out completely.

Gann rode in silence as they cut through the blackness of the desert night, but he couldn't keep his hands totally still. To show all of them that once again he was right, and it was only because of him that they even would *have* Gordon Mitchell to bring to trial—*ha!* His cheeks almost hurt from grinning.

He didn't know why the thought of an accomplice hadn't occurred to him sooner—of *course* Gordon had to have a connection down here to put the money in the bank for him, to make sure everything was ready for when he killed his wife and had to make a dash for the border. *Of course, of course.* He wanted to slap himself in the head, but decided Perez wouldn't find that comforting; after all, Perez was sticking his neck out to help him—a risk that would be rewarded when they brought Gordon in.

So all he had to do was check Gordon's cell phone records, see who he was calling during the trip, look that person up—maybe give a call, catch Gordon answering the phone, *yeah*—then get the New Mexico police looking for the car and the RV. It would all be over before the sun came up. Wherever Gordon had planted the money, Gann would make darn sure he never got to it.

10

Night in New Mexico, even in June, is *cold*, especially walking by the side of the highway without so much as long sleeves. Gordon had crossed to the southbound shoulder and stuck his thumb out again and again, then realized the only people his age who would be hitchhiking were rapists or escaped convicts. After that, when a semi would approach, he'd jump up and down like he was in great distress, try to look like maybe he was a father with a kid in some car run off the road.

It worked. Within ten minutes, he had his ride, a trucker who looked puzzled that Gordon's distress was left behind as soon as he climbed in.

"You okay?" the trucker asked him, no doubt wondering now if Gordon was an escaped convict.

"Never better—just looking for the next town down the road, get something to eat, make a phone call."

"Socorro'd do ya, probably—they got a Denny's."

They were already moving, the loud grinds and rumbles so familiar to Gordon from his years driving a rig. "Mind stopping there?" he yelled over the noise.

The trucker gave a wave of his hand: *No problem.*

Gordon smiled at that, realizing Wanda was probably right—he *didn't* give a shit about anyone but himself. Here was this trucker going out of his way; when Gordon was driving semis, not only did he never stop for stranded motorists, he'd always give a blast on the air horn to let them know he'd seen them and that they could go fuck themselves.

Socorro was at least a few dozen miles closer to Truth or Consequences, and it did have a Denny's, which was good, because Gordon was starving. He'd have plenty of time to eat, too, waiting for his little New Mexico Philly, Janey, to come from T or C to pick him up.

His cell phone was still on the damn coach with that psycho kid who was probably hacking Wanda into little pieces right then—Gordon smiled warmly as this thought crossed his mind—so he got on the pay phone and called Janey, collect.

"I should *not* even take this call," she said as soon as she had accepted the charges. "Where the fuck have you been?"

"Baby doll, calm it down. There've been developments."

"I should hang up right now."

"It's about Wanda—"

She hung up. He dialed again.

"Why the hell am I even taking these calls?"

"Easy, honey—listen: Wanda's gone."

There was silence on the other end of the line. Then: "Gone? *Gone* gone?"

"Pretty much."

"What does that mean?"

He quickly added up the pros and cons of telling her the truth, and decided against it. "Run off—she's found herself another man, took the coach and everything. Surprised the living hell out of me, let me tell ya."

"What?" She didn't sound convinced. "She'd never leave you. She just loves you *sooo* much."

"I'm telling you."

"You said you were gonna push her off the cliff at Coyote Jump! What, did she meet somebody on the way down?"

"Don't worry about that, honey—she's someone else's problem now. Fuck, forget 'pretty much'—she's *gone* gone."

Janey let out a raucous squeal of joy. "Oh my *God!*" she screamed into the phone, and cackled. "Where are you—it's midnight! I want to be with you *right now!* We have to—oh my God oh my *God!*"

"Knew you'd be happy."

"Where *are* you? I'm coming to get you right now!"

"Socorro—you know where that is?" he said, looking around him to see if anyone had heard the screaming and squealing coming from the phone. Didn't look like it.

"Socorro? That's like an hour from T or C, baby. How'd you end up there?"

"Long story. I'll tell you when you—" There was a *click* on the line. "Janey?"

"I've got another call. Should I take it? It's probably my mom."

"Go ahead, it's your nickel."

She switched lines, leaving Gordon to listen to nothing but the Denny's low-playing country Muzak. The restaurant was half-full with truckers and tired-looking couples, nobody that Gordon could see causing him any trouble. And this time, he could eat a meal in peace, not have to worry about making everybody in the place sick with romantic bullshit heaved at his wife.

He wondered if Spike was being "romantic" with Wanda right then, and smirked.

The line clicked again, but no voice came from the other end.

"Janey? You back?"

"Gordon," she said, flat as Kansas.

Oh, shit. She was calling him *Gordon.* "Take it that wasn't your mother."

"They know about me. That was them on the phone."

"Them? Who's them?" he asked, but he had a feeling he already knew.

"The detective from Elkhart—Detective Gann. He said he knows I'm your accomplice."

He blustered soundlessly for a few seconds, clenching his fists in the air, before he could finally say—quietly—"Accomplice? To *what?* You haven't done anything!"

"He don't know that, Ronny. He said the police found a motorcycle at the lookout, at Coyote Jump, and he says it's mine."

The lookout? How the fuck did Gann know about the lookout? Gordon's mind raced, but nothing came. "But—did you tell him you don't have a motorcycle?"

"Right. I told him I have a car. And he—"

"Asked what kind." He rested his head against the wall next to the pay phone.

"Yeah."

"Don't tell me you told him."

"He was breathing down my neck. What was I supposed to do?"

Bang. His head sent a shudder through the wall.

"This isn't happening, Ronny—you told me they wouldn't know anything about me until we were in Venezuela. Now that detective is here and he's calling *me?* I don't *think* so—"

Gordon snapped to attention. "Whoa. What?"

"What what?"

"*Who's* here?"

Janey spoke distinctly, as if talking to a particularly slow child. "*Gann.* The *detective*. The guy you've been telling me about."

"He's here? In New Mexico?"

"That's what I said. I said he found a motorcycle at the lookout—"

"No—said the *police* found a motorcycle at the lookout."

"Whatever. Look, Ronny, you said there was no chance of me getting involved. I can't be involved in all this shit. I'm not—"

"What did you tell him?"

"What? Nothing. I said I didn't know you."

"Good girl. What'd he say to that?"

"He said that you call me a lot for somebody I don't know. I just acted like I didn't know what he was talking about. And you know what? I *don't.* I'm not getting involved in this."

"I'm at the Denny's just off twenty-five in Socorro. Need to come get me, *now.*"

"Aren't you listening? I just said I'm not getting—"

"Listen, Janey. Honey. You *are* involved, okay? We're both fucking involved, all right? And you're gonna fuck everything up if you don't get up to Socorro now and get me, so we can get the fucking money in the morning and get the fuck out of Dodge, okay?"

He could practically hear her pout through the phone. "I don't like it when you talk to me like that," she said.

"Oh, sweetheart, stress, you know? Got to get all this stress behind us, then we'll be good. Just like we said. Come on—it'll take you an hour to get here, then we can go. Got to get some distance between us and Johnny Lawman."

Long silence. "And Wanda's really gone?"

"She's disco."

"Disco's coming back."

Je-SUS. "Well, Wanda's not. See you in an hour."

12

Gordon could barely taste the food, his concentration on what Janey had told him: Gann was there, in New Mexico, lurking somewhere to jump out and haul him in; he must've waited until the floor-plan checker was finished and then flown out right away. Now he knew what kind of car Janey was driving and that they were in this together. *Son of a bitch!*

Well, actually Janey was right—she wasn't actually involved as far as taking part in any crime, even though she knew the plan to knock off Wanda and flee the country. Was that enough to arrest her on? *Was* she an accomplice? And, saying that maybe she was, how in the hell did Gann know it? How did he know about Coyote Jump? Had Wanda talked to him? No—if she had, Gann wouldn't have been out there looking for her. Well, not for *her*, exactly—just for her...

He froze, a forkful of Grand Slam Breakfast hanging in the air. *Fuck me,* he thought. *Gann was out there looking for her goddamn body.* How the fuck did Gann do this shit? Nobody knew about his plan except Janey, nobody had even seen him in New Mexico, except at the lookout when he had to scare off—

He dropped his fork. The hippies. Mary Mother of God, the hippies.

They saw him acting strange and running them off and they told the cops—it had to be. That was the only connection, the *only* flaw in the execution of his plan. Except for Spike, of course.

But he could see now that if Spike hadn't stepped in the middle of it, stopped him from tossing Wanda off the lookout like a sack of trash, Gann would have found her body before it was even cold! There would be an all-points out for Gordon, sure as shit, and that would have been the end of his grand adventure right there. Border patrols don't check for embezzlers; murderers are another story.

But the kid *had* stepped in, and then kidnapped Wanda to boot. The cops might end up finding the abandoned RV with Wanda's dead body inside, but the *kid* would be the suspect, not Gordon. Spike kidnapped her, so Spike would have to face the music on that one.

Except...

Except no one knew the coach had been hijacked or Wanda had been kidnapped. No one knew the one thing that could end up making Gordon look like the victim instead of the perpetrator—that the kid had stolen the coach and made off with Wanda, told Gordon he was going to rape her and kill her. If her carcass turned up anywhere in the state of New Mexico before he got over the border, then he was looking at some very difficult questions from the state's finest, with Gann added as a special bonus.

That is, unless he went on the offensive.

He looked at the yellow-stained clock above the cashier's station and saw it was almost one a.m. Twenty minutes and Janey would be there. Plenty of time to report a stolen vehicle, an easy-to-identify thirty-five-ton Rambling Vacationeer.

He borrowed the phone book from the front counter and looked up the Socorro police, put his quarter in and dialed. At the first ring, he gulped back a big swig of his glass of water, sucking in a good breath at the same time. He coughed half of the water out onto the floor, catching stares from most of the restaurant, but when the dispatcher picked up on the other end, Gordon sounded amazingly like he had just been crying.

He reported the coach stolen, and told the dispatcher who it was who had stolen it—his estranged wife, one Wanda Mitchell. And the new boyfriend she had run off with, a kid name of Trent Jones. And be careful, he told the dispatcher to tell any officers that found it: The kid's got a gun.

"Does the vehicle have a global positioning system?" the dispatcher asked him.

"It's got everything," Gordon said, then reminded himself that he wasn't trying to sell her one. He gave her the code, so they could pinpoint the coach's exact location. Technology had made it all so easy now—for those who could afford it. Redundant systems were insurance made into something you could touch.

The dispatcher said she would send an officer out to ask him some questions. Gordon said that would be just fine, and, upon his return to the table finding his Grand Slam had become cold while he was on the phone, just smiled to the waitress and ordered an entirely new one so he could try it again.

13

It was one-thirty when Janey Briggs walked into the Denny's and scanned the place for Gordon. When she spotted him, he was sitting and talking to a cop.

She walked right back out the door.

Before she could back her car out, Gordon came flying out the door at her. "It's okay! Just reporting the coach stolen. Park, come back inside, come on."

"They're *looking* for me!" she said, the car stopped but still in gear. "How could you bring a cop here?"

Gordon sighed. "They're not looking for *you*. Gann can't do anything—he has no jurisdiction here. Get done with this officer of the law, we'll be out of here, okay?"

"Ronny Mitchell, you play too close to the edge."

"Thought that's what you liked about me."

She gave a little smile at that and let him go back inside while she parked. She stayed in the car for a while, waiting for him to finish his business with the cop, which took forever. Just as the officer was standing to leave, it hit her what Gordon had said: *He was reporting the RV stolen!* They were going to find the RV—and Wanda—for him! He wanted her back! But—he called her, Janey, and had her come up, right? He didn't love Wanda, he loved *her.*

She was dizzy, and by the time the cop left and she slipped inside, she was mad, too. She'd get his two-timing ass down to T or C, all right, but he was going to have some explaining to do on the goddamn way.

The officer, Merry, six-foot-six of Midwestern farm boy, looked Gordon over as he approached the table, no doubt taking in his tousled hair and dusty clothes. "Did you want to report a stolen vehicle, sir?" Merry asked him, and sat down.

"Don't know if I should consider it *stolen* exactly," Gordon bullshitted, "because it's my wife who's got it. And, uh, her boyfriend." This was his story now, and he knew to stick to it.

Merry's eyebrows popped up. "Boyfriend."

"Yep. She and I were having problems, and were taking this trip, delivering a coach—see, I sell recreational vehicles—"

"Why did your wife take the RV, sir?" All business, this Officer Merry.

"Why? I don't know. Surprised me, all right."

After a minute or two of writing, Merry looked up from his notepad. "Are you interested in pressing charges, sir?"

Gordon took this one slowly—he was dancing around in enemy territory in the first place, calling the police in. But he had a big feeling they didn't know anything and wouldn't know anything until a warrant was issued in Indiana and worked through the channels. Now he had his confirmation.

So he weighed what to say. If Wanda was dead in the coach, he didn't want to sound vindictive, make the cops think he had something to do with it. But he wanted them to go after her and Spike, so he had to make it sound important enough to pursue, not just a half-ass plea from a jealous husband.

He said, "Just want to make sure she's all right. This isn't like her, stealing the coach we're supposed to deliver. Knew things were bad, but hell, another man? It's his influence—I think she's scared of him. Got a violent history."

Merry seemed to sift all of this through his mind slowly, looking for anything out of place, anything to raise a red flag. Watching him, Gordon was damn glad he had chosen his words carefully. "You think he might hurt her?" Merry asked.

Score! "He's very jealous of her being married to me in the first place."

The officer nodded. "I've seen that many times. The 'other man' or 'other woman' feels that he or she has a more legitimate claim on the subject than does his or her spouse, precisely because this 'other person' has heard nothing but complaints about the spouse. It's not uncommon for their jealousy to rival the wronged spouse's."

"Uh, right." At least the officer seemed squarely in Gordon's court. "So…"

"You told dispatch that there was a global positioning system on the RV?"

"Right. I gave her the code for access."

The officer checked his notes, then read off the code.

Gordon checked the card in his wallet. "Correct."

"Apparently, there's a malfunction with the equipment on-board the vehicle. We couldn't get a response."

Gordon grimaced. He'd said to the kid: *I can track this thing, you know,* right before he stepped off the Vacationeer. Finding the transmitter wasn't hard if you knew where to look. One point for Spike.

But redundancy, the insurance you could touch…the score was tied.

"Sir? You all right?"

"Just worried," Gordon said. "Can you still find it, find my wife?"

"Don't worry, Mr. Mitchell," the officer said as he stood and shook Gordon's hand. "We'll just have to do this the old-fashioned way. Is there a number where we can reach you?"

Think fast. "Yeah, um, Albuquerque Motel 6, room 118." It was bull-shit off the top of his head, but hopefully, by the time they had something to report, he'd be long gone and it wouldn't make any difference.

"Okay. We'll have something to tell you in no time." With that, Officer Merry marched out through the front door, not even stopping for coffee and a donut.

Thirty seconds after Merry walked out, Janey walked in. And she didn't look happy.

"All set?" Gordon asked without getting up.

Janey stepped right up and slapped him, hard, across the face. "You want your goddamn wife back!"

"I do?"

"Why are you getting the police to look for her? What kind of game are you playing? We're not going anywhere until I get some answers." She stood there with her arms crossed, leaving Gordon to stare at her with this hand against his stinging cheek.

"Gonna sit down so I can tell you?"

"We can talk in the car on the way down."

He stared at her. "Thought you said we weren't going anywhere."

"Shut up. You are *so* lucky I trust you."

"This is lucky? This is trust?"

She bent down and put her arms around him, giving him a kiss on his hurt cheek. "I trust you to tell me what's going on, okay? Let's not fight now—we've got the rest of our lives to fight."

Ain't that the truth, Gordon thought, and, after a minute of seriously weighing his options, followed Janey out to the car.

Spike worked his fingers over Wanda's neck, enjoying feeling the interesting texture of her forty-something muscles and skin as he manipulated them. She was different than the girls he had known at Carnegie-Mellon—this was no bred-for-success, overaerobicized president of a sorority. This was a real *woman*. She knew how to draw him into a kiss and make him want her with everything he had.

In the end, he'd been strong—strong enough, anyway, and resisted doing anything he would regret—mixing it up with a robbery and kidnap victim could result in the Helsinki Syndrome, and Spike was not in this business to cause mental hardship on anyone. But the romantic involvement, small though it was, made what he had to do that much more difficult, and unfortunate.

He turned her captain's chair around to face him and knelt down to her, slipping the thirty-eight from his belt as he leaned forward. "Wanda, I've had a very nice time with you, but I'm afraid it's time for you to turn over all your money now."

"You don't need that, honey," she said, pushing the gun away.

"Okay," he said, and tucked it back into his belt behind him. "Let's have it then, okay?"

"You don't look like a robber to me." She said it softly, like she was glad of it.

"It's my trademark that I steal only from those who can afford it."

"*I* can't afford it, Spike—I'm a new widow," she said, winking at him. "Lonely, too."

He felt a stirring deep inside. Her skin had felt *so* nice, rougher than what he had grown used to and bored with. Her lips, her mouth, smooth and rough at the same time…*Shit.* He shook it off.

"Besides," she continued, stretching her foot so her toes rested on his knee, "there might be a way we can help each other. Gentleman bandits don't have a code against that, do they?"

He could feel the weight of the pistol pressing against his back. He wanted so badly to just grab it, feel its heft in his hand so he could rob this beautiful woman and be gone, live the life of the quintessential American lonely desperado. But with the gun stuck back there, out of reach for all practical purposes, he was paralyzed, mesmerized by her words, her full, slathered-in-red lips, her bright lavender eyes, her white-coated skin with patches of red so carefully applied…

He struggled. "No, Wanda—*ma'am*—not that I know of. But my price for rescuing you from your husband, that's non-negotiable. I have to rob you."

"Are you in this for the money?" her red lips said.

He shook his head. "It's deeper than that."

"Anything else interesting to you?" she asked, leaning back and undoing the top button of her floral blouse. She…*wanted him?* Wasn't she supposed to be scared right about now? The kissing and the rubbing, they were one thing, but he'd kidnapped her! Saved her life first, yes, but he'd kidnapped her! Didn't that count for something?

He supposed not, remembering the sexual attractiveness embedded in the entire Western desperado archetype, which Wanda was no doubt powerless to ignore as she tapped into the collective unconscious.

Then it hit him: *You put your gun away, genius. If you're going to rob someone, keep the gun out.* "I want your money," he said, and pulled the gun from his belt. "Stick 'em up."

"Nobody says that in real life anymore, Spike," she said, and dropped her blouse to the floor, revealing her freckled, beautiful chest shrouded in mystery by a shiny, teasing Playtex Living Bra. "But I'm glad to obey."

He now could feel an erection raging against his black jeans. The motor home was parked and the night outside was chilly, but his face felt as hot as if he had just run a marathon in the heat of the New Mexico afternoon. He cleared his throat and said, "Come on, I need the money."

"And you'll get it," she said in her flat, sexy voice. "But I need something from you first."

He set the gun down on the dash as she stood up and stood him up, glancing her hand across the bulging crotch of his jeans, and led him through the lush accommodations of the living area, through the convenient ergonomic kitchen, past the free-standing dining set and full-size bathroom, past the kitchen area with its island gas range, past all of the upper-middle-class comforts that somehow this gorgeous older woman didn't seem to belong in.

Spike, loving her touch as she led him by the groin to what looked to be the bedroom of the RV, thought the splendiferous Wanda belonged in a home with a waterbed, three televisions, velvet paintings, and a Precious Moments figurine collection at the very least. A couch on the porch. An old freezer in the yard. Her natural habitat, if you will.

Then a thought hit him, a thought that filled him with joy and affirmation—Wanda and her rotten husband *lived in the RV!* It all made sense—they were going to Truth or Consequences, a town made up almost entirely of people who lived in trailers and recreational vehicles! This was their *house!* A giant grin split his face as he realized that knowing this made everything right, even as it made the pounding in his crotch even more severe.

They reached the door of what he assumed to be the bedroom when Wanda said, "Close your eyes."

He did. He got a good whiff of her perfume, which smelled a lot like Giorgio but not exactly. He pictured her face in his mind, smiling at him, promising him, winking at him. He heard something like rustling—a paper bag?—and then the sound of paper falling onto the bed. A smile was frozen onto his face.

After a few seconds of sound he couldn't quite place, he heard the *thump* of something hitting the bed and a new, fresh smell, like a field of flowers, like a spring day, wafted into his nostrils. He ate it up.

Finally, Wanda said, "Okay. Open."

He opened his eyes, which became almost as wide as his grin.

Wanda lay on the bed, nude—totally nude, except for her earrings, necklaces, rings, and anklets—on her back, propped up on her elbows, her knees bent and spread the tiniest bit to give Spike just a glance at her nether region, clouded in a dark reddish brown nothing like the reddish brown of the hair on her head. Her freckled and tan-lined skin also didn't match the white beauty of her made-up face, but the sight of her naked, wonderful body made him yearn for all of it in its entirety.

Then he noticed what she was lying *on*.

Underneath her butt, her elbows, her back, everywhere, were dollar bills which looked suddenly familiar. These bills had not one zero, not two zeroes, but *three* zeroes after the one.

They were thousand-dollar bills, just like the two Gordon had handed him as hush money by the side of the road. And the bed was covered with them.

"I told you that you didn't need that gun, Spike," she said, spreading her legs a bit wider. "But bring your pistol if you want to play."

He whipped off his shirt and vest and shucked off his jeans and shorts, revealing his trembling, shiny-with-tautness erection, which was purple with the pressure of premature release.

Wanda opened her legs to him as she rustled a handful of bills—*what was that in her hand right there, fifteen thousand dollars?*—and said, "And you know what else?"

He was so excited he was about to burst. "What?"

"Compared to what Gordon's got stashed in T or C, this is chump change."

Electricity surged through him, galvanizing him as he exploded, showering the edge of the bed and Grover Cleveland's face with his seed. He was mortified, but Wanda simply smiled and then said something he realized, with love, that he never in a million years would have heard from the mouth of a girl from Carnegie, or Colgate, or Vassar, or Wesleyan:

She said, "Don't sweat it, honey. The easy one's no fun anyway."

He leapt onto the bed then, overwhelmed with love for this woman of his deepest dreams, and they made love like he had never known possible, her playful, teasing, "punishing" words only serving to make him want her more.

They lay in bed, the heat of sex still heavy in the little room at the back of the bus.

They kissed and stroked.

Wanda asked him, "What are you doing here?"

Spike smiled. "Isn't it obvious?"

"No, I mean, why are you a robber? You're so smart—you're like a genius. What are you doing holding people up by the side of the road in New Mexico?"

Spike propped himself up on one arm and looked deeply into this wonderful woman's eyes, this woman with eyes like pools of crystal brown water. "My parents are rich."

"I figured that. Your nails are perfect."

"I was supposed to follow in Pop's footsteps, major in business management at Carnegie-Mellon, then on to business school itself, Harvard or Yale, of course. See, I was bred to be part of this new breed of young Turks who would reverse the destructive, short-term profiteering of the junk-bond kings and liquidators of the 'eighties as well as rebuild after the currency traders did their dirty work blasting away at the economies of Russia and Asia all during the 'nineties. Both of these groups dropped American business to its knees thanks to hostile takeovers by corporate giants which wanted only to sell off the pieces of the once-great American blue-chips and thanks to currency devaluations necessary after decades of bad loans took their toll on once-venerable banks all over the world.

"Follow so far?" he asked Wanda.

She nodded, whether she did or not, so he continued. He had practiced this little autobiography a hundred times riding his bike through miles of nothing all over the West.

"Well, this vanguard I was supposed to be a part of, the vanguard that was coming up through the ranks at the big schools, undergrads and MBA students alike, it was poised to redefine business in the next millennium, building indestructible companies, hiring the best in each field at salaries tied half to simple reputation and half to financial performance. I was one of the best of the best of the best—if I may repeat what others have said— a genius among the blue bloods who make up the top echelons of the business world. Talent, drive, charisma, you name it—I had it all. There was only one problem."

Wanda's eyes said it all: *A problem with all this?*

"The new vanguard was as greedy as the old guard. They just went about it differently. What business magazines and the rest said was geared toward saving the American corporate identity was really designed just to make sure fortunes stayed put where they were.

"It was all a plan by the rich to get richer.

"And I *hate* the rich."

"But," Wanda said slowly, "I thought your family *is* rich."

"No, I know, I know. I hate them. I've felt this way since I was six years old, when my family's cook would tell me how lucky I was and then tell me about his own life and family, how they had to hang on to each other for support, for love, for dear life, without any of the comforts that a lucky little rich kid like me took for granted.

"But I didn't want what *I* had. I wanted what *he* had, you know?" He leaned back and stared out the moon roof, watching Wanda watching him out of the corner of his eye, and kept talking, spilling it all out, telling everything to the woman he had found. "One of my family's two cleaning ladies, Tara, explained to me how lucky my mother was, since she didn't have to put her career on hold to spend time with her child. No, she had nannies to take care of that for her. Of course, she didn't make time for me when she got home—hey, the nannies were still getting paid to work, weren't they?

"Tara said she thought I was a very sweet boy and she would've loved to take me home—then she would always squeeze my cheeks, which made me giggle—but she had three boys of her own back at her apartment and she, unlike my mother, had to cook dinner for them herself every night when she got home."

Spike chuckled. "You know, even the hired help in my starched and scrubbed home were pretty well starched and scrubbed themselves. Everybody wore uniforms, nobody was allowed to wear jewelry beyond what my mother thought was tasteful, nobody smoked on duty, nobody drank, nobody *lived* at all.

"Especially me. Nobody showed any signs of life."

Now he smiled wide. "Except one guy. One guy—Spike Manning, the lawn maintenance man."

"That name rings a bell."

He looked at her and shared even more of his smile. "He was in his fifties, balding, paunchy, and to my prepubescent eyes, he was the very embodiment of life itself. He'd mow the lawn, spread the fertilizer, trim the hedges, sweep the walk, all with a bent cigarette hanging from his lips while he hummed a song I couldn't recognize.

"I could hardly wait until the day every week when Spike would come—he'd let me ride with him on the little golf cart he used, he'd sneak me cigarettes I never had the nerve to light up, and he'd tell me stories about life back at the Mobile Acres."

"Oh, God," Wanda said, obviously trying not to laugh. It was okay—it *was* kind of funny. He had wanted to tell this story for so long, to share it with someone who would understand and enjoy it, and here he was.

Here *she* was.

"I mean, to me, what Spike Manning was talking about—*that* was living, you know? He lived with his common law wife, Goop—"

"*Goop?*"

"Well, her real name was Gertrude. He lived with her and their two kids, one from one of Goop's earlier relationships, in their very own single-wide manufactured home on four acres just on the outskirts of Pittsburgh—not too far from the Jones spread, now that I think about it.

"I mean, imagine what this was to me—Spike Manning had dogs his kids could play with whenever they wanted! They ate, like, macaroni and cheese and watched TV until they fell asleep! They didn't dress up for barbecues. They didn't always say *please* and *thank you* and bow and curtsy and all of that. And best of all, since Spike was self-employed—that's why he could get away with the cigarettes and everything while he was working—and Goop was on disability, they could spend lots of time with the kids. Too much time, Spike used to say with a laugh, but I knew that had to be a joke. There was no such thing."

"Wow" was all Wanda said.

"You know, at Carnegie, I hardly even remembered Spike Manning—consciously, at least. But I did remember vividly that there was a whole other world out there beyond what I and my fellow Masters of the Universe had been raised with. I completely pissed off my father when he found out my degree was in sociology so I could learn about native and indigenous people, the people who were run over by the heartless business machine of the modern world, throwing traditional farmers off their land in Guatemala so vast banana plantations could be planted for Dole; hooking South American turtle fishermen on cheap baubles and hatchets so they'd give up their way of life to come and work for the white man; and uprooting and pushing aside completely innocent trailer park residents in Pennsylvania to make room for a new superhighway to serve an elite which cared only about getting rich and getting laid, you know? Money and sex, that's all it is to the upper ranks of society, that's it.

"I wrote a senior thesis titled *Ain't that America: Ruinous Greed and the New Business Vanguard.* It got an A and a special plaque from the famous holdout Marxist who ran the class. It also got me disinherited, everything except my platinum American Express.

"That's when I decided to put into practice what I learned, to take up the cause of *all* of those who themselves had been disinherited by the American system, become a Robin Hood for the new millennium, spreading understanding while supporting myself on fines I would levy against the rich. That's when I realized I needed a new identity—and Spike Jones was born."

"But how do you spread understanding? I don't see how people learn anything by having a gun put to their heads, except not to stop and help people," Wanda said. She was thinking. That was exciting.

"I always give a little lecture—maybe you could even call it a sermon—about the evils of greed and how Fat Cats are ruining the country and the world with their intense focus on money and sex."

"But *you're* stealing money."

"True, that's true. But I'm doing good with it—or, I mean, I'm going to. With the money I get from…" He almost said *you*, but remembered that things had taken quite a different little tack now. "…from people on this trip, I'm going down to old Mexico to liberate some poor child prostitute from her squalid life, give her a few thousand *dineros* to let her start a brand new life."

"That's why you're doing all this? To help somebody you haven't even met yet?"

"And to teach Fat Cats a lesson, don't forget that," Spike said, feeling a little defensive all of a sudden.

"Listen, Spike, you need to learn your lesson—you're working hard for this money, you're suffering for it, *you're* doing all this, not some Mexican streetwalker. Learn your lesson—keep the money you earn."

"But...that would take away half of my reason for doing this."

"That still leaves you with half of a mighty fine reason."

"It's a thought," he said, just so this conversation could end. Wanda seemed to take the cue, because she just enveloped him in her arms again and brought him to her, laid him down with her in the pile of money. He didn't resist, of course, but all the way he reminded himself that he was doing this for good, and that he would never debase himself for money or sex ever again.

Twenty minutes later, Wanda watched as Spike mopped some of the sweat from his brow with a thousand-dollar bill and tossed it back on the pile between their glistening, naked bodies. The moon roof above the bed of the two hundred and eighty thousand-dollar Vacationeer was open, and the chill of the desert evening wafted in on their reddened faces.

"Happy?" she asked softly.

"Silly question," Spike answered, kissing her. "The stars are shining and fate is smiling upon us. You?"

She propped herself up on an elbow, drinking in all of her buff young lover and his romantic talk. But it was time to see if he was going to play with the big dogs or just stay on the porch like a puppy. "I don't know, Spike. There's something I've got to tell you."

This got his attention. "You don't have syphilis, do you? It's prevalent in certain socio...Never mind."

She put her hand against her eyes and said suddenly, dramatically, "Oh, hell, Spike, I'm no better than you. You know I didn't come by this money honestly."

"Most people that do probably don't have sex on it."

"My husband—Ron—he…was planning to kill me for it, run away to Venezuela," she said, afraid that the fact that this was true probably didn't make it sound any more believable. But Spike was *there*—he saw Gordon ready to chuck her off the cliff. Maybe there was a chance…

"I can hardly believe anyone would hurt a hair on your beautiful head."

"It's true. And this is only seventy-six thousand."

Spike blinked. "I'm sorry—*only?*"

Easy now, she reminded herself. Gordon had shared some of his sales secrets with hers over the years. One of them was not to try to make the sale too fast, just let the concept, idea, RV, whatever, sell itself first. "Gordon 'Ron' Mitchell is a dangerous man, Spike. He's not above stealing—no offense."

Spike shrugged it off. "Only?" he asked again.

"What I mean is, he'll kill for this money—you saw that. Twenty-five years of my life I've given to this man, and this is how he thanks me."

"What do you mean, *only* seventy-six thousand? How much more is there?"

Wanda steeled herself—just saying the words sent shivers through her body. "There's a million and a half dollars waiting for us in Truth or Consequences," she said, biting her bottom lip in a grin she hoped looked conspiratorial. She had been careful to say "us."

Spike was speechless. His mouth moved, but nothing came out but air.

"I want that money, Spike," Wanda said, "and I want you. Can you help me?" She ran a finger, the one sporting the Rubyite stone in its ring, down his chest and into his pubic hair.

"That—that's dishonest, Wanda."

She raised her stylishly penciled eyebrows. "And armed robbery isn't?"

"No, exactly," he said, getting excited, "that's exactly what I mean. Sticking some Fat Cat up with a thirty-eight and making him hand over his filthy lucre—"

Filthy lucre?

"—that's *honest*. That's up-front and laying things out like they are, who's got power and who doesn't. It's empowerment, my darling Wanda, putting the responsibility for one's own life in one's own hands."

Wanda stared at him for a few seconds, at his eager pea-green eyes, his animated way of talking about something he obviously felt passionate about, and said, "I don't get a word you're saying."

"Look, if I put a gun in your face—not that I would do that anymore to you, my love—but if I did that and told you to give me your goddamn wallet or a sandwich or whatever, you know what's going on, right? You know that I, a lowly robber, am leveling the playing field with you, a Fat Cat, right?"

"Okay..." *What fresh bullshit was this?*

"But if I sneak into your bank and clean you out, not only will I be profiting disproportionately from my actions—the same thing I accused you (not *you*, but my hypothetical victim) of doing—but I will also leave you without an understanding of the reasoning behind my actions. I will not have taught you a lesson, which is what I as a gentleman bandit strive to do."

Wanda weighed all of this. "Teach lessons to sons of bitches? That's what you do?"

"Pretty much," he said, stroking her leg contritely. "But I would like to—"

"That's what this *is!*" She sat up, her breasts still showing an admirable amount of bounce for a woman of forty-three. "I want that thieving, cheating, murderous son of a bitch to learn a *lesson!*"

Spike's gaze lingered on her naked body and then scanned the small fortune in cash littered around the bed, no doubt picturing a million and a half more. "Well, why didn't you say so?" he said, and pulled her back down to him.

From the time that Gordon explained his scheme to her, Wanda Mitchell had thought and thought about what she would do with a million dollars. She knew full well that that amount wasn't even that astronomical anymore; if they were staying in the United States, they still would've had to *work*, for Chrissakes. But a million dollars, all at once? She and Gordon could have a big house, servants, horses (she loved horses), anything and everything their hearts desired.

That was before Detective Gann told her about the single ticket to Venezuela, though. It was certainly before Gordon tried to push her off the cliff. It was only on this trip that she realized her husband had no intention of sharing the million and a half with her. He had no intention of sharing anything at all with her, even—especially—himself.

He wanted her out of the picture. Be with his hussies down in South America. Spend the money *she* had brought to New Mexico time and time again in her oversized purse on anything and everything *his* heart desired. She loved to be contrary with him, give him a hard time, make him pay a little bit for all the lousy things he did to her—but *this?* Just when they were going to be able to be happy as a couple?

Well, he hadn't even *seen* her contrary yet. She'd rather have burned the money than let him have it at that point. She'd rather have killed somebody herself before she'd let him get at the money, let him laugh about how he fooled her, fooled everyone.

She'd rather kill *him.* No—even better, make him want to kill himself. Take away the most important thing in the world to him: the money. Leave him going to jail for the rest of his life for a million and a half dollars he never even got to hold in his hands.

As she lay on the queen-size bed standard with every Vacationeer class motor home, watching the quiet sleep of the first new lover she had taken in twenty-five years, turning thoughts over in her mind the way one can only do in the cold dark middle of the night, she noticed the New Mexico driver's licenses, two of them, mixed in with the money. She sat up and picked one up—it was Gordon's picture, the man in the picture had a ridiculous fake moustache but it was definitely Gordon. They had gone to Kinko's to get the pictures taken—"passport" pictures, they said—and it was one of the few times in the past five years Wanda could remember them laughing like they were on a first date. Gordon's license had another name, of course: "Richard V. Modine." *R. V.*—Gord's little inside joke. Stuck onto the back of the ID was the moustache.

Without putting that one down, she picked the other up, the one with her on it, the one with the name "Edie Modine." The one she produced when she had to drop the thousands into the safety deposit box for Atchison to change into smaller bills. She had a curly blonde wig on in the picture, and she smiled as she remembered that she and Gordon had shared a good laugh over that, too—

Looking at the license, she stopped smiling.

The woman in the picture, "Edie Modine," was not her. Wanda's picture, the one with the wig, had not made it onto *this* license. The blonde-haired girl in the picture—the one with *real* blonde hair—was not her.

She knew who it was. This was *Janey*, the one Gordon had been talking to on the phone. This was *honey*. This was *sweetheart*.

She stared unbelieving at the two pictures, side by side, the lovers, fake IDs showing husband and wife, and Wanda could feel something deep inside snap, like a damn giving way.

Then, slowly, the downturned corners of her mouth crinkled back on themselves and folded into a mirthless smile.

She was going to do what Spike did.

She was going to teach that son of a bitch a lesson.

Slowly, quietly, so as not to disturb her lover, Wanda got out of bed, put a face on, and used the cellular phone to call the Elkhart, Indiana, Police, telling them it was an emergency and she had to speak to Lieutenant Detective Douglas Gann. She didn't have a plan about what exactly she was going to do or say, but when they told her Gann was "on vacation" in *New Mexico* and gave her his motel room number in Truth or Consequences—Gann was in *Truth or Consequences*, Gann was there!—all at once everything fell into place.

She clicked off the phone and shuffled back over the carpet to the bedroom, pausing only to peek through the curtains at the stillness outside. Spike had picked a terrific secluded spot, had made love like a champ, had saved her life and given her the chance to get Gordon back for flushing twenty-five years of her life down the crapper.

As she looked at his face in the dim glow of the automatic nightlight, she figured he was just about perfect. Now she would give him the chance to prove it.

"Spike," she said, waking him with a rub to his shoulder. "I'm hungry."

"Mmm. Of course, darling. We're not ten miles from Albuquerque— it's midnight snack capital of the world, if you don't mind trucker chow. There's a Denny's."

That was perfect. She cupped her face with her hands and let out what she hoped sounded like a sob. "Oh God. We need money."

"I'm sure they have some kind of special."

"No, more than that. Traveling money, Spike."

"There's like twelve thousand dollars stuck to my butt."

She shook her head. "Those are no good except at the right kind of bank—Gordon's bank, with his connections. If you took those into your local branch, the Treasury Department would be all over you in a heartbeat."

"They're illegal?" He looked stricken.

"They'd have lots of questions. They're supposed to be just for currency transfer."

"Between the rich. Fat Cats again."

"The point is we can't spend it. We can't do nothing with it until we get to that bank in the morning. And we need some traveling money. Oh, what are we going to do?"

Spike stroked her face. "Not to worry. I've got six hundred bucks in my vest pocket. Ill-gotten booty, if you will. We'll just tap into that, get ourselves some breakfast at Denny's, they're open all night, okay?"

"Denny's," she said, trying to look sad. "I come all the way from Indiana to New Mexico, and I end up eating at Cracker Barrel and Denny's."

"My roommate at Carnegie's thesis was on that—the death of regional cuisine, you know? They've got the money to stay open twenty-four hours a day and give people exactly what they want whenever they want. It's pretty unbeatable economically. But hey, some eggs and bacon, some coffee, we'll be good as new."

She nodded, not looking so upset now but screaming inside. This isn't how she wanted this to turn out, not at all. Hell, Gordon could *buy* breakfast. "That sounds great," she said, wheels turning in her head.

"You sure? You don't sound like it sounds great."

She leaned into him and gave him her tongue. That clouded him up in a hurry. "Go clean yourself up, young man. We got a long way to go before we're through tonight."

He gave her a smile and another kiss and padded out to the full-size bathroom clutching his jeans. In one motion as he left the room, Wanda swept herself onto her feet, shutting the door with one hand and whirling the other to yank his vest off the floor. She checked one pocket—empty. Another—empty. She was beginning to think he meant to say the money was in his pants—the pants he was putting on right then—when she found a hidden inside pocket, and hooked a huge wad of bills with her pinky.

She slid the side window and screen open and poked the money through, spilling it out onto the rocky ground. Then she slipped back into bed, arranging herself to look as casual as possible and tossing the vest back onto the floor.

The door opened and her young lover beamed. "To Denny's," he said.

"To Denny's," she echoed, and smiled at her own deviousness. Hell, she thought, she was enough older than him to say what she was doing was for his own good. "Are you gonna bring your gun?"

He did a little double-take. "What for?"

"I'm pretty hungry. If we didn't have enough to pay…"

"Six hundred dollars buys a lot of pigs in a blanket, darling," he said, and whipped the pistol—it was there the whole time—out from his belt. "But if that won't cover it, we may just have to take breakfast by force."

"Now you're talking," she said. He was going to go all the way for her. Goddamn if he wasn't going to go all the way.

16

"I need an APB put out on this car," Gann said, and placed the information on Janey Briggs' silver LeBaron on the desk of the new officer on duty at the NMSP station. "Sergeant Perez was working with me on this—"

"Perez went home forty-five minutes ago. This is his case?"

"Uh, no—it's mine. He was assisting me."

The new sergeant, Frick, sighed mightily. "And you are?"

"Douglas Gann, Elkhart Police Department. Indiana. *Detective* Douglas Gann." He pushed the paper toward the officer. "This is the accomplice's vehicle."

He pushed it back. "Accomplice to what?"

"Possibly murder."

"*Possibly* murder, huh?" Frick said, and breathed a tiny chuckle. "Look, I took a peek at Perez's shift report. There's nothing here. If something happens, we'll help you, okay? This is our jurisdiction here—any help you want to give us is welcome, too, you know."

"I'm trying to help. This is the accomplice's car. Find that, and we find the perpetrator, Gordon Mitchell."

"Again, perpetrator of what? Indiana hasn't put out a warrant yet, you know that, won't have one until at least eight our time. Then we'll talk, okay?"

"He's planning to flee the country. I just need this car, then I'll wait for the warrant, I swear to God."

Frick stared at him for a few seconds, then slid Gann's paper back so he could read it. Perez was right—this guy was a Boy Scout, and just as charming. "All right, we'll find the LeBaron. But after that, you're on your own, okay? We're not arresting anybody without a warrant."

Gann nodded, giving Frick a good thank-you smile. Everything was falling into place. Which was good, because he was so dog-tired he was beginning to lose track of what he had to do, who he had to convince of what, where his duty lay. If Gordon and his accomplice, this Janey Briggs, were in the silver LeBaron, then Wanda was truly not with them. Which meant…she was dead, right? In the RV, because the RV was gone, too. He had given a call to the reputed customer who was supposed to take possession of the vehicle, a David Atchison of Truth or Consequences, and learned that he was still waiting for the delivery. He'd heard nothing from Gordon or Wanda, Atchison had said. Gann could tell the man was agitated about his vehicle going lost—he was as nervous and pent-up as anyone Gann had ever interrogated, let alone just called for verification of some facts.

But *jeez!* He needed to find the RV if he was going to make anything stick to Gordon, not just the LeBaron! His sleepy head reeling, he rushed to his briefcase and copied all of the information on the Vacationeer down on a sheet of legal pad, then ripped it off and ran it over to Frick, who hadn't yet had the chance to move from the desk.

"This too," Gann said as he reached over to slap the page from the legal pad on top of the LeBaron description.

Frick's brow furrowed as he looked it over. "Now *two* vehicles? Are they supposed to be together?"

Gann shook his head. "The wife of the perpetrator—the victim—she's in the RV."

"The victim of what, the murder?"

"Mitchell probably hid her body in the RV, then hid that. The accomplice drove."

He whipped the paper back at Gann. "Get the fuck out of here with this."

"But it's vital—"

Frick raised the LeBaron paper. "You want this sent out, right? Then get out of my face, okay? I'm not supposed to be doing this anyway."

Gann spread his hands in a gesture of surrender, backing away from the desk, and sat down in one of the plastic waiting-area chairs. He watched as Frick gave the paper to another officer, just a young kid, to call in the APB on the LeBaron.

Red-eyed and dragging as he was, Gann kept his eyes glued to the kid. Frick would have to take a bathroom break eventually, and then Gann would be able to just tell the kid he forgot to add another vehicle to the APB.

Gordon and his accomplice in the LeBaron. Wanda, or Wanda's body, in the Vacationeer. He'd have everything he'd need to send a very bad man away for the rest of his life. And all of it done before the muckety-mucks back in Indiana even got a warrant together.

He closed his eyes and allowed himself a couple of Z's, keeping his ear open for any sound of Frick shuffling off to relieve himself. It didn't take long.

Truth or Consequences lies on historic Route 66, and makes the most of this fact in tourism brochures and gift shops. Old—that is, "classic"—motels line the T or C business strip, and while perhaps they don't offer all of the latest theme-hotel amenities, they have beds, and pools, and color, even cable, television. Gordon didn't care much about pools or TV, but the bed at the "Motel 66" sounded mighty good to him.

However, once they checked in, standing between him and it was Janey Briggs. "This isn't working," she said, not responding to the wistful way he was eyeing the queen-size mattress. "Wanda is supposed to be *dead*. That was part of the plan."

"Not the important part."

"Not—? That was the *most* important part!"

He could see that her blood was rising, but his was too. "Know the plan, do ya? Know the most important parts?"

Her eyes narrowed. "You think I don't?"

"Asking you a question."

"And I'm answering it! I know the plan, Ronny."

"What time we need to be at the bank?"

"Nine o'clock on the dot." The look on her face was pure self-satisfaction.

"And what do we do once we're there?"

The smug look slid away. "We get the money." Pause. "Right?"

"We get the money," Gordon repeated, and nodded at her, his whole field of vision going red. "How do we get the money, Brainiac?"

"Isn't it in a special account?"

He was going to snap her neck. "Don't know the plan."

"Well, maybe I don't remember every little detail..."

"What time was I gonna kill Wanda?"

She cocked her head at him. "Wha? Between four and five p.m. What's that got—"

"Why was I gonna do it then?"

"It—it was because that's the least likely time for witnesses." She was eyeing him with outright fear now.

"Where was I gonna do it?"

"Coyote Jump lookout. Just outside T or C."

"Why was I gonna do it there?"

"'Cause no one would find the body until we were out of the country. What are you doing, Ron?"

"Just seeing how well you remember the plan. Or parts of it."

"I remember every part having to do with killing that fucking wife of yours, the wife you say you don't love, the wife you say you *hate*—"

"But you don't give a rat's ass about the money, or me going to jail, that it?"

Her expression collapsed and she started to sob. "No! Sweetie, I...I get a little obsessed."

"No shit."

"I got excited that she'd finally be gone, that's all. She'd be dead, out of our lives forever," Janey said, and stepped up to put her arms around Gordon. "I'm sorry."

"Get that money, we're history. No more Wanda, ever. But you gotta know the goddamn *plan*, sweetheart. We go at nine sharp—what's my name?"

"Huh?" She stuttered, "G-Gordon Mitchell. Ron Mitchell."

"Jesus *fuck*," he said, and ran a hand through his hair. She was a great lay and lots of fun to be around, but what exactly the fuck was he doing here? He shook that off and said, "My name at the bank is R. V. Modine."

"That's right, shit. Right. A fake name, so they wouldn't know it was you."

"Got connections that are worth something, darling. Now, you're standing behind me in the bank. What's my name?"

"R. V. Modine. You got the fake ID and everything. Now I remember."

He relaxed a bit; she was remembering all right now that he had taken the focus off of goddamn Wanda for a goddamn second. "What's your name?"

"At the bank?"

"And on the plane, and for the rest of your Venezuelan life."

"It's...shit." She screwed her features into a twist. "Edie! It's Edie Modine."

"Halle-fucking-lujah. What next?"

She was getting serious now. "We get the money from the bank, all small bills that your connection changed for you, then drive down—"

"Drive what?"

"Rental car."

"Good. Then?"

"Then we drive down over the border and into Mexico City, and hop the plane to Venezuela to start life as Mr. and Mrs. Richard V. Modine."

Gordon allowed himself to give her a smile at last. Keep her brain off Wanda, and she did just fine. "Then what?"

Her eyes grew wide. "Uh..." she muttered, plainly scouring her brain for what she had forgotten. "Oh shit, I don't remember. I'm sorry."

He laughed and swept her up. "Then we fuck like wild animals for a month."

She gave him a serious look and said, "Oh, that's right." She took him in for a good long kiss, and he felt her fantastic shape. There were good, damn good, reasons for bringing young Ms. Briggs down to Venezuela. Two of them pressed into his chest as they kissed.

When they finished and Gordon finally got to lie down on the bed, Janey said, "You know, I haven't even seen how my ID turned out. Can I see it?"

Gordon chuckled. "These aren't like chop-shop fake licenses you get so you can get into bars, sweetheart. They look just like the real thing."

"Well, can I see mine?"

He paused a minute to string her along, pretending to size up her worthiness. "Oh, I suppose. They're—" He stopped dead. He could feel his face go white.

Janey rushed to him. "Ronny? Are you okay? Are you having a heart attack?"

"I'm fine," he lied. The IDs were in the sack with Morihita's money. The sack with the money was still in the Vacationeer. And the Vacationeer was Christ knew where. "Think I need a drink."

"A drink?" She moved back a bit, trying to read him. "It's almost two in the morning. What's going on?"

"Nothing. Just need a drink. Been under a lot of pressure."

"Hey, what about the IDs? Don't I get to see them?"

"Cool it for a second." Jesus, he was fucked. Without the licenses, he couldn't get the money, couldn't get across the border, couldn't get on the plane. He needed to get on the horn and order two more up, fucking pronto. He'd blown two grand on a stripper and two on Wanda's kidnapper—not that it didn't turn out to be worth it—so he supposed spending another thousand for two more IDs wasn't anything he could complain about. He still had some dough left from selling Chunky Dan the minihome, though spending the Clevelands was a lot more fun.

"Ronny—"

"Where's the closest bar? Just need to clear my head a little."

"My dad was an alcoholic, Gordon. Don't go getting like that. I can't take it."

He gave her a sappy smile. "I'm fine, sweetheart, really. Everything's fine. Just now that we're almost in the clear, need a little liquid courage to see me through. Okay?"

"You probably need sleep more."

"Janey, just...just..." he started, then sighed and rubbed his eyes. "Just...Janey, where's the goddamn bar?"

The Pine Knot Saloon had to have the greatest view of any middle-of-nowhere drinking establishment in the country. Across Highway 151 is a glorious view of Truth or Consequence's Elephant Butte mountains, and there's plenty of parking. Gordon didn't notice the mountains, it being pitch black at two in the morning, but he did see the welcoming sign of the Pine Knot as he rounded the bend. Even though the bar was on one of the main stretches outside T or C, the road that led to it was pretty much completely empty on a Sunday night. The place was isolated, at least until you got to the parking lot full of locals.

It was a big place, like a giant barn, much like ones Gordon had seen in desert retirement areas before, so when he walked in the door no one really noticed him. There was music and activity and that was just fine with him. He didn't need or want to be noticed by anyone. He just wanted to suck down a couple of Scotch-sodas, make a late, *late* call to his bank connection here in town to get a couple more fake licenses, then get on back to the motel room for some sleep before the sun came up.

Atchison, his contact, would *not* be happy to hear from him again. His position at the bank created a lot of opportunity, he had explained to Gordon when they first met to hunt down a late payment five years earlier, but that could also be an opportunity for big trouble, the kind that lands a man behind bars for a good chunk of his life.

It was a lot for a bank man to say an hour after he met someone, but Gordon got people talking. It wasn't too long after Atchison described one or two "special services" he could provide that Gordon started thinking about what life would be like if he were rich. Converting thousand-dollar bills, the currency that got the whole ball of wax started (Gordon had showed Atchison a couple of them, a good conversation piece), into totally untraceable smaller bills was one of these services.

Another was contracting for fake identification. There were a lot of people in the desert southwest who were there because they needed to start over, Atchison had explained. Now, five years later, Gordon needed to start over starting over, with some replacement IDs. Thank God he knew people; he might've been a freaking RV salesman the rest of his life.

But Atchison wouldn't want any more contact with Gordon, now that their business was supposed to be done. It wasn't, though, that was all. There was one more thing Gordon needed. Maybe he shouldn't have needed it, maybe it was stupidity on his part to need it, but he needed it just the same. And Atchison was the man to arrange it for him. Hell, it'd be another grand in his pocket anyway; how could he refuse?

He sucked down the first Scotch, then nodded for another. He was already beginning to relax, because he had a plan again. Janey knew the plan, he knew the plan—plus the one tiny little bit of additional headache he now needed to take care of thanks to leaving the licenses in the RV when the young stud decided to play tough. All was well. He sipped the second drink. No need to rush; he'd need to get a good blush on before making his call.

Truth or Consequences is a small town, and most businesses shutter long before two in the morning. So when Douglas Gann mentioned to the kid putting out the APBs that the LeBaron was probably in T or C—and oh, here's another vehicle to add to the bulletin—it didn't take a whole lot for the police to locate it, parked outside the Pine Knot Saloon on Highway 151. There was no arrest warrant associated with the APB, so the officer simply called it back in to the NMSP, where Sergeant Frick took the report and handed it to Douglas Gann.

"There's your vehicle," Frick said. "Now that's it, right? We're done until a warrant comes through, okay?"

Gann nodded with a sleepy smile. He had been right all along! And soon they would find the Vacationeer—*shit*, he thought. Frick didn't know about that. "Well, not totally done, officer."

"I think we are."

"There's still the RV to find. It could have the body in it."

"The body."

"Of Mitchell's wife."

"Do we have a description of this recreational vehicle?" Frick asked.

Gann started to answer, but the young officer behind Frick who had taken the information from Gann spoke up. "Got it, Sarge. The full description and license number are out there," he said, obviously pleased to be able to help.

Frick turned back to Gann, sucking in his lip. "Goddamnit, that's *it*."

"Listen, sergeant—"

"Cancel that all-points, officer. Okay?" he called behind him.

"Yes, sir. Canceling."

"Now get the hell out of my station, *detective*. If a warrant comes down, *we* will execute it, okay? We don't need your help. You've gotten all you're getting out of us."

"But Mitchell's wife—"

"Do you need an officer to escort you out, detective?"

He didn't. He got his briefcase and padded out the glass door into the night. The NMSP parking lot was well lighted, but beyond that was just desert darkness, no other businesses in sight, nothing. He looked at the report locating the LeBaron. He now knew where Gordon and his accomplice were—drinking it up at a local watering hole. Only he could keep Gordon from getting away with it all. He alone could bring justice to bear.

He cast one last peek over his shoulder at the hulking sergeant glaring at him through the glass, no doubt ready to call in reinforcements if Gann should take a step back toward the station house. He wished Perez had been working a little longer. That was someone who understood what he was trying to do.

Perez. A light went on in Gann's addled brain. He needed an officer to help him bring Gordon in. There was only one officer he could call.

He got in the car, drove a few yards out of Sergeant Frick's line of sight, then dialed local information on his cellular phone. Fifteen seconds later was on the phone with Luis Perez.

"Sergeant Perez? Douglas Gann here."

"I'm dreaming, right?"

Gann let him hear a little chuckle. "We need to make an arrest."

Perez made an odd sound—a groan?—and said, "You found the body."

"No, but we found Gordon Mitchell. Well, his car. His accomplice's car."

"No body?"

"They're working on it," Gann said. A little misrepresentation, but…

"Who they? The New Mexico police?"

"They put an APB out on the RV half an hour ago." This was at least true, although he left out the part about it being canceled. "We have to get a hold of Mitchell."

There was a long pause on the other end. Then Perez said, "Why isn't the officer on duty at the station handling this?"

"I need *your* help. You understand what's going on."

"Detective, I have exactly no freaking idea what's going on."

Gann shrugged that off. People knew more than they realized, oftentimes. "Can you meet me at the Pine Knot Saloon on 151?"

"When?"

"ASAP."

"Oh, Christ almighty," Perez said with a sigh, and Gann started to smile, because he knew that was a yes. He was just minutes away now from finally, finally nailing Gordon Mitchell.

19

Anywhere is romantic when you're with the right person. A garbage dump, emblematic of the wastefulness of Western society, could become a magical place touching and squeezing in a wrecked car; a Wal-Mart, that Grand Central Station of American commercialism, could seem as romantic as Paris when a newlywed couple was shopping for accessories for their new home; and even a Denny's, picked for its easy cash and big breakfasts by two hungry robbers, could glow with sweet expectation when two people were there with eyes only for each other, a plate of pancakes, and the contents of the cash register.

But as they looked over the menu, only Wanda knew they were going to be facing an imminent, severe money shortage and would have the chance to make romance out of an armed robbery.

The waitress, an exhausted-looking, skinny woman who smelled like stale smoke but gave them a nice smile when she spoke, set their beverages down—Wanda had coffee, Spike had hot tea with a sprig of mint—and said, "Ready to order, folks?"

"Hungry," Wanda said, then fixed Spike with a playful look she made sure he saw the waitress saw. "Hope you're loaded tonight."

Spike and the waitress laughed. "I think I'll be all right," Spike said. "Ready?"

"Top sirloin and three eggs," Wanda said. "Double hash browns."

"You *are* hungry! To drink?"

"Large orange juice. Price is no object, right, honey?"

"Uh, right." He wondered why she was making such a point of that. Had the materialistic urge overtaken her, or did she just want her male to make the show of power expected in modern capitalistic society, and cover a big check? "How about the Western Omelet and a small O.J."

"You got it. Need anything else, my name is Rhonda," the waitress said as she whipped the menus out of their hands and zipped back to the service line to clip the lone order to the wheel for the manager to cook.

Wanda leaned forward. "You're sure you have the money for this."

"After all you've been through, I can understand your apprehension, my sweet. But I've got enough for us to get through the night right here—" he said, and fished into his vest pocket for the six hundred he had stuck there earlier.

He kept his eyes on Wanda, but cold panic rushed through his brain, icy fingers seizing his heart. *The money was gone.*

"Are you okay?"

Spike quickly poked into all of the other pockets in his outfit. "Problem," he said at last, shakily. "Oh, a problem."

Wanda sipped her coffee. "What is it?"

He sat there, glassy-eyed, not knowing what to say. Finally he just said, "I can't find the money."

She almost dropped her cup. "Tell me you're kidding."

"I'll check the RV. It probably just fell out of my pocket during…you know." He stood up and darted out through the double glass doors to the parking lot.

But the money wasn't in the RV. It wasn't anywhere he could see. It was gone, daddy, gone, and they were in deep shit. Somehow he didn't think Denny's could break a thousand-dollar bill at two in the morning.

"We've got to cancel the order," he said as he sat back down, ashen-faced. "I'm sorry, dollface, but I don't have any way to pay for this."

"Oh, but I'm so *hungry*."

He turned this over in his mind. "We could skip out on the check."

"That's not very romantic."

Romantic? What was she—? A wave of understanding passed over him, and he said, "You want me to take breakfast by force."

"Just like we talked about, remember?"

"That was *talk*, Wanda. I don't rob establishments, just individuals."

"Denny's is an establishment now?" She looked greatly disappointed.

He couldn't stand her to look like that, but…"Besides, I don't know anything about doing this kind of job—'job' in this usage means criminal act, not like a job job, you know. All I know about robbing a restaurant is what I saw in *Pulp Fiction*."

"Then do that."

"And look, in that movie, it didn't turn out well for the robbers or their victims. It's just too violent for my taste."

"We need the money, Spikey."

"Spikey, huh?" he said with a smile.

She shrugged demurely. "I need a man who's not afraid to get violent."

"I'm not *afraid* to get violent. It's just against my whole philosophy. It's—"

"Sometimes you need violence," Wanda said, her hands stretched across the table clasping Spike's. "You've got to wound people who need to be wounded, show them who's boss. That's what a man does."

"I don't agree. Showing a gun gets as much done as shooting a gun."

"But isn't showing a gun still a kind of violence?"

He supposed it was. "That kind I can live with. The kind where no one gets hurt. Maybe it's threatening, but no actual physical injuries occur."

"It's a small step," Wanda said.

Spike knew what she meant by this, that if he could do one, he could do the other, but to him, "it's a small step" meant that he could fall over to doing the other—hurting someone for money—so easily he'd barely even realize he'd done it until it was all over. "I think I liked it better when I didn't characterize what I do as violent."

Wanda smiled sweetly at him. "You're the expert here."

God, she was a treat. Here he was, a total novice at this particular kind of thing and she was getting him excited at the prospect. But still…"I don't know much about group dynamics during a heist, darling," Spike said, "and I have no idea what to expect as a take from a restaurant holdup. I just don't have enough background. Not to mention the fact that a Denny's doesn't exactly represent the Fat Cat power structure I'm trying to subvert."

"Not true," Wanda had said. "These are *franchises*. Who do you think owns Denny's franchises? Rich people! Your Fat Cats."

"I don't know…it's so indirect."

She leaned over the table and kissed him softly. "If we don't pay this check, the police are gonna come after us anyways."

Spike chewed his fingernail. The woman had a point. The police, protecting the Fat Cats, would never tire of upholding the power structure and trying to crush people like himself and Wanda. If they did it—if *he* did it—he would literally be taking something away from the "franchised," he thought, and smiled at his own cleverness.

"That's a positive expression," Wanda said. She was watching him. She was testing him.

"All right. All right, all right," he murmured. "All right, I'm in."

Wanda just smiled that one-of-a-kind smile at him. "Well, all right."

He could do it. Watching the coming and going of the twenty-four-hour crowd—it was just after two a.m., Monday morning now, and so he and Wanda and one other couple made up the few customers there were—he knew he could do it. *They* could do it. He had a wonderful lover now working with him, a literal partner in crime!

"What are you thinking about?" Wanda asked as she sipped her coffee.

"Just...you and I are going to go places." He took in her face as he spoke. "After we get the money, well, we can do whatever we want, can't we?"

"First things first. We need traveling cash."

He winked at her. "Don't you worry about that. Let's have a nice breakfast, then we'll take care of business, yeah?"

Her beautiful lips, filled in with a gorgeous stop-sign red, pulled up into a half-smile. "You'd do anything for me, wouldn't you?"

"Darn straight. And I can prove it," he said, and grinned as he made his fingers into little six-shooters.

Rhonda interrupted them with a massive round tray full of eggs, bacon, hash browns, pancakes, steak, the works. She quickly placed each plate on the table, along with the check—Spike wondered if they should pay it and then steal their own money back, but then remembered they didn't have anything but the thousand-dollar bills—and was gone.

Spike surveyed their meals. "What did I tell you? This is the new authentic New Mexican cuisine."

"Probably truer than we know," she said, and they laughed as they dug in.

Half an hour later they had eaten their fill, and had drunk all the coffee they were going to drink. There was practically no one in the restaurant except them, the manager, the tired waitress, and one other couple in a far booth. The street outside was almost completely deserted.

It was now-or-never time, but Spike found himself paralyzed in his seat, his hands and feet gone cold, his courage buried under a mountain of pancakes and eggs.

Wanda said, getting excited, "Do you have the gun?"

Spike nodded weakly. "Wanda, I don't know about this..."

She gave him what he thought was a very comforting smile, and stretched her hand across the table again to take his. "Please, honey. It's for us."

He looked at her beautiful face one more time. "Go get the RV started up. We're going to have to get out of here in a hurry."

"I can't watch?"

"It'd be better."

She nodded at this, then gathered her purse and marched quickly through the dining room and out the door.

He steeled himself, gathered up the check, and walked to the register, his legs feeling like lead weights. He didn't believe in institutional crime, teaching no one a lesson except maybe an insurance company, which would learn only not to insure certain types of businesses or maybe just to raise rates, but here he was. Sometimes love meant doing something you didn't necessarily believe in, but your partner did.

Partner, he repeated to himself, and smiled. Like Butch and Sundance. Ma and Pa Barker. Bonnie and Clyde.

Of course, all of them had ended up shot to death, hadn't they?

Wanda pulled the Vacationeer up across six parking spots so he could see her waiting there. They were ready. Spike waited patiently at the counter.

But no one came to the register. He stood where he was sure to be noticed, and cleared his throat a little bit in case they were listening for some sign of a customer wanting to pay.

No one came.

Wasn't there some kind of little bell or something he was supposed to ring? He looked but all he could see was the sharp stick for paid checks, a stapler, nothing that made any kind of noise.

He picked up the stapler and clicked it a few times. Nothing.

"Hello?" he said, not very loudly. He didn't really want the couple in the far booth to take too much notice of him. If he was lucky, he could get out of there with almost no one realizing there had been a robbery.

"Hello?" he said again, louder this time.

No one came. Were they having sex back there? He'd heard about that kind of thing happening with people who were forced to be on their feet all the time.

Just as he finished thinking this, the waitress zipped out of the back, smoothing her apron. "Sorry about that," she said with a shy little smile, still looking tired but with a little more spark than before. Spike kind of hoped she was having fun back there.

"That's—" he said, then sputtered out as he noticed the couple walking up from their booth in the back, no doubt figuring they'd better get their check paid while the help was already up front.

Spike looked out at Wanda in the RV. She gave him a "get on with it" gesture, and she was right—they didn't have the money to pay the check, so they were going to be committing a crime one way or the other.

"Um, can you folks have a seat just for a minute?" Spike said to the couple as they came up behind him at the register.

"For what?" the male half said with bluster. "What are you, the manager?"

"Sorry," Spike said. "Why don't you just go ahead?"

The man eyed him suspiciously, his enormous belly no doubt exceeding the design parameters of his striped polyester shirt. "No, why don't *you* just go ahead?"

The waitress leaned forward and said, "Is everything all right, sir? Is there a problem?"

"I'm really sorry," Spike said, took a deep breath that only made him feel the butterflies in his stomach even more, and pulled out the thirty-eight. "But I've got to have the money in the register, okay? Now, please."

The female customer shrieked and her companion yanked her right out the door. "We don't want no trouble! Just leave us alone!" Belly yelled as they backed out both sets of glass doors. Spike could see through the side window that once they were clear they ran for their car around the building, stopping to write down the license plate number of the Vacationeer, which they had obviously noticed was running with a getaway driver waiting inside.

*Oh, man…*Spike took the gun off the waitress and tucked it back in his belt. "I'm not going to hurt anyone. I just need the money in the register. This is a robbery."

"No kidding," she said, and hit a series of buttons that sent the drawer sliding out. "You seemed like such a nice young guy, too."

"This isn't like me, ma'am." He took the money she held out to him and shoved it in his pocket. "I've never done this before."

"Sweet vehicle you got there for a first-timer."

He glanced out at the Vacationeer. "Oh, that's not mine. That's my girlfriend's."

"Mmm."

The look on her face, one of betrayal by someone she thought was "nice," was sending a dagger of guilt through his heart. But what could he do? He had to take care of the person he loved. Speaking of which…"Where's the manager?"

She jerked her head toward the back and said, "Waiting for me to get back there. He won't be happy he has to get his pants on and call the police."

He made for the door, then stopped and gave her a twenty from his pocket. "That should take care of the bill."

"You're paying your check," she said, holding the twenty in disbelief.

"Keep the change. Have a good night."

Finally, she fixed him with a smile. "I knew you weren't such a bad guy."

He stopped again and gave her another twenty, savoring her reaction. His guilt was beginning to subside; that was worth all the money he had.

He hurried through the first set of doors and was about the hit the second leading outside when he noticed Belly standing outside, his legs spread wide in a shooter's stance. And with good reason—he had a massive pistol, a forty-five automatic by the looks of it, aimed right at Spike, who kept his hands up for wont of anything else to do.

"Hold it right there, fucker!" Belly yelled, almost drooling with glee as he held Spike immobile between the two sets of doors. "You hold it—

the police'll be here any second. They're probably calling them inside right now."

Spike glanced back at the waitress. She wasn't calling anybody—yet.

"Come on outta there, you little chickenshit," Belly yelled at him. "Let's get you down on the ground here."

Spike didn't move, instead just gazed mournfully at Wanda in the still-running RV. Belly seemed to have decided to ignore her. Spike hoped she would just drive away to safety; there was no reason for both of them to go down for this.

"Come on, goddamnit. I'll blow your stinkin' little head off, pal, don't think I won't."

Violence begets violence, Spike thought, and shook his head at what his bad judgment had wrought. One job, and he was through with institutional robbery. It just didn't reach any of the objectives he—

"Out! *Now!*"

Spike moved for the front doors when he heard behind him, "Hold it right there, asshole."

He turned around slowly to face the voice coming from inside the restaurant. It was the manager, his pants back on now, pointing his own gun—what was that, a Magnum?—at Spike's head through the back set of glass doors. If anyone fired, he'd be cut to pieces by the flying glass even if not one bullet touched him.

"Rhonda here called the police, jerk-off," the manager said, but behind him she shook her head slowly.

That was a lesson Spike had learned early on: *Tip big.* You never knew when you'd need a favor from someone in the service industry.

"They should be here any second. Just cool your heels and get back in here," the manager said, and Spike turned to go back into the restaurant proper. Wanda still hadn't moved. He wanted to yell for her to get going, get the hell out of there, but he thought making any sudden moves or loud noises was probably a bad idea right then.

"*Hey, where the fuck are you going?*" Belly screamed outside. "Another step and you're hamburger."

Spike elected to take Belly at his word.

"I want you out here, on the fucking sidewalk, face down, pal. *Move!*"

Hesitantly, Spike moved for the outside door.

"Hey, not another step, fuckface!" the manager yelled, and Spike could see him trying to look around him at the helpful citizen outside. "Got it covered here, sir! Thank you!"

"*What?*" Belly said, his non-trigger hand cupped to his ear. "I got him right in my sights, Jack—let's just get him out here!"

"What the fuck is he saying?" the manager yelled to Spike, who just shrugged. Let them figure it out. No one was supposed to ask the criminal anything, were they? "Put the gun down, sir! I'm handling this!"

"Did he say put the fucking gun down? I'll put this fucking gun down his throat!"

It was amazing what people could and couldn't hear through two sets of glass doors, Spike thought, and eased himself a bit to the side of the entry area to let them read each other's lips a little better.

The manager's eyes bugged, and he turned to Rhonda to say, "Did that asshole say what I think he said?"

Rhonda didn't have much to say on the matter. In fact, she seemed to have sudden pressing business in the back, behind a few bullet-stopping walls.

"Hey, fuck you, buddy! I'm the manager here, all right?"

"Fuck *me?* Fuck *you!*"

Spike crouched down and grabbed a real estate ad magazine to cover his face.

"You want a piece of this? This is a goddamn three-fifty-seven Magnum, fucker!"

"What's this, a water pistol? Huh, asswipe?"

Good, Spike thought. *He got the curse word in.* He tried to become one with the floor, which was sticky and littered with fly carcasses. That secured it for him: He'd never eat at one of these dog-nasty places again.

Just as the two men started choking on their own testosterone and Spike could hear the safeties clicking off, a huge rumble rattled the glass doors.

Wanda!

The Vacationeer's engines revved to the max and he could hear the giant vehicle round the curve leading to the door. Then he heard Belly crying "*Jesus Christ!*" and the screeching of God knew how many sets of brakes.

Spread out on the floor, Spike gambled the manager couldn't see him, blinded as he was anyway with male rage. He kicked the near glass door open with his foot and scrambled out on all fours, getting to his feet just as he rounded the back of the RV and ran into Belly, who didn't seem to have his gun anymore.

"That bitch knocked me down with that thing! She coulda killed me!"

"That *what?*" Spike said, and laid the fat-ass out flat with one punch. Then he ran to the Vacationeer door, his knuckles screaming, and jumped in before the Denny's manager could even get out the doors to see what had happened.

"Way to go, Wanda!" he screamed with joy as he got into the shotgun seat. "I love you!"

"You love me! Now I've got you right where I want you!" she screamed back with a laugh, and peeled out of the parking lot and back onto the highway. In the huge side mirror, Spike could see Belly and the manager, letting bygones be bygones in the great phallic parade, already making their way back inside with all the information the police would need to find the bandits and haul them off to jail. But there was no way Spike would allow that. They would have to be out of the country as soon as they got the money.

"You know what?" Wanda yelled, even though there was no noise she had to yell over. "I love you too!"

Spike whooped and kissed Wanda as she drove onto I-25 back down to Truth or Consequences. They were really in this together now. Partners.

The Albuquerque Police Department responded to the robbery call, getting a full description of the robbers and the recreational vehicle they were reported driving. Rhonda the Denny's waitress kind of hoped the nice guy would get away—there had been only two hundred dollars or so in the register anyway—minus her tip.

The big-bellied customer and his wife, who had been sitting in the car digesting the whole time, and the manager left out any mention of their bravado gunplay.

An APB was put out over the NMSP system and in Albuquerque on the robbers and the Vacationeer, with all the relevant descriptive information. Seconds later, the bulletin came over the wire at the Truth or Consequences post with all the information about the Vacationeer. The young officer read it with disbelief and brought it immediately to his boss, Sergeant Frick.

Frick actually laughed when he read it. "I'll give the son of a bitch an E for effort," he said, and handed it back to the officer. "Make sure Albuquerque knows this has been canceled already, okay?"

"How did he get it on the system again?" the officer asked, bemused.

"That Detective Gann, I admire him—he could sell condoms to a eunuch. He sweet-talked some poor sap at another station into putting this out."

"He really wants his man."

"Well, he's really gonna have to wait for his warrant."

Frick and the young officer shared a chuckle over that, and then they made sure the APB on the Vacationeer was canceled again. The vehicle had been reported used in a robbery, but Frick saw right through that little ploy. Again, it was a nice try by Gann, he thought. Hell, didn't they all want to be Supercop from time to time? They did, and that's exactly why there were rules for this kind of thing. In five hours or so, Gann would probably have his warrant from Indiana—for the RV thefts, not for some missing person—and then they could all go get "his man," but by the rules this time.

After downing shots of Scotch with beer chasers, when it was just ten minutes from closing time, Gordon had drunk up enough balls to call Atchison and get him working on those new licenses. What a fuckup this was—but hey, at least Wanda was out of the picture. He stood up to make his way to the pay phone by the john—

—and found himself looking right into the face of Douglas Gann.

"Motherfucker," Gordon said. "Give me a goddamn heart attack."

"Good to see you too. Got a minute?"

"On my way out. Sorry."

Gann grinned. "No, that's perfect. I'll follow you."

This is it, Gordon thought as he made for the door, slowly, maybe a hundred sixty pounds of Indiana flatfoot trailing right behind him. They must have found Wanda's body, and of course they thought he did it, because Spike was long gone, naturally. "What's this about?" he asked, the only question to ask when you knew exactly what a police visit was about. They stepped outside.

"Where's your wife, Mr. Mitchell?"

"Don't you read your police reports? Run off with some fruitcake biker in the Vacationeer. Sure you noticed I'm driving something a bit more modest."

"I don't read the reports here. I don't have jurisdiction."

Oh? "Then I don't really have to talk to you, do I?" Gordon said, and moved to get to the LeBaron, stopping dead as he saw the State Police squad car pull into the gravel lot.

"No, but you might want to talk to him," Gann said, and swung the cuffs on Gordon. "I am hereby arresting you on the charge of murder in the first degree. Mr. Mitchell, you have the right to remain silent. Anything you say can and will be used—"

"Jesus, what are you doing?" the Hispanic state cop said without even getting out of the car. He just pulled his squad car up to them and stuck his head out the window.

"I'm arresting him, on your authority."

"On *my* authority? Shit, Gann, get the cuffs off him. I didn't know you were arresting anyone. I thought we were trying to find the body."

"*Body?*" Gordon gasped, trying to act shocked. "Whose body?"

"You know whose body, you son of a bitch," Gann said.

"Heard the officer—get these cuffs off me."

Gann roughly uncuffed Gordon but stuck him in the back of his car. "Stay," he said, and climbed into the passenger seat of Perez's prowler.

"Detective, you're gonna get in a hell of a lot of trouble. People lose their badges for shit like this."

"In five hours, I'm going to have a warrant. Everybody wants me to wait, but you know and I know that he'll be long gone by then."

Perez looked at the sad soul sitting in the back of Gann's car. "If he's so hot to leave, then why is he taking his time drinking at the Pine Knot Saloon like he don't have a care in the world?"

"Maybe he's waiting for his accomplice."

"I thought that was the accomplice's car."

Gann mulled this over. Truth was, he had no idea why Gordon was sticking around when he knew half the state's police must be looking for him or his wife's still-warm body.

"If you wanted me to come here so you could arrest him, no offense, but you're shit outta luck, detective. Unless," he said slowly, "you have some kind of witness—not like the hippie kids, but like somebody's who gonna say 'Mr. Mitchell was gonna kill Mrs. Mitchell.' You know, without a body, that's the only way we can do this."

He waited. Gann didn't say anything.

"So, do you have a witness, detective?"

Gann stared at Gordon through the windshields. His hunches had brought him this far—now what? "You mean the wife."

"Yeah, I mean the wife. She make a statement?"

He shook his head. "They're looking for the RV as we speak. Her body's in there, I know it is."

"What about the boyfriend?"

"Who?"

"She ran off with her boyfriend, that's what Mitchell said, right? Well, where's the boyfriend?" Perez said.

"That's a bunch of bull puckey. He killed her and hid the body and the RV. There's no boyfriend, never was."

"Then we got nothing to go on. What, were you gonna hold him for five hours until the warrant came in? Hold him where, in your car? For five hours? He'd be the last son of a bitch you ever arrested, I guarantee you that. His lawyer'd stomp you flat. I'm doing you a *favor*."

Gann shook his head sadly. Perez was right, of course. He had nothing to hold Gordon on, nothing at all. But…"How about one more favor?"

"No," Perez said, then reluctantly added, "What is it?"

Jesus, this was so very, very fucked.

Gann's car had door handles in the back, but when Gordon tried them, the door didn't open. Child-and criminal-proof locks, he guessed.

He could see Gann and the Hispanic cop, Perez, getting into it, with Perez doing a lot of head-shaking and Gann making a lot of gestures toward Gordon in the car. He had no idea what they were saying, whether it was good for his position or not.

Perez had said Gann couldn't arrest him, didn't he? He'd heard that much, and then Gann had taken the cuffs off him. But then he was stuck in the back of this car—hey, this was unlawful confinement! He could sue! Of course, that wouldn't do much to improve his quality of life in prison, which was exactly where he was headed if he had to stick around there much longer.

He'd driven a truck for years and seen the darkness of Midwestern skies at midnight, but this desert night was so damn *black*. Even with the cop's light shining onto the rocky parking lot, the inky night pressed in just out-side of the glowing circle.

Then the Pine Knot shut its lights; closing time. It was like half of the world fell away, and Gordon could feel himself floating in space, between the Earth and the moon, with the cop's spotlight as the sun. He was weightless, and he could go either way, floating forever, free, or falling to Earth, screaming, crashing, burning. What he did now would make the difference.

They weren't going to arrest him, maybe—but then why were they fucking around? Rules, rules, cops were all rules. They couldn't hold him without some kind of paperwork or something, right? *Right*, he told him-self, but he didn't feel much better, especially when Perez stepped out of his squad car and backed Gann up as he walked toward Gordon in the car.

He'd do what they said; that was the only way to get out of this, he knew that. Get Janey, get the goddamn money at nine on the damn dot, then make a run for the border, just like Butch and Sundance. Who got shot to death, he remembered, and shook the thought from his head.

Gann swung the door open.

"Look, I'll cooperate—"

"Zip it, Mitchell," Gann said, obviously puffed up by the uniformed offi-cer within his jurisdiction standing behind him. "You're darn right you'll cooperate. Sergeant Perez and I want to know where your wife is, *now.*"

"Told you, she ran off with—"

"Then why can't we reach her by cellular phone? Why isn't she answering? What did you do with her?"

Gordon sat frozen in the double stares of Gann and Perez. This wasn't anything he could agree to—he didn't know where they were! He could use the cell phone trick his RV positioning software rep told him about, but that took the cops. Then the cops would know where she was…and then he'd really be in the shit.

"You'd better start talking, Mr. Mitchell," Gann said. "In a little less than five hours, a judge in Indiana will be sending down a warrant for your arrest, you know that, don't you? The New Mexico police won't let me arrest you now, but…but *goddamn* if I'm not arresting you the *second* that warrant comes down. And when we find Wanda's body—"

"She was kidnapped."

Gann frowned and looked at Perez, who shook his head noncommittally. "Kidnapped."

"Look, the boyfriend—he kind of hijacked the coach, and took Wanda with him."

"Just like that."

"Just like that. Listen, he said he'd kill her if I brought in the police."

"How convenient," Gann said.

"No, seriously," Gordon said, seeing the small window of opportunity his years of sales experience had trained him to look for every time, "he said if he saw one cop, he'd blow her brains out. The guy's crazy."

"So he's after the RV, or he's after Wanda? He'll kill his *girlfriend*, as you say, if the police approach for the theft of the RV. Does that sound reasonable to you?"

"Don't know. That's what he said."

Gann spit on the ground. "And you, you're so upset, you come to the Pine Knot Saloon and have a couple of drinks. Driving your friend's car. You're beside yourself."

"I reported the coach stolen. It's not illegal to have a drink while your wife's screwing around, is it?"

Gann looked at Perez again, no doubt looking for some sign he could arrest Gordon now, but Perez shook his head again. *No chance.*

Undaunted, Gann crouched down to Gordon's level in the car and leaned in. "You think you're the cleverest son of a gun in the world, but you've just been lucky, and luck runs out, mister. I'm going to find you before you can skip the country, don't doubt it. Roadblocks looking for a Gordon Mitchell and companion. I'm going to arrest you for stealing the RVs from Major Dale's, and if I haven't heard from Wanda by then, heard her voice telling me everything's all right, then you're going down for murder, too."

Gann was grinning that cop grin right in Gordon's face when Sergeant Perez gave him one light tap on the shoulder for him to come up and talk.

He said it quietly, but Gordon could hear the question: "What if the judge don't get the warrant down first thing? Could be the middle of the day by the time we get it."

Even from behind Gann, Gordon could feel the detective's face freeze. A complication he hadn't thought of! Well, he couldn't very well throw up a roadblock for someone who wasn't even officially wanted, could he?

When Gann turned back around and bent into the car, not crouching this time but coming at Gordon from above, Gordon wanted so badly to give the little asshole a shit-eating grin, but thought the better of it. "Really want to cooperate in any way possible, *sir*," he said, twisting the last word a little. Couldn't help it.

"Oh, I'm sure. And you know what? I'm going to give you just that opportunity."

"You—you are? Good. Great." He was suddenly really glad he'd kept his triumphant grin to himself.

"Well," Gann said, warming to his task, "I think you killed your wife, or you were going to kill her, anyway. See, I've got a sixth sense about this stuff."

"Really."

"Yes, really. Literally. I've developed my extra-sensory perceptive abilities to the point where I can know just what certain elements—for instance, criminal elements such as yourself—are planning to do, sometimes before they do."

"I'm sure that's admissible in court."

Gann waved it off. "That hardly matters, once I know where to aim my sights. And I aimed my sights at you once I talked to your lovely wife. One ticket to Venezuela? Smooth move, Gordon."

"Don't know what you're talking about."

"No, sure, of course not," he said, and winked—*winked!*—at him. "But listen, I know what's going on in that head of yours, and I know what you did to Wanda. Something weird happened, I can feel it, and maybe she's not where I thought she'd be. But you're going down, because I'm going to find her eventually, and when I do…"

Enough, Gordon thought, and said, "And I can help you how?"

"Oh, well, you're innocent, right?" Gann said with a smirk.

"Get on with it."

"Well, since you're innocent, and since Sergeant Perez here has pointed out that we might not get a roadblock for the RV thefts in time to keep you from leaving the country, then all I need is the second part of what I was talking about."

"Which is?"

Gann gave him a look of mock surprise. "Your *wife*, Mr. Mitchell! I need to hear Wanda's voice by, say, eight o'clock, or the roadblocks are going up, I promise you. And they'll go up a lot faster for murder than they would for embezzlement, I promise you that, too."

Gordon stared at him. "Don't know where she is."

"Then you'd better find out."

"How'm I supposed to do that?"

"I don't know," Gann said, standing up again, "and actually, I don't care. I want to take you down anyway. Now get out of my car."

Gordon unfolded himself from the back seat and faced Gann and Perez. The New Mexico officer looked less sure of this than Gann did, but Gordon recognized a fellow silver-tongued devil when he saw one. That silver tongue was probably the reason Perez was there in the first place.

"See you in about four and a half hours, Gordon," Gann said, and walked around to get in his car.

"Hey, what's your number?"

"I don't think you'll need it," Gann said with a smile, and started up his car and drove off.

Gordon stood there, in the dark of the gravel parking lot, watching the last stragglers come out of the Pine Knot and stagger to their cars. Perez was still there, too.

"What the hell's going on, officer? Come on, this isn't right, what's happening here."

Perez's face was hard to see in the dark, so Gordon couldn't read what he might be thinking. "You got a way to find the vehicle, don't you?"

"What do you mean?"

"That thing's got every gadget you can get, don't it?"

"Not sure what you're getting at."

"Hey, I'm trying to help you here," Perez said. "You wanna bullshit me, I'll be on my way."

"Okay, yeah, got everything, loaded."

"Cellular phone?"

Gordon nodded, knowing exactly what he was getting at, of course.

"There's that special way to track it, if the phone's got the right hardware, right? I know what these things have—hell, ninety percent of the people in this town live in mobile homes and RVs. That's probably why you're here in the first place, huh?"

He nodded again; the cop may have gotten sucked in by Gann's vision of a perfect police state, but he was no dummy. The Vacationeer cell phone had the right hardware.

"Why didn't the police track it when I said it was stolen?"

"The positioning stuff, there's a couple different ways to do it, right? You can use a separate transmitter that works off the cellular antenna, if the vehicle has one, and yours does, I'm sure. Or you can use the company tracking system, the one that they said is malfunctioning. Or there's the third way, just using your cell phone. As long as a cell phone is on, it can be tracked."

"But the police didn't ask about that one."

"The cell phone thing—you know this—it's private. We don't do it unless we get asked. You have to give us the code. Come on, don't bullshit me, just don't."

"Look, I didn't kill her."

"Fine, then find her and get her on the horn to us. We'll get it to Detective Gann—he's at some motel around here."

Gordon didn't know what to say. Finally he just said, "Thanks."

"No problem," Perez said as he lowered himself into his prowler again. "Oh, and if Detective Gann is right, and you did do it?"

"Yeah?"

"Then fuck you."

With that, Perez drove off, leaving Gordon in the darkness of the empty lot. It was a minute before it hit Gordon that Perez had left out a fourth way to find the coach, one available only to the rich, only to those who could afford Vacationeer's fantastic twenty-four-hour service. One that didn't take the cops.

It wasn't much of a ray of hope, but when it's that dark, anything looks bright.

Driving the long, long five-minute drive back to the motel, Gordon felt like his heart was going to simply refuse to keep beating. Shards of pain, driven by the fact that he was finding it hard to catch his breath, radiated out from his chest down his arms and back and up into his neck. He was worried enough about Gann and his mission, sure; but what had him aching and praying he really would have a heart attack was the realization in the parking lot that he would now have to go back to the motel room and face Janey.

Uh, Janey, sweetness, love, got some bad news. Wanda needs me.

He could almost feel the slap.

Janey, hey, I feel much better now, thanks for giving me some time to clear my head. Oh, and we have to go rescue Wanda.

His balls hurt just thinking about the kick.

There was no good way to broach the subject, he knew. But he had to call Vacationeer's twenty-four-hour line and find the coach. And he would have to tell Janey they needed to spend the next couple of hours saving Wanda from…from…

From what, exactly? He didn't know. From her new boyfriend? Oh, that would go over well. His balls were really starting to ache at the thought of Janey's reaction.

Wait, wait—forget about saving *Wanda*. Janey wouldn't want to hear one word about that; Janey'd light herself on fire if she thought it would give Wanda blisters. Gordon would have to couch in talking about saving *himself*. And Janey! Yes! They'd have to find the old buzzard so they could get away scot-free!

He swung the LeBaron around on the narrow road and headed back toward the Motel 66. That ache was fading fast.

"Gimme my keys."

Gordon's hand instinctively fell to cover his pocket. "Need to calmly sit down and work this out—"

"You son of a bitch! You want me to be calm? A year of my life I've given to you!" Janey cried, still standing with her hands clenched. "And now you want Wanda one last time. I can't freakin' believe it!"

"You know it's not like that. The police want to see she's alive."

"Fuck them! You wanna work with the police now? Gimme my keys— I'm getting outta here."

"Think it's getting too emotional here, sweetheart. Just take it easy and let me tell you what we're gonna do."

Her lips pursed into a tiny pink circle. Gordon gathered he had not used the right choice of words.

"All we got to do is find her and her boyfriend, just get her to make a call to this crazy detective, say she's all right, then we're home free," Gordon said. "There won't be any roadblock or people looking for us, none of that."

"Looking for you."

"Not a team anymore? What happened to you and me against the world?"

"You invited Wanda," she said, spitting out the name.

"Fuck I did. Listen—we get her on that phone to Detective Gann, then shit, you can shoot her yourself if you want to. Our job's done."

"Shoot her? There's gonna be shooting now?"

"Her little boyfriend's got a gun."

"The boyfriend's gonna shoot her?"

"It'll look like that, won't it?" he said, and gave her a million-dollar smile. "And you, darling dear of mine, can pull the trigger yourself if you want. Let Wanda know how much you really think of her."

"Holy shit!" Janey screamed, loud enough certainly to bring the motel management, but that was fine with Gordon; they were checking out early anyway. She leaped up on the bed and Gordon tackled her. "She's gonna die! She's gonna die!"

"Let's don't advertise too much, sweetheart, okay?"

"Sorry," she said with a giggle, pantomiming locking her lips and tossing away the key.

If only, Gordon thought, and smiled to himself.

Janey's little face scrunched up at an apparent thought. "But Ronny— what about the boyfriend? Won't he say something like, 'I didn't do it'? 'The husband, the ex-husband, did it?' Or 'the new wife did it'?"

"Who's gonna believe him? He's a multiple felon."

"We should just skip it. Let's just get out of here, please?"

"Babe, gotta get the money at nine, remember? Even if we just get the bitch to talk on the phone, that buys us the time we need, get it?"

"I want her to die," Janey said, unnecessarily.

"And I want to kill her. But first we gotta find her, right? Then we gotta track her down. Then we gotta see if she'll listen to reason."

"Reason? She don't seem the most reasonable to me. We should keep as far away from her as humanly possible."

"She could find us," Gordon said.

"Then we should kill her."

Gordon laughed. "Shit, woman, what do you want to do? Said five different things in five minutes here."

"Kill her, let her live poor and miserable, which is better?"

"'Bout equal, I suppose."

"Then do them both!" Janey said, collapsing into his arms with laughter.

This was a little unnerving, but better than giving her the keys back and getting his balls kicked in. And God, she felt good against him…

"Hey, got a minute?" he said, reaching down to grab a handful of firm ass.

"Shit, I got all night," she said, and grabbed him right back.

Gordon knew they really didn't have much time, but a good screw would hopefully keep her mind—hell, his too—off of the fact that they were jumping back in the lion pit now to face the biggest hellcat of them all. When they were done, they scooped up their clothes and their stuff and pulled out of the Motel 66 with a little less than four hours to go before they'd be out of time and out of luck.

24

Wanda could not stop smiling. She beamed at her new lover, manly and strong in the shotgun seat, counting the money he'd just brought in for her. With him, she could do anything—he'd do anything for her, and now he'd proved it. Sure, it put some money in his pocket, but he'd done it just for her, a reason Gordon never would have dreamed of considering. This kid, this young boy practically, had risked his life, ready to kill for her, his gun full of bullets he'd be willing to unload into anybody who got in his way.

For her.

She realized, of course, that Spike had gotten pinned between two guys wanting to blow his head off and she'd had to basically run one of them over with the coach, but that was hardly the point. She had a man on her side who would draw his gun, stand up for her, not weasel out and buy single plane tickets because he wanted a divorce and was too chickenshit to ask for it.

Except Gordon hadn't really wanted a divorce, had he? He'd wanted her dead. It took Spike, gun in hand, to save her. Spike and his gun—they had saved her life, they had proved themselves worthy of her at the Denny's, and now they were going to help her teach Gordon Mitchell a lesson he'd never forget.

Now where was that call from Detective Gann? Didn't he ever go back to his motel room? All he had to do was pick up the phone and he could hear all about her rotten husband and his attempt to kill her. Then, with Spike's help, she could clean out his "R. V. Modine" safety deposit box, money he'd be looking forward to as his just reward after spending what, five, ten years in prison, the son of a bitch would come out and think he was starting his life all over, come down to New Mexico again, thinking there was all that cash just sitting in nice bricks after getting his attorney to make sure the box was paid for each month, the money waiting for him as a reward for hanging in there, being a model prisoner in some country club institution, maybe regretting that things didn't work out but knowing that he'd be a rich man, spend his retirement years rich and fat and happy with some little chippie sucking his dick and all he had to do was wait it out, he would win, he would *win*, goddamnit, and there was no way on God's green Earth that she was going to let him win.

She smiled. All she needed was one phone call from Detective Gann. She had a good, strong man and she'd have the million and a half in cash. But better than that, she'd fuck Gordon over and he'd sure as shit know who'd fucked him. He laughed at her for twenty-five years, and now, now it was her turn.

She glanced at the cell phone sitting silent in the custom holder between the front seats. *Come on, damn it, ring.* There was a *reason* she left a message!

She looked at Spike, who was just as silent, staring at the barely pinkening eastern sky, and reached over to brush her hand over his thigh.

"*Wha!*" he yelled, jumping and twisting in his seat. His eyes were wide and watery in the dim light of the coach.

"Jesus, are you okay?" Wanda said, trying not to make the concern sound too motherly. "You look like you're about to cry."

He shook his head, but to no effect; the boy looked *scared*.

"We'll be over the border by lunchtime. They're not gonna find us, if that's what you're worried about."

"They're not, huh?"

She shifted in the seat, checking the mirror for any headlights following them that might…lessen the effectiveness of her argument, to say the least. "We're twenty miles from Truth or Consequences again, driving south at what, sixty miles an hour? That brings us into town how soon?"

"Twenty minutes. Mile a minute."

"Well, as soon as we get into town we pull this thing into an empty residential lot and pull the plates. Do you know how much of this town is made up of RVs?"

He shook his head again, looking like he was ready to be comforted now.

"All of it. I don't know if I've seen two wood-frame houses here."

He sat up straight, the wheels turning. "God, you're right. Was that part of the plan all along? Is that why you and Ron picked this place, 'cause you'd fit in with this thing?"

"No, Gordon picked it because there's a crooked banker in town."

A look of understanding washed over Spike's face. He said, "Someone who could launder the big bills. Sierra Savings and Loan. It's where he told me to go with the…"

She looked at him. "The what?"

"With the, uh, money. The thousand-dollar bills." He was back to looking sickly scared again. "He gave me two of them to come into the RV and tell you he was a swell guy."

Her lips were pursed so tight they were turning blue.

"I—look. I was going to rob you guys anyway—that's why I was by the side of the road in the first place! He gave me money instead, that's all. Once I saw you…" he said, but didn't finish. He didn't have to.

"Once you saw me, you realized what a dirty thing that was to do to somebody."

"Well, yes. Not right away, but—"

"And that Gordon was a fucking manipulative bastard."

"Definitely."

"And that every day, when they bang on the bars of his tiny cell to wake him up for another full day of getting fucked up the ass, he's gonna regret he ever did this to me. That's gonna be *my* dirty little present for *him!* Twenty-five years…maybe now *he'll* waste twenty-five years…"

Spike was quiet for a few seconds, then said, "I didn't realize."

"No one did," she said. But that wasn't true, was it? One person realized, one person who tried to stop her before all of this started, but she hadn't listened because she had believed, she had believed her husband, that bastard, and she had wanted the money and the time with him that it would bring.

But Douglas Gann knew better. He had *realized*. And now he had come to New Mexico to finish what he had started; all it would take would be one phone call.

She was tired of waiting for him to call back. She picked up the cell phone and dialed the motel.

25

Gann was lying on his face, wearing only boxer shorts and a T-shirt, trying to fall asleep, taking a break on orders from Sergeant Frick, who hadn't been amused when Gann came back to the station looking for news. He knew he looked like shit, probably didn't smell too great either, and was completely and totally beat, not to mention despondent. His threat to Gordon—what did that amount to? What could Gordon do? If Gordon really had killed her, he wouldn't go and find the RV or the body for the police, and since no one around there really took what Gann said seriously enough to put the heat on Gordon, there wouldn't be any real pressure for him to find the body, would there?

And if Gann had been wrong, if Gordon actually hadn't killed her and she had been kidnapped, how was Gordon supposed to find her? The New Mexico police could have found the RV in an hour—if it was on the road, not somewhere hidden with a dead body in it, of course—but they'd canceled his APB. There was nothing, nothing. Gordon could be slipping over the border right then and there was nothing anyone would do about it.

He was trying to sleep, honestly.

But the thought kept creeping into his head, the question Perez had asked: If what Gordon had to do was done, then why the heck was he sticking around, sucking down drinks at a bar an hour from the border instead of hightailing it out of there?

Gann flipped onto his back and stared at the ceiling. It would probably help him sleep if he turned the light out, he thought, or maybe if he took off his shoes. But he wanted to be ready if the NMSP needed him.

So why, why was Gordon still there? There were two reasons Gann could think of that would keep a man who was just hours away from being arrested remaining in the States when he could just jump over the border like a kid playing hopscotch. The first was that he had failed to get the money he had undoubtedly stashed in some local bank, maybe more than one, under an assumed name with fake IDs and all the trimmings.

But that was insane. No one waited until the last minute to get their money, and not from a place so near the border, where they could be thwarted from getting it. No, much more likely was that Gordon had stashed the million or so in a bank in Oklahoma or thereabouts, probably not far from where they had stopped for the night. There would have to be a spectacularly compelling reason for Gordon to stick the money in southern New Mexico, and Gann couldn't think of one, no matter how much he tried to get into the criminal mindset.

The second reason why a soon-to-be-wanted man would hang around a state crawling with cops looking for him—okay, *one* cop actually looking for him but the rest ready to do so at the drop of a warrant—was the need to get rid of anything that might reveal his getaway plans, might tell the authorities where he was going to spend the rest of his wealthy days. This kind of knowledge was inconvenient to have around, since even countries that didn't extradite could make exceptions under enough pressure. And there was only one person who knew where Gordon was headed.

Gann sat up, his heart racing.

Wanda! She was still alive!

Still alive, somewhere near.

And Gordon knew it.

Now Gann's mind started churning as fast as his heart. If Gordon had failed to kill Wanda—if Wanda really was kidnapped, or had just gotten away, if she was still alive—then Gordon was trying to find her.

And kill her. He was still going to kill her.

He slapped his hand against his forehead. And he'd just let Gordon go!

It took a few seconds to realize that it wasn't as bad as that—that it was, in fact, much, much worse. He hadn't just let Gordon go; he'd let him go *and told him to find his wife.*

He slapped his forehead again.

Ordered him to find her.

Whap! Slapped it again.

Then *let him go.*

Whap! Again.

This was the end. If Gordon hadn't already killed Wanda, who he figured now must have known a few things about the thefts but kept them quiet for fear of her husband—immunity, this case had immunity for the testifying wife written all over it—then he was definitely going to find her and kill her now, after he put a gun to her head and told her to call Gann and tell him everything was peachy.

Whap!

Dead tired and now woozy from the beating he was giving himself, Gann still knew the NMSP and Sergeant Frick and the rest of them would laugh at him for being such an idiot if he called and asked for help again. *Wait for the warrant,* they'd say. *We canceled your APB, and we're not putting out another.*

But he had to try. If they could find her alive after all, they could get her into protective custody and get her statement, keep her alive until they could get the almighty warrant and get Gordon Mitchell off the street.

There were two ways to do it—get Gordon behind bars or get Wanda in custody to protect her from her husband. And since they wouldn't allow him to arrest Gordon…

As he made his decision, three things happened exactly simultaneously: He reached for the nightstand phone, he noticed for the first time that the message light was blinking, and the phone screamed out its shrill ring, making him jump and nearly knock himself off the bed.

He picked up the receiver. "Gann here."

"Detective Gann, it's Wanda Mitchell." It sounded like she was crying.

"Wanda—how did you know I was here? I fell asleep, didn't I? This is a dream."

"I need help, please, I need help," she said in a whimper. "I called you in Elkhart. They told me you were here, on vacation."

"Wanda, I came to help you. That's why I'm here. This is no vacation for me, do you understand?"

She was silent for a moment, then said, softly, "I'm scared."

"Is it Gordon?"

"Oh, God…" she said through a sob.

Gann pumped his fist in the air. *Yes!* "Tell me," he said.

She told him.

Most of the people who bought recreational vehicles from Major Dale's RV World were done with the productive times of their lives, and they were ready to rid themselves of some of that hard-saved cash, spend it on something huge, something that would let the world know that they had arrived and could afford every single bell and whistle.

Airstream trailers, hell—they were nice for retired truck drivers and their chatterbox wives, but the real rich, the chairmen emeriti of the world and their society wives, they got themselves behind several hundred thousand dollars of Vacationeer or Mirage or some other massive Rambling Industries product and hit the road with enough food in tow for weeks of hard traveling, taking the interstates with the windows rolled up and the air conditioning set on high. *Ain't that America,* Gordon thought, and thanked his lucky stars for it, because all of those money-dripping, bronze-tanned, slicked-back oldsters wanted to know everything that was available for their new prized possession, every gadget that would help keep them from getting lost, getting stuck, or getting ticketed. Gordon, being on salary plus commission, was always more than happy to help, of course, and that's how he learned about the secondary global positioning system that a wealthy traveler could call on when the primary system went down—not that that would happen, Gordon would assure his customer, but don't you want to take every precaution, what with the interstate signage system in such disarray these days?

Naturally, they did, and Gordon sold the service—developed by and still proprietary to Rambling—to just about every moneybags that drove off the lot.

And he had, just in case it was needed, added the service to his Truth or Consequences customer's order for the drive down. Just in case, and here he was, on Janey's cell phone in the middle of the desert in the middle of the night.

Major Dale's customers liked *full* service, Gordon thought, and smiled as he listened to the ringing on the other end.

When the automated system picked up the line, Gordon blazed through the computerized menus as he had done so many times when hapless wayfarers would call him at the office, clueless and more than a little desperate.

He had the VIN, he had the social security number and access code, and within two minutes he had his location in latitude and longitude down to a hundred yards.

Well, not *his* location. The RV's. *Wanda's.*

And their heading—direction and speed.

He shut off the phone and said to Janey, "Bingo."

"You found it." She didn't sound overly thrilled.

"Bingo again."

"How do we know the police aren't using the system, too? Can't they access it just like you? They're the *police.*"

"Don't have a warrant." That much was obvious from Detective Gann's little ploy. "They got nothing on me but his suspicion, and since New Mexico is a bit outside his jurisdiction, that ain't worth squat. They don't have a warrant, they can't do nothin' with the tracking systems I don't personally request."

She mulled this over. "What about when they get a warrant?"

"Be long gone by then."

"Then…then why do we have to go see Wanda?"

Come on… "Janey, we're not going to see her—we got to get her on the phone with Gann, show she's alive—the only way we're not gonna have a roadblock on our ass at the border is if we can show we didn't kill anybody."

"*You* didn't kill anybody, you mean."

"What I mean, all right."

"Fine," she said, and sat back in the seat in a huff as Gordon looked for a good place to pull off the road, but then added, "Funny all this happens as soon as your wife finds another man."

He took a deep breath. "Funny *what* happens?"

"You suddenly develop this great need to rescue her. Make sure she's alive. You've got to do this as soon as she runs off with another man. Quite a coincidence."

"Been kidnapped, darlin'. Little different."

"Still."

"Still what?"

"Still, you best just do what you need to do when you find her, and get her bitch ass talking on the phone, and then get the hell back out here to me," she said. "I don't find this all that amusing."

Gordon started to say something, a lot actually, but instead just stuck it in his hat and pulled the LeBaron over. He whipped out Janey's map, checking it against the coordinates he got over the phone. "Best map you got?"

"What am I, Triple-A?"

That wasn't even worth a nasty glance. "Looks like they're on twenty-five, going south."

"Towards T or C," Janey said, not looking at him either.

"Near there, yeah. We can get down to them, half an hour at the most."

"Towards the money."

Now he looked at her. "Money *happens* to be in T or C, Janey. Sure they're just finding a good place to..." *To what?* His brain struggled to find the words, but there were none.

"To get the money!" she yelled. "Jesus Christ, Gordon, didn't you say this guy was a robber? An *armed* robber?"

He shook it off. "Wanda's not gonna tell him where the money is," he said, and then froze dead still in his seat.

She didn't have to tell him where the money was.

Because Gordon already had.

Sierra Savings and Loan, that's where he told the kid to cash in the Clevelands. It wouldn't take much for Spike to figure there was more there, especially if he found the seventy-six thousand in the bag with the fake IDs.

"Fuck me," he said slowly to himself.

"I'm right, aren't I?" Janey leaned over, around the map and into Gordon's face. "They're going after the money. That guy and that fucking bitch *wife* of yours."

"Might be right."

"And now you want to go find her, rescue her from her boyfriend."

He took a pen out of his pocket and made an X on the map where the coach was. "Gonna find her," he said as he folded the map back up and gunned the LeBaron back onto the interstate. "And then I'm gonna kill her *and* her little boyfriend."

"Then who can you blame it on?"

"Don't worry about blame, darlin'—time the cops get around to blame, we'll be sunning it in Venezuela."

Janey planted a kiss on his cheek and said, "That's what I like to hear."

He bet it was. She wouldn't have liked to hear that he was going to have her come up into the coach, take an actual look-see at Wanda's body—no way she could resist that—then shove the gun in her mouth and make it a nice jealous murder-suicide. Then all his problems would be solved.

Should've done this solo from the beginning, he thought. He hadn't really needed Wanda, except as insurance that maybe Dale wouldn't act as quickly suspecting his niece was involved. And while he had needed Janey, would've been in a real jam without her and her car—and he would've hated to miss out on that body of hers—she was quickly becoming Wanda Jr., and that was about the last thing he needed.

So the Vacationeer was on I-25, same road they were on, and just minutes away from them. He had a surprise for the young kidnapper and his quarry, not to mention for Gordon's emotionally needy goddamn partner in crime there. *Bang,* Wanda's dead. *Bang,* Spike's dead. *Janey, come on in and survey the damage—in fact, why don't you put a bullet in Wanda yourself?* Get the evidence on her fingers that she fired the gun. Then *bang,* she's dead, too. Then no one knows where the money is, no one knows where he is, all the loose ends are neatly tied up, and he is gone baby gone, a future of warm beaches and warmer women who can accept and forgive the goddamn fact that he was married once, for the love of Christ.

And oh, yeah, he gets his R. V. Modine license back. And the seventy-six thousand he left behind when that moron forced him off the bus.

At last, the perfect plan had presented itself again. Everything was falling into place. He hit the gas.

Gann used every second of investigative training he had ever received and every ounce of extrasensory ability he had ever developed as he listened to Wanda describe the trip out across Illinois, Missouri, Oklahoma, Texas, talking with Gordon about the future—she admitted he said he had a lot of money saved up but she swore she didn't know he was doing anything illegal—and finishing with Gordon ready to push her off Coyote Jump. He believed every word she had to say.

So he'd been right all along—not only was her stinking husband going to do away with her, but he was going to do it exactly where Gann had said he would. He gave himself a little mental pat on the back. "But," he said, "how'd you get away?"

On the other end, Wanda started to cry.

He had to take this more slowly. "Listen, where are you now? Are you all right?"

"My husband," she choked, "tried to *kill* me."

He nodded to himself, then realized he should be tape-recording this. *No matter—she'll be coming in anyway.* "I know, I heard you before, I'm listening. Now, Wanda, where are you right now?"

"I…I'm not sure. New Mexico somewhere."

"In the RV?"

There was a moment of silence on the other end of the line, almost as if she was unsure of what to say. Finally she said, "Yes."

"Is there a problem with being in the RV, Wanda?" He could pick up on these things.

"That's it, that's right. Afraid of being in the RV. Gordon might get me. You've got to stop Gordon! Arrest him—he tried to kill me!"

"I'll do that, all right, but first I'm going to bring you in to safety."

"What?" she cried. "*No!*"

Gann hesitated a moment, then said, "It's only for a day. It's not jail or anything—we'll put you up in a nice motel, just 'til we bring your husband in."

"No, *no!* Arrest *him,* not *me!*" Wanda was upset, he could hear it. But upset about what? This was for her own protection!

"Wanda, I need to talk to you, get your statement, find out what your husband is up to. I need to bring you in to safety!"

"I—I shouldn't have called. It's just—Gordon—you've got to arrest him!"

Gann had a lot of experience dealing with hysterical people, and this was no exception. The important thing was to understand what was *really* bothering them, not just what they said. In this case, Gann saw, it was easy. She was afraid for her life, afraid her monster of a husband was really going to get her, even if she was safely ensconced in a Truth or Consequences motel room guarded by state law enforcement officers. Of course, nothing could be further from the truth—she would be completely safe there. No one could get in or out, and no one could possibly hurt her there. He'd have her back to her old, comfortable life as soon as possible. If necessary, he would put her on a plane back to Indiana himself, escort and protect her every step of the way.

But first, he'd have to bring her in to safety.

So he changed tacks. "I need a statement from you to issue a warrant for Gordon's arrest, Wanda. If you really want him out of your life, I need a statement."

"I'm giving you my statement: Gordon Mitchell is trying to kill Wanda Mitchell. Okay?"

"In person, ma'am." A bluff, but if it worked...

He could hear her hand covering the mouthpiece and a muffled curse. *Boy, was she scared!* He had never encountered anyone so opposed to coming for police protection. He didn't know what Gordon Mitchell did to his poor wife behind closed doors, but he had her as scared as a jackrabbit in traffic.

"Wanda? I need you in the flesh."

Waiting for her answer, Gann rubbed his tired eyes for a long, long minute. Finally, she said, "I'll meet you. In Truth or Consequences."

"Gordon's not going to get to you if you're in custody, Wanda."

"You want a statement? I'll meet you. No cops."

No cops? What was this, a Cagney movie? "Where?" he said.

"Outside of town. No people."

"How about the Pine Knot Saloon on Highway 151? I, um, passed it driving around today. It looked pretty remote." Just reel her in, nice and easy...

"Fine," she said. "Just the two of us. Nobody else. Early."

"How about now?"

"No! Not now. I—I need some time."

"How about seven? Seven in the morning. That's a few hours."

"Good," Wanda said. "There shouldn't be anyone around a bar at seven a.m."

She was talking like a fugitive herself. Hadn't she ever heard of protective custody? It wasn't like *custody* custody. She was acting so strange. There was no reason for it, unless...

She wasn't alone.

His fingers gripped the receiver hard. "Listen carefully, Wanda, and just talk normally. Is someone there in the coach with you?"

She made a little strangled gurgle, startled-sounding.

"Is there?" he asked, his pulse pounding.

"Seven a.m. Meet me at seven, detective, okay? Seven at the Pine Knot, you said."

"Wanda—" he called, but the connection was lost.

Gordon found her, Gann thought as he raced to throw his clothes on and get to his car to rush out to wherever she was, *he found her and he's going to kill her!*

There was no way he was waiting until seven—three hours!—to bring in his charge. He was sorry to have to set her up in the first place, but he would slap cuffs on her if he had to in order to bring her to safety. He *would* save her. He knew best.

That was, if she even lived until then. *Oh, to have her so close, just to lose her now!*

But how did Gordon find her so fast? He couldn't have, could he? Found her and gotten on the RV? It didn't seem possible, unless—

Holy shit.

She *had* been kidnapped.

Gordon had been telling the truth, or at least his version of it. Because it was fairly obvious now that Gordon and the mysterious "kidnapper" were working together. Wanda was frightened because she had been hijacked along with the RV, but she had thought there was nothing she could do.

And now Gordon would find her, get her to call, and finish her off, blaming it on the "kidnapper."

Very clever, Gann thought, *but not clever enough by half.* Did Gordon Mitchell think he was the first person in the world to dream up such a scheme? He'd seen all of this before, in training material and the like. And what did they say in that training material? *Stay with your original suspect.*

Let him lead you to where you need to go.

He'd been so intensely focused on Wanda that he had forgotten completely about the old scam, forgotten about it until it was almost too late. You send the original suspect out to nab the "real bad guy," someone supposedly worse than him, and then the victim ends up dead—hey, along with the *real* bad guy, who maybe the original suspect himself has to take out in "self-defense." Then disappears.

Not this time. He had to go out into his car to hunt for Janey's cell phone number in his briefcase—Gordon had accomplices on him like fleas—but when he found it and dialed the number, he knew he was seconds from getting a bead on Gordon, and then on Wanda. He'd get Gordon, and if he failed at that, there was always the Pine Knot Saloon at seven as a last resort, take Wanda into custody and *then* get Gordon Mitchell and his bevy of accomplices.

He dialed Janey Briggs' number. The line was busy.

He cut the connection and hit redial. Still busy.

He cut the connection and redialed.

Again.

Again.

Again. If Gordon thought Douglas Gann was going to let this go, the man was sadly mistaken.

He cut the connection and redialed again. Busy.

Gann wondered who in the heck Gordon could be talking to at almost five in the morning. Whoever it was, when Gann got Gordon behind bars and yanked the phone records again, the person on the other end of the line was going to deeply regret ever having met Gordon's acquaintance, he'd make darn sure of that.

28

Wanda said into the phone, "Seven a.m. Meet me at seven, detective, okay? Seven at the Pine Knot, you said."

"Wanda—"

She hit the disconnect button. Spike was staring at her. "Problem?" she said.

"I'd say so, Wanda dear, if you're inviting the police to join us. We *are* wanted for a violent crime, you'll remember."

"What, violent? Nobody was hurt. Besides, Detective Gann doesn't even know about that. He's just here to help me get away from Gordon."

Spike didn't seem convinced. "Sounded like he wanted to arrest *you*."

"Protective custody. It's not happening."

"If he wants—" Spike started to say, but the phone's ring cut him off. Wanda just looked at it and said, "Probably Gann again."

"This just isn't a good idea. We should just avoid contact—"

At that, she picked up the phone and answered. "Detective?"

"Wanda, listen," the voice on the other end said, and she could tell the person was on a cellular phone. In a moving car.

The voice on the other end was Gordon.

Instinctively, she started scanning the road for cars that could be containing her husband. "This is a surprise," Wanda said. "Where are you?"

"Who is it?" Spike whispered, but she ignored him.

"Don't worry about that. Answering the phone yourself? Gotta be a good sign," Gordon said. "Spike decide to spare your life?"

"If he did, he'd be one up on you, wouldn't he?" Wanda said. "Where are you, Gordon?"

She could see Spike hitting the roof out of the corner of her eye.

"'Bout to ask you the same thing. Think we need to meet up."

"What for? So you can finish what you started? Huh? So you can kill me?"

"Wanda, that was a bad mistake. Didn't do it, did I?"

"Spike held us up, remember? At gunpoint?"

"Listen, listen," Gordon said, brushing that aside, "need to know where you are, so I can rest assured that kid didn't make good on his threat. Honey, we had our differences, I know that, but I can still care about you, can't I?"

"*What?*" Wanda could hear a shrill female voice cry in the phone. "You son of a bitch!" the young woman's voice yelled.

That about figures, Wanda thought, and said, "You sound busy. Maybe I should just let you go—"

"Hold on now, hold on. Detective Gann's been asking about you. Needs to know you're all right."

"Gann, huh? How'd you happen to talk to him?" she asked, trying to get his goat, but then wondered: *If Gann had talked to Gordon, why hadn't he arrested him? What exactly the hell was going on?*

It seemed like a long, long time before Gordon said anything. She could hear the wind whipping across the cell phone's microphone, so she knew he was still there, but thinking. She knew his pauses, and she knew he was going to lie to her, but she didn't know how. That kept her waiting on the line.

"What's he saying?" Spike said at last, his face crunched in worry.

"Who's that I hear?" Gordon said. "Are you still in danger?"

Surely you fucking jest, she thought.. Gordon did *not* talk like that. "Save it," she said. "Now *you're* gonna be in danger if you don't tell me how you happened to talk to Detective Gann."

"That's not important. Just need *you* to talk to him and tell him you're okay."

"Not important, huh?"

"Jesus Christ, Wanda. I told him you got kidnapped—thought *that* was important. I'm trying to rescue you here, for Christ's sake."

"I *knew* it!" went the shrill voice on Gordon's end. Wanda could hear that and she could hear Gordon telling the girl to shut the fuck up.

"Wanda? Isn't that good enough, I'm trying to save your life now? Spike—he's still with you, isn't he?"

Why would Gordon care if Spike was there, or if he'd chopped her into little pieces, for that matter? Why did he need to know where she was? He knew Spike had a gun and so he'd be killed himself if he tried to kill them. And Gann—*Gordon* wanted *her* to call *Gann?*

And this was right after Gann had talked to her, too.

Something clicked in Wanda's head.

"Tell me to get the fuck off the phone," she said to Spike as she pressed the receiver against her chest.

"What? Why?"

"Goddamnit, Spike, Jesus."

He raised his hands in surrender. "Okay," he said, and waited for her to lift the phone again. When she did, he screamed, "*Bitch, get the fuck off that phone before I put a bullet in your goddamn head! Who the fuck are you talking to? Did I give you permission to answer that goddamn phone?*"

"I'm sorry!" she yelped, and cut the connection as she smiled at Spike. "I—God! I never heard you talk like that."

"Sorry," he said sheepishly. "When I studied inner-city youth—"

"No, I liked it," she said to cut him off, and gave him a good, long kiss. "But we got problems."

"Problems?"

She nodded. "Detective Gann must have arrested Gordon for the Major Dale's thefts, and now he's trying to use Gordon to get to me."

Spike looked honestly perplexed.

"I'm just as guilty as he is, honey. Don't think he wouldn't turn on me in a second."

"Guy has no honor whatsoever."

"He wanted to know where I was, wanted me to call Detective Gann and let him know I'm all right."

"But you just talked to Gann."

"And I wouldn't tell *him* where I was, either."

"They repeated each other."

She nodded again and said, "They must be together."

"Together?" Spike chewed on that one. "But the detective was going to *arrest* your husband. How can they be together?"

"Obviously, obviously Gann's already gotten to Gordon, already arrested him. And now, Gordon obviously wants me arrested since, he's already been, so I can't get at the money before he does. He knows I want my share, and if I'm in jail, I can't get it. He's working with Gann to bring me in."

"But he tried to kill you!"

"Doesn't matter. 'Protective custody,' my ass—Gordon's turning on me, and that goddamn idiot Gann is playing right into his hands."

Spike watched the sign for Truth or Consequences pass by at seventy miles an hour. "So now what?"

"Now we pull off and talk, make some decisions. I have a plan."

29

"Son of a—" Gordon muttered through clenched teeth, and damn near chucked the phone out into the brush. His hands were shaking and his head felt like it was ready to explode. The kid was still with her, still in command of the vehicle, and that meant trouble, because Detective Gann didn't give a rip if the woman had actually and truly in fact been kidnapped or if she had run off with some young stud with more guns than brains—all Gann cared about was "saving" Wanda from Gordon, the big, bad husband who right now was trying to *save* her stupid ass.

Save her long enough to let her make a phone call, anyway, get himself off the hook.

Gordon knew that he and Janey were within minutes of the Vacationeer, all thirty thousand pounds of it—not likely to be too many of those on the road at that hour, the sky rapidly lightening to the east as five o'clock approached. He'd seen a couple of coaches, though, even some class A's—this was RV country. But the Rambling Vacationeer was a singular vehicle, and he was ready to spot it.

Getting on board was another problem altogether. But he had a plan. "Janey?"

She had become interested in the sunrise herself. At least she looked that way, arms crossed and staring out the window away from Gordon.

"Enough with the pissed-off routine. Need you to drive for a while."

That got her attention. "What, you getting sleepy all of a sudden?"

"Getting close to the coach," he said. "You've got to drive, so I can…"

"Can what?"

Yeah, can what? "Get their attention."

"What are you gonna do, wave and tell them they have a flat tire?"

He pulled the LeBaron onto the shoulder and stopped, got out, walked around the car, pulled Janey's door open, and said, "Drive the fucking car."

The look she gave him was pure ice, but he'd had twenty-five years to get used to that expression. He just stood with the door held open, counting the seconds until he could get her on the coach with Wanda and Spike, give them all a piece of his mind they'd have just a few seconds to appreciate, but that he'd never forget.

Janey just sat there for a minute, drawing it out, maybe testing to see how Gordon would handle a little insubordination now that he really needed her. "You want me to drive, huh," she said flatly.

"Right," Gordon said. "Want you to drive, so I can get their attention, get them to pull over."

"So you can rescue Wanda, make sure she's all right."

"Jesus Christ." He turned and trudged a step away from the LeBaron, kicked the dirt.

Now her switch was flipped. She got out of the car and stepped up behind him. "You never even tried to kill her, did you?"

He kept his eyes on the mountains just becoming visible as he said, "Meaning?"

"Meaning you didn't want to kill her in the first place. And now, now that she's in trouble, you want to *save* her!" She got into his face, careful of the steep drop-off just a foot or two behind her. "You didn't get interrupted, did you? *Did you?*"

"The fuck I didn't."

"Come on, how hard is it just to push somebody off a cliff?" she said, then stopped as she realized she had nothing but air behind her, two hundred feet down.

"Not hard at all," Gordon said, and lifted his hand to push.

"Ronny, no—"

She tried to dart out of the way, but his hard hand grabbed a hold of her blouse and held her still in place. Her eyes fixed on his, wide, begging.

Gordon leaned in close. "Not hard at all," he said again, whispering into her ear. "That's why we have to *trust* each other." And let her go.

She didn't move from the spot in front of him, smearing a tear with her hand. "I'm sorry," she said. "You got interrupted. You did want to kill her."

He took a deep breath, regained his composure. "Goddamn right I did. Still do. I trust you, sweetheart, now you got to trust me. Let's go."

Janey rushed over to the driver's side without argument or hesitation. As she pulled them back out onto I-25, Gordon couldn't suppress the smile that crept onto his face. *Sincerity*, he thought. *Fools 'em every time.*

30

"This is getting too complicated," Spike said as Wanda eased the coach off the exit and applied the pneumatic brakes. "We're losing sight of the basic philosophy of what we're doing here."

Wanda took his hand and led him back to the sectional, sat him down and immediately started her hands roaming over him. "I know my philosophy, Spike, and you do, too—you taught it to me. I want Gordon to learn a lesson he'll never—"

"That's not enough, though, is it?"

She eased off of him, and said guardedly, "It's enough."

"You want the money, too, though."

"I want him in jail and I want the money, yeah. That's part of teaching him the lesson. And besides, it's my money, too."

"I never shot anyone, you know," Spike said.

"Never…What are you saying?"

He got himself in a comfortable position and now he would start talking with his hands; she had known him twelve hours, and she already had him down. *Christ.* "I would hold people up—the usual Fat Cats, retirees sponging the Social Security and Medicaid systems, people like that—but I would take their money and run. I never shot anyone just to show them who had the power in the exchange. Showing the gun was enough; they got the picture."

"And so screwing Gordon over, getting him in jail, is enough here. We shouldn't go after the money. That's what you're saying."

"He'll get the message. He'll learn his lesson."

She sat there wordlessly, a lump growing in her throat as she struggled not to cry. After all this—the sex, the restaurant holdup, everything—he was saying he didn't want to go all the way for her because it went against *his philosophy.* Well, fuck that and fuck his philosophy—*she* was going all the way.

And she needed him to go with her. He had the gun and he had the criminal know-how. After she was done with him, fine, fuck him, let him go off in search of his philosophy. She should've known better than to think a man was going to do anything for her anyway. She'd been kept so low so long that down had looked like up to her.

She'd been without love so long she thought Gordon was making a new life for both of them.

She'd been starved for affection so long she thought Spike Jones' attention was the end-all and be-all of the world, instead of the misplaced charity work it was. Inner-city youth? Socioeconomic stratum?

Losing sight of the basic freaking philosophy?

She was just another case study to the boy, and she was just now realizing it, being so awestruck at young hands that wanted to touch her, a young cock—Gordon would say *cock,* she would never say *cock*—a young *cock* that she wanted inside her, that she never stopped to think what the fuck the kid wanted from her. She had assumed money, because that's what everyone wants, isn't it? But it wasn't money at all.

The boy wanted to *save* her, didn't he? *Savor* her and *save* her from her blue-collar existence. Fine—that's just what he could do.

"Wanda?" Spike said at last, watching her get teary-eyed. "You've done it—you've made him learn his lesson. He'll be arrested any time. You can just hide out, or maybe turn state's evidence against him. That'd be quite the how-do-you-do, wouldn't it?"

"What then?"

"Then…then you get your life back. Whatever. Travel, journal, you know," he said, shrugging a little, like this was the most obvious thing in the world. "Life stuff."

"Life stuff takes money, Spike."

"You'd be surprised how little. I mean, I—"

"He'll get the money," Wanda said, looking straight ahead now. "He'll get out and get the money."

"When he's old and gray."

"He'll be old and gray and rich. I'll just be old and gray."

"But you will have won."

"Not without the money! I don't win if he gets it all, and all I get is a trailer and a TV set, a goddamn *job!* What about my salon? What about everything *I* should get?"

Spike stared ahead himself now and looked like he was thinking, hard. College boy hit with a word problem. *A real-life scenario,* they used to call it in school. Well, this was real life, all right. And this was one exam he had better pass.

Then, out of all the things he could have said, all of the countless options available to him, he chose exactly the wrong set of words.

He said, "It'll work out. You're still relatively young."

Now she turned to look at him, her eyes narrowed to slits.

"And I love you, don't forget that," he added, but it was too late.

She grabbed his shirt and pulled him toward her. "You—you love me," she said, like a dare.

"Wanda, you know I love you. All I meant was—"

"You don't love me. You're just in this for *yourself.*"

"Wanda—"

"I *trusted* you. I *believed* in you. Your—your *philosophy*, everything you said about *Gordon*, about *Fat Cats* and *teaching people lessons*—I *listened* to you!" She was spitting the words in his face now, but he was immobilized, taking it all in as she clutched his shirt and held his face in front of hers. "I need that money, Spike. It's the only thing that can save me."

"S-Save you?"

"Save me. And I need you—*Richard V. Modine*—to get it for me." She slipped the driver's license out of her pocket and held it in front of Spike so he could see it. The mustache was taped to the back of it, and she made sure he could see that, too.

She could see it all dawn on him. "But—how will the money save you? I've found that when a person comes into a large lump-sum of cash—"

"No—not the money," Wanda said. "The money isn't what'll save me."

Spike's eyes said it all. *It's not?*

"It's *you*. You getting the money is what will save me. Because if I lose my faith in you—the only new man I've been with, that I've *loved*, in twenty-five years—then I lose my faith in everything." She let go of his shirt and let him fix himself, but didn't take her eyes from his. "You said you were gonna help me teach that bastard a lesson. I say that taking the money is the only way he'll learn."

Spike squinted into the dawn and said, "Then I guess we take the money."

Wanda threw her arms around him and hugged him tight.

"Now let's go before Detective Gann has a chance to find us."

"Where are we going?" Wanda said as she started the coach back up, but Spike didn't really have to say anything, because she knew: *Wherever they could disappear for a little while.*

They were back on the road by the time the cell phone rang.

31

The cell phone rang. The cell phone *was ringing*.

Spike kicked the dashboard.

This is what he got for going against his philosophy. Dozens of armed robberies that went off without a hitch, then the Denny's where he almost gets his head blown off, and now the telephone is ringing with a cop on the other end of the line.

What could he do? Wanda was gesturing for him to answer it, make like the good kidnapper, but what if they actually got stopped, got caught? What would be there to say that he hadn't actually kidnapped her, even raped her? They *had* had sex, there was evidence of that—and he *had* told her husband that he was going to rape and kill her. All of that would come out, and he'd be put away forever, and no one would understand the point of what he actually *had* done.

He'd just be another robber, doing it for the money. Not for the money to survive, mind you, the way he did, but for the big take itself.

Not answering, however, was clearly not an option. Wanda was glaring at him now, and he was finding he'd do just about anything to get away from that.

"Yeah," he said into the phone, trying to sound as criminal as he could.

"This Spike?" It was Gordon. Of course it was—the detective was laying low while he put out the bait again.

"What do you want, 'Ron'?

"Know what I want—Wanda's got to talk to the cop."

"Then put him on the line," Spike said. "He's with you, right?"

"With me? He's not with me."

"Come on."

"You think I got the cop with me? What am I, crazy? He wants to know Wanda is alive and well, okay? There's money in it for you—"

That did it. "Look, *pal*"—his father would say that to people when they got on his last good nerve—"Wanda didn't do anything, and there's no way you're going to turn the tables on her!"

"*What?*" Gordon yelled. "She's *my* wife and *I'm* responsible for her, ass-hole—now pull that thing over and let me on!"

"Pull...?" Spike started, then felt ice go down his spine and turned white-faced to Wanda and said, "Honk the horn."

"Do what?"

Spike covered the mouthpiece of the phone, then reached over and leaned on the Vacationeer's horn.

He could hear it, loud and clear, on the other end of the line.

Not taking the phone from his ear, Spike jumped up and ran down the length of the bus, ran all seventy feet, yanking apart the curtains when he got to the bedroom window all the way at the back.

Gordon was right behind them.

"Howdy," Gordon said into the phone as he stared at the butt end of the Vacationeer, and gave Spike a little wave. "Now stop that thing, and let me talk to my wife."

Spike didn't move.

"Or I'll start shooting."

"You have a gun?" Spike said, still staring out the bedroom window.

"Me to know, you to find out, asshole."

"I don't believe you. Let me see it."

"You see it, it's the last thing you ever see, boy. Stop the fucking coach."

"You don't have a gun, do you?"

"Don't piss me off further, Spike."

"Who's that girl?"

"Counting to three here. One."

Spike didn't move.

"Two."

The shades fell shut as Spike ran away from the window.

"Three."

The Vacationeer didn't stop.

"Said three, Spike."

Nothing. Then, "You don't have a gun, do you?"

"Spike—" But the line was dead. "Son of a bitch!"

Janey said, "What's this *She's still my wife* bullshit?"

Gordon waved an irritated hand at her. "Get alongside them."

"You have to remind me she's still your fucking wife?"

"Wasn't reminding *you*," Gordon said, and motioned for her to get next to the damn coach already. "Reminding the stupid asshole on board the RV."

"Consider me reminded," she said, and finally stepped on the gas to bring them up next to the driver's side of the Vacationeer. "But I'm telling you—"

"Enough already, for the love of Christ. *Wanda!*" he yelled at her profile in the window, yelled and waved his arms, plenty visible in the convertible with its top down. She was ignoring him, of course. "*Wanda, it was all a mistake! Just need you to tell the detective!*" He was standing in the foot well now, yelling at a closed window.

Wanda kept driving, her eyes on the road.

"Get in front of them!" he yelled to Janey. "Get in front and *slow down*."

"All a big mistake, huh?" she said, but gunned the gas and got them in front of the coach.

Janey was really burning his ass, but there was nothing he could say to her just then, seeing as how he was climbing over the back seat and onto the trunk. "*Okay, keep slowing down!*" he shouted back to Janey, then turned and yelled, "*Wanda, stop the coach! Pull it over!*"

"*Fuck you!*" Wanda screamed back. "*I'm not going to jail!*"

Jail? What was that all about? He wanted her dead and buried, not in jail, where she could cause him any more problems. "*No one's going to jail!*" he yelled, which he hoped to God was true. "*Just need you to talk to the detective!*"

Janey was still slowing the LeBaron down, so they were going maybe twenty-five miles an hour now, enough still to kill Gordon instantly if he fell off the trunk and under the Vacationeer's wheels, but not so fast that the wind was going to whip him right off the car.

He could see Wanda thinking; after so many years, he could practically smell the wood burning when she had an idea, and this was one of those times. So he had an extra second to prepare for whatever it would be when Wanda suddenly wrenched the wheel of the Vacationeer and hit the gas, trying to whip the coach around the LeBaron.

Only problem was, there was only about a foot between the front of the RV and the back of the car. Not near enough turning radius for a huge bus, and so the Vacationeer's front bumper smashed the back of the LeBaron, shoving the car forward about five feet down the road.

And leaving Gordon standing on air.

But he saw Wanda was doing *something*, and so had braced himself enough to jump up when the RV slammed into the convertible, his foot leaving the trunk just as the car was shoved out from under him.

He jumped and grabbed—grabbed at anything, grabbed at the air, grabbed at the massive grill of the Rambling Vacationeer, his fingers finding just enough purchase to keep him from falling to the asphalt and bouncing back up into the workings of the RV. He supposed a person *could* fall *between* the wheels at a low enough speed and survive, but didn't think his luck was running that way lately.

Wanda and Spike stared at him in amazement through the panoramic windshield.

He looked behind him. Janey was going to the shoulder, getting out of the way.

Didn't I tell her to keep slowing down? Gordon thought as he turned back to see Wanda look out at the open road ahead, and start to accelerate.

Janey Briggs sat in her crumpled silver Chrysler LeBaron convertible, sob-
bing in the early morning sunshine. The cell phone rang, and she almost
let it go, thinking for a second that Ronny was still there, that he'd pick it
up like he always did.

But he wasn't there anymore. The bitch had made off with him, and
now she was going to kill him. She used her womanly wiles, her painted
face and aerobicized body, to entice him back and kill him.

She picked up the phone. "Hello?" she choked out.

"Ms. Briggs, this is Detective Douglas Gann again. I'm sorry if I'm
waking you."

The detective! Her eyes searched up the road for Ronny, for him to tell
her what to do, but he was long gone. "You're not waking me," she said.

"You're on the road with Gordon Mitchell, aren't you?"

"He's not here."

"Janey, I'm a police officer. It's a crime to lie to me."

"Ron—*Gordon*—isn't here. He went with…"

"With whom?"

"With his *wife*. With Wanda."

The detective was silent for a moment, then said, "Now, why would he do that?"

Janey put a hand to her eyes and let out a wet sob.

"Why would he go with her, Janey?"

"He—he still loves her," she said, and felt a tear roll down her cheek. "He wanted to rescue her from the kidnapper."

"Janey, you know and I know there's no kidnapper."

"From her boyfriend, then. Oh, God…"

"Take it easy," the detective said. "Look, don't you want to see Gordon Mitchell punished for what he's done to you? Set you up and left you all alone for his wife, after he promised you the moon?"

"Punished?"

"He's a bad person, Janey. You can make sure he never does this again. You can get him back. They're in the RV, right? All you have to do is tell me where they're headed, and I'll get Gordon in the Sierra County Jail before he can hurt anybody else."

Janey choked back another sob and took a deep breath. Maybe Wanda didn't know what love was. Maybe even Ronny didn't know what love was. This detective, maybe he thought love was about revenge; he didn't know what love was.

Janey knew what love was.

"One more time," Gann said. "Where are they headed?"

They were going south, towards the border, she knew that. So she took a deep, deep breath and said, "North."

"North?"

"Albuquerque," she said.

Gordon had long since lost the feeling in all his fingers by the time he gave up yelling at Wanda to stop and decided to try to move around the side of the Vacationeer. The wind whipped against him as he held on with his right hand clutching the fiberglass grill and his feet sliding around on the bumper, and eased his left hand over to the edge of the grill. When he found purchase on the grill with that hand, he eased his entire body over, his right hand giving only with extreme reluctance and agony in his fingers.

He could feel bugs slapping into him, exploding against his back and his head, just like he'd explode if he fell now under one of the coach's huge tires. All it would take would be one slip, and he'd be broken in half—if he was lucky. Way things had been going, he'd probably just end up in a wheelchair like Christopher Reeve, blowing into a tube if he wanted to visit the far corner of his jail cell. Hell, all they'd need to incarcerate him then would be a fucking curb.

But that was thinking negatively; sales required positive thinking, and getting inside the RV was going to be one hell of a sale to make, even if he lived long enough to get around to the door.

The asphalt was whooshing by beneath him, mesmerizing him whenever he stopped to catch his breath and looked. Wanda had the damn thing cranked up to at least eighty now, and even a fall off the side into the dirt would be fatal at that speed.

"Wanda!" he tried to yell, but he didn't have the breath. She wasn't going to stop anyway, that much was obvious. At least, not voluntarily.

He put out a hand carefully, carefully around the curve of the bus, finding the side-view mirror just at the very end of his reach. He put the hand back on the grill and slowly slid himself over another arm's length. Then he reached across himself with his right hand and got a hold of the mirror tubing, hoping to God that it would hold him when it counted.

He took a second to wipe the sweat from his eyes with his arm—not his hand, he didn't need either of them slippery just now—and looked at Wanda and Spike inside the coach, watching him as he made his way across the front. They didn't look amazed, exactly; more like sitting on the edge of their seats. *Fuckers.*

He got ready now, his right hand threaded through the tubing of the mirror, his left hand ready to go for it. He braced himself, and—

HWONNNNK! Wanda let loose on the horn.

It almost made him recoil his way under the Vacationeer. Almost. He took a few more seconds to remember to breathe again, then took his left hand, put it up where Wanda could see it, and shot up his middle finger.

Then he wrapped that hand around the mirror tubing, and swung over to it, all of his weight threatening to pull him right off as he swung down and around and finally stopped himself by shoving a foot against the side of the coach.

His arms were shaking like a bitch. Somehow this was a lot different from impressing customers by showing the mirror could hold a man's weight, hanging on for five seconds every couple of weeks on a vehicle that was nice and motionless.

His feet slid off the smooth sidewalls. There was nothing for him to put his weight on, like he could on the bumper in front. All of his weight was on his arms and hands now, and they were starting to become slick with sweat.

He looked down. He wasn't supposed to look down, he knew, but he had to see what he was heading for.

It wasn't good. If, for some reason, he wasn't killed on impact at eighty miles an hour onto the rocky shoulder, there was a pretty good chance he'd bounce right off the edge, have a nice long time to think about how he'd fucked everything up on his long way down to the desert floor.

But it was really okay. He probably wouldn't survive falling off the RV in the first place.

His arms were giving out. All of his weight was on his hands now, and they were getting slippery. If he didn't do something *now*, he was going to fall.

Sweat poured into his eyes. The burning and the blurring hardly bothered him, considering he wasn't going to be feeling anything ever again in a matter of seconds. He had to pry his left hand off the mirror, had to get it over to the door.

He slipped his fingers off the tubing, and his exhausted hand fell free. Now all of his weight was on his right hand, which wouldn't last long.

He swung his arm over to the door handle and tried it.

It opened.

The wrong way. He couldn't climb in from his position if the damn coach had been stopped. He hung there from the mirror, the asphalt three feet below him whooshing by at eighty miles an hour, and the door popped open the wrong goddamned way, making an impassable wall between him and the inside of the Vacationeer.

But the door swung open, and Gordon could hear Wanda and Spike—both of them—scream like teenage girls in a horror movie.

The door was open only for a second before the wind got it, ripped its handle out of his fingers, and hurled it shut. Groaning, the air whipping in his ears, Gordon brought his hand back over to the mirror and looped it inside the tubing. He felt like his wrists were going to snap, but he had bought himself another second or two before he'd lose it and be smashed against the ground.

He hauled himself up a little with the very last of his arm strength and could see Spike inside, fumbling for the lock, which on the Vacationeer wasn't your average push-down chrome affair. Spike was obviously holding the door handle, trying to insure against it opening again while he tried to lock the door.

This was it. Last time, now or never.

Gordon swung again and latched onto the outside handle just as he could feel Spike slamming the lock home. But the kid was too late—Gordon got his hand around the handle and yanked with everything he had left, which wasn't much, but enough to haul the Vacationeer's door open one more time.

And bring Spike out with it.

One of the kid's feet went *whack* on the ground as he fell out, went *whack* and bounced up and backwards, straightening and stretching out Spike's body as it tried to absorb being yanked in two directions at once. Hanging on the mirror, Gordon was sure Spike was going to splat flat on his face, fall right out of the coach and roll in a broken little ball until he was no longer in sight.

But Spike's fingers must have just held on to the door handle, a few fingers on one hand saving him from a bloody death. The kid hung there on the handle with his left hand—Gordon could see Spike's right hand around the door whip out as his body was stretched, then come back in as he struggled to stay with the coach. After a second or two, Spike's feet drew up so he wouldn't get dragged onto the rocky ground and get yanked nearly in half once again.

Spike let out a long, terrified wail.

Gordon could hear Wanda yell, "*Spike! Oh my God!*"

She slammed on the brakes, and the coach stopped almost like it hit a brick wall. Spike smashed into the door, which snapped off like part of a broken toy and whipped around against the sidewall, shearing the mirror off the coach like a razor lancing a bit of stubble, shearing the mirror off not two inches away from taking all of Gordon's fingers with it.

Spike hit the ground, still holding onto the door, which dragged him like a boogie board through forty feet of rocks and dirt down the shoulder ahead of the coach.

Gordon also hit the ground, but went out instead of forward, swinging out away from the RV and slamming down on the shoulder so that his body, head, and arms absorbed the impact, and his hands—still holding the mirror—went over the edge of the drop-off. The mirror kept going, chucked down the side of the cliff, and if Gordon hadn't gotten his fingers untangled when the wind was knocked out of him, the momentum of the mirror would have whirled him right off with it, lifted him up and over the side hundreds of feet to his death below.

As fast as he could—before the bitch could get the coach moving again—Gordon staggered to his feet and over to where Spike lay on top of the door. In some places, like where they almost drove off the edge the day before, the mountain drop-off was a hundred feet from the road. Other places, like this one, it was less then ten. Spike was lucky his little surfboard had gone forward instead of out and taken him right over.

But not all that lucky. Gordon's hands were shaking from the exertion, his fingers in agony, but he was able to gather Spike up, yank him off the broken door, and get him moving to the RV. He shoved Spike inside and climbed in right behind him, not saying a word. Then he followed a list of steps he promised himself, hanging on the mirror, that he'd follow if he ever made it back on the bus:

First thing he did was punch Wanda right in the mouth.

Second thing he did was count his broken fingers.

Third thing he did was look around for Spike's gun—and there it was, sitting plain as day on the end table.

Spike was looking at it too. That wasn't on the list.

Fourth thing he did was turn to Wanda and say, "You like to drive, huh? Then you can…" He stopped dead, looking at his kabuki-faced wife with a mixture of dread and amazement. He could not fucking believe it.

There was a hickey on Wanda's neck.

In an instant, he understood everything: They were in this together. She had the fake IDs; she had the traveling cash; she had the RV. Maybe Wanda had somehow plotted the whole time to have the kid meet them at the lookout, gang up on Gordon, it was all coming together now, Wanda and Spike.

And Spike…well, he had a special spike all his own, didn't he? He was using it to screw Wanda—and Wanda was going to use it to screw Gordon. Goddamn if they weren't fixing to get the money and skip out on *him!*

It was the oldest trick in the book, the wife and her lover against the unsuspecting, hard-working husband.

Of course, the second-oldest trick in the book was that of the *suspecting* husband who shot his conniving wife and her young stud dead as Dixie.

If he could get to the gun first. Otherwise, talking about a different story.

Gordon could see Spike moving—glacially, but definitely moving—for the gun. Their eyes met and stayed pinned on each other, Spike inching from the kitchen area up front to the living room's end table, Gordon now stepping away from Wanda, shifting his weight forward to look like he was just gliding ahead, nothing to worry about, no reason to rush—

"Don't think so," Gordon said to Spike, and he could see out of the corner of his eye Wanda turning all the way around in her captain's chair. "Give it up, boy."

Spike, bruised and bloodied, just grinned at him as he eased himself closer to the end table. He was closer to it than Gordon, by a good two feet, and was closing in.

Gordon realized that if the kid really was fucking Wanda, he had to have a screw loose, and that gave him his only shot at beating him to the gun. "How's it feel nailing a circus clown, huh? She make you want to go to a KISS concert or what?"

Spike stopped. "What's that supposed to mean?" he said, looking at Wanda and then back at Gordon again.

Not stopping but still inching his way forward, trying to look and sound casual with the kid standing there paralyzed by his hard-on, he said, "Ever see makeup like that? Puts it on with a roller."

"Hey..." Spike said, his blood rising now, and took a step towards Gordon—and away from the gun, or at least not directly towards it. "I love her, you bastard."

Another little step. Another. Now he was just as close to the end table as Spike was, and Spike was facing the wrong direction—towards *him*, not the gun. "*Love* her? You fucking insane? What happens now, huh? Gonna spend the rest of your lives together, you and the Kabuki dancer?"

"I don't like violence," Spike said.

"Good," Gordon said, and took another little baby step.

"But for you, I'll make an exception."

Just at that moment, just as Spike lunged at Gordon and tried to take him down, Wanda must have realized why the men in the RV were moving so slowly and strangely—she must have seen the gun, because just as Spike jumped, as Gordon ducked out of the way and around the flying body, Wanda screamed, "*Get the gun!*"

Spike seemed to stop in midair and try to turn around, reverse everything and get back to the table and the gun before Gordon, who was falling into the side of the couch and sliding the thirty-eight off the table and under him as he fell.

No one moved. Gordon lay on his stomach and listened to Spike's careful footsteps approach. Then, when he was almost on top of him, Gordon spun around onto his back and almost got the barrel into the kid's stomach before Spike grabbed it and held it away. Finally, Gordon rammed a knee up into his balls, and that got him to let go of it. Now it was back where it belonged—pointed right into the kid's stomach.

"Gordon!" Wanda yelled. "Leave him alone!"

"Gonna visit the bank this morning, *honey?*" Gordon snarled, looking up at her without moving the gun. "Take a little withdrawal out of *my* account?"

"That's *our* money, Gordon. Half is mine."

Gordon stood and staggered over to her. "But you weren't just gonna take *half*, were ya? Or maybe a half for you and a half for Studley over there?"

"He doesn't know anything about any of that. Leave him alone."

His back to the steps and ripped-open doorway, Gordon scratched his head with the gun and said, "So, just gonna treat your boy-toy to the carefree life, cruises and shit? Everything we talked about, only with his cock in you instead of mine?"

"You never wanted that thing in me anyway. It would've interfered with your social life."

"Brave talk for a dead woman, Wanda."

"*No!*" Spike screamed from his crumpled position by the cooking island. "This is all *my* fault—don't hurt her, come on!"

"Gee, Spike, usually I don't like violence, but for her I'm gonna make an exception," Gordon said. He put the gun right up against Wanda's forehead, then stopped and turned to Spike. "Really love her, huh?"

Tears in his eyes, Spike said, "I do."

"Tough," Gordon said, and pulled the trigger.

35

Click.

Wanda jerked hard in the recliner, then slowly opened her eyes. *Wha—?*

Gordon's face, every feature creased with anger, now gave way to an expression like that of someone trying to take that eleventh step on a flight of ten stairs, like the whole world had just been yanked out from under him.

He pulled the trigger again, and again. Just *clicks*.

"No bullets, Fat Cat—I don't believe in them," Spike said, springing to his feet with a smile and grabbing the gun out of Gordon's hand. "Let that be a lesson to you: Don't assume all robbers are killers."

Dazed, Wanda slowly started to actually listen to what her young lover was saying, to what the man who she would ask to kill for her today was saying: *He didn't have any bullets in his gun!*

She let out a groan. *No bullets?* No bullets meant he had never...he was never...

It meant she was alive, but it also meant she was alone again, didn't it? That she had always been alone, no matter how she'd fooled herself.

But...what was the Denny's thing, if there were no bullets? What was his scuffle with Gordon, if there were no bullets? What did anything he did mean, if there were no bullets?

"You okay, darling?" Spike asked her, then turned to Gordon, who was just standing there in front of Wanda, stunned. "That's right, Mister Man, I said *darling*. I love the woman you threw away. I *value* her, get it? And she values me, *Ron*, more than she does you, because we think alike. I know her kind of people, I understand them. That's why she's including *me* and not *you*."

"What in the hell are you talking about?" Gordon said at last, but Wanda had a sinking dread that she knew. "Include you in what?"

"The *money*, Fat Cat."

Oh, no, Wanda's mind screamed. *Shut up, shut up, SHUT UP! Gordon didn't know for sure—he was only guessing!*

"Suppose you tell me what money," Gordon said, crossing his arms, "or maybe I already know." With this, he looked back at Wanda. "So you *were* set to cut me out, give my share to the boy-toy here."

"That money's half mine," she said.

"And the other half is mine," Spike cut in, "to teach you a lesson you'll never forget. Ever hear of sharing the wealth?"

Wanda had lived with Gordon Mitchell for twenty-five years, since Nixon was in the White House and Elvis was thin enough to sing on national TV. She had seen him happy, mostly smelling of perfume, sad, mostly on anniversaries—and angry. She had seen him explode. He had never hit her—well, not until today—but he had destroyed a few things around their house in his day.

Before he would explode and start on a rampage, his meaty face would turn a bright pink and his eyes would narrow to wrinkled slits. His hands would clench into fists by his sides and start to shake. His thin lips would peel back to expose his small teeth in an animal snarl.

This was what Wanda was seeing now, and her Spike—who she desperately needed for her meeting with Detective Gann, especially now, since they had no goddamn *bullets* in the gun—was standing right in front of the powder keg.

"Bank opens at nine sharp, boy," Gordon hissed through his snarl. "Guess it's a race to see who's first."

"Not if it's like my darling says and we have the IDs that match the deposit box," Spike teased, pushing it way too far. "And the disguise. We're about the same height, wouldn't you say?"

Gordon's shaking fists came up. "*You lousy punk son of a b*—"

But before her husband could so much as lay a finger on Spike Jones, Wanda hurled herself up off the recliner and, calling on twenty-five years of bottled frustrations and five years toning at the aerobics center, slammed the heel of her foot full force into Gordon's gut, knocking him off his feet and sending him reeling backwards over the passenger seat, down the sharp steps and through the gaping hole where the door used to be, slamming him flat on his back on the rocky ground not two feet from where the shoulder ended and empty space began.

Spike, useless pretend man Spike, was standing right behind her, between her and the driver's seat, an unbelieving smirk on his face. "That—that was—"

"*Move!*" she yelled, and he scrambled out of the way as she stomped into the cockpit and jammed herself down into the driver's seat.

She turned the ignition key halfway, waited for the diesel engine signal to give her the okay as she looked out on Gordon still unmoving on the shoulder of the highway, and she fired the fifteen-ton behemoth to life, stomping the gas pedal to let the monster roar.

"What are you going to do?" Spike peeped as he belted himself in.

"Didn't you hear the man?" she said as she dropped the Vacationeer into gear. "It's a race now."

She looked at her watch: It was almost six. The sun was up. They had a little over an hour before they had to meet Gann at the Pine Knot Saloon, convince him that it would be a very bad idea to take her into custody.

And now, thanks to Spike, somehow they still had to stop and get bullets.

36

Lying sprawled by the interstate in southern New Mexico, somewhere south of Truth or Consequences and somewhere north of Las Cruces, Gordon realized he had never seen such a blue sky. Maybe it was because it was everything he saw, lying there, so much blue, blue reaching out into infinity, blue light, blue lights…

…blue *flashing* lights.

The brown face of a New Mexico State Police officer leaned into the perfect blue sky and looked down at Gordon. "Sir? You okay?"

It took ten seconds, maybe more—Gordon couldn't tell, his head had whacked against the ground pretty hard—for him to look at the cop.

"You need to go to a hospital, sir?"

Hospital? Did he need to go? Was he broken? He moved his feet and dragged his arms on the little rocks of the shoulder. He was hurting pretty bad. He thought maybe he should go and get checked out—

Then he remembered *why* he was on his back by the side of the road in New Mexico, looking up at the morning sky. And he remembered he had what, three hours to get to Sierra Savings and Loan and stop the cunt and the kid from draining his retirement fund.

"No," he said after a while. "Think I'm all here."

The cop straightened himself. "All right then, sir, then you have the right to remain silent. Anything you say can and will—"

"Whoa! What am *I* under arrest for?"

"I have ten witnesses reporting they saw a man about your size hanging off the front of a moving recreational vehicle not five miles from this spot," the cop said, and paused, no doubt to check for some kind of self-incriminating look from Gordon, which was not forthcoming. Finally he added, "That's reckless endangerment—against the law, sir."

Gordon groaned and closed his eyes again. "What makes you think it was me?"

"You mean, instead of all the other people laying by the side of I-25 with the door to an RV laying next to them?"

He groaned again and said, "This the kind of thing you can post bail for?"

The cop took his hand and hefted him up. "That's for the judge to decide, when he gets here at nine."

"At—at nine?" Gordon sputtered as the cop clicked the cuffs on him. "Gonna be in jail until nine o'clock?"

"Not necessarily—that's just when the judge gets here. Could be ten or later 'til you get in to see him." With that, he pushed Gordon's head down and sat him in the car, then walked around and got in himself and whipped a U-turn to head back towards Truth or Consequences.

Didn't really matter when the judge set bail anyway, Gordon realized, watching the dusty town come back into view, because Gordon didn't have ten dollars to his name. Or the ID that would let him get to his Sierra safety deposit box. Or a car to get over the border. Or his plane ticket.

What he did have was a warrant that would be coming down on his head at right about nine o'clock—figure New Mexico is an hour behind Indiana, and it might take an hour for the law to get the okay for the warrant and get it together to send across the country—a warrant right at nine, just when the good Sierra County judge would be looking over his docket with Gordon Mitchell standing right in front of him, looking just peachy after a couple of hours in a holding cell.

Should've taken the hospital, he thought, and leaned his head against the window.

37

Douglas Gann lay on the motel bed and stared at the ceiling, his eyes red and his face wet, his breath ragged in heaving sobs. He had failed.

If the Mitchells were headed for Albuquerque, there wasn't a darn thing Gann could do now to stop Gordon. The New Mexico police didn't believe him; his own department wanted him to wait for the stinking *warrant*, which would come in maybe just over two hours now, nine o'clock, and would be completely useless because Gordon would have definitely killed Wanda, knowing—thanks to Gann—that she was the witness he needed to eliminate. They could bring him in now—if they could find him before he got his money and got the heck out of the country—but that wouldn't help poor Wanda. No, thanks to the girlfriend, the accomplice, Janey Briggs, Gann knew now that he had totally, absolutely and completely fucked this one up.

Elkhart might knock him down to sergeant for this.

They might want his badge.

They might even *prosecute*—impersonating a police officer. Was that illegal when you actually *were* an officer, just on vacation? Or was it obstruction of justice, since he let Gordon know they were after him?

Or…accessory to murder. Gordon wouldn't have known how vital it was to get rid of Wanda if it weren't for Gann's meddling. He might have decided not to kill her. Gann pushed him over the edge, so sure that he'd get his man.

He sat up on the bed and stared at himself in the bureau mirror. His aura was dark, streaked with brown and gray; he was low indeed. There was one spot, just one spot, that was a bright, even shining, white—it flickered, but was definitely there.

A ray of hope? Gann wiped his teary eyes and—

The phone rang.

He jumped, the way you do when you're not expecting the phone to ring, or even forgot there was a phone, and after a second collecting himself, scrambled over to pick it up. "Gann here," he choked out through the lump in his throat.

"Detective, glad you're still in town," the deep voice said. "This is Sergeant Frick over at the state police station."

Gann sighed. "Look, I'm sorry about the trouble. I know when I go back—"

"We've got Mitchell in custody, detective."

"You—*what?*"

"Gordon Mitchell—that was the one you were after, right? Came in not ten minutes ago, picked him up for reckless endangerment, hanging off the front end of an RV on I-25."

Gann jumped ,to his feet and started looking for his shoes. "He's there now?"

"I'm looking right at him, in the holding cell."

"What about the wife?"

"Don't start in with that, okay?"

"But," Gann said, pacing in the room, "my informant told me he was in Albuquerque."

"Do you want to come by and see him for yourself?" Frick said. "You have to ask?"

Spike Jones had never, ever put even one bullet in his gun, had never fired the thing in anger or in any other way. That wasn't what it was for. When he bought the thing, the shop owner asked him how many rounds of ammunition he wanted, and when he said "None," the man fixed him with a look that made Spike think he was going to take the gun back.

"Not gonna be much use without bullets, son," the shop owner said.

"Deterrence is what I'm after," Spike had said. "Like with nuclear missiles, the other side just knowing you have the weapon is all you need."

The shop owner said, "You know nuclear missiles got warheads on 'em, right?"

"Of course."

"Well, so do the Russians. If they thought we just had missiles but no bombs, shit. It'd all be over in a heartbeat, no contest."

"I don't plan to *tell* anybody I don't have bullets."

"Son, buy a couple of rounds, at least. Gun's no use without bullets, unless you're planning to be a stickup man or something. Even then."

Spike cleared his throat. "Are we all done here?"

"Take some bullets. Christ, they're on me."

"I'll pass."

"What the hell's wrong with you, boy?" the shop owner said. "I'm giving you these goddamn bullets, all right? Free with the thirty-eight."

"Thank you, but I don't want them. I don't believe in violence."

"You don't believe in violence." He sounded stunned.

"That's right," Spike said.

"But you're buying a *gun*."

Spike grinned at him as he collected his purchase and started for the door. "True, but remember: Guns don't kill people—bullets do!"

But Wanda—Wanda was a different animal, from a different background and upbringing and a completely alien set of rules and expectations. Wanda believed in bullets, because—and this was just the way she was raised, he knew this, he wasn't casting aspersions—she believed in violence. No doubt in her blue-collar upbringing there had been frequent use of physical punishment for even minor transgressions, and of course her husband had just tried to throw her off a cliff.

He couldn't blame her for her violent nature, but, because he loved her, neither could he allow her to get sucked into perpetrating further violence. There would be no bullets for his gun, not now, not ever. Gordon had come after them twice, and both times it had been fine without any shooting—in fact, she'd be dead now if the gun had been loaded. They didn't need bullets to protect them from Gordon.

When Wanda broached the subject again, the RV parked and locked down right outside the only twenty-four-hour pawn shop within a fifty-mile radius of T or C, he told her as much.

She didn't take it well.

Wanda silently counted to ten, trying to keep her anger down so she didn't shove her lover out of the RV through where the door used to be and try to run him over. He was so damn sure he knew what was best, just like all the men she had known her entire life. He knew best they didn't need bullets, huh? She'd show him. She'd—she'd—

One Mississippi. Two Mississippi. Three Mississippi...

"Darling?" Spike said, touching her hand. "Are you feeling all right?"

She clasped her hand around his and stood, pulling him with her. "Let's lay down for a minute."

Naturally, he seemed to think that was a good idea. Why had she thought he was so different from everyone else? Even from Gordon? He was a criminal, all he really wanted to do was fuck, he was a smooth talker who knew all the answers before the questions had even been asked...the only difference was that he was young and attractive.

Well, Gordon had been, too. Just give Spike twenty-five years and see how close a match we get, Wanda thought as she led him through the living area, the kitchen, the dining area, and back to the bedroom, where she put him on his back on the bed and climbed on top. "I think we need to talk," she said.

"Nice way to do it," Spike said with his smarmy man's smile.

Her patience was running thin. It was time for Spike to put up or shut up, show her what he was made of.

And, if need be, take the rap for what was about to be done. What had to be done.

She said, "Spike, do you love me?"

His ears perked up. "Yes, darling, yes."

The "darling" thing was starting to grate. She took his face in her hands. "I love you, too, you know," she said, mustering what she could in the way of sincerity in light of the fact she wanted to rip his little fucking face off, "and there's something I need you to do."

"Anything."

"I need you to get some bullets for your gun."

He sighed. "Gordon is not going to threaten us again—and I just told you, being armed just increases the likelihood that someone is going to end up getting shot."

"That's what I want."

"Why? The gun does all the talking. That's a lesson I've learned well in my time on the road," he said, and moved to kiss her.

She averted her lips. "We need the gun loaded, Spike."

"*Pour quoi?*" he asked with a mischievous grin. "That means *why?*"

Her fingers tightened around his cheeks as she demanded his full and immediate attention. "Why? Because you're going to shoot somebody."

His grin melted away. "Oh, no. No, no, I don't think so."

"I want that money."

"So let's get it!"

"There's someone in our way, someone who wants to stop me—us," she said slowly, remembering why they were together in the first place— there was some kind of love thing supposed to be going on here. Spike didn't believe in violence? Fine. He believed in love. "Someone who wants to stop us. Someone who wants to come between us. Jesus, I've waited all my life for you, and now…"

Spike shifted underneath her as he tried to put his arms around her. "Darling, darling, no one's going to come between us. We don't need to shoot anybody."

"No, Spike. The cop we're going to see, he wants to break us up. He wants to bring me in for questioning—he wants to arrest me, really—and leave you behind."

"Let's not go see him, then."

"No—he'll find us. He's a tracker; he'll keep us from getting into Mexico. There's a million eyes on this RV."

"Then let's ditch the RV."

"*Goddamnit, Spike!*" she cried. "We need to buy bullets. We need to kill Detective Gann. You have to shoot him."

"What's gotten into you, Wanda? You're not like your husband—you're not a killer. There must be another way."

"I—I'm desperate, Spike. I want you to be a part of my way of life," she said, trying to think fast, "but there are people who oppose that. Gordon. And Detective Gann."

"Why is it your people always have such trouble with the police? I've always—"

Wanda slitted her eyes at him, the drawn curves of her makeup enhancing the effect. Spike stopped speaking immediately. "You like teaching people lessons? Then teach Detective Gann a lesson. Teach him not to come between a woman and the rest of her life."

"I'm not killing anyone," Spike said with finality.

"Well, you're buying those goddamned bullets," Wanda barked, then stopped herself. That wasn't the way to do it—God, hadn't she learned anything from this whole thing? Hadn't she learned any smoothness from the salesman who shared her bed for twenty-five years?

Now she put her hands on Spike's chest, stroked him. Then she bent down to kiss his neck, then his chest, then moved down to unbuckle his belt, her lips tracing every inch of the way. "Please, Spike, please…"

She could feel him try to resist for a few seconds, then put his hands in her red hair and press the tips of his fingers against her head. "God, Wanda."

"Can't you see how desperate this all is, baby?" She put her mouth on him for a second, letting the warmth sink into him. "Can't you see how important? We're nothing standing up to the world if we're holding an empty gun." She put her mouth on him again and gave him everything she had.

"All right, I'll buy the bullets," he said after a while, "but I'm not killing anyone."

"That's all I'm asking," Wanda said. But of course, it wasn't. Not by a long shot.

Spike loved the feeling of his darling woman's mouth on him, touching him in the way that no "good" girl ever would, girls with breeding and self-respect and all the rest. But even through the haze of oral sex, he wondered, *Why do I have to buy the bullets?* He owned the gun, sure, so he'd be the one who knew what kind of ammunition it took, but he could pretty easily tell her that, couldn't he? With the doorless RV parked in the dirt lot of an all-night pawn shop, he couldn't understand why she needed bullets for his gun so badly if she knew they weren't going to kill anyone.

He wasn't going to kill anyone, anyway. She was an adult, she could do whatever she wanted and was willing to pay the price for, but leave him out of it. Now that he thought about it—as much as he could think about anything right then—he realized he didn't even have to let her use the gun. He could buy the ammunition, say *See what a cooperative fellow. I am?* and then put all of it away, hide the gun *and* the bullets so he and Wanda could go meet up safely with Detective Gann and get all of this worked out.

And what was up with that, with meeting the detective? Why did she want to kill him? She'd said because he wanted to come between her and Spike. But Spike got the feeling that wasn't the real reason at all. All she had to do was run off with him, and they could be together. No one had to get shot or killed.

But Wanda wanted him to shoot Gann, kill him.

She'd said *We* need to kill Detective Gann.

But it was *You* need to shoot him.

People at Gordon and Wanda's social stratum didn't understand the abstract idea of leveling power with a weapon without using it as it was designed. It wasn't about violence, it was about power. It wasn't even really about power—it was about exploring the balances of power. That was his thesis statement, if he could be so droll, and the experiment he'd been on was the thesis itself. But Wanda with the whole bullet thing, she was taking the experiment away from its original parameters and moving it directly into applications.

That wouldn't do. What he had to do was get things back on track—if they were going to go for the big power balance, the big steal, and get the million and a half Wanda and her husband had stolen, great, that could be a natural and exciting conclusion to his short life of crime. He could take his part of the money—heck, have Wanda by his side—and use the money for good.

But Wanda had to understand it was never *about* the money, and it was certainly never about violence. She would have to understand. He would have to make her understand. Only problem was, she had his penis in her mouth right then and didn't look quite ready for an attitude adjustment.

Still…"Wanda."

"Mmmph?"

"Listen, stop for a second."

She stopped, and crawled over next to him and kissed him, that musty taste still in her mouth. "You rang?" she said playfully, which now made him nervous instead of putting him at ease.

"It isn't about Gann coming between us, is it?"

The playful look was gone. "What isn't?"

"Killing the detective. The reason you want me to get the bullets. It has nothing to do with us, does it?"

"You already agreed, Spike."

"Then you have nothing to lose by telling me the truth. Why do you want these bullets so badly?"

Wanda bit her lip and looked at him a while before saying, "We're fugitives."

"Fugitives? I haven't hurt anyone—"

"That doesn't matter—Jesus! The cops, they don't care if you hurt someone or just hold them up. It's still *against the law*."

"The people I robbed should thank me for opening their eyes."

"For helping them learn a lesson."

"Exactly," Spike said.

"And if you ever got caught, your rich parents could hire the best lawyers, get you right out of trouble, couldn't they?" Wanda sat on the edge of the bed now. "You don't even need the money."

"Wanda, this whole thing isn't supposed to be about the money."

"*The hell it isn't!*" she yelled, and stood to pace around the tiny room. "If I don't get the money, Gordon will—whenever he gets out of jail—and then he wins and I lose! It's always about the money!"

"Gann doesn't have to die for us to get it. Why does he have to die?"

"He wants to bring me in *for my own safety*, Spike—he wants to put me in custody until he can get Gordon. He wants me under police protection, so no bank for me, no money, no nothing. He's going to let Gordon win!"

"You're talking about *murder*, Wanda—killing another human being. Prison, the death penalty, eternal damnation, you know?"

"What are you, religious now?"

"Do you hear yourself? Are you hearing *me?* You don't have to shoot anybody, you don't have to kill anybody! You—*we*—can just lay low, avoid the police for a while. I've got experience with this, you don't, remember?"

"Your richie rich parents—"

"They couldn't get me off of a murder charge, and you know it. There's no reason to kill *anybody*, and if we don't have bullets this won't even be an issue, unless you're planning to beat Detective Gann to death."

"I want those bullets, Spike—I want the insurance. Gordon tried to kill me—to *kill* me, can you understand that? *I* have the experience here!"

"How do you know Gordon isn't arrested by now himself? We left him lying by the side of the road, pretty conspicuous."

"Then Detective Gann'll bring me in to testify against Gordon."

"We just have to—"

"*We have to get rid of Gann!*" Wanda screamed, and banged her fist against the wall. "Goddamnit, you men are all exactly the goddamn same!"

"Hey, wait a minute—"

"You like the blow job, huh? You'll buy the bullets when I'm sucking your cock, but when it comes time to show me you love me, show me you'll fight for me, I'm just shit out of luck, aren't I? Because you're just the same as Gordon, the same as my father, the same as *everyone!*"

Spike sat up on the bed, looking out the side window at the pawn shop. He wasn't the same as anyone his lover knew, not a single person. His life was being spent in pursuit of something good, spreading the word that wealth should be shared. It wasn't ever about hurting people, shooting people, *killing* people. Wanda didn't understand this, he guessed, but he could make her understand.

He loved her. He could make her understand. But only if he could keep her near him, and she was going through a bad patch right now—the stress of her husband trying to kill her and then unexpectedly finding her true love in the form of a Gentleman Bandit, well, Spike realized that all could be a shock to the system. That's why she wanted the bullets; heck, at this point he couldn't blame her at all. The poor woman was scared out of her wits, and if getting some ammunition that would never be used was one way to soothe her, then he would do as she asked. It was the very, very least he could do.

He stood up, breathing hard through his nose, and took Wanda in his arms and kissed her, hard. "I'll show you something," he said, and zipped himself up, got his shoes on, walked all the way up through the bus and was just about to walk out the doorway to see if he couldn't go get his darling what she needed when Wanda called, "Spike!"

She ran up and peeled the mustache off the back of the R. V. Modine driver's license, then took Spike's hand and walked him back to her dressing area, sat him down in front of her makeup mirror and knelt down and started to apply some sticky stuff to his upper lip, rubbing with her finger to blend the flesh-colored substance in with his skin. That done, she took the mustache and gently stuck it to his face.

They both looked at him in her mirror. The effect was amazing.

When he thought it would be safe to talk, Spike said, "Why are you doing this right now, Wanda?"

"Don't you need ID to buy ammunition?"

"I do have a license of my own."

She eased back on her heels to look at the picture on the license and the person sitting in front of her. Looked at him. Looked at the license. Looked at him.

"Mr. Modine," she said at last, and smiled. "Call it a dry run, okay?"

When Gordon Mitchell was driving the big rigs cross-country for
Schneider, then J. B. Hunt, and then his own truck, he'd been on the
brink of death plenty of times; driving all day and all night, all the time,
was just too dangerous not to face some hairy situations once in a while.
One time he was rocketing through the Appalachians a few miles outside
of Nashville, huge eight-point grades yanking you down the mountain
darkness, when his electrical system gave out, just stopped working and
the entire truck went completely dark: No headlights, no running lights,
nothing. He was encased in a pitch black tomb, screaming down the
mountain at near seventy miles an hour. It was a few seconds of blind,
utter panic, seeing himself simply drive off the road, off the edge of the
mountain, because he couldn't see the road. There were no streetlights,
not even any other cars, and he couldn't stop, couldn't even slow down
without burning out his brakes.

· He wished he had visited one last time with that girl at the truck stop,
the one with the Roy Orbison tattoo on her thigh.

That time, he was just getting ready, after fifteen seconds of straight road that he knew had to curve any second, to bend over and kiss his ass goodbye, when he came up on a little Datsun that at least had taillights he could see. He drove white-knuckled right behind the little rice burner, no doubt scaring the shit out of the guy driving it—who saw a truck with no lights on two car-lengths behind him, smoke pouring from its brakes—but that little goddamn Datsun led him all the way down the mountain, where he could pull off and make a phone call to his dispatcher and drink until he passed out. That was a hell of a scare—he had to take a week off before he'd get behind the wheel again.

And that, Gordon thought now, was nothing compared to sitting in the Sierra County Jail waiting for the ax to come down. He sat in the tiny holding cell, watching the cops and the way they tried to act tough but bored, like they'd seen it all before. This wasn't like the big-city—he was thinking Elkhart here—holding areas with the caked piss on the metal john, the dead-eyed gang-bangers packed thirty to an eight-man cell, no guards in sight for hours. No, this was a small, small-town cell. It was clean, at least, and he could see into the station itself.

He could see a clock. He could watch his dream floating away second by second.

The cops seemed amused to have an actual person in custody. One of them even leaned against the bars of the cell and asked, not even looking at him, "So what they get you for?"

"Reckless endangerment, supposedly."

The cop chuckled and said, "*Supposedly*. I like that. Don't admit to anything."

Gordon didn't even bother to mumble anything under his breath.

They got him in there, booked him for "reckless endangerment," tried to get some information out of him about whom, other than himself, he was apparently trying to "endanger"—they wanted to know who was in the coach, as if they didn't know already, and he told them he wasn't saying a damn thing until he got a lawyer—and then stuck him in the holding cell to wait for a bail hearing sometime after the judge got there at nine.

They also told him that he could make a phone call. A *local* phone call.

A lot of good that would do him. Janey was God-knew-where—if she had gone home, which was pretty likely, giving up on the man who was going to give her everything, she'd still be long-distance. Any cronies he could call back in Elkhart would find it *very* interesting indeed that he'd been put in jail in New Mexico, and wouldn't be too likely to accept a collect call in the first place.

Who was he supposed to call? Wanda on the Vacationeer's cell phone?

He buried his head in his hands, thinking: *I never even got in touch with Atchison to get the new IDs—*

Atchison! His bank contact! He could call Atchison!

Gordon sprang to his feet in the cell, his eyes wide at his one chance to get the hell out of Truth or Consequences with his money and his sanity intact. He had to call David Atchison—he could get him the new ID, get him to his money, help him! Hell, Atchison was as deep into this as he was, practically! He *had* to help him out! And it was a local call!

"Officer! Officer!" Gordon shouted as politely as possible. "I'm ready to make my phone call!"

Truth or Consequences, New Mexico, located one hundred and fifty miles south of Albuquerque, started life as Hot Springs, so designated because of its rich supply of hot mineral springs some say are the secret to health and long life. In 1950, when television and radio producer Ralph Edwards—still honored by the city every year with his own fiesta—asked that some town in the United States show its respect to the venerable game show by changing its name to Truth or Consequences, Hot Springs answered the call, and has been rewarded with more TV and radio publicity than any other town its size. Not bad for a town of just seven thousand souls.

One other quality Truth or Consequences had was a steady supply of tourists, foreign and domestic, thanks to its location on that historic piece of Americana, Route 66, and to its unusual name, which looks great on a postmark. When one of its two banks, Sierra Savings and Loan, hired its own expert on foreign currency, David Atchison, they made a great choice. Knowing wealthy Europeans and Asians alike preferred to bring over large-denomination bills not circulated by U.S. banks, he made a move for their business, since Vista received a fee from the federal government every time it took a five-hundred-dollar bill or larger out of circulation.

David Atchison drove a beautiful Rambling Centennial mini-home, paid for (among other things) by the commission he derived from turning Gordon Mitchell's eye-catching thousands—brought by that oddball wife of his every month or so—into everyday hundreds, fifties, twenties, and tens, which he then put in a safety deposit box Mitchell had rented. If questioned, Atchison knew absolutely nothing. The money went into the Sierra books as thousand-dollar bills, but that just looked like normal overseas currency transfer—and of course, there was no account statement on a safety deposit box.

David Atchison also owned a villa by Sierra County's beautiful Elephant Butte Lake, on weekends flew his New Mexico Aerospace Cessna, and on nights when he told his wife he was working late enjoyed the affections of a kept twenty-three-year-old in a luxury apartment a client had provided to Atchison rent-free down in El Paso.

He made lots of money, got lots of perks, and he did it while keeping his nose completely and spotlessly clean.

His clients were many, and generous. David Atchison insisted all come to him, not vice versa. Truth or Consequences was his hub. It may have been inconvenient for some—the RV salesman, Ron Mitchell, came to mind as one who bitched plenty, even though the whole dang town was nothing but RVs—but it kept everything simple, neat, and on his terms, which nicely helped him avoid both truth and consequences.

And which was why, when his night-table phone rang at quarter to seven in the morning, he didn't want to pick it up.

It rang, and rang, and rang. Fifteen, twenty times before his wife, still in the throes of her Sunday night Bloody Mary binge, said, "Is the phone ringing?"

Letting her answer what could possibly be a business call was a bad idea, so, waiting another half-dozen rings, he rolled over and grabbed the receiver, mumbling, "God, what."

"David! Ron Mitchell."

Atchison put a hand over his eyes. "Our transaction is done, Mr. Mitchell."

"Been, um, a little bump in the road. Identification's been lost. My important identification for the *bank*, you know?"

"I can't help you with that," Atchison said. "That was through a third party. A fourth party, really. I can't help you."

"Fuck."

"Have a good trip, Mr. Mitch—"

"No, no, hold on, wait. Need to, ah, get access to the box. Might be another party looking to gain access." Mitchell sounded really strange, like somebody was with him, or listening in. "There any way you can block access?"

"Look, there's no way anyone's withdrawing anything without the proper ID, if that helps." Atchison was awake now, sitting up. "Where are you, anyway?"

"That's another thing. David—Mr. Atchison—this is very embarrassing. I need...I need somebody to come and bail me out."

"Bail you out."

"I'm in the Sierra County Jail. Gonna have a hearing at nine or so—"

Jesus H. Christ! "Uh—hey, who is this? You have the wrong number."

"Oh, David, please don't hang up—please—"

Atchison hung up.

He sat there on the edge of the bed, holding the receiver in his hand and staring at it. What the hell kind of trouble had Mitchell gotten himself into that he expected him to come and announce to the world that he was in cahoots with a criminal? He'd laundered millions and never gotten so much as a parking ticket—he'd be goddamned if he was going down to the freaking jailhouse to bail out some fool who couldn't keep himself out of trouble long enough to withdraw his money and get the hell out of town.

Then he realized he should've taken his fee out of the cash he moved for Mitchell, because how was the son of a bitch supposed to deliver that Vacationeer to him now? Twenty percent—that was about three hundred thousand dollars worth of vehicle he was owed, and now Mitchell was too hot for Atchison to collect it.

Unless... He looked at his watch. Almost seven. He could get down to the bank and take his cut out of the cash in the box before Mitchell could even get there. Hell, the dumb jerk had lost his ID anyway, so he'd probably have plenty of time to get over to Sierra, subtract the three hundred grand, and get out before Manager Bob even had the bank open.

Fucker thought he was going to pull a fast one on me, Atchison thought as he trudged over to the shower, then remembered that Gordon Mitchell was sitting in a cell at the Sierra County Jail and probably didn't think he was pulling a fast one on anybody. Poor sap was probably going to sit in jail until the authorities from wherever he was from—Illinois? Indiana? Iowa?—came and collected his sorry ass, then put him away for fifteen or twenty years. *Don't do the crime if you can't do the time.* Naturally, Atchison couldn't even conceive of how horrid it would be to do time for the various financial crimes he had committed, but he hadn't gone and gotten himself arrested, had he?

Atchison was chuckling to himself as he stepped into the hot water and got started scrubbing. It was funny, but Mitchell was the first "client" of his ever to get in legal trouble while his money was still in one of Atchison's special accounts. A couple of embezzlers, or maybe drug dealers—he couldn't remember, he hadn't paid all that much attention—had gotten arrested and extradited after fleeing the country, but he'd long since erased any trace of their accounts by the time they might have mentioned Sierra Savings and Loan. Besides, the laundered money that they took with them had always been transferred to another bank by that time—

Sierra was just a way station for the cash. Gordon Mitchell was the first to be arrested while the money was still there.

He froze and repeated the words in his mind: *While the money was still...* *Oh, shit.*

If Mitchell blabbed about Sierra, about *him*, and the cops found the money...

Oh, shit shit SHIT!

Atchison stood there under the water, trying to *think*. He had been so very careful, and now it could all be crashing down around him, Mitchell would lead the cops right to the account, unless—unless...unless *the box was already empty*. Ron Mitchell was a bullshit artist—the cops would think this was just one more example of his quick-thinking bullshit, trying to stall them.

But where would the money go? A million and a half dollars...

Mitchell said he thought "other parties" were going to try to "access" the box, hadn't he? And he said he didn't have his ID anymore, hadn't he?

All Atchison had to do was grab the keys for the box, get one next to it for himself, and move the cash. That was one thing you learn in the banking industry—cash is a wonderful, untraceable thing. So are safety deposit boxes.

Besides, hell, he'd be doing Mitchell a favor—he wouldn't want all that hard-earned cash *confiscated*, would he?

"Thanks for the call, Gordy," Atchison said out loud in the shower, and chuckled. A million and a half dollars, all for him. And, what with Mitchell going up the river for the next twenty years or so, there wouldn't even be anyone around to miss it.

Gordon clutched the receiver for a few more seconds, repeating, "David? Mr. Atchison? Hello?" until the officer eased it out of his hands.

"No luck, huh?" the officer said, and took the phone back to his desk. He shook his head in a way that showed Gordon he'd seen all of this before. "Maybe we'll let you try again after the judge talks at you."

This was it. Wanda was going to get the money—they had the ID, and Spike with the mustache would be convincing enough to get into the box and grab the cash, then get out of the country. Gordon was going to get sent back to Indiana in leg irons, with nothing to show for his years of toil but a bitch wife getting her back lotioned by Spike the MENSA member while Gordon was getting butt-slammed by some giant Black mass-murderer.

By the time he got out of jail, he'd probably be seventy years old.

He knew no one here; he'd fucked over everyone he knew back home; and even if the judge reduced his bond to a hundred dollars, he didn't have it, and so he'd have to sit there until that warrant came from Indiana and they decided to raise it just a bit—like to half a million—or to not set any bond at all.

Which wouldn't be impossible for him to round up if he could just say, Can I go over to the bank three blocks from here and get some of my embezzled cash so I can make bail and flee the country? I'd have my wife go do it, but ever since I tried to kill her, woman's been a little cranky.

At least Wanda, even with the money, would be long gone, and he wouldn't have to deal with attempted murder charges on top of grand larceny. With all of that stacked against him, the only way he'd be leaving prison would be feet-first.

There was nothing for him to do but sit and wait until nine, hope that whatever desert rat judge they had in this county had his act together, could get him in right at nine, maybe release Gordon on his own recognizance. Or maybe not.

But he had definitely hit bottom now. At least things couldn't get any worse.

"Well, hello, Gordon," a cheerful voice said as the guard unlocked the cell door.

It was Douglas Gann.

"I can't believe I'm seeing this with my own eyes," Gann said as he came in, sat down on the bunk next to Gordon, and the cop locked them both inside. "See, what you really have to do is *believe*. I *believed* this would happen, and here we are."

"Can hardly believe it myself," Gordon said.

"Oh, I bet, I bet. The RV you were hanging onto—Wanda was in there, I take it?"

"Not saying a goddamn word to you, detective."

"She's alive, then. That's good for you, Gordon, really." Gann cleared his throat and leaned in close. "See, I was tracking you—and her—all night, but the folks here wouldn't let me move in. Of course, you know that, don't you? Officer Perez made me let you go, and I sent you off after your wife, trying to get you to show me she was still alive. I didn't know then that I'd be hearing from her not half an hour later."

Gordon could feel his eyes bug, but tried to play it off. "That so?"

"You bet. See, she and I talked on the phone, made an agreement to get together and have a little sit-down, talk about you and all the trouble you've been causing her. I don't know why you didn't kill her when you were planning to—something got in your way, and it wasn't your conscience, was it?"

"Didn't plan to kill anybody."

"Oh, sure, sure. Well, we'll find out all the answers soon, won't we?"

"This is where I'm supposed to ask you what that's supposed to mean."

Gann looked at his watch. "Oh, in about five minutes I'm supposed to go meet your lovely wife, get her to come in and make a statement. I'm sure she'll get all of this cleared up."

Gordon looked between the bars at the clock on the wall. It was just about seven. Gordon knew how slowly police business went—in two hours, she could be just finishing up with Gann, or, if she was making some of the shocking claims Gann clearly expected her to, it could be a lot later than that. Filing attempted murder charges—hell, Gann got a hold of her, it could be ten, eleven o'clock before she could get away. It would probably be hours before she could get back to business.

Before she could get to the bank.

But, if all went right, not before Gordon could.

Wanda had to know this. "No way in hell she's gonna come down here and file a report," Gordon said.

"Not voluntarily, maybe, I grant you that," Gann said, and moved in for the kill. "That's why I'm putting her under protective custody. I'll slap the cuffs on her and haul her in here if it means she'll be safe from you until these guys nail you on her complaint or the Indiana warrant. Your ass is *grass*, mister."

Gordon looked at him now and tried to stifle a crazy grin. "Gonna make sure she isn't anywhere I can get at her, that it? Keep her locked up here all day if need be?"

"You heard me. I'm going to get every ounce of testimony out of her, even if it takes all day. And then I'm going to nail you to the wall."

Keep your cool, Gordon told himself. He wanted to jump and scream for joy—Detective Douglas Gann was the only thing standing between Wanda and Gordon's hard-earned money. The only thing—but enough. "Well, go get 'er, tiger," he said, finally unable to hold back his smile.

Gann said, "You may think this is funny now, Mitchell, but I promise you it won't be funny when I set up a roadblock at the border. They'll do that for attempted murder, you know."

"Don't doubt it," Gordon said, and figured that he would be long gone by the time Gann coerced Wanda into giving up going after the money and got her to make the full statement with all the trimmings he wanted. All he needed was two hours.

Actually, first he needed money for bail—if the judge would even set it. Then he needed some way to convince the bank he was R. V. Modine. Then he needed a car.

Shit—and all he had was two hours?

Gann stood and motioned for the officer to come let him out of the holding cell. "You just stay here," he said, "and I promise I'll be back—with your wife."

Gordon smiled at that. "Not an easy woman to deal with, you know."

"I think I know what I'm doing. Remember, Gordon, I've seen all of this before."

He watched Gann stop at the front desk to chew the fat with the sergeant up there, then slide his cop sunglasses on to go meet Wanda wherever the hell he had that set up.

Then Gordon just sat and watched the clock. He couldn't believe Wanda was just going to let the man take her in, no matter how bad she wanted to get back at her husband, when she could get at all that money. Hell, what was he saying? She was a weak woman, and would always be a weak woman. The stickup man had a thing for her—what a freak—so maybe she was feeling full of piss and vinegar, but in the end she would give up and give in, just so she could have something to bitch about later.

That was the way Wanda had been for twenty-five long years, and he didn't imagine a taste of young cock was gonna make all that much difference.

So let Gann take her in, take her into "protective custody," and let him get the hell out of there, make bail, give them his watch, his shoes, anything, and he could get out the door and shit, *run* the three blocks to the bank. Wanda could spin her tale of woe all day if she wanted—Gordon could be in Caracas by one in the afternoon.

But not unless a miracle occurred, and he somehow got the money to post bail.

He watched the minutes go by on the grungy clock on the grungy cinder block wall of the grungy police station. He watched ten minutes go by and depression sank on him again like a wet blanket.

That's when the officer said, "You're a popular guy, Mitchell," and unlocked the cell door to let in another visitor.

"Ronny," Janey Briggs said.

43

Spike, naturally, had no idea how to load the thirty-eight. He could vaguely remember what he'd seen in movies and on TV, good and bad guys—only good guys came to mind when he really thought about it now—frantically counting out bullets and slipping them into chambers or a clip, all the while keeping up a steady stream of chatter designed to mislead their opposite number into thinking they had plenty of shots ready to go. It always worked in the movies.

Real life was different. The pawn shop guy, after checking the ID and Spike's scribble—luckily, the signature of "R. V. Modine" was one loop and a bumpy line, easy to reproduce, very much unlike Gordon's real signature, Wanda had said (and no doubt why Gordon had chosen to use it)—counted out six bullets and asked, "You sure that's all you want? More you buy, more you save."

"I'm not planning even to use these," Spike said, trying not to move his mouth too much, lest his mustache pop off. He took the tiny bag and paid the guy, then stopped about halfway to the door and said, "Hey, um, can I ask a stupid question? How do you, um, *load* these exactly?"

"You should know how to load your weapon," the pawn shop guy said. "State of New Mexico, you can't get your permit without taking the gun safety course." He stared at him, and Spike was glad the guy didn't have the fake ID to refer to anymore. "That includes safely loading and unloading your weapon."

"Oh, right, no, I know. It's just been a while."

The guy nodded, unconvinced. "Be careful, now."

That'd be a lot easier if you'd cut the lectures and tell me how to load the darn thing, Spike thought, but kept it to himself and slipped out the door and back to the RV.

"You got them," Wanda said as soon as she saw the bag, sitting—literally, Spike saw—on the edge of her seat. "How many?"

"Six."

"*Six?* How many chambers are there?"

"Six, I believe. That's why I got six bullets, Wanda."

"But that's—that's not even one reload! *Six?*" She sat back on the sectional and let out a huge, disappointed sigh.

Spike gingerly placed the tiny bag on the dining area table and sat down on the bench stool, as far from Wanda as he could and not make it look like he was trying to stay far away from her, and said, "We don't need enough to reload the gun. We don't even need six in the first place. Nobody is shooting anybody."

"The hell they're not. Ten minutes, you're shooting Detective Douglas Gann."

Spike leaned his elbows on the table and covered his eyes. God, was he tired. "That's not my job."

"Not your—not—" Wanda sputtered, standing and stomping towards the table. "You little *shit!* You think you can—you can just come in here and take my honor, and not take the responsibility for it?"

Spike put his hands down and looked at her. "Your *honor?*"

"I am a *married woman*. You *fuck me* and expect to just *walk away?*"

"Um, Wanda? You wouldn't be walking anywhere if I hadn't come along."

"That's what you do, get women away from their husbands and seduce them?"

"Seduce—?" Spike started, then took a deep breath to get a hold of himself. "Excuse me, but I believe it was you who started rubbing my crotch while I was driving."

Wanda folded her arms and narrowed her eyes at him. "You had me at gunpoint."

"I don't think the gun was even out of my belt."

"You had a gun and screamed—in front of witnesses—that you were going to rape me and murder me."

"Witnesses? You mean *your husband?*"

"You had a gun and kidnapped me, Spike, with declared intent to rape me."

Declared intent? Spike didn't know if this was an actual legal term or Wanda's creation pieced together from television police dramas, but it sent a chill down his spine as he realized what was going on. "The gun is empty," he said quietly.

"I didn't know that when you said you were going to rape me."

"You know it now, and you're still with me in the parked vehicle."

"There's a bag of bullets right there," Wanda said. "A man with a gun, a man who forces my husband off our coach—"

"The husband who was going to *kill* you—"

"—says he's going to rape me and murder me, leave my body in the RV. I figure it's better to play along, take him to bed voluntarily, not make him angry—"

"That's not what happened!"

"I've got your cum inside me, Spike! And I've been punched! My face is bruised!"

"*Gordon did that!*"

"You've stolen my money, robbed a restaurant, and raped me! *Raped me!*"

"You know that's not what happened!"

"Doesn't matter. What matters is what I *say* happened. Your rich parents can get you off a robbery charge, right? But not rape. Not kidnapping and rape, Spike."

Spike grabbed the thirty-eight from the table and popped it open, loading each bullet carefully while he talked. "I helped you. I *helped* you. Forget that you were going to die when I saved you, forget that. Just remember the part about us being together—I gave you my love, Wanda. You can tell the police or whoever that I hit you and kidnapped you and raped you, but you know the truth: I loved you."

Wanda coughed a tiny, bitter chuckle. "'Loved'? With a *d*?"

Spike swung the chamber closed and pointed the gun at her. "With a *d*," he said. "I should've realized—studies do show that when members of a couple come from opposite sides of the tracks, it usually doesn't work."

"I'd call this not working, all right."

"Don't make me do this, darl—Wanda."

She didn't look scared; she looked resigned. She took a deep breath and kept her eyes on Spike, not on the gun, which was unusual—he'd heard that for the most part, people on the business end of a weapon stare at the weapon, not its owner.

Spike guessed it was different when you deserved to get shot.

"I don't even want the money," he said, sliding out off the bench and standing to keep her in his sight in the event she tried to run. "I just want to walk away now. We had something beautiful, but I guess it's over."

"Guess so." She didn't move, didn't look at him.

"I would have done anything for you, Wanda."

She laughed at that. She *laughed*. "Honey, the going got tough, and you got the fuck out. You wouldn't do nothing for me you didn't already want to do."

"Bullshit," Spike said, then regained his composure and started inching towards the front of the bus, trying to get past Wanda. "I'm walking away now."

She blocked him. "You want to walk away, you got to shoot your way out."

"I don't—damn it, you know I don't believe in violence."

She reached up then—she didn't have to reach out very far, he was right in front of her, trying to pass—and slapped him. His whole head turned with the force of her hand, and when he turned back, his face was red and his eyes were full of tears.

"Well, for me, you're going to have to make an exception," she said, and pulled the barrel of the gun to her stomach.

Spike looked down at the gun buried in the woman he had thought he loved, and let out a huge sob. "Don't make me do this. Please."

"You'll shoot me, but you won't shoot the detective. *That's* love, isn't it?"

He stood there with the gun against her, his hand shaking.

"Spike, you don't shoot me, you try to walk away, I'm gonna cry rape and anything else I can think of to put you behind bars until you're old and gray. Think of it, honey—field study with the lowlifes for the next forty years, all because you couldn't shoot somebody one lousy time."

His finger stiffened on the trigger, then he looked at her, looked into her blue-shrouded eyes, and saw that she was right. He lowered the gun and sat in a heap on the bench. "And if I shoot you, they'll find you full of my seed and bullets from my gun—"

"And you'll never see the light of day again anyway. Now you got it."

He laid the thirty-eight on the table. "Then I'm not shooting anyone."

There was the sound of tires crunching on the ground outside.

Wanda smiled and said, "Oh yeah. Yeah, you are."

44

It didn't take ten minutes for Gann to get from the police station to the Pine Knot Saloon. It wasn't open at seven in the morning, which was fine by him. He didn't need the whole world seeing him arrest a forty-three-year-old housewife for her own protection, putting cuffs on her if necessary. Doing *whatever* was necessary to bring her to safety. He had seen this before with his colleagues, seen chances to save endangered women slip away, leaving only regrets and "what-ifs" when she was killed by an angry spouse, a dealer trying to cover his tracks and remove witnesses, a jealous girlfriend of her husband's.

But this would not happen to him. Not Douglas Gann. He would do what it took to insure that. He fiddled with the cuffs for awhile, sitting in his car and taking a look at the damaged vehicle, and the stuffed them into his back pocket. Wanda would be protected.

It was a few minutes after seven, but he wasn't too late. He got out of the Caprice and walked around to where the Vacationeer's door used to be. Wanda was sitting stiffly in the driver's seat.

Gann smiled at her. His heart was soaring. "Alone enough for you?" he called to her.

She wasn't smiling, however. As she set the brake and climbed down from the liner, Gann could see her eyes were rimmed with red, her cheeks drawn, her makeup unable to cover the anger on her face. Gordon's betrayal must have been hitting her pretty hard.

"I'm glad we could talk," Gann started, the morning wind whipping across his face. "You coming all the way out?"

Wanda remained in the doorway of the coach. "What did you want, detective? If you need a statement, take it. I have plans."

Plans? "I want you to reconsider my offer. I want you to come in to safety."

"I'll be safe enough when you arrest Gordon."

Gann tried to keep his calm, but he was getting very nervous. Wanda's husband had Gann's satellite communication outfit and could find the RV in nothing flat. He had to get Wanda out of the RV and into the car he borrowed from the deputy. Fast. "Can we sit for a minute so I can get your statement?" he said, and motioned towards the car, which, in the back seat, could not be opened from the inside.

"Can't we take it here?" she said, looking back into the RV for something. "I don't feel safe. Why don't you come on board here?" She looked back again. What was back there?

"No, no good." *Why?* "Um, the recording equipment is in my car. Not allowed to remove it from the car, sorry."

Wanda was acting very peculiar. "Can you hang on a second?" she asked, and without waiting for a reply ducked back into the RV. Three seconds later she was back.

"Everything okay, Wanda?" he asked, patting himself for his sidearm, which, God, was still in the car. "No one's bothering you, are they?"

"Can you come a little closer, detective? I can't hear you."

As he stepped forward, he could see just from eyeballing her that something was terribly wrong: She looked agitated, sweaty, about to crack.

Enough was enough. "Wanda," he said, reaching into his back pocket, "I need to bring you in. It's for your own good."

She stood rock-still, her wide, liner-drawn eyes boring straight into him.

A shock of premonition hit Gann right before Wanda's face broke into a scream.

"Spike! *Now!*" she shrieked. "Jesus Christ, Spike, do it!"

Gann skidded to a stop on the gravel lot. Time slowed to a complete halt. He could see the barrel of the gun come around the corner of the RV wall next to and behind Wanda first, peeling out inch by inch. He swung his arms around to change direction, get back to the deputy's car, get out of the line of fire.

He threw a glance back as his feet struggled for purchase on the gravel, seeing a pale, almost green-faced kid holding the thirty-eight in Gann's general direction. His joints seemed wobbly and he slipped down one of the plastic-covered stairs of the RV, losing any aim he had on Gann, giving him a few extra seconds.

Gann's feet finally bore down on the packed rocks and dirt as Wanda grabbed the gun from the kid, held it hard and tight in her hand and launched herself off the RV's stairs toward him, opening her mouth and emitting a long, loud, inhuman cry of anger, tears, frustration, like the sound of a caged wild animal finally turning on its handlers after years of abuse.

Gann got to the deputy's car, hurling himself at the door handle just as Wanda squeezed off the first shot, running towards him and screaming her paralyzing wail. The bullet exploded *thwok* right through his back, piercing his lung, and shattering his sternum before it punched a hole through the car door, shredded the seats, and ripped a hole exiting the door on the opposite side.

Gann held on to the door, his fingers grabbing the open window's frame. He could feel Wanda Mitchell running up behind him now, pulling the trigger and shattering his shoulder blade, his collar bone, filling his chest with shards of ivory.

Still, he held the door. He wouldn't let go. To let go would be death.

Finally, he felt the hot muzzle right against the back of his skull—*why hadn't he sensed this? Why hadn't he seen this coming?*—then heard the first instant of the pistol's *crack* as the lead exploded against his brain, and then knew no more.

Gann's fingers clamped the door in a death grip even as his body slumped down against the blood-splattered and punctured metal. He did not let go.

Three

Wanda stepped over the body of Lieutenant Detective Douglas Gann, the man who tried to keep her from her destiny, from punishing the one who had taken her life away. "I'm sorry," she said to him, and shoved his body away from the car. It slid down to the ground, smearing blood against the Caprice's blue paint.

"This wasn't for nothing, Doug. Your death won't be in vain."

She looked at Spike, who turned by the front of the coach and puked. The weak son of a bitch *puked*. Had he been the man of her dreams just the night before?

She chuckled to herself. There *was* no man of her dreams. Only bits and pieces of a larger nightmare.

"Got that out of your system?" she said, a smirk cocked on her face.

"Oh God, Wanda, you just murdered that man! You *murdered* a *policeman!*"

"He was gonna stop us."

Spike took a lunging step towards her. "*Stop us?* What the hell did we come here for! He didn't even know where we were!"

"He could've found us."

"They're *going* to find us, Wanda. They're going to find us and we're going to get the gas chamber."

"Not part of the experiment, huh?"

Spike's face was a mask of outrage, bits of vomit stuck to his chin and streaming from his nose as he yelled. "This isn't funny—this is *it!* You can fulfill whatever white-trash destiny you want, end up on Death Row, but this is *it* for me!"

Wanda stared, impassive. "I thought you loved me, Spike."

"You just put a man to *death*, an *innocent* man, a *cop!*" He put his hand to his forehead, looking like he was going to throw up again. "I can't love someone who would do that!"

"I thought you were gonna go all the way for me."

"Go—? Wanda, do you even understand what has happened here?"

Enough of this bullshit, she thought, and moved in with the heart-breaker. She stuck the gun in his hand, aimed it out towards the mountains behind the Pine Knot Saloon, and squeezed her finger over his in the trigger.

Spike's look as the gunfire echoed back said it all. *What the hell was that?*

"Yeah, I understand what happened. The man who kidnapped me—and raped me—shot the policeman who was gonna bring him in. Shot him in cold blood."

Spike was frozen to his spot, unblinking as he stared at her.

"He bought bullets and everything. Used a fake ID and disguise."

After a few more seconds of wide-eyed incomprehension, Spike said, "You incredible bitch. I can't believe I ever loved you."

She sauntered over to him and relieved him of the gun, tossing it next to Gann's body. "It doesn't have to be that way, though."

Spike just stared at her again, but his eyes narrowed.

"You just have to get off your high horse and finish what you started, Gentleman Bandit. Stop saying *this is it*, because it isn't a goddamn research project anymore. Stop puking because there's a little blood. Fuck, what you just saw? That's been coming for twenty years. I almost did that to Gordon a hundred times."

"What stopped you?"

"What do you think?" she said, and laughed her bitter little laugh. "Love."

The judge was fifteen minutes early, and Gordon was the only resident of the Sierra County Jail holding cell, so as soon as the clock struck nine, he was escorted into chambers to stand next to his public defender while Janey waited and watched from the gallery. At the prosecutor's table was a weary-looking lawyer along with the arresting officer and the duty officer who was just getting off when Gordon was brought in, Sergeant Frick; for some reason, he had chosen to stay late and add his two cents to the proceedings. There was an empty chair at the table; Gordon hoped to God that wasn't for Douglas Gann.

The judge asked the prosecutor to state his case, which he did: The defendant, Gordon Mitchell, matched the description of a man seen hanging from the front end of a moving recreational vehicle on Interstate 25 south of Truth or Consequences. The state believed Mr. Mitchell was attempting to coerce the driver of the vehicle into an accident, thereby putting the occupants of the vehicle as well as himself in mortal danger. Mr. Mitchell was later apprehended on the shoulder of the interstate, having apparently fallen from the RV and having his fall cushioned by a door, which seemed to have been broken off during the event. There was no report of an accident involving the RV.

"You're a very lucky man," the judge said.

Gordon, knowing Janey was sitting not fifteen feet behind him, couldn't have agreed more. "Truly a stupid thing to do, Your Honor," he said.

The judge said, "You bet your behind it was. Now, you want to just plead *no contest* and get this over with?"

Gordon's "lawyer" wasn't making a sound, which was fine—Gordon didn't need anyone coming in and messing up the rapport he was building up here. He said, "Sounds great, Your Honor."

"There's a fine, all right?"

Gordon nodded. This was working out even better than he—

"Um, judge?" the prosecutor said with a little tremor in his voice. "Sergeant Perez here says this man is wanted on interstate embezzlement charges."

Gordon swung around. *Perez?*

There the brown-skinned officer stood from what was an empty chair two minutes earlier, giving Gordon a little look he didn't care much for. But Detective Gann was nowhere to be found.

The judge's eyebrows raised, and he looked through his bifocals at the docket on the bench, then at Gordon. "Is that right, Mr. Mitchell?"

Gordon swallowed hard. What was on that sheet of paper in front of the judge? He couldn't read the old man at all—he'd hate to face him in poker. "Not that I know of, Your Honor," he said, and wondered where that silver-tongued devil he used to know had gone.

"Huh. Counsel, I don't see anything about embezzlement here," the judge said to the prosecutor. "Sergeant? What do you know about this?"

Perez cleared his throat and said, "At this time what I know is that there was an officer, a lieutenant detective came down from Indiana to bring Mr. Mitchell into custody for grand larceny back in his home state."

"Is there a warrant? Where is this detective?"

"I don't know, judge."

"Don't know what? If there's a warrant, or where this detective is supposed to be?"

"Um, either one, sir," Perez said, glancing back towards the door to chambers, through which no one was entering.

"Well, I'm sorry, but if the lieutenant detective is gonna come all the way from Indiana, he should at least show up at the hearing for his guy," the judge said, and took off his bifocals, chewing on an end of them while he stared at Gordon. "Let me just ask you one thing, Mr. Mitchell, all right?"

Gordon nodded and swallowed. Here it came, the chance to fuck up his open door.

"Just what in the heck were you doing hanging off a moving vehicle?"

Gordon looked back at Janey and shook his head slightly before facing the judge and saying, "My wife had stolen it and was driving off with another man."

"No kidding," the judge said.

"Seriously, Your Honor."

"You got life insurance, Mr. Mitchell?"

"Yes, sir."

"How much?"

Gordon thought. "Hundred thousand or so."

"Well, you almost went and made your cheatin' wife a rich woman, didn't you?" the judge said, and laughed. "Think of that next time you go getting any more brilliant ideas like trying to stop an RV with your bare hands. Fine is set at one hundred dollars. You can pay at the bailiff's station."

"But judge—one hundred—it's a felony—" Sergeant Perez began to say, but the judge banged his gavel and fixed him with a stern look, and that was that.

3

Janey paid the fine for him, out of cash Gordon had given her as a contingency fund months earlier, money Gordon had forgotten about completely. He kissed her; he hugged her; he looked at his watch.

It wasn't even five minutes after nine. The whole thing hadn't taken five minutes. There was still time. "Got to get to the bank," Gordon said before their embrace outside the courthouse adjoining the jail was even through.

"I'm not going, Ronny," was all Janey said before she started crying.

"Not—? Sweetheart, we're *this* close." He put out of his mind for the moment the fact that he was going to shoot her dead when he had finished with Wanda and Spike. "Bank's three blocks away—you and me can be over the border by noon."

She looked at him with those big, wet eyes and said, "What about your *wife?*"

"What, back in there? I just had to say that to the judge, you realize that, don't you?"

"No—I mean, did she give up or what?"

The finely tuned engines on his mental P-38 had been sputtering for a while now, but he was still sharp enough not to tell a bald-faced lie that would be turned around on him five minutes later, so he said, "Probably gonna be at the bank."

"The bank right now?"

"She's made my life a living hell since I was twenty-one—think she's gonna stop now?"

Janey nodded, biting her lip to fight back more tears, but they came anyway. "I just can't do this anymore," she said. She took a step towards her LeBaron and looked at him again. "That bitch—that *bitch, that bitch!*—is still a part of your life, and she'll be like that forever, won't she?"

"She—"

"Don't even answer that, Ronny." She stepped forward and kissed him on the cheek, like an aunt at a funeral. "I know the answer. Don't, okay?"

"How about a ride?" he said, trying to look appropriately mournful.

"I just can't," she said, and went to her car, got in, and drove away.

Gordon watched his lover go for all of five seconds before he took off running as fast as his tired legs would take him in the direction of Sierra Savings and Loan.

Two minutes hadn't clicked off the grungy clock inside the New Mexico State Police post when the fax line rang and began receiving a transmission from the Elkhart City Police. It was an arrest warrant for one Gordon Reeve Mitchell.

Sergeant Perez, pissed off at himself and ready to go home at last and sleep this whole goddamn shift off, walked by the fax on his way out the door. He was almost to his car when he said, "Son of a bitch," and high-tailed it back inside, his weary brain almost hoping the name on the fax wasn't what he thought it was.

But it was.

He bust back out the door and scanned the parking lot, thinking maybe the cocky shit was still around. Then he got back inside and showed the warrant to the duty officer. "He can't be far," Perez said, adding to nobody in particular, "All night that detective from Indiana is riding me—would someone please tell me where the hell he is now, when I actually need him?"

Spike didn't really care anymore what socioeconomic factors did or didn't contribute to the way Wanda Mitchell thought and acted; what he did care about was getting away from her, getting away from the bloodshed, the violence that had engulfed him and this killer, this woman he thought he knew and loved. But no, no—the "score" was still on, the "job" she wanted him to do still had to be done.

He didn't want to do it. He didn't want anything to do with this. There was innocent blood all over it.

Soon his blood could be all over it. His life, his freedom, gone as he's framed for rape and murder. But if he went through with ripping off what Wanda's husband had already ripped off...

If it was the only way out of this, it was the only way out. After all, how could he stand on principle after he'd held up a restaurant, something that had exactly nothing to do with helping anyone understand anything, and bought the bullets his lover—the Bonnie to his Clyde—had used to mur-der a police detective? Nothing he did now was going to bring Gann back anyway, and if it meant he might escape with his freedom, even his life…he *was* a college graduate. He wasn't an idiot. He could do what it took and then put all of this behind him and help the underprivileged with his cut of the money like he had always intended to do.

"So what's the plan?" he asked her as she parked a block away from the bank and engaged the brakes on the Vacationeer. "Do we go in with guns blazing?"

She shook her head. "It's *my* money already, Spike. All we have to do is get it out. It's in a safety deposit box—all we have to do in go in, show the manager your ID, and use our key while he uses his key to open the box."

"Then what? Say thanks, and by the way, could you help us with this million dollars? It's kind of heavy."

Wanda dumped the contents of her huge purse—a dozen plastic clamshells of makeup, lipsticks, papers and pens, candy bars, eyeglass and sunglass cases—onto the table and held the leather bag open for Spike to see. "I think it'll fit. Besides, once the manager turns the key for us to take the box out, we get to use the little room. Very private. Just load up the purse and walk out."

"We could use my backpack."

"No, the purse'll do fine. Nobody notices a purse."

"It seems too easy."

She put a hand on his knee, and immediately, despite himself and the fact that she had used that very hand to take down an innocent man, he felt that familiar stirring. "Gordon planned it to be easy. Can you imagine showing a fake ID and asking for a million and a half in cash from a teller? That might attract some attention. That's the whole point of the safety deposit box."

"You're amazing," Spike said, and he meant it. "We're really going to get the money. Really."

"Really."

"I'm sorry I called you a…a bitch. Blackmail has that effect on me, I guess. And witnessing a murder."

She gave him a smile, deep red lips opening around her slightly crooked teeth, and said, hand moving up slightly on his thigh, "Well, it was for your own good."

He took a deep breath. "Then—you didn't mean what you said? You weren't going to turn me in?"

"Don't worry about that right now. Let's make up," she said, and moved her hand up to his crotch, feeling the growing bulge there.

"Do we have time for this?"

"Not right this second. But I'm about to tell you the plan, and I need your complete and undivided attention."

That sounded good to him. He remembered suddenly how he could love her after all. He would let himself be useful to her one last time, let her get the last of Gordon's influence out of her system and get her fortune, before he put his foot down and made darn sure they started acting according to his philosophy once again. He'd let her use him—that's what she was doing with the pilfering of the safety deposit box, it had nothing to do with her romantic feelings for him, he knew that—and then, he knew this too, she would have no further actual *use* for him, allowing them to live purely and on love, if that's what she had ever wanted with him. If they were meant to be together at that point, they would be, and it would be according to his rules, his philosophy.

That was the lesson he would teach her—money was great, but principles, philosophy, were greater.

Wanda smiled to herself as she remembered the crazy shit she'd yelled into Spike's ear the first time they had sex, screaming for him to give it to her, show her he was a real man, and on and on.

But it was really true this time, wasn't it? Time to show her he was a real man.

And that real man was one R. V. Modine.

She told him the plan—a simple one, basically *go in and get the money and come back out*—then got the list started on the makeup she needed to slather Spike in to make him convincingly match the ID Gordon had made with his little chippie. They had the mustache already, of course, but she had to lighten Spike's thick black hair a bit, put some powder in it maybe, and thin the locks back a little to mimic Gordon's receding hairline. The boy may not have liked it, but it would be done before he even had a chance to protest.

She didn't want to have to threaten him with the whole rape-and-murder thing, but he was going to have to be a real man, probably for the first time in his young life, and she had to do what she had to do as well.

She looked at Spike's slim face.

Gordon—or R. V. Modine, whatever—also had about sixty pounds on young Spike, but Wanda knew, just as in her days as a cosmetologist when she could make weight seem to disappear with the right stroke of a brush, so could she make a slight double chin or even a little jowl. It was just his face that they'd be looking at, if they even looked at that, so she could get him at her makeup table and in five minutes have the job done.

Which was good, since it was a little after nine already. The bank was open, and waiting for them. Five minutes.

6

Sweat poured off Gordon in rivers, soaking his shirt, making his khakis feel like they were going to slide right off of him. His feet were drenched inside his black socks and topsiders. The last time he ran, really ran, was so distant in his memory that he couldn't bring it up.

His gut bounced and sent ripples all through his torso—he'd always had a bigger top than bottom, and now his skinny legs, coated with sweat, were threatening to give out on him before he even made it the three blocks to the bank. His gut bounced as he ran, his back screamed out each time a foot would make contact with the roadside, his neck muscles were straining as he shook salty stinging drops out of his eyes.

There would be plenty of time for working out once he got his cash and got down to Venezuela, he told himself, but knew that was only if he didn't give himself a heart attack first. What a day it had been already—hanging off the Vacationeer, belting Wanda a good one in the face, running three blocks in the desert heat.

He kept himself focused on the cool drinks they'd have on the plane to Caracas.

Finally, his whole body about to give out from the exertion, Gordon padded up to the side of Sierra Savings and Loan, a place he hadn't seen in person since his first visit with Atchison almost a year earlier. He leaned his head on the stucco wall, and knew immediately something was wrong.

Cool down, he told himself, *supposed to cool down.* High school and football—the last times he had really bothered to use his muscles except for pumping hands and humping women—were echoes of the distant past, and it took a few seconds to remember anything about his physical conditioning. He couldn't remember *why* he was supposed to cool down, only that he was.

So he took a step or two away from the bank wall, and felt his gorge rise up and come spewing out of his mouth, his nose, puke rioting out of him and splattering the sidewalk in front of the bank. His stomach felt like it was turning itself inside-out as everything he had eaten for the past day and a half shot up and out, bending him in half and making him bark out loud as he expelled the nasty stuff down his chin and shirt and onto the plants and sidewalk.

That was why he always had to cool down, he remembered now.

He stood there, near the entrance to Sierra Savings and Loan, dark vomit stuck to his face and clothes, sweat matting his hair down and sticking his clothes to him in great dark blotches. He didn't have his R. V. Modine ID or his box key, and he certainly didn't look like someone who a bank employee would let into a safety deposit box on his good word alone.

He ran a hand through his wet hair and remembered Atchison, his contact, his savior, the one person who could help him through this nightmare. Sure, he didn't want to come and bail him out of jail—shit, Gordon would've been the same way! But the man wanted his fee, didn't he? Of course he did.

Gordon wiped some of the crap off his face on the leaves of a plant outside and stepped into the beautiful air conditioning of the bank lobby.

David Atchison had made an entire career out of playing it safe, taking large bills from overseas transfers and changing them into smaller bills, for a fee. Mixed in there was laundered cash, lots of it, but it was visually indistinguishable from the bona fide exchanged stuff. He'd played it safe and always come out *okay,* certainly not hurting for his effort, but never making the big score, either.

Now it was ten minutes after nine, and thanks to Ron Mitchell's moronic bumbling, Atchison was finally going to be able to make that score and leave the world of banking behind for a while. He was stealing the money, he understood as he got a hold of both the keys to the safety deposit box belonging to "R. V. Modine," but he was stealing it from someone who could never report it stolen!

And that was important, because it was vital to Atchison that no one ever, *ever* make a link between himself and Ron Mitchell; that would open him up to investigation, and that would open up a lot of sensitive information on people who expected their transactions at Sierra to stay completely confidential, forever.

Losing his job, even his money, would be the least of David Atchison's problems, if somehow he were linked to Gordon and that link revealed other links. Horrible, painful death would be more of a pressing problem. He had only dealt with professional criminals—mob guys, drug kingpins, the occasional jewel thief—until Mitchell, and he had learned the hard way the lesson not to do that. Now Atchison had to pack it up and get going before the whole house of cards he had built so carefully came fatally crashing down on him.

Pack it up and get going with Mitchell's million and a half bucks, of course.

Atchison entered the vault with both keys, put the bank's in one lock and was just sliding the other home when one of the tellers poked her head around the steel door and said, "Mr. Atchison? There's a...customer wanting to speak to you."

"Have them take a seat in my office."

"He says it's urgent, sir. He says to tell you it's Richard Modine."

Atchison's hand recoiled from the lock. He tried to compose himself before he mumbled to the teller, "I'll be right there."

He slid the bank's key out of the lock. Mitchell was there? He was using the fake name, good, because no one would remember him as Gordon Mitchell. No one could link Mitchell and him if they didn't know it was Mitchell, right? What link could there be? What link could there possibly be?

People could remember Mitchell's face. Shit, they could pick him out from the surveillance cameras, say "That's him, that's the man I saw talking to Mr. Atchison!" And the cops would see the link, see the connection, right away. In a matter of days, records could be checked, names could be named, and Atchison could be found hanging from a bed sheet tied to a pipe in his jail cell, an "apparent suicide" ordered by one of his former clients whose books had been unexpectedly opened.

He had to get out of there. He had to get past Mitchell with no one linking the two of them. If he didn't, he was a dead man.

Mitchell, you stupid fucking bastard! Can't you even keep track of your lousy ID and key? Jesus! He gets arrested, he gets his RV—shit, *Atchison's* RV—stolen, then comes around here looking to be let into the box! *Bullshit!*

Atchison could feel a trickle of sweat crawl down his forehead and into his eye as he stood frozen in the vault, the incriminating, *linking* keys to Mitchell's box in his hands.

The teller stepped around the door. "Mr. Atchison—"

"Here!" he said sharply, and shoved the keys into the teller's hand. He moved quickly through the back area, trying to remain hidden behind the other tellers there that early.

"David!" a voice, that damned familiar voice, called from the other side of the counter, "It's Gord—Richard! Richard Modine! R. V. Modine! *David!*"

The tellers were turning to look at Atchison. The man calling him, Ron Mitchell without a doubt, was caked with puke and his hair was greasy-looking. His face was red. He was sure to leave an impression—*as he called for him!*

"Mr. Atchison!"

The customers were looking at Atchison now, the tellers, the cameras, everyone. He was still walking, almost running now, as he stared at everyone staring at him, and as he yelled to Mitchell, "I don't know you!" he *did* break into a run, started running and punched his fists against the emergency exit at the back of the building.

A piercing alarm sounded and everyone immediately threw their hands up to their ears—everyone except Atchison, who counted off the fifteen seconds before the door would open, then burst through it and started running back behind the building, through the drive-through, and towards his car. He would think of something, anything, to erase whatever link it was people were trying to make between that puke-covered man in the lobby and the squeaky-clean bank officer now making a mad dash for escape from a certain death sentence. He would think of it on his way out of town.

8

It all happened so fast Gordon wasn't sure what he was seeing. First, Atchison speed-walking out of the vault, then running, then "I don't know you!" and the fire alarm going off. Nobody knows what to do, they all cover their ears like they're in a fucking combat zone, people hitting the floor, going crazy, because when this shit happens in a *bank*, it usually means robbery, and that means there's gonna be shooting.

But if this was a robbery, where was the robber? In the vault? *Fuck me,* his brain suddenly shrieked, *are Wanda and Spike robbing the fucking vault?* In the confusion, he stepped up and leaned back behind the counter, peeking into the U-shaped area lined with hundreds of safety deposit boxes. No one was inside.

"Sir, did you need some help?" a teller yelled over the pulsating fire alarm. She took in his whole appearance; Gordon was sure it didn't invite confidence in his banking plans.

He held his hands out in front of him and backed off, showing that he was no harm. Then he saw Atchison through the window to the drive-through, running past at full speed to his car in the parking lot.

What the hell?

Atchison was his only hope of getting into that box without his key or the Modine ID—if Atchison went on break or whatever the hell he was doing, Gordon wouldn't be able to get the money! He had to get out there and talk to the man!

He whirled around and made for the front door just as he heard a new kind of high-pitched whine. Fire trucks.

And police cars.

He couldn't be in the bank—he had to get outside to Atchison, get outside before the police got in there and locked everyone in until they had a handle on what was happening. That was standard procedure.

He made a leap for the door, but someone was already swinging it open. He made a dash for the outside and slammed up against the shoulder of someone entering the bank.

"Excuse me—" he muttered, looking ahead at Atchison's Stingray tearing out of the parking lot and three police cars and a fire engine screaming down the street towards the bank.

He almost didn't notice that the person he had bumped into was Wanda, and she didn't see him at all.

Spike Jones—hair dusted gray and mustache in place—was holding the door. Spike looked right at Gordon, his eyes behind cheap sunglasses, but didn't seem to recognize him as he darted inside.

Wanda. And Spike—wearing a mustache.

Gordon was frozen. They were there—they were *right there*—but now the police were pulling up and were on their way inside, and all Wanda had to do was point at him and they'd drag him away. He had chunks of fucking *puke* on his shirt, for Christ's sake; he looked like a freaking vagrant, and he got the feeling that even if he weren't wanted on a variety of creative criminal charges, the police of Truth or Consequences probably frowned on vagrants bothering people in the city's banks.

He unglued himself from the sidewalk and trudged half a block with his head down, picturing Spike and Wanda with the money, fucking him out of everything.

Then he saw the doorless Vacationeer parked out of sight of the bank, and almost kissed it as he stiffly walked up, took a quick look to make sure no one was watching, and climbed inside.

"Y'all having a fire?" Spike said, trying to sound *déclassé* as he put his key into one of the safety deposit box locks. "Whole lotta excitement around here."

"No, no problem, Mr. Modine. We just had someone…become ill and had to use the emergency exit, that's all." The teller slid out the box and led him and Wanda to the beveled glass room where they could conduct their business. "The police haven't asked us to shut the doors—we can still accommodate our customers."

"Whoeee—no fire." Spike pronounced it *far*. "Quite a relief, huh, sugar?"

"Quite, R. V.," she said, then added as soon as the teller shut the door to the privacy booth, "I think you're laying it on a bit thick."

"What? Don't you think I've done research into how people of different economic backgrounds talk?" He said it defensively, but smiled. They were safely ensconced in the room with their booty now—with plenty of police lurking around in the lobby, making sure everything was okay, but *they* weren't doing anything illegal. This was Mr. Modine's box, and here was Mr. Modine! "It's show time."

Wanda took a deep breath, then put her hands on the box lid and eased it open, almost afraid to look.

When she did, she saw a million and a half dollars in hundreds, fifties, and twenties, crisply arranged in rows of bills and bound with paper bands, just like in the movies.

All she had ever put in the box had been small stacks of thousand-dollar bills; Mr. Atchison had done the rest.

Atchison. She hadn't seen him around the bank while they waited for the girl to get the bank key to their box; she wondered if anyone had ever caught on to his little scams. Probably not—guys like that were usually too smooth ever to let themselves get linked to anything dirty.

"We did it. Gordon didn't beat us to it. You've gotten what you wanted now."

Wanda didn't say anything, just stared at the piles of money. Her money. *No,* she thought as she looked at Spike and took his hand. *Their* money. "Spike," she said. "I love you."

Spike's eye twitched. "I thought you didn't want this anymore."

"Spike, we can do it. We can be together."

"Is that relief talking, now that you've won? Or do you just see one final way to get back at your husband?"

She gave him a half-smile as she said, "I don't know what would piss him off more than me being happy."

"Is that what this, all of this, has been about? Getting back at Gordon?" He still held her hand, but looked at her now with new eyes, eyes that bored into her and made her transparent, eyes she felt could see right through her. "You were going to send me to prison. You were going to frame me for rape and murder."

"I—Spike. That was just talk."

"You killed a man. You wanted *me* to kill him."

She blinked back what felt like a tear. "I was wrong. I was insane. I wish I had listened to you—that poor man would be alive now. I'm...I'm sorry, Spike."

He looked like he wanted to believe that so much.

She gazed back into his eyes for a moment, then once again took in the sight of all that money, which was hers now. There was no way in hell Gordon could do anything about it; she had won. It was the ultimate rush. The least she could do was give Spike the truth, the whole truth, everything.

Which was what, exactly? That she had let herself fall in love—and in bed—with him, her first new lover since her husband—in other words, her second lover ever—because that lousy son of a bitch finally pushed her too far, or would have if Spike hadn't come along and saved her wretched life? That she would like to get to know Spike now, and not have to wonder if everything she felt for him was because of Gordon? Was that the truth?

"Yeah," she said to Spike at last. "It was all to get back at Gordon…at first."

"And what is it now?"

"I thought you weren't a real man because you wouldn't shoot Detective Gann."

Spike nodded. He was a sensitive type; he knew what had been going through her mind, hadn't he? And maybe that had added to his hesitation, not wanting to commit the ultimate crime for a woman who had such a low opinion of him in the first place.

"Spike, I…"

He waited, not giving a thing away.

"I fell in love with you," Wanda said. "You saved my life, and I love you. I never met anybody like you."

He hesitated. "So—if I go with you—it's not just to burn Gordon? It's not just to get him back? You're finished with all of that?"

"Spike, I *love* you. I want you with me."

"That's good, 'cause I love you, too," he said, and after a few seconds said, "And let's not forget—it would also piss off your husband to no end."

She smiled. "That's just a bonus."

She took him in his arms then, and let him kiss her neck, make her feel like a real woman again, a free woman, a woman who would never have to suffer the insults and abuse, the stings and arrows or whatever, of her husband ever again, now that she was wrapped in the arms of a loving, *real* man.

When he came up to meet her lips with his, she closed her eyes and saw the future, saw the sun fat and orange and low in the sky, just dipping its oval in the water of the horizon as she sat back in a lounge chair and sipped a strawberry daiquiri and let the hands of her young lover find their way all over her back and neck, her arms, her stomach, down and down—

"Hey, whatcha doing down there?" she said with a thrill.

Spike grinned and said, "Just seeing if maybe we can consummate this new understanding."

Wanda looked at the locked door and made sure she couldn't make out anything on the other side of the beveled glass. She lifted off her shirt, then said "Wait," and dumped the cash out on the table. Then she slid out of her pants and got on top of all that money.

"This is getting to be a habit," Spike said, and took her.

When they finished and got zipped up and smoothed their hair into something looking at least halfway respectable, Wanda and Spike high-tailed it out of the safety deposit room and out of the bank, giggling all the way at their trespass over decent behavior. They hung onto each other like high school sweethearts, the purse stuffed full of money hanging heavily between them. The bored-looking police and firemen had already unlocked the front doors—the fire alarm had been tripped by an ill employee, Wanda heard somebody say. She imagined there would be some time answering questions in a windowless room for whoever that poor bastard was.

She scanned the street as they made their way out of Sierra Savings and Loan, looking for one man, who wasn't there. Finally, he wasn't there—he wasn't there to dog her steps, bring out the worst in her, make her feel like shit for her just being herself.

He wasn't there to try to kill her or take her money away.

She gripped Spike even tighter as they got to the coach and he took her hand to help her inside. The Gentleman Bandit. It was a good nickname, she thought, and, for the first time since Gordon had brought up the idea of stealing a fortune from her uncle's lot, getting the money didn't look like something that had to take everything else away.

9

Not even waiting for Wanda to start up the RV and get them moving, Spike launched himself into the Vacationeer's bathroom and threw the door shut. He fell to his knees and hacked dryly into the toilet.

It's not about the money, he told himself as he sat with his backpack still on his back, pressed against the sink cabinet, and tried to catch his breath.

Then it's about the sex. You took Wanda—again—on a pile of money. You fucked her again on a big pile of filthy lucre. It's about the money and it's about the sex and any little señorita you were going to save from some Mexican brothel can just get her little caboose back to work. That's true, isn't it?

Spike swore it wasn't. *It's about love.*

Love? he answered himself. *When are you going to learn your lesson? Love and saving the world—these things are possible only with money. And with sex.*

Did he honestly think he'd feel what he felt for Wanda if she hadn't made love to him? And why was he planning on going down to Mexico only if he was loaded up with cash? And for God's sake, rescuing a *prostitute?* Could this be more psychologically loaded with sex and money? *It's about love,* he repeated to himself, and let out a chuckle as the final seasoning of the Freudian stew suddenly sprang into his mind:

It's about violence.

He shut his eyes tight and rocked against the cabinet. That's what it was—it was all about sex, about money, about *violence.* He "fell in love" with a woman because she was something physically he had never had, not because of her social views or any kind of charming blue-collar history. He made a mini-career out of robbing people, culminating now in this million-dollar take, not because of the good it would do some mythical Mexican or the Fat Cats he held up, but because it lined his own pockets. He bought bullets, not because his woman wanted him to, but because he must have secretly wanted violence to result. He must have secretly wanted Detective Gann to die.

No, his mind said. *Maybe lust, maybe greed—but never violence.*

Prove it, his mind said.

Spike opened his eyes as he felt the Vacationeer rumble to life and start moving. He hung on as the RV went around a long corner—maybe an on-ramp—and then smoothed out. They must have been on the interstate now, heading south towards Las Cruces, then El Paso and over the border into Mexico, where he and Wanda would start a new life.

And it *would* be a new life. He would prove to himself that violence was not a part of Spike Jones. Neither was greed. Or lust. From now on, it would be as it should have always been—peace, love, charity.

From these would come hope, which he had felt slip away as he watched the woman he loved shoot dead an innocent man. He would get his hope back again.

He stood up and flushed the toilet, filled the sink to splash some water on his face. That's when he heard the bedroom door next to the bathroom open up. The click was quiet and the door hardly creaked, but the bathroom door was thin as cardboard and Spike could hear each sound quite plainly.

The vehicle was rocking gently—Wanda was driving. That meant there was somebody else on the RV, somebody coming out of the bedroom. Somebody trying to stay very quiet. Somebody who had amply demonstrated he had absolutely no problem with violence.

It was Gordon, of course, with his score to settle with Wanda and him. Of course it was, Spike thought, that was how these people were.

The great anthropologists and sociologists all report the same phenomenon: When immersed in a culture of great psychological distance from one's own, the researcher will start to sympathize with the practitioners of that culture, begin to—if not see things from a native's perspective—at least lose his initial revulsion at the "backwards" rituals and practices of that culture.

But staring at himself in the Vacationeer's bathroom mirror and wondering what exactly he was supposed to do, Spike decided that particular theory was a load of shit.

Then, before he could even realize what was happening, the whole world lurched toward him and the mirror shattered against his face.

10

The desert highway stretched out forever in front of Wanda as she guided the coach south. How far was it to the border? Two hours, three? She knew it had to be that far at least, miles ahead of her that would have to be crossed before she'd be free. Maybe with Detective Gann out of the way, the police would be a little slower to find her and end what she had worked so hard to start.

Truth was, she had no real idea what she was supposed to do next, now that she had all but beaten Gordon and gotten away. *Drive south*, that was all she could think of, *Drive south and get the hell out of the country before anybody figures anything out. Get out of the country before Gordon has a chance to drag you down with him.*

That was really what it was, she realized. She was doing all this to get away from Gordon. Never mind that he was going to spend the rest of his life in prison—she had built up a barrier against ever even visiting him again, now that she had to stay out of the country or end up in jail herself. She never wanted to ask for a divorce, told herself that she still loved him, the whole time hating him for what he did because *he* was unhappy being with *her*...

Oh, Gordon, she thought, and let out a little chuckle. She wished she could see his face one more time, tell him how stupid they both had been, see for herself the look on his face when he really understood that she was the smarter one, that she had won—

She heard a creak behind her and automatically looked up at the inside wide-angle mirror. She could see that the bedroom door was open.

Her breath caught in her throat.

She could also see her husband's face. He was right behind her.

Of all the wishes to finally get, she thought, and slammed on the brakes.

The Vacationeer seemed to throw an anchor down into the ground, pulling it violently backwards. Gordon flew between the custom leather driver and passenger seats and went head-first into the windshield. He didn't crash through, as Wanda had hoped he would, but instead sort of bounced off it, whacking hard against it and then ricocheting backwards, absorbing all of the impact in his skull.

Take that, bastard! Wanda screamed to herself—her jaw was locked too tight to make any actual sound—and mashed both feet hard on the accelerator, launching the coach forward again like it was attached to a rocket. Wanda felt herself pressed hard against the seat and watched in the wide-angle mirror as Gordon tripped backwards and stumbled, dazed, a good twenty feet until his head cracked once again into the corner of the dining area cabinet.

She was going to win. *She was going to win!*

That's when she saw Spike, covered in broken bits of mirror and soaked in blood, swing open the bathroom door and lock eyes with Gordon. "You!" he yelled.

"You!"

"Kill him, Spike!" Wanda screamed.

"It's not like that anymore," Spike said. "No more killing."

This seemed to clear Gordon's head, because he stood up straight from where he had been sprawled against the counter, stood up straight and smiled despite the huge red welt on his forehead and the blood streaming down past his ear from where he had cracked his head open on the cabinet. "Come on, Spike," Gordon said, "just a little more," and threw his fist into the boy's face. Spike didn't raise his hands or even resist.

What the hell was he doing? Wanda cursed under her breath and thought, *Should've dropped that wimp when I had the chance.*

Gordon punched Spike's face, head, body, but he would not hit back. Blood streamed from the kid's nose, his face and neck were a storm of swelling bruises, but still Spike—who had no problem screwing Gordon's wife and stealing his money—would not fight back. It made Gordon think something was coming, and he didn't need any more surprises.

"Put your hands up, punk," Gordon yelled as he swatted Spike in the side of the head and jammed his knee into his ribs. "Gonna kill you if you don't."

"Then kill me," Spike said through fat lips. "Wanda's worth dying for. It's not about the money. It's about *love.*"

"Then where's the money?"

"In her purse—"

"*Spike!*"

But Spike just smiled. "I told you—it's about love, not money. And not violence, either."

If he hadn't been so enraged, if he hadn't hated everything the kid stood for—if he understood what the hell it was the kid stood for—Gordon might have laughed right then at the sheer absurdity of anyone thinking his crabby, nit-picking, hateful, war-painted wife of twenty-five years was worth breaking a nail over, let alone dying for.

He also would have laughed if he didn't know goddamn well it was about a million and a half of *his* dollars before it was above love or anything else. "Sorry, asshole—it's about money, and it's about violence. Now you gonna fight back or not?"

Spike jutted his bloody chin out defiantly. "Not a chance."

That did it. Red flames of fury, stoked now by the pacifist stance of this little bastard, obscured his sight, but he could still see well enough to punch Spike in the stomach, double him up, and—not bad for forty-five years old—pick the fucker right up off the carpeted floor and carry him nearly over his head towards the front of the slowing coach.

Gordon watched as his wife's eyes grew wide with horror, and then, roaring at the pain, hurled her lover at the back of her head.

The force of Spike's body dislocated the fine leather chair, snapping it loose from its metal bolts and smashing Wanda up against the steering wheel, possibly breaking her neck in the process. Spike then bounced and spun forward, hard up against the wrap-around windshield, shattering it into a hail of white shards as he dropped out of sight in front of the coach.

But Gordon had no time to enjoy the moment or feel for the bump of the Vacationeer running over his wife's lover, because Wanda's weight as she was rammed against the wheel shoved it to the left, sending the RV careening sideways at fifty miles an hour.

Gordon held on tight to the counter. He could feel them leave the road and start bumping across the rocks and dirt, the whole coach skidding out of control—

Holy shit.

Gordon ran for the front of the bus, catching a glimpse in the early morning sunshine and seeing exactly what he prayed he wasn't going to see.

The edge of the world was fifty feet away. And they were screaming toward it. The coach was slowing down, but there was no way it was stopping before it flew right over that four-hundred-foot drop.

Like he was in a dream, seeing his stunned wife slumped over the steering wheel as their vehicle was about to be destroyed, seeing the woman who he had pledged to love and honor through good times and bad, for richer and for poorer, forsaking all others, Gordon Mitchell knew exactly what he had to do to make things right.

He grabbed the purse full of money and made for the shattered window.

Forty feet. He slammed a foot down on Wanda's back and readied himself to leap out the front window and hope he landed out of the coach's path.

But just as he tensed to jump, Wanda's paint-slathered talons reached up and picked the purse from his arms like she was jerking a cherry tomato from a garden salad and plunking it in her mouth with a grin.

Twenty feet. He stopped himself in mid-spring, wrenching in horror as she ran stumbling to the back of the bus, to the bedroom, clutching the heavy purse to her chest like a schoolgirl with a diary.

Ten feet. The Vacationeer was swinging hard now, doing a three-sixty. The front end—Gordon's end—was just at the edge of the abyss and going over.

He tried to turn and plant his foot to run after Wanda and the purse, but suddenly the world lurched out from under his feet and the back of his head hit the floor.

The front of the bus had sailed off the cliff. It was dangling in space.

Then the back axle must have caught something, because the coach stopped dead, throwing Gordon up into a standing position against the dashboard and giving him a sickening look at the scenery. He could feel his hamstrings pull as he used his legs to keep himself from flipping right out the shattered windshield.

The undercoating creaked as the Vacationeer, perfectly balanced, teetered on the brink. Slowly, carefully, Gordon turned around to see his wife frozen in place thirty feet away, holding the purse tight.

They stared at each other.

"We're gonna die," Wanda said.

"Give me the purse," Gordon said. He had come too far now to be able to say anything less.

His wife had no expression, just stared at Gordon with her white face, the corners of her mouth drawn down. "Is that all you want? The purse?"

Gordon nodded. There was no point in trying to hurt her anymore. He just wanted the purse. "That's all I've ever wanted," he said, and reached out his hand. "I never wanted to hurt you."

"Still the silver-tongued devil."

He smiled. "I just want the purse, Wanda."

She nodded then, and a tear drew her eyeliner with it down her cheek. She zipped open the purse. "I know, Gordon," she said, "and that's what I'll give you."

Watching her husband's face, Wanda then slid open the side window and dumped the million and a half dollars' worth of bricks of hundreds, fifties, twenties, and tens onto the mesa outside, and crumpled the imitation-Gucci purse in her hands.

It took a second for Gordon to understand what she was doing.

But only a second. He screamed and started to run for Wanda's end of the bus.

But too late. Grinning her last bitter grin, Wanda hurled the purse her husband had asked for, threw it with every ounce of her strength, whacking him across thirty feet, whipping him in the face and tearing his cheek open with its zipper.

Gordon fell backwards, and the force of his body slamming against the floor tipped the delicate balance of the Vacationeer. He held on as the whole coach reeled, everything sliding off of tables and out of cabinets as the angle steepened and his legs started to dangle.

Then it stopped. He was hanging on with his fingertips now, and anymore pull would surely have sent him falling to his death. But the coach *stopped*.

He held perfectly still. "Wanda?" he said, very quietly.

She was tucked under the bolted-down dining room table. She didn't respond.

"Gonna make it. It stopped falling. Gonna be okay if we just stay still for a minute here."

That's when Wanda stood up, leaning against the table for support.

"Jesus, Wanda—stay still! *Stay still!*"

All it would take was one jump to get the coach going again.

Wanda jumped.

The Vacationeer creaked, groaned, and finally slid right off the edge of the mesa.

Spike's swollen eyelids stung as slowly cracked them open. Blood had caked in places he didn't even know he had. He couldn't feel his left arm, so badly was it dislocated. He spit out two teeth after the explosion woke him up on the dirt and rocks of the mesa. He was broken, but he was alive.

As he stood, he could see the winding skid marks going right to the edge. He could smell burning, the acrid smoke of diesel fuel in flames, and hear a cacophony of sirens growing steadily louder.

A violent end for violent people, he thought, and wished he could have joined them at the bottom of the valley. He wasn't cut out to be a robber; Spike Jones was never a real person. He would have to crawl back to the world and start again, live life on its terms, not his own. He would give up lest he turn out like Wanda and Gordon—this was what happened when people lived by their principles.

He smiled despite the pain. After everything he'd seen, it had just hit him that Wanda and Gordon were the ones who actually lived by their principles, not him.

Lived by them, and died by them.

He was just turning around to head back down the highway when he noticed a pile of grayish bricks fifteen feet or so from the edge of the cliff. Although his every bone and muscle cried for him to stop, he shuffled over to it.

It was money. Wanda and Gordon's money. Their blood money.

As best he could with his dislocated shoulder, he pulled off his back-pack and stuffed the bricks inside it, then slung the package over his good shoulder and gingerly started walking to somewhere he could get a bath, clean clothes, and a doctor.

Trent Jones turned and took one last look at the thick black smoke pouring from the remains of the Vacationeer. He had loved an exciting woman of a different culture, only to lose her forever. He had eschewed violence, only to hasten two peoples' fiery deaths. He had professed disdain for money, only to buy bullets so a man could be killed for it. He had dared to dream of a better world than what he had thought possible, only to witness his hopes crumble like a house set on fire.

Spike Jones was dead now. It was time to start over once again.

He turned back around and headed for home.

He had learned his lesson.